The
Rememberer

For my family

With love

ONE

The morning sun streamed against the blinds of Walt Walters' half-pulled shades. His first waking thought was "Saturday! No school today!" and joy surged through him, but only for a moment, until he heard his Dad's voice from down the hall finishing the sentence he'd begun when Walt was still half asleep:

"...outta bed before we miss the good stuff."

Saturday. Garage sale day. The joy subsided.

"Aw, Dad," Walt moaned, not loud enough for his father to hear.

Walt hated garage sale days only half as much as he hated school days, which is to say, a lot. And throughout the late spring, through summer and into mid-fall, *every* Saturday was garage sale day. Seven months of the year, you could count on someone in the neighborhood or a nearby subdivision seizing a warm weather weekend to unload the junk—from their garage, their attic, their growing kids' closets, their ever-increasing pile of clutter—and ruin Walt's Saturday with a sale.

"C'mon, you sleepyhead. Or we'll leave without you!" Walt's father threatened. Walt could hear him heading down the hallway.

"Go ahead!" Walt called his bluff. "Leave without me."

"Walt!" When Mr. Walters shouted his son's name and nothing else, it meant "end of discussion."

Reluctantly, Walt scootched to the end of the bed and pulled on a sweatshirt and the slacks he'd kicked off and left there the night before. He found two shoes but only one sock so he decided it was warm enough outside to do without the socks.

In two minutes, he was heading down the stairs where his father—the self-proclaimed "garage sale king"—and his two sisters were waiting for him near the front door. Walt launched immediately into his familiar complaints, knowing it would get him nowhere but feeling an overwhelming compulsion to go on:

"I hate garage sales. Why can't we go out for donuts like normal families?"

"We're not a normal family," Walt's sister, Zelda, reminded him. Zelda was two years older than Walt and had resigned herself to life with the garage sale king.

"Where are your socks?" Walt's father asked.

"I couldn't find any. Why can't I stay home, Dad? I'm old enough."

"What if six men came to the door wielding tire irons. What would you do?"

"Dad. . ."

"When you can answer that question, you can stay home. You're only twelve years old."

"I'd call 911."

"Where are your socks?"

"If you can't dress yourself, you can't stay home by yourself," Zelda added.

"Shut up."

"You shut up."

"Children!" Mr. Walters hollered, putting on his jacket. He handed Walt a jacket, too. Zelda was already wearing hers. She was ready to go. Walt's younger sister, Acey, had her winter coat on, along with her hat and gloves. She was five years old. She was always cold.

"Why can't we just have one Saturday where we get out of the house without whining or complaining?" Mr. Walters wondered.

"Why can't we have one Saturday without garage sales?" Walt wondered back.

"It's only an hour or so. I think it will be a lot of fun."

"Think again, big guy," Walt responded, just under his breath.

"There's an old house over on Mill Street I want to see. There'll be a lot of cool old stuff."

"You know, some parents would like to see their children have a hearty breakfast before they drag them out into the morning chill," Walt tutored him.

"I had parents like that," Walt's dad responded. "It was a nightmare. Had to have a good breakfast every morning before I left the house." He led his children out into the morning chill, unto the small porch and turned to lock the door behind them. "'It'll make you big and strong' my mother used to say, and look at me—barely tall enough to scratch my own head."

Walt's dad was actually quite a tall man. He was lean and gawky and wore pants that were just a little too short, which made him look nerdy. Walt had only noticed this recently and it had become a real source of embarrassment whenever he and his father were out in public together.

The old van sat patiently in the driveway, waiting for the Walters family to give it purpose. It was the "garage sale van"— an old clunker—that Mr. Walters bought specifically to use on Saturdays to patrol the neighborhood for sales. They had been driving it all summer, every Saturday, from sale to sale, looking like gypsies whenever they piled out of the van. When they bought it, it only had two front seats, but Mr. Walters had found two more bucket seats—at garage sales, naturally—and bolted them almost securely into the back of the van so that they faced the cargo area.

"Shotgun," Zelda called, unnecessarily. She always rode shotgun no matter who called it first.

"Are you warm enough?" Mr. Walters asked Acey.

Acey didn't answer. She rarely said anything unless she was cold and then she said, "I'm cold."

"I think we're going to have fun today," Mr. Walters repeated to no one in particular as they piled into the van: "Let the adventure begin!"

Saturday morning garage sales had been a tradition with the Walters family since their mother disappeared four years earlier. One Saturday morning, about six months after she disappeared, Mr. Walters bundled Acey—who was just eighteen months old at the time—into the stroller and went out to "get some air." That was when Grandma Walters lived with them. She had moved in after Walt's mother disappeared, providing a maternal influence for the family until Walt's own mother was found. Grandma Walters ended up staying for three years before deciding that she was no longer needed and that Walt's mother was probably not coming home.

That first garage sale morning—when Mr. Walters went out for air—he was gone for almost six hours. Grandma Walters was worried sick and about to call the police to report this second mysterious disappearance when she saw Mr. Walters making his way up the sidewalk toward the house. He was moving exceptionally slowly because, in addition to pushing the stroller where little Acey sat in docile indifference, he was pushing a wheelbarrow and pulling an old wagon, both of which were completely loaded with what Grandma Walters immediately and most accurately described as "junk."

Saturdays became "Garage Sale Saturdays" from then on. While Grandma Walters lived with them, Walt and Zelda were saved from having to go. But, Mr. Walters and Acey would boldly set out every warm-weather Saturday, be gone for hours, and return with more useless stuff than anyone should be allowed to own.

But when Grandma Walters moved back to her own home 200 miles away, "Garage Sale Saturdays" became "Family Garage Sale Saturdays." Walt and Zelda were too young to stay home on their own, so they joined the pair of bargain hunters and followed their father through the neighborhood.

At first, they'd walked the neighborhood sales. Later, Mr. Walters agreed they could get more stuff if he took the car. And finally, this most recent spring, he'd bought the garage sale van.

If you had asked Walt Walters that morning whether there were any streets in the entire town of Lexington he didn't know, he would have answered, emphatically, "no."

All summer long, he and Celia Washroth, his best friend since fourth grade, spent hours riding the roads and byways of Lexington, discovering new routes and shortcuts, testing their courage on the main thoroughfares and all of their side routes miles out to the county line. Walt Walters was sure he knew every road of his hometown.

Until they turned onto Mill Street.

"Where are we?" Walt wondered to himself. Just moments earlier, they'd been on Concord Drive, old familiar Concord

Drive, no more than half a mile from home. Then, suddenly, his father turned left where Walt would have sworn there'd never been a road before, onto--Mill Street?

"Where are we?" Zelda asked, taking notice. She, too, was in unfamiliar territory.

"Mill Street," Mr. Walters explained, matter-of-factly.

"I'm cold," Acey announced.

Aside from being previously unknown to Walt and Zelda, there was nothing very remarkable about Mill Street. It was a two-lane asphalt street, narrow in the way of older roads, with no sidewalks or shoulders. Just lawns and fields and houses. It obviously wasn't a new road. The homes that sparsely dotted the side of the road were fifty years old and more and many looked empty and abandoned.

Mr. Walters brought the van to a halt by the side of the road, just before a dead end. "Last stop!" he announced, "I promise," and bounced out of the van before anyone had a chance to respond.

The three Walters children piled out and, as they did, a chilling wind picked up, blowing strong and steady right down the street. They were happy to see that this last garage sale was largely picked over with only a few straggling pieces of landfill-ready furniture in the front yard of a modest, moldy, slate-shingled ranch house. They wouldn't be here long.

"Where's Dad?" Zelda asked, scanning the yard.

Mr. Walters had dashed out of the van quickly and disappeared.

"Dad?" Acey squeaked, drawing her jacket around her tightly.

Walt surveyed the lawn and the front of the house and didn't see his father.

An elderly couple sat in front of a small utility table near the front porch with a tiny, shoebox cash register before them, staring blankly, unenthusiastically, for final customers, but Mr. Walters wasn't there.

A panic rose up Walt's spine. As children of a mother who had vanished without a trace, they were easily alarmed when their remaining parent was unexpectedly out of sight.

"Over here, kids," they all heard at once from a distance. It was the unmistakably ebullient voice of their father in a garage-sale thrill and they turned around together to see, across the road, in front of a house set fifty yards from the pavement, another yard sale where Mr. Walters was waving at them.

Walt, Zelda and Acey hadn't seen the sale at all when they first drove up, spotting only the smaller, sadder one on the south side of the street.

"Oh, no," Zelda said, because, unlike its neighboring sale, this one was packed with all kinds of junk of the sort their father would find "fascinating." It looked as if not a single shopper had stopped in to diminish the treasure trove of bargains. Perhaps others, too, had missed seeing it altogether.

"Over here," Mr. Walters called again, and signaled for them to join him.

The three made their way across the road and the lawn leading up to the house and its cluttered yard sale. It was clearly the oldest house on the block. A two-story, wood-sided home, painted white with green shutters. The paint was chipping off the clapboards. It reminded Walt of an old-fashioned farmhouse and may have been one once when all the land around it was still alfalfa and sorghum fields. A half a century ago, almost all of

Lexington was farm country, miles outside a major metropolis. Now, it was practically a suburb, but with a few remaining houses and old barns here and there to remind itself of its farming roots. This house looked as if it hadn't been lived in for years. A real estate sign at the edge of the property near the road announced that it was "For Sale."

Mr. Walters continued waving his hands and shouting "over here," until the children were within ten yards. He was standing before a wooden picnic table that was the checkout lane for this yard sale. Behind the table an old man sat—smiling and alert, but wrinkled and crooked and gray and worn. He wore a big brimmed hat that partially hid his face. He went perfectly with the ancient house behind him. He studied the children carefully as if recalling fond memories. His smile was cheery and inviting, and Walt had the odd feeling that he had met the man before.

Walt took a quick survey of all the "merchandise" scattered for sale in the yard, most of it set out haphazardly between two huge, century-old oak trees that dominated the front lawn. The items for sale included everything from an old-fashioned washboard with the words "Missouri's Ozarks" stenciled across the top, to a refrigerator, to a rusted tractor with a flat front tire. There were a few tables of knick-knacks: books, salt-and-pepper shakers, skewers for holding corn-on-the-cob and a framed photo of three monkeys. There was even a chipped and battered kitchen sink, removed from its countertop and resting against one of the huge trees. None of the items were priced and it looked as if someone had dragged the contents of their attic to the front lawn and dumped it there before deciding to call it a "sale."

"Some pretty cool stuff here, kids. What do you think?"

Mr. Walters asked as they approached.

Walt was thinking that the old man behind the table couldn't possibly have carted all of this stuff into the yard on his own.

"That's a lot of junk," Zelda said, undiplomatically.

The old man laughed, good-naturedly.

"Zelda."

"I mean, cool junk," Zelda tried to recover. "Nostalgic, I mean."

"I'm so cold," Acey said. The wind continued to blow in cool gusts.

A small, round table of old hardware caught Walt's eye and he wandered over to it. It was filled with tools and fasteners of a sort used 100 years earlier. There were hammers and pliers and vises alongside dozens of other items Walt didn't recognize— tools of a bygone era that had been replaced in contemporary carpentry by some electrically powered invention.

"Lots of antiques," Mr. Walters was saying to Acey. "So much character."

Zelda had walked over to another table during her father's antiquities lesson. She picked up a wooden mask painted in the manner of an Indian war chief and held it up to her face. "Hey Acey," she called and when Acey looked over, she screamed "AHHHH!" in mock warlike zeal.

"Eek!" Acey responded, startled.

The old man laughed and then Acey spotted a big, dilapidated dollhouse set on the ground unceremoniously. It was nearly as tall as she was, obviously handcrafted by someone's father or grandfather.

Walt was now looking at an old transistor radio with only an AM dial. It was probably forty years old and when he opened the battery compartment, he found rust and corrosion that made it useless.

"Not much here to interest a young man," the old man behind the picnic table called to him. His father and the others were out of earshot. "See anything you like?" the man asked.

"Not yet," Walt said.

"Lot of old junk," the old man pronounced. "Nothing to interest a boy."

"Some of these old tools are kind of cool."

"Did you see the portfolio? Now that's something you might like."

"The what?"

"The portfolio . . . on the table."

Walt looked again and, there, right in the middle of the table, as if framed by the hardware, was a thick case in the shape of an oversized notebook, leather-bound and ancient, closed and held shut by a leather strap and metal clasp, as if protecting secrets. He had not seen it there moments earlier, when he was looking at the tools. It was as if it had suddenly materialized, called forth by the old man's pointing it out.

"What's a portfolio?"

"Oh, it's lots of things," the old man explained. "It can be anything...hold anything."

"Looks like a notebook," Walt said. He walked over and picked it up off the table. It was much heavier than it looked, as if it were weighted with lead.

"It's like a notebook, isn't it? It could hold your schoolwork, I suppose, or your drawings or anything."

"Is it yours?" Walt asked, carrying it back to where the old man was sitting. He wasn't especially interested in the answer, but felt obliged to go along and amuse the old man.

"Belonged to a girl who lived here in Lexington many years ago. Started collecting things in it when she was about your age."

10

"Your daughter?"

"No, no." The old man lowered his head so that his eyes were shadowed in the brim of the hat. "I don't have any children."

"Why does she want to sell it?"

"Oh, she's been gone many, many years. Left that in her attic. I found it." The old man paused as if considering whether to provide any further elaboration. Finally, he said, softly, "Found it in a closet in her attic."

"Did you know her?"

"I found it...after she...moved out."

Walt turned the portfolio over in his hands. It had a title on the cover, embossed on an attached, rectangular, tin plate. But whatever it had said was gone now, rubbed away.

"It's neat," Walt fibbed, wondering why the old man had ever thought this crusty, cracked artifact could appeal to him.

"It's yours," the man said with a meaningful nod.

"Oh, no, no," Walt held the portfolio away from his body, as if it were contaminated. "I couldn't take it. Thank you anyway..."

"Take it," the old man said gently, but firmly. "I think you'll like it."

"I...well... I..."

"Free. It's a gift."

"But..." Walt did not know what to say. He didn't want the portfolio but the friendly old man was making such a point of giving it to him that he felt guilty rejecting it. Walt was just formulating a kindly excuse about his father not allowing him to accept gifts from strangers, when he felt a friendly clap on the back.

"What've you got there, Kiddo?" his father asked.

11

"Um…portfolio?"

"Oh, cool." Mr. Walters took it from Walt's hands and turned it over. "My father used to have something like this for his work." And then, to the old man, Mr. Walters offered, "They don't make them like this any more."

"I'm giving it to your son."

"Well, that's very generous of you. What a nice offer. What do you say, Walt?"

"Thank you."

Mr. Walters examined it closely, appreciating its age.

"But be careful with it," the old man said, looking directly into Walt's eyes, almost whispering.

"Be careful?" Walt asked. What was there to be careful with? That it might fall apart? It was an old notebook, a little smelly from sitting in a damp attic, but otherwise harmless.

"Do you know the combination?" Mr. Walters asked and held the portfolio so the old man could see how the strap around it was held by a clasp and lock that had a tiny, three-number combination dial on it.

"No. I don't have the combination," the man reported as Mr. Walters tried to open the clasp.

"Maybe I can just use it as a paperweight," Walt offered, resigned to being stuck with the portfolio now that his father had admired it. Maybe he could pawn it off on Acey.

By profession, Mr. Walters was a cryptographer who spent most of his work hours cracking codes and deciphering unknown languages and symbols. The combination did not look difficult to break. "Oh, I'd imagine I can figure out a simple combination like . . ." Mr. Walters began, but was interrupted by Zelda who walked up from behind.

"Dad? Are we done, yet? I'm hungry."

12

"Hey, Sweetie, seen enough?" Mr. Walters put his arm around his daughter and, unconsciously handed the portfolio back to Walt.

"Plenty."

"All right, all right," Mr. Walters conceded. "Let me just check out this . . ."

But before Mr. Walters could finish his sentence, a stiff wind swirled across the lawn, knocking over several of the tables, spilling garage sale merchandise, on the lawn. It was an odd blast of wind, Walt thought, because it seemed to come from all directions at once and blow up toward the treetops rather than down. And then, Walt could have sworn he felt an earthquake—a mild but distinct tremor that accompanied the stiff gust and made the ground beneath his feet tremble.

The wind took Mr. Walters by surprise and the quaking ground made Acey lose her balance as she hurried back to her father.

And it startled the old man, too, for he looked around him quickly as if expecting to find someone at his side and then stood up and announced abruptly, "Garage sale is over," before the gust had even subsided.

"Blustery," Mr. Walters commented.

"The garage sale is over," the old man exclaimed again, agitated. "I've got to get this stuff in." He started scooping items up off the tables around him.

Mr. Walters was perplexed. "Do you need some help?" he asked. "That's a lot of work for one person."

One old, frail person, Walt thought and started to pick up one of the tables that had been knocked over.

"No, no," the old man insisted, again checking over each shoulder and looking off down the road. "Get the boy out of here. I'm fine." And then, the old man stopped and took a deep breath as if trying to compose himself. "I mean…my niece will be here at any moment to help. Please."

The Walters hesitated and another cold gust of wind accompanied by an almost indistinct tremor of earth struck the yard sale from every direction causing the table Walt had just set up to tumble over.

The mishap frightened the old man and he looked Walt directly in the eyes. "You should go," he said, as if talking only to Walt. "Take the portfolio and go."

"I'm freezing," Acey piped in.

"All right, all right," Mr. Walters replied, relenting. "Let's get going." He turned to the old man one last time, "Are you sure you don't need any help cleaning…?"

The old man forced a weak smile. "No, no," he reassured, "I've got my niece and I'll be fine. Go, go."

"All right," Mr. Walters said, reluctantly. "Good luck."

"Thank you, thank you. Have a nice day. Good-bye."

Walt knew his father did not feel right leaving such a crooked old man to clean up such a large mess by himself. And, as the Walters walked to their van, Mr. Walters checked over his shoulder several times to see if the old man was doing okay. Walt turned around, too, when they got to the van, only to discover that the old man was gone.

TWO

It was almost a year before Walt Walters thought about the portfolio that the old man gave him. But he thought a lot about the old man and his house in the days immediately after the sale.

The following Monday at school, he'd told his friend, Celia Washroth, "I discovered a new street in Lexington." She was surprised, and a little skeptical especially when, after school the next day they'd ridden their bikes to find Mill Street and Walt was unable to retrace his way back. "It was somewhere around here," Walt kept saying.

Celia looked at him suspiciously. "It was!" he insisted.

And when he told her about the creaky old house and the friendly but mysterious, old man. Celia had asked, "What's so mysterious? He gave you a book. Old people do that."

"I don't know," Walt told her. "There was something weird about it. Not creepy, but . . . mysterious."

Eventually, though, Walt forgot the encounter with the old man. Every once in a while, as they drove down Concord Road, he would look to find Mill Street, but that curiosity, too, faded and the whole day receded into the back of his mind.

And the portfolio? Walt had noticed on the ride home from that garage sale, sitting in the enclosed van, that the portfolio gave off a strong, moldy smell of damp leather and he just wanted to get rid of it. But, because it was a gift given so deliberately to Walt—because the old man seemed so intent on Walt having it—he couldn't bring himself to throw it in the trash.

So, rather than doom it to the landfill for eternity, he'd done the next best thing: he put it in his closet.

Walt's closet was famous among all those who'd ever seen it for its uncanny similarity to a rubbish heap. Anything Walt didn't know what to do with or had grown tired of went into the closet, ceremoniously placed there with a fling of the arm, or a strategic shove and, if necessary, a kick.

No one could say when the closet was last cleaned out. It had been at least since Walt's mother disappeared, for she was the only one in the family who could work up the energy against his stiff resistance to make him tidy it. Since she'd gone, Walt had been free to pile as much in there as he could with only an occasional, half-hearted observation "You should clean out that closet" from his father.

Then, almost a year later at dinner one night, Mr. Walters was asking Acey what she wanted to be for Halloween.

"I'm thinking of being a furnace," Acey explained. The previous year she had been "The Lady of Many Coats" and wore several pieces of outerwear around the neighborhood trick-or-treating.

"Don't you want to be something a little more…" her father started.

"Normal?" Walt offered.

"Well, no," Mr. Walters went on giving Walt a corrective look. "I don't know. A little more…Halloween-ish?"

"You mean like something scary?"

"No, not necessarily. You could be a cute pumpkin."

"Could I hold a lighted candle? It would keep my hands warm."

"It might be hard to keep lit."

"I heard something scary," Zelda offered, nonchalantly.

"You can't carry a candle, Sweetie," Mr. Walters went on. "But you could wear a couple of warm sweaters under a pumpkin suit."

"It was coming from Walt's closet."

"A pumpkin suit?"

"The scary noise."

"What scary noise?"

"The one I heard today."

"You heard a scary noise?"

"Coming from Walt's closet."

"You did not," Walt interjected. Zelda was launching an unprovoked attempt to get him in trouble.

"I did."

"What kind of scary noise?" Acey asked, getting scared merely at the mention of a scary noise.

"The scary kind."

"You did NOT."

"What did it sound like, Zeld?" her father wanted to know.

Zelda made a crackly noise blowing her breath against the roof of her mouth. It sounded like a radio that was not tuned in.

"Stop it," Walt said. "You did not."

"I did. It was coming out of your closet."

"What were you doing in my room?"

"I was walking by. I wasn't even in your filthy room."

"You're just trying to get me in trouble."

"Did you really hear a sound coming from Walt's closet?" Mr. Walters asked, mixing concern with a bit of skepticism.

"It sounded like scratching or thumping."

"You did not."

Zelda made the sound again.

"That makes me cold," Acey announced.

"Oxygen makes you cold. There was no sound coming from my closet."

"Zelda, seriously," Mr. Walters said, seriously, trying to get to the bottom of this, "Did you hear something coming from Walt's closet?"

Zelda looked straight at her father and said, deliberately, "I did" and seemed so earnest about it that a slight shiver went up Walt's spine. He was not so confident now when he retorted, "You did not."

"Now, Walt, I wouldn't be surprised. That closet is a mess."

"It's a health hazard to all of us, really." Zelda had turned sixteen over the summer, gotten her driver's license and a boyfriend and apparently had decided she would help her father rule the house.

"It's not a health hazard. Shut up."

'But I wouldn't be surprised," Mr. Walters went on, "if some squirrel or chipmunk or something got in and found his way into your closet to make a nest."

"A raccoon, maybe. With babies," Zelda speculated.

"There's nothing in my closet."

"Nonetheless," Mr. Walters pronounced, "tomorrow, I want you to go through your closet and get rid of the junk in there.

"Beware the raccoon."

"Don't smush the babies," Acey pleaded.

"There's no raccoon. And there's no junk in there. It's all very valuable," Walt assured his father, though he couldn't honestly remember anything that was in his closet.

"Well, then, use the two-year rule: if you haven't used it or played with it in two years, throw it out."

"That would be everything in his closet," Zelda speculated.

18

"Dad, I need all that stuff." Truthfully, Walt knew, he wouldn't mind if it all got thrown away, but he didn't want to be bothered with the labor of throwing. "Besides it would take up my whole Saturday to clean it up."

"Walt," his father said, firmly, "it's time. Clean it up."

And so, the next morning, Walt woke up bright and early at the crack of 10:30 to get a jump on cleaning out his closet. When Walt turned thirteen, his father gave him leave to stay home alone on garage sales Saturdays, but Zelda continued to go because her father let her practice driving and Acey continued to go because she was too young to stay with her brother.

So, when Walt woke up on Saturday, he was alone in the house and got right down to work cleaning the closet after he had breakfast and read the newspaper and watched TV and wandered from room to room looking for some legitimate distraction from the chore. When he couldn't find one after a half an hour of wandering, he went to his room, stared at the closet door, and tried to prepare himself mentally for the task ahead.

Then he lay down on the bed to rest until the phone rang.

It was Celia.

"Want to go riding?"

"I have to clean out my closet."

"It's the end of the world as we know it."

"Sarcasm doesn't become you."

"Why do you have to clean it out?"

"Zelda betrayed me. She said she heard scratching sounds coming for my closet and now Dad thinks there's a raccoon in there."

"I once read about a guy who found a muskrat family living under the hood of an abandoned car."

19

"Fascinating."

"Do you want some help?"

"Would you really help?

"I'd watch. I'm bored to tears."

"You can watch if you want. It's not going to be pretty."

"I'll bring some trash bags."

Even though Celia hadn't offered to help, Walt saw no point in starting before she arrived, so he made himself a sandwich and waited for her. When she got there, they went straight up to his room.

"Get ready," Walt told her, grasping the doorknob to his closet to prepare her for the avalanche.

"Bring it on," Celia said. She was sitting at the desk in his room. Walt had been trying for a year to deny his growing awareness that Celia was becoming a very pretty girl. They had been friends for almost four years now. He looked away when she smiled smartly.

To their surprise, nothing tumbled out when Walt opened the door. It was a mess inside the closet, but a stationary one.

"Where to start?" Walt asked.

"You need to make two piles," Celia recommended. "One for stuff you want to throw away and the other for stuff I want you to throw away."

Walt reached in randomly, and pulled on the handle of a tennis racquet, but that caused the entire closet pile to shift and groan as if preparing to cave in.

"Try the birdcage," Celia suggested.

Walt saw the birdcage near the top of the pile and pulled it out. It was old and bent and rusted in several places. There was no bottom to it.

"Why do you have that?"

"I found it in the woods when I was seven."

"Oh," Celia nodded.

"I thought it might be useful one day."

"What's that black thing?"

Walt seized the black thing that he hoped might turn out to be a kite—it had a nylon texture like the more expensive kites. But when he pulled on it, it turned out to be his father's favorite umbrella that had mysteriously disappeared last year. It, too, was bent and maimed to the point of uselessness.

"My dad's been looking for this." The handle fell off in Walt's hand.

"He'll be pleased you found it," Celia noted.

"We can fight off the raccoons with it," Walt suggested and took a couple of jabs at the empty air, fighting off imaginary four-foot-tall rodents.

"Put it in the discard pile."

And the process of cleaning Walt's closet went on like that for a half an hour, as he pulled, at Celia's direction, individual items from the unruly pile in his closet and made an unruly pile in the middle of his room with them. Then, just when Walt was ready to call for a snack break, he came across the old portfolio.

He was about to toss it in the junk pile without comment, but Celia stopped him.

"What's that?"

"It's called a portfolio." He started to toss it again, but Celia held out her hand.

"It's cool looking. Where'd you get it?"

Walt brought the portfolio over and sat down on the floor beside her. "Remember I told you about the garage sale last year with the mysterious old man."

"On the non-existent street? I thought you made up that whole thing."

"This is the book he gave me."

"It's not a book."

"Well, it looks like a book. He really wanted me to have it," Walt explained—that day replaying in his memory.

"It looks ancient."

"I think he said it was his when he was a boy and he was about two-hundred-and-fifty-years old."

"Did you open it?"

"It's locked," Walt told Celia, remembering his father's effort to open the portfolio at the garage sale.

"Try it."

"It's locked," Walt repeated, and then he pressed the latch on the clasp to show her the futility of the effort. "I guess we could break…" he began, but to his surprise, the clasp latch released and opened. "Hey!"

"What's in it?"

Walt opened the portfolio which unfolded like an upside-down book—with the binding to the right side. Inside the front flap were several small pockets on the cover flap of a much larger pocket, designed to hold a book or thick notepad. The smaller pockets were empty except for an old, rusty pen and a tiny scrap of paper sticking out of one opening.

Walt pulled at the tiny scrap, which stuck slightly against the leather before coming out. It turned out to be not a scrap at all, but a photo, black and white, square, very old. It was a picture of a little girl holding a small dog.

"Who's that?" Celia asked.

"Dunno."

"Maybe it's the old man when he was a little girl."

The girl in the photo did look vaguely familiar to Walt. She was, perhaps, seven or eight years old. She had dark, wavy shoulder-length hair and dark but lively and mischievous eyes. She wore a dress and tights and dress shoes and an overcoat, as if outfitted for church or a social outing. Under her arm, she was holding a small white terrier that looked earnestly at the camera, perhaps expecting a treat for good behavior.

"Does it say anything on the back?"

Walt turned the photo over and on the back was scribbled the useless description, "Me with Dog."

"It's her," Walt explained, "with her dog."

"What's in the big flap?" Celia pointed.

Walt unfolded the portfolio flap so he could reach his hand into the bigger, central pocket, which held a book--the binding side facing through the opening. He pulled at the binding and drew out a hardbound volume, on the cover of which was engraved the letters "A.S." Walt slowly opened the book. It was obviously old and probably hadn't been opened in many years. It smelled musty.

On the inside cover, the words *"Property of Alice Shaworth. DO NOT TOUCH!"* were written boldly in black ink.

"Alice Shaworth," Walt announced.

"A. S.," Celia echoed.

"I wonder if she's the one in the photo."

Walt thumbed past a couple of blank pages until he came to the first page of text, an unlined journal page, half-filled with a pretty, neat, girl's handwriting.

This is the top-secret diary of Alice Shaworth, begun on this date, Tuesday, October 6, 1934. In it, I intend to record the important events of my day, the secrets of my heart, and the ordinary and extraordinary circumstances and happenings of my existence.

"A little flowery," Walt observed.
"I think it's endearing."

Today, I have been utterly ill at ease due to the unusual circumstances of the preceding evening. It was an ordinary evening in every regard, until bedtime, when, after kissing Mother and Father good night, I came up here to my room and began reading as I am wont to do before I retire...

"'Wont to do before I retire...?'" Walt questioned, mockingly.
"Clearly," Celia defended, "she's an aspiring writer. She's just trying to sound like the books she reads. Plus, this was decades ago."
"Sounds like centuries ago."
Celia adopted a hick accent. "We all can't write as purdy as you, Walt Walters."
The diary continued:

I read in various states of rapture and complacency for about an hour or so, until I heard my parents clump up the stairs and to the bedroom for the night. I intended to read for only a few minutes more before going to sleep myself. But as I was finishing up a chapter of my book, I heard a faint, strange scratching sound emanating, so it seemed, from the floor above me—from the attic. We have had squirrels in our attic before along with other small, wild animals...

"Raccoons, maybe," Celia suggested.

...but this was somehow different: disturbing in its deliberateness, eerie in its distinct rhythm. Moreover, it was not quite the sound of scratching, I realized, but something between the sound of scratching and the croak of a raspy whisper.

A chill ran along Walt's back and he felt the tingle of anxiety on his skin, so he said, "Oooh, scary," so Celia wouldn't suspect his apprehension.

My parents had obviously fallen asleep, for they did not respond at all to the creepy sound which seemed to be growing louder by the moment and was accompanied, after a short time, by a faint thumping, like the slow beat of a tom-tom or the contemplative pace of a peg-legged man.

"Well, now, she's gone too far," Walt said, throwing a hand in the air. Immediately, he felt less frightened. The peg-legged intruder smacked too much of hokey legends and campfire ghost stories to be real. This girl, Alice Shaworth, was obviously working in fiction. Or perhaps it was not Alice Shaworth's writing at all. Perhaps, decades earlier, the old man from the garage sale had written this diary as a horror story about a character named Alice Shaworth. Perhaps he had forgotten the story was in the portfolio altogether.

"It is a bit much," Celia agreed, but she and Walt both kept reading.

As the thumping grew louder with the passing moments, I crawled under the covers of my bed, hiding my head, hoping for the noises to go away, fearing what it meant if they did not.

"Go wake your parents!" Celia advised the manuscript, chiding it toward safety.

"Where's the fun in that?" Walt replied.

For what length of time I remained hidden under covers in this manner, I do not know. I only know that I awoke, several hours later to the sound of my mother, rapping on the door to my room while the bright morning sun streamed against the blinds of my window. The night had passed, the noises from the attic had ceased and I was safe and sound in my own warm bed.

The diary entry stopped at the end of a page and Walt flipped to the next page to see several shorter entries for several other dates.

"Do you think it's real?" Celia asked him.

"No, are you kidding me?" Walt said without a lot of certainty. "I'll bet it's just a made-up story someone was writing."

"But those other entries look real."

Walt looked at the next few entries. They did seem to include dull descriptions of teenage-girl interests—what he would have expected from a girl's diary. There were descriptions of friendships and rivalries, of desires and dreams and fantastic plans for the future. The entry for October 1st read:

I have determined to become either a great female aviator, or a nurse. Both, of course, would take a college education, so I

*am assuming money will not be so tight in five years when I'm
ready to go to college. Father encourages me, as he always has,
to pursue my dreams without caution. Mother is kind but will
only repeat that my dreams might change in the next several
years and that I should not settle too early for one vision of the
future. I get so frustrated with Mother sometimes. Her advice is
often more enigmatic than useful.*

The entry for October 4th was brief and to the point:

"Billy M. is a pickle. I hate him!"

"Are there any more about the creepy sounds from the
attic?" Celia wondered.

Walt thumbed ahead through the pages, glancing through
entries for key words that might signal an attic entry. It didn't
take long. On October 9th, the person writing under the name of
Alice Shaworth recorded this:

*The noises were back last night! And they were worse than
last time! They grew so loud, at one point, that I felt as if the
whole house were vibrating. I couldn't believe my parents did
not awaken. I expected at any moment for one of them to burst
into my room, scream of some geologic cataclysm and to rescue
me. I, myself, could not move.*

*As with the previous occurrence, the noise had seemed
relatively innocuous at first, like the faint scampering of a small
animal. I hardly noticed until, again as in the previous instance,
a persistent thumping began, accompanying the scratching
sound. Once more, the thumping was deliberate and measured,*

like a steady pace, and my heart began to race as I heard the thump move across the attic floor ... toward the attic door!

My impulse, of course, was to flee from my bed, to run down the hall to my parents' room to awaken them. In doing so, of course, I knew I would have to pass the attic entrance, and what if the thing pacing its way to the attic door were to exit, just as I passed. The thought gave me a moment's pause which, as it turned out, was a blessing of good fortune, for only a moment later the room—indeed the whole house—began to shake and vibrate furiously as if being tossed about in a tremendous storm. My bed felt as if it were riding a wave of vibrations across the room.

And still, the thumping persisted, louder, more menacing. My bed shook so violently, I was afraid to step off of it and, instead, clung to my headboard for dear life. The thumping grew, louder and louder, and I thought I heard the screech of the attic door!

It's coming, I thought, it's coming!

The roar within my room was like a freight train traveling by at top speed. The thumping and scratching felt as if they might rip the very wallpaper from the walls. Anticipatory terror filled my entire body as I held on to my shaking bed frame for dear life, contemplating seriously a dive through the window as an only hope for escape. The thunderous quakes grew louder and, in that instant, I saw the door of my room swing open...!

At that very moment, coincidentally, the front door to the Walters' house flew open and Walt and Celia heard a loud bang as Mr. Walters entered the living room off balance under the weight of a heavy armful of garage sale booty and swinging the door against the doorstop and the wall.

Walt and Celia both jumped involuntarily at the sudden noise. Mr. Walters heard their screech and called up anxiously, "Walt? Are you okay? Walt?" He dropped his treasures and bounded up the stairs.

Walt's heart was beating fast and it took a full five seconds before he could recover. By that time, Mr. Walters was at his bedroom door.

"We're okay," he said weakly, as his father ran into the room.

"What hap...?" Mr. Walters started, and then saw the heap of junk from Walt's closet piled in the middle of the floor. "What the hay?"

"We were cleaning out the closet. You scared us."

"You really did," Celia confirmed. Her voice trembled. "Hi, Mr. Walters."

"Hi, Celia," Mr. Walters' eyes were fixated on the mess in the middle of the room. "I didn't know you were coming over."

"I came over to help."

"Well," Mr. Walters said. "Looks like you're making some... some.... progress." Mr. Walters sighed. "Is everything okay?"

"You just surprised us," Walt told him, not knowing how frightened Celia had been or how frightened he wanted to admit to being until he knew about her.

"Sorry." Mr. Walters stared for another long moment at the mess in the center of the room and then, with resignation, said, "We brought some burgers home for lunch. There's plenty, Celia, if you want to stay. Wash up and come down to the kitchen."

"Thanks, Mr. Walters."

"Okay, Dad."

As soon as Mr. Walters left the room, Celia and Walt looked at each other to see what the other was thinking.

"Were you scared?"

"Nah," Walt said. It wasn't exactly a lie because he could tell Celia didn't believe him.

"Me, either," Celia said. Walt didn't believe her either. Celia nodded toward Alice Shaworth's diary and added, "Let's see what happens before we go down for lunch."

Their reading of the diary had been interrupted by Mr. Walters' entrance just as they reached the bottom of a page. With more than a little trepidation, Walt turned to the next page of the diary to find out what had happened to Alice Shaworth the night her house started shaking.

"It's blank," Walt reported, surprised.

"What?" Celia asked, though she, too, was looking at the blank page.

"It's blank."

"Maybe two pages are stuck together."

Mr. Walters called them from the kitchen, "Walt! Celia! Lunch!"

Hurriedly, Walt rubbed the pages between his thumb and forefinger to see if any were stuck to a preceding page.

"No."

"What happened?"

"Maybe the pages got ripped out."

Walt quickly leafed through the rest of the volume to discover that all the subsequent pages were blank, too. It didn't seem as if, from where the pages were bound to the cover, any had been torn out, but it was hard to tell.

"Strange."

"That's a rip-off," Celia decided. Her voice was returning to normal. "I wonder why she stopped writing?"

"Maybe she got devoured by the peg-legged man," Walt suggested. He couldn't tell if he was joking or guessing.

"I hate when that happens."

"Walt! Celia!" Mr. Walters called from downstairs.

"Get down here, dweeb-heads. Lunch is ready!" they heard Zelda add and then Mr. Walters chastised her, "That's not so helpful, Zelda."

"Speaking of devouring…" Walt said to Celia.

"I wonder what happened?" Celia asked. She took the diary from Walt and thumbed through the pages herself, looking for a continuation.

"Like I said," Walt reminded her. "It's probably just a big hoax. Come on, let's go get some lunch."

Celia looked carefully through the rest of the diary before closing it and setting it on the floor. "I guess you're right," she admitted. "Let's eat."

THREE

After lunch, Mr. Walters followed Celia and Walt up to Walt's bedroom to supervise the rehabilitation of the closet. What he saw of their progress before lunch led him to believe that some adult supervising was essential. With as much commanding authority as he was capable of, he directed the sorting, disposal and organization of the things they pulled from the cluttered pile.

And as soon as the work began to look more productive and determined than fun, Celia lost interest and decided to go home.

"Let me know if you come across something good," Celia had said as she left.

"It's all good," Walt assured her.

His father thought differently and suggested that almost everything in the closet be placed in the discard pile. At first Walt balked at the disposal of his priceless treasures, but then, when he realized how quickly the sorting went when everything was put in the same pile, he warmed up to the idea. He worked diligently for several minutes before his mind wandered.

"Dad, do we have an attic?" he asked. The diary of Alice Shaworth had piqued his interest about attics and what they might contain.

"An attic? Well, of course we have one. It's above the house…somewhere."

"What's in it?"

Mr. Walters looked puzzled. "Nothing. Just insulation."

"There's not a room or anything? Where someone could walk around?"

"It's not that kind of attic. People had those kinds of attics in the old, old days in the old, old houses. Nowadays, people just have insulation."

"How do you get there?"

"Get where?" Walt's father was a very smart man—his job included code-breaking and highly-advanced encryption techniques. But in daily life he was often easily confused.

"To our attic," Walt explained.

"Oh," Mr. Walters paused. "Let's see… I know we have one. Where is it?"

Walt watched his father think. The door to the attic could not be in an obvious place. They had lived in this house since Walt was a baby and he couldn't recall ever seeing the attic.

"Is it in the basement, maybe…" Walt's father went on, "No, that wouldn't make much sense. Where is it? Your mother would remember. She had a memory for those sorts of things."

"A memory for attic doors?"

"Wait…wait," Mr. Walters urged. He was on the verge of recollection. "Ah, yes, yes." He looked at Walt, triumphantly. "There's a panel in one of your closets." Mr. Walters was exceptionally pleased with himself. "Either yours or Acey's…or possibly Zelda's. Or maybe it's in mine." To find out, he walked to Walt's closet and looked up at the ceiling. "There it is." He pointed up.

Walt went to stand beside his father. In the ceiling of his closet, a two-by-three-foot panel covered the opening to the attic. It was painted white, like the ceiling, and easy to miss. Obviously, Walt had missed it in all the years he had used the closet for his dumping ground.

"How do you get in?"

"You just push on that panel and it goes up. Scoot it to the side and climb in."

"Can I look?"

"In the attic? I told you, it's just insulation."

"I know, but I've never seen one."

"Well, you've never seen a housefly drown in eggnog, but that doesn't make it worth seeing."

"C'mon, please? Can I go up and take a look?"

Mr. Walters sighed. "If we get this closet cleaned out before suppertime than you can take a look. But you can't walk around up there. Too dangerous."

It was vague promise, but at least some modest motivation for Walt to get back to work. "It's a deal," he told his father.

For the next several hours, Walt and his father worked steadily to get Walt's closet cleaned out. They sorted almost everything that came out of it into the discard pile and a few things into the "store in the basement" pile, and only a handful of items to go back in the closet—a football, a racquetball racquet, Walt's beginnings of a coin collection, a sweater his mother had given him. By four o'clock they were through and they bagged and dragged the stuff in the discard pile out to the front for the trash.

When they came back in, Walt reminded his father about the promise to show him the attic.

"Oh, all right," Mr. Walters conceded. They went to the garage for the stepladder and carried it together to Walt's room. Mr. Walters positioned it carefully in the closet so that the top step of the ladder was right below the attic panel. It was a tight fit of the ladder into the closet, and an uncomfortable climb around the shelves and clothes racks, as if the attic were deliberately intended to be hard to reach.

"What do I do?" Walt asked.

"Just climb up and push the panel to the side. Make sure the insulation doesn't get into your eyes."

Mr. Walters' voice betrayed the weariness of a parent reluctantly indulging a child's curiosity despite his better judgment. Walt heard the patience running thin and hurried up the ladder. It was dusty and cramped at the top where his shelf closet rested over the clothes rack. He put both hands on the attic panel and pushed up, not knowing what kind of resistance to expect.

There was no resistance. The panel pushed up easily and Walt felt like a superhero lifting the roof of a building. The panel rose with Walt's pushing for eight inches or so, above the two-by-fours that created the frame for the panel in the attic floor, and above several inches of insulation, until he could see the natural light of the attic room.

"Just push it to the side a little," Walt's father coached from below. "You don't have to push it totally out of the way. Just enough to get your head and shoulders through. Mind the insulation."

Walt followed his father's instructions and gently set the attic panel down on top of the insulation. Then, while holding onto the panel frame for support, he climbed up the last two steps of the stepladder, until his head and shoulders were through the attic access and he was looking out over the top of the insulation.

It was, Walt had to admit, one of the dullest things he'd ever seen. The attic contained nothing but pink, fluffy insulation and rafters. The afternoon sun was still directly on the roof, so enough light shone through cracks and vents to light the space.

And it was stuffy. Though, outside, it was a pleasant Indian summer, inside the attic it was at least 20 degrees hotter and with the stuffiness of a room that had been closed off forever.

"What do you think?" Walt's father asked. If Walt did not know his father better, he would have guessed there was a hint of sarcasm in the question.

"Um… neat," Walt lied. "Really neat."

"Not what you were expecting?"

Walt wasn't quite sure what he'd expected, but his mind had conjured up all kinds of images reading Alice Shaworth's diary, and none of the images matched what he was looking at now.

"Any sign of the raccoon getting in?"

"There's no raccoon, Dad." In a far corner, Walt could see where birds had squeezed into the attic and built a nest, but the nest could have been decades old. There were no other signs of any animal life. "It's too hot up here for any animals."

"That's the way it should be," Walt's father said, logically. "You done?"

Walt had to admit his father had been right: there was nothing worth seeing, but he lingered for a moment to deny his dad the satisfaction of thinking Walt was wholly disappointed.

"One more sec," Walt said, "I just want to…take it all in."

He searched the dark corners for something interesting to observe to justify the lingering and there, in the shadows at the farthest corner, where the roof angled into the ceiling, he saw what looked to be another access panel. Like the one he'd just lifted to get into the attic, the panel was perhaps two feet wide and three feet tall. It was surrounded by a frame and painted white, standing out against the natural grained plywood of the roof.

"What's that opening in the corner for?" Walt called down to his father. He knew just from looking at it that, if the panel opened, it could lead nowhere but to the roof of the house for there was nothing above the attic but tar paper and the roof's shingles.

"What opening?" his father asked.

"That one in the corner," Walt explained. "It's like another access panel."

His father was curious. "Let's see." And Walt felt Mr. Walters climbing up the stepladder below him. He scootched to the side of the step he was on so that when his father got to the top, he was able to squeeze his torso through the opening and stand on the step with him. Together, they looked over the insulation to the corner where Walt was pointing.

"Hmm," Mr. Walters mused, studying the panel from twenty feet away. "That's curious. I've never seen that before."

"What is it?'

"I don't know. Nothing, I guess. Maybe just a patch where there was a hole in the roof."

"Why would they put a frame around it?"

"That's a good point," Mr. Walters admitted. "Maybe they had planned on putting in a skylight when they built the house, but changed their minds."

That made more sense to Walt. The panel seemed like the perfect size and place for a skylight. Sometimes his dad could be pretty smart.

"Huh," Mr. Walters said finally, after looking at the panel for another moment. "As long as it doesn't leak, I guess it doesn't matter. Come on, let's get down and go have a lemonade."

With that, he ducked his head through the attic opening and descended the ladder, patting Walt on the back as he went down, and repeating, "Come on."

Walt looked across the space one last time for good measure, then ducked his head to climb down. Seeing the attic had been, he admitted, anticlimactic. He scooted the attic panel back in place, then climbed down to the floor.

As he did, he could have sworn he heard a noise above him, a vague but repetitious sound from the attic. He didn't say anything to his father, who seemed oblivious to the faint noise, because he didn't want to admit what it sounded like: the deliberate scratching of a small animal's claws, like those of a raccoon.

FOUR

Mr. Walters was very proud of and worn out from the cleaning of Walt's closet that evening. So, he declared a celebration of the pizza variety and took his children out for deep-dish pepperoni. Afterwards, he was so pleased with himself for avoiding cooking that he rewarded the family with an ice cream cone. It was well after nine o'clock before the well-fed Walters returned home, content but at the limits of family togetherness. So, they each went off to do their own thing except Acey who wanted to do her own thing with her father.

Zelda went to her room to watch television. And Walt could hear Mr. Walters, talking to his younger sister in her room, answering for the millionth time all of Acey's questions about her mother. She never tired of asking the same questions—what their mother was like, how much had she had loved her, how did she disappear. But Walt had to admit, he, too, took consolation from his father's patient, reassuring replies.

Walt had been thinking about the diary of Alice Shaworth throughout the evening, and so, when he went to his room, he found the book and began re-reading, trying to decide what it was: a real diary? The phony diary someone named Alice had written for amusement? A total work of fiction by an anonymous author in order to entertain or scare whomever found it?

More slowly than he had with Celia, he read Alice Shaworth's account of the footsteps and noises coming from her attic. There was something familiar about the description, but Walt couldn't put his finger on what it was. He read again about the rhythmic thumping above Alice's room, about Alice, huddled in her bed, waiting for the sounds to subside, about the thudding steps pounding toward her bedroom door. As it had when he read the passages earlier, Walt's heartbeat quickened:

Anticipatory terror filled my entire body as I held onto my shaking bed frame for dear life, contemplating seriously a dive through the window as an only hope for escape. The thunderous quakes grew louder and, in that instant, I saw the door of my room swing open...!

When Walt got to the end of the passage, he automatically—in the natural habit of reading—turned the page, though he knew from earlier in the day, that the rest of the diary was blank.

But it wasn't! The next page, he was shocked to see, was filled with more of Alice Shaworth's handwriting. He was so surprised that he didn't even read it at first, taking a moment instead to make sure he hadn't somehow paged backward or missed the next page altogether.

But there was no mistake. It was, without a doubt, the next page. He rubbed it between his thumb and forefinger thinking he'd unwittingly loosed pages that were stuck together. He was sure that he and Celia had looked through the rest of the diary, thoroughly. It was as if this new writing had appeared out of nowhere—as if his intense curiosity had reached across time and prodded Alice Shaworth to a new, explanatory entry.

Slowly, as if trying to understand a confusing instruction manual, he began reading the new page. However, this new entry was not as enlightening as Walt had hoped. Rather than picking up where she'd left off—with the door to her room flying open, Alice took up the story the next morning:

I awoke very late with the bright sun streaming through the shades of my window. I was surprised to find myself safe and secure on my own bed, beneath comforting blankets surrounded by familiar objects, all quietly sitting, unshaken and unmoved despite the earthquake intensity I'd felt in the last moments before I lost consciousness last evening. For it must have been that I had lost consciousness, I was sure. The terrifying events of the preceding evening were so real and vivid in my mind. I could remember so clearly—or thought I could—the sheer terror of the moment as I watched the door open. I was certain I was about to confront some malevolent fiend intent on my destruction.

Yet, as soon as I assured myself that I was indeed awake, safe and alive, I jumped from bed and rushed downstairs to the kitchen where my mother stood, calmly stirring the breakfast oatmeal. I hesitated. Everything seemed so normal, so ordinary, that immediately I began to wonder what had happened the night before, what had been real and why it's terrifying actuality had not seemed to change my room, this house and its routine, the world one solitary iota.

My mother stood at the stove in her house dress and apron, stirring patiently and humming. She greeted me brightly as I entered, as if nothing in the world had ever been amiss, so immediately I questioned her: Did you feel that shaking last night? Did you hear footsteps?

She looked at me, very puzzled, and so I told her the whole story, everything I could remember from the night before but, mysteriously, as I explained, the images that had been so vivid in my mind only moments earlier began to fade in the retelling—as if they had been impressed in a sand that was slowly being blown aside by a strong wind.

"That sounds like an awfully scary dream," my mother told me. And, although I had been certain it was real, when she mentioned the word "dream" the memory faded all the more and I began to think of it as a dream and marvel at its sublimity. My fears subsided quickly.

At school today, Darcy asked me again about her party...

And Alice Shaworth went on from there about Darcy (whose upcoming party she was not so thrilled about), about money (which she apparently she had none of), and about someone who's initials were U. U. (whom she had a crush on but was too shy to talk to): *Should I tell U.U. what a big crush I have on him?*

Walt rifled ahead through the pages, searching for more entries or further information, but this time, clearly, there was not more writing after a couple more bland descriptions of her daily events. The diary ended on the very next page with no other mention of the noise from the attic or footsteps in the hall. He scanned the final page for key words to suggest Alice's fate, but the last entry, which ended halfway down the right-hand side of one page concluded with a brief, school-girl reverie on the sweetness of U.U.:

He is a wonderful boy and I only hope he will notice one day my interest in him lest I be doomed to harbor my affections unrequited.

"Ah, woe is me," she ended the entry, with mock melodrama. And that is where Alice's diary ended, somewhat anti-climatically.

Walt set the book down beside him on his bed, disappointed. Instead of a satisfying resolve to the taut entry he'd read before, he'd found only a tamer cliffhanger. It was frustrating, like the bad sequel to a favorite novel or movie.

In the hallway outside his room, Walt could see the lights in the house being turned off, room by room—his father's ritual right before going to bed. His conversation with Acey was over and the hum of Zelda's television had stopped as well.

"Goodnight, Zeld," he heard his father call as he passed her room, but Zelda gave no reply, perhaps already asleep. A moment later, Mr. Walter's stuck his head into Walt's room.

"It's getting late," he told Walt.

"I was just reading. I'm done."

"I'm heading off to bed. Don't forget to brush your teeth."

"Okay."

"Love you, Kiddo."

"Love you, Dad. Thanks for showing me the attic."

"It's the least a father can do for his son." Mr. Walters smiled. "Goodnight."

And then Mr. Walters went into his own bedroom, right across the hall from Walt's, looking tired and thoughtful. Walt watched him close the bedroom door and then Walt went to the bathroom to brush his teeth, finding himself irrationally irritated by Alice Shaworth and her inconclusive diary. There was no reason to be frustrated by Alice who had lived (and perhaps died), many years ago. Yet, in his mind, he pictured her like one of the girls at school who giggled when they passed and yet, when you asked them why they were giggling, just couldn't say. Alice, too, just couldn't seem to eek out of her tantalizing pen, the answers to the questions Walt most wanted to ask: What was the noise in the hallway? Did it ever return? And, if so, what happened to Alice when it finally entered her room?

Walt finished brushing his teeth and headed back down the hallway to his room. He shut off his bedroom light and pushed his window open a bit to let in the crisp autumn air that always smelled so clean. A streetlight at the curb a few doors down threw a tiny shaft of light through the window and along the wall near his bed. He lay back, tired and surprised to see on his clock that it was nearing midnight. Re-reading Alice's diary had made the past two hours fly by.

He wondered what Alice's life had been like many years ago. Her diary covered her teenage life but never mentioned the little things that added so much flavor to daily living and that Walt found himself thinking about: How was her room decorated? What kind of appliances did her family own? How many steps was it from her bedroom to the kitchen?

And he thought about how difficult it must have been for Alice to lay down to sleep the night after her terrifying experience with the noises in the hall—although her subsequent diary entries made no mention of her fears.

But when she crawled into bed that next night, she must have felt some apprehension. Walt imagined her, lying there, listening tensely for any noise that might be a portent of the wild commotion of the previous evening.

And Walt found himself listening, too, trying to center his hearing on his closet door because that was where the entrance to the Walters' attic was and the attic in Alice Shaworth's house had been the origin of the mysterious clumping that had terrified her.

And then he heard it...

It started very faintly, so much so that Walt felt sure he was imagining it, conjuring it with his speculation on Alice Shaworth's experience. And then it disappeared and Walt was certain his mind had been tricking him.

And then he heard it again...

More distinctly this time—two clumps, not faint but clear. Like someone dropping one shoe and then another in the attic above him.

And then nothing for a long time. He was telling himself it was "just the house settling" as his father would have explained it, when the next clumps sounded, several of them in a row, moving across the attic rapidly, scurrying.

He remembered the raccoon his sister Zelda had suspected and thought, that could be it. It kind of sounds like the scurrying of tiny rodent feet.

He had convinced himself of that for only a moment, however, when the next series of clumps sounded across the ceiling of his room. Not rapid scurrying, but slow, deliberate thumps like heavy footsteps pacing with menacing patience in the attic above his head.

FIVE

"You're just trying to scare me now, Walt Walters," Celia Washroth claimed, though she didn't seem scared at all. She seemed skeptical.

"I am not, I swear." Walt hadn't told anyone else about the noises from his attic because he felt sure he'd be called a liar or the noises would be attributed to movements of the mammoth raccoon his sister Zelda had reported. If anyone would believe him, he'd thought, it would be Celia.

"It was probably that big raccoon," Celia suggested, impatiently.

"It wasn't a raccoon."

"Maybe it was bats."

"Bats generally don't stomp around on the floor."

"Maybe it was a bat with a chip on his shoulder."

"I have no idea what that means."

It was Monday morning and they were standing near Celia's locker in Lexington Junior High before first period. For two nights in a row now, Walt had heard the distinctive, rattling above his bed, coming from the attic.

The first night, Saturday night, the vibrations sounded for less than five minutes and then ceased suddenly, leaving the house eerily quiet. The second night—last night—they had gone on much longer and Walt had eventually covered his ears with his pillow and hummed childhood lullabies. The next thing he knew, it was morning and everything was back to normal.

"I have to get to class. I have a test," Celia told Walt, looking at her watch. "Just give me the diary and I'll give it back after school."

He pulled the volume from beneath his arm where he'd been carrying it while he told Celia about the footsteps. He'd already told her about the additional diary pages he'd discovered Saturday night.

"We must have just missed them. They were probably stuck together," Celia explained, reflecting Walt's reasoning.

Walt was going to show her the new entries, but she took the book from him.

"I'll find it, Walt. I've got a test."

"When are you going to read it?"

"This hour."

"I thought you had a test."

"I can finish early if I don't get hung up on accuracy."

"Give it back after school."

With that Celia Washroth hurried down the hallway to her first class. Walt watched her bustle away. He felt oddly possessive, letting the diary out of his sight—as if it were something he knew, intuitively, he should hold on to. Yet, if there were one person in the world he could trust with it—he could trust with anything—it was Celia.

She was a bit of a wiseacre sometimes, but a loyal and trustworthy friend.

She'd been a salvation to Walt after his mother vanished. For months after the disappearance, none of the Walters children went to school. They stayed home, at first, while the police investigated the mysterious and sudden absence, anticipating wordlessly her imminent return. But as days turned to weeks and weeks turned to months, it became clear that she wasn't coming back. Still, Walt, Zelda and Acey stayed at home with their father who was, first, anxious and worried to distraction and, then, inconsolably heartbroken.

After almost three months, however, the extended family convinced Mr. Walters it was time to return his family to a normal routine, and so Walt was sent back to school where he sat in class and stared at his teacher unable to comprehend how life could go on as usual without his mother. For a long time, he was oblivious to almost everything that went on in the classroom, including his schoolwork, and his teacher, Mr. Wentworth, kindly let him occupy a seat without asking anything of him.

And then, after several weeks, Walt began slowly to take notice of his world and his classmates and one of the first things he noticed was that a new kid had been added at some point. Had she been there when he first came back to school? Was this one of her first days? He couldn't have said. All he could say was that one day he looked around the classroom, as if just waking up from a dream, and saw a girl who looked to be as lost as he felt.

She sat in the back of the classroom and never spoke to anyone—not to any other students, not to Mr. Wentworth, not to anyone. Not only did she not speak, she didn't make eye contact with anyone either. She stared at her desk, her book, her papers or out the window. And if you happened to catch her eye for a moment, she would look away quickly as if afraid of being acknowledged by the world.

Walt was too wrapped up in his own grief to take more than a passing interest in the quiet girl except to feel a brief kinship of loneliness. But a few days later, when he was standing on the playground blacktop watching the other children play, he heard a quiet voice behind him ask, "Are you the kid whose mom disappeared?"

Walt turned around to find the girl from the back of class staring at him—not sympathetically but curiously—as if she had never encountered this alien species.

"Who are you?"

"I'm Celia. My parents are dead."

"What happened to them?"

"They died."

"How?"

"Not sure. How did your mother disappear?"

"Not sure."

"Do you think she's dead?"

"Not sure."

"Never give up hope," Celia said. "You want to play two-square?"

"Okay."

And they had been best friends ever since. That was the last time they talked about Celia's parents or Walt's mother. Their friendship took off so fast that they didn't have time to talk about anything substantial.

Celia lived with her uncle in a big but shabby two-story house in the older section of Walt's neighborhood. Walt had only seen her uncle once or twice during the entire time he'd known her and then only in fleeting meetings. Celia said he had to work all the time to make ends meet and keep the house and was always napping, worn out from being a father and mother and uncle to his orphaned niece. Walt had been in Celia's house perhaps ten times in the last three years. It was sparsely decorated and the furniture was a throwback to a previous decade. From what Walt had seen, he guessed they didn't have a television, and once he had even observed Celia's uncle—in a brief glimpse and from the back as he and Celia passed down the hallway—sitting in a poorly-lit living room listening to a ballgame on an old-fashioned box radio.

By contrast, Celia had been in Walt's house many times and had become almost a member of the family. For a young girl, she was an excellent cook, and she often came over after school and cooked with Zelda and Walt while Acey watched. Then Mr. Walters would come home from work and Celia would sit down with the family for dinner. Her uncle, she explained, was working anyway, and it was either eat with the Walters or eat on her own. Mr. Walters had told her many times, "Celia, you're always welcome. You're an honorary member of the family." Even Zelda, who referred to most of Walt's friends as "loser-creepy-cretin-nerd-dweebs," liked Celia. That was something.

So, when Walt gave the diary of Alice Shaworth to Celia, he was sure it was in safe and trusted hands. And yet, he was anxious about it all morning. Not that he feared Celia would lose or damage it. But he had a growing intimation that there was more to the diary than met the eye. The more he recalled Saturday and going through the diary with Celia, the more certain he felt that they had checked and double-checked to ensure that the diary ended—abruptly—where it seemed to end. And so, the appearance of the additional entries—very different in tone and intensity than what had preceded it—felt all the more glaring, though it was clearly written in the same, distinctive, and proper feminine hand.

And he kept remembering what Alice had written about her memories being swept away slowly like sand on a windy beach. The image was disconcerting in its impermanence and yet the appearance of additional diary entries made it seem as if details were being added to the mystery rather than dusted away.

Walt was mulling this murky image around in his brain during third period when he heard his name being called, sternly, and was jolted out of his ruminations.

"Mr. Walters!"

Walt sat up straight in his desk. He felt as if he were coming out of a deep sleep. He looked around to see if, in fact, someone had truly called his name.

"Mr. Walters!"

Someone had. And it was Mr. Murphy, his third period Modern European History teacher.

"Are you with us, Mr. Walters?"

Mr. Murphy called everyone in the class "Mr." or "Ms." He said he did it out of respect for the men and women they were becoming but everyone in the class knew they were just kids and that being called "Mr." or "Ms." only made it weightier when you got in trouble.

"Yes, I'm here," Walt answered, uncertain of the context of the question. "Present," he added, just in case Mr. Murphy had been taking roll.

"Glad to hear it, Mr. Walters," Mr. Murphy said, not sounding very glad at all. "Perhaps you can answer the question then."

Walt looked to his classmates for some clue but got nothing from their blank faces. "What question?" He almost asked and then realized that would only reinforce Mr. Murphy's assumption that he hadn't been paying attention—which he hadn't.

Walt asked, "The question?" thinking that was much less incriminating.

"The question, Mr. Walters. Do you know the answer? It was in the reading you were supposed to do for homework this weekend."

Things were only getting worse for Walt. Not only didn't he know the answer and question, he didn't know he was supposed to have done any reading over the weekend.

"Ah, yes," Walt said, as if enlightened.

"Did you do the reading, Mr. Walters?"

"Is it General Grant?" Walt asked.

"Is what General Grant, Mr. Walters?"

"The answer to the question."

Walt guessed from the titter of giggles that went through the classroom that "General Grant" was not the correct answer, but he knew Mr. Murphy would take delight in pronouncing the failure publicly.

"No, Mr. Walters," Mr. Murphy started, more amused than angry at how wrong the answer was. "'General Grant' is not the correct answer to the question 'In what year did France officially withdraw from the Vietnam peninsula?' Nor is it the correct answer to any question I can think of regarding modern European history, though it might make a fine answer to a question about American Civil War history."

The class roared with laughter at the wrongness of Walt's answer and Walt slumped in his seat.

"Not so quickly," Mr. Murphy cut them off. "Clearly, Mr. Walters did not do the reading for today, but I'm guessing, from the total absence of hands that went up when I asked the question, that very few people did."

The class was suddenly quiet.

"Honestly, now," Mr. Murphy said, looking at them as if he truly wanted a straight answer, "How many people actually read the assignment?"

Six or eight hands went up throughout the class.

"The whole assignment," Mr. Murphy added.

Six or eight hands went down.

"People, people, people," Mr. Murphy complained, shaking his head. "I know that simply reading about history from a textbook can be dull sometimes. But I don't ask you to read an unreasonable amount."

Almost to a student, the class slumped in their chairs to match Walt's deflated posture.

"And I only ask you to read because it is so important. So terribly important." Mr. Murphy took a deep breath and his chest swelled, and the entire class knew what was coming next—Mr. Murphy's favorite quotation about the importance of his beloved subject: "For those who do not study history," he pronounced, "are doomed to repeat it."

He paused after the quotation but then quickly elaborated, recognizing that he had their shamed attention, "Read, study, and, most importantly, remember. Why do you think so many monuments—of war, of fallen heroes, of people who have sacrificed or been sacrificed—are inscribed with the words 'lest we forget'?"

This time, Mr. Murphy was not looking for an answer.

"Because the people who have seen and suffered and studied and understood know that the only true way to prevent recurrence of the horrors of the past are to remember them, to remind ourselves of them, often and sincerely."

Mr. Murphy cast a wise and mournful look over the entire class and repeated slowly, "Remember. Read and remember."

The bell in the hall rang, as if to punctuate Mr. Murphy's admonition and to toll its significance. Mostly, however, the class was relieved to have the lecture over and, impatiently, the students gathered up their books and papers and bee-lined it for the door.

Walt was the most relieved of all since, after being caught daydreaming and unprepared, he felt certain Mr. Murphy would have some extra assignment or other punishment to mete out. So when the bell rang he thought he might just escape, especially since Mr. Murphy had very mercifully spread Walt's shame at being unprepared over the whole classroom. As inconspicuously as possible, Walt picked up his notebook and history text and slinked toward the door, trying to blend in with the other students.

He made it halfway to the exit. "Mr. Walters."

Walt stopped, knowing what was coming. He didn't even have to look at Mr. Murphy. The teacher was at his desk, studying the stack of quizzes he'd collected earlier in the period.

"That's your third missed reading this month."

Walt nodded. There was no use in denying it. Perhaps ready admission of guilt would win mercy. "Yes."

"Three strikes and you're out, Mr. Walters," Mr. Murphy reminded him, not looking up from the quizzes.

"Yes, Mr. Murphy," Walt mumbled humbly, trying to sound contrite.

"Half hour detention, Mr. Walters. I'll see you at 3:00."

"NO!" Walt shouted, unintentionally. He was so set on seeing Celia right after school to hear her thoughts on Alice Shaworth's diary that the idea of postponing it an extra half hour seemed intolerable. He had shouted "NO!" more forcefully and defiantly than he intended, so much so that Mr. Murphy looked up from his stack of papers.

"I beg your pardon, Mr. Walters?"

"I mean . . . I mean . . ." Walt was so distressed by the punishment that he couldn't think up a quick excuse about why he couldn't stay late after school. "I mean...yes, sir."

Mr. Murphy smiled. "See you then," he said, returning to his work.

Walt was miserable as he walked out of his third period class. He didn't mind having made a fool of himself in class, but he hated the idea of missing Celia and the diary. He hurried through the hallway, determined to get to Celia's locker before next period to see if she had read the diary. But her locker was at the other end of the school, and by the time he got there she'd already left and it was too late to catch her before class.

As a result of traveling across the school, he was late to his next class and had to miss the first ten minutes of his lunch as a punishment and so he missed seeing Celia, as he usually did, between her lunch period and his. And the rest of the day went like that—Walt trying to catch Celia between classes and always just missing her and then being late to his next class.

By the end of the day, he was tired of being scowled at by teachers for his tardiness and rather than try to catch Celia after school, he went straight to his detention in Mr. Murphy's class. Mr. Murphy put him right to work cutting out names and dates of important events in late-twentieth century European history for the timeline he was creating. Walt worked for twenty minutes resigning himself to this unrelenting boredom before he could head over to Celia's, when he heard his name over the school's public-address system.

"Mr. Murphy," the authoritative voice of Mrs. Frick, the vice principal called. "Do you have Walt Walters in your room for detention?"

"Yes, I do," Mr. Murphy answered pleasantly from his desk, as if proud to have nabbed such a dangerous criminal.

"Have him collect his things and come straight to the office."

Mr. Murphy looked puzzled for a moment and turned to Walt who shrugged his shoulders. "Will do," Mr. Murphy called.

Walt had gathered his things and was hurrying down the hall in an instant—his first thought being relief from the last few minutes from detention. But his second thought was that you didn't get called out of detention to go to the principal's office unless something were very wrong. His sense of doom increased as he approached the office and saw Vice Principal Frick waiting by the door in the hall for him.

"Were you supposed to pick your sister up after school today?" Mrs. Frick asked, with an accusatory lack of expression.

"AHHHHH," Walt yelled. Monday! Zelda's volleyball practice! Walt's day to get Acey at the elementary school! He'd forgotten!

He was in big trouble.

"AHHHH…." he said again because he couldn't think of anything better to say.

"Your father is on the phone," Mrs. Frick reported, opening the office door to let him in.

Walt would rather have fallen to the floor and melted into inert matter than talk to his father, but he slunk inside the office and to the phone on Mrs. Frick's desk.

"Press the flashing red light," she directed.

Walt picked up the phone and pressed the red light. "Hi, Dad?" He spoke cautiously, not knowing what was coming.

"Are you all right?" his father asked urgently.

"I'm sorry, Dad," Walt said quickly. He was afraid he might cry in front of the vice-principal and then it would get all around the school and then he'd die. "I got a detention and I forgot."

"What did you get a detention for?"

"I forgot to do my reading."

"My gosh, son, you're forgetting everything these days."

"Sorry, dad," Walt said again. He blamed Alice Shaworth for this whole mess. Her diary had distracted him. Since he'd read about her life in her journal he couldn't help thinking about her and what might have ultimately happened to her.

"We'll talk about it later," his father said. "Right now you need to get over and get Acey. She's at Mrs. Harrison's."

"Mrs. Harrison's?"

"Mrs. Harrison was at the school to pick up her kids and saw Acey come out. When nobody was there to meet her, she took Acey home and called me." Mrs. Harrison was a very good friend of the Walters family. She had been very helpful and generous with her time when Walt's mother first disappeared.

Now Walt felt especially awful. He could picture Acey standing outside the school door waiting expectantly for Walt, becoming quickly alarmed and panicked at the idea that no one was there to pick her up. She always got nervous when people didn't show up as expected.

"You need to get over to Mrs. Harrison's and get her," Walt's father finished.

"All right, Dad," Walt tried to sound very reliable. "I'll be there, don't worry."

"Call me if there's a problem."

"All right, Dad," Walt said. "I'm sorry," he added.

"I'm glad you're safe. We'll talk about it when I get home."

Walt hung up the phone feeling awful. He had let down his sister and his father and Mr. Murphy and caused Mrs. Harrison some inconvenience that reflected poorly on his father and on him. Mrs. Frick could apparently sense his contrition, because she didn't even give him a withering look when he hung up and walked out of her office. Instead, she said, with encouragement, "Tomorrow's a brand new day."

Unfortunately, Mrs. Harrison lived almost a mile away from the Walters' home, which was more than a mile and a half from Walt's middle school. And Walt had missed the bus that would take him home because of detention. So, by the time he got home, picked up his bike, rode over to Mrs. Harrison's and walked backed home with Acey, it was five-thirty—almost time for his father to come home from work.

On the walk back from the Harrison's, Acey hardly spoke a word except to remark that the Harrison's kept their house pleasantly warmer than most. Walt apologized to her again and again and she kept telling him, "It's okay, I was just worried about you," but he could see she was remembering the sinking feeling of waiting outside school and no one coming to meet her. Walt felt terrible.

It didn't help when they got home to find Zelda returned from volleyball practice and having somehow learned of Walt's big goof-up.

"That was dumb," Zelda said to greet Walt.

Mr. Walters pulled up in his car a few moments later and had a few things to say about Walt's forgetting as well, mainly, "Next time don't forget." Once he saw that Walt was sincerely sorry, he eased up and kept the lecture focused on responsibility, organization and remembering.

But, Walt continued to feel awful through dinner and into the early evening. It had been a miserable day, all in all. He couldn't remember having had such a consistently bad series of events occur in so short a time. He couldn't remember ever having let so many people down at once.

He was so busy feeling badly about his behavior and feeling sorry for himself, that he almost forgot about Celia and Alice Shaworth and her diary or any of the preoccupations that had gotten him in trouble in the first place.

And then, at eight o'clock, the phone rang.

"Where have you been?" Celia practically yelled at him over the phone. "Where were you after school?"

"I got a detention," he reported. "And then I had to go get Acey." He decided to leave out the part about forgetting to pick her up in the first place.

"I need to talk to you. It's the diary. I'm coming over."

"What happened to it?"

"I'm coming over. I read it!" Celia sounded excited and anxious.

"What did you think?"

"I read it before lunch, Walt. All the way to the end, where it stopped."

"So, what did you think?"

"And then I waited to give it back to you after school and when you didn't show up I took it home with me."

"Celia, did you lose it?"

"Then after supper, I opened it up again. To the last page."

"Yeah?"

"And there was more written!"

"What?"

"Walt, I'm coming over."

SIX

October 11

How I wish I could say what was happening to me, what horrible illness is affecting my brain, creating these delusions (if they are delusions!) and destroying my memory.

Oh, how I hope they are delusions. How I hope that what I am about to do, and what I have been doing these last several hours are part of a fevered nightmare that has caused my brain to envision what is really not there.

I'm frightened, and yet, not, because I know everything will be resolved in the next few moments.

But I get ahead of myself and am losing track of my purpose, which is to tell you, diary, what has happened and what I intend to do now, in hopes that, if I do not return, if I never record another thought within your pages, you will remain here to survive and explain. . . in hopes that the world is not frozen, as it seems, and that someone will come along to read this and know what incredible things have transpired.

So, I will diligently write everything that has happened down to record the truth (if what I think I have experienced is true) before the experiences become shrouded in the fog of mind.

Two days ago, I sat down to re-read this diary and was shocked to find entries describing tremors and horrifying sounds coming from the attic. And though, as I re-read, the events came back to me in some detail, they had apparently completely been washed from my mind otherwise, despite their singular, extraordinary and terrifying nature. It was as if they had never happened. And yet, as soon as I re-read them, I knew they had happened—at least in my mind.

Walt read these new words in Alice Shaworth's diary with intense interest. Celia sat by his side in the Walters' living room. When she arrived, she had handed him the diary without speaking, and as soon as they could find a quiet place to sit, he'd opened it to what had once been the last page to discover the new writing Celia had reported over the phone.

It was "new" writing for sure. This time, there could be no mistake. The script had not ended at the bottom of one page with the possibility of other pages being stuck together after it. This new writing appeared *on the same page* as the previous entry. But, it was clearly the same distinctively beautiful handwriting throughout. It was as if the diary were writing itself when the book was closed.

"Turn the page, turn the page," Celia was prompting excitedly.

Walt quickly turned to the next, not really needing Celia's prompting.

As I write it is one o'clock in the morning and, if they are real, I have just experienced the most unnatural and unnerving events I have ever heard of outside books and fantasies. I am writing because I have resolved to take actions to bring the truth of the matter to light and, perhaps, to discover some way to rescue my parents from the frozen state they are in.

Only moments ago, I recall being up in the attic searching for the origin of the clattering vibrations that have so frightened me. And yet, even as I write these words the details and clarity of

61

events are fading and seeming unreal—like a terrifying story I heard or imagined but never experienced.

I don't know why I'm so terrified. For all I know, what I will discover in the attic is as likely to be benign as dangerous. I have no reason to believe one way or the other. Perhaps the tremors were the lure of a heavenly messenger come with a peaceful message. Perhaps the placard was a sign of good fortunes to come.

Oh, yes, the placard (you see, I almost forgot!) with the strange markings. I told myself to memorize them, but they've completely left me now and even a memory of the placard itself had fled until I wrote of the messenger and then it came back.

So, let me begin again, start at the start, as it were, so I can capture it all in the order it happened so that the world will know:

It began, as I have said, with the re-reading of my diary entries and discovering in them passages and events that had apparently slipped my mind despite their extraordinary nature. It was like experiencing the phenomena anew and I became wholly frightened.

I was lying upon my bed when I started reading, with the intent of falling asleep after a few minutes, but had become so engrossed that, when I finished, I was completely awake and the clock in my bedroom revealed it was midnight. Then, as soon as I closed the book—concerned, curious, afraid—the very moment I closed my diary and secured its clasp, the vibrations described in its pages, the noises from the attic, the thundering footsteps, etc.—THEY ALL BEGAN AGAIN!

But, wherein they had started (according to my diary, for I could remember very little) softly and slowly before, this time, they began with the ferocious intensity of a hurricane, pounding and rattling through the attic, bent on destruction.

I was determined this time not to be paralyzed by my fears, but to confront them head-on, for I knew now that remaining where I was and waiting for the stomping steps to find me could leave me without any further knowledge of the origins of these ominous sounds and might cause me simply to faint again without ever learning the truth.

So, quickly, I raced across my room and opened the door, not sure what might lie beyond it. The floor shivered beneath my feet. The hallway, though filled with the thundering noise from above, was otherwise empty and I poked my head out cautiously to see if anything might be lying in wait.

The coast was clear, and down the short hallway was the door to my parents' room, only seconds away and yet it seemed like miles, for situated between me and my parents' room was the entry-way to the attic—the doorway from behind which the crashing sounded.

There was nothing to do but run, to run as fast as I could past that attic door in hopes that I would be too quick to be grabbed by anything that might be waiting behind it.

And that is what I did. I ran, fast, with my eyes tightly shut but alert in every other sense to the possibility of whatever might try to stop me.

And then I was at my parents' door and I think I may have even cried out in triumph and relief when I reached it. Saved and safe at last, I thought—I would open the door and run to my parents' bed like a toddler and wake them (if they were not already awake from the thundering noise) and they would know what to do. They could protect me. They could rescue us all.

But when I burst into their room, I entered to the strangest scene I have ever witnessed in my life.

There was my mother, lying peacefully in her bed, despite the earthquake shaking the house to its very foundations. And my father was sitting in his chair across the room, with a book in his lap and his reading glasses on, but both of them unmoving as if they were frozen. I approached them, quickly but cautiously and laid my hands gently upon them, at first, but when they did not move, I shook them more vigorously and yelled loudly. But they did not stir. No, they were not dead, I feel certain of that. But rather, they seemed to have been momentarily suspended in time and, indeed, when I turned to rush from the room to call the police, I noticed the clock on their bedroom wall read only ten-fifteen though I knew it was now past midnight.

And that is why I say they were "frozen," for it was as if everything in their room—or perhaps it is everything outside MY room—had stopped in time at ten-fifteen, about the same time that I had started reading my diary that evening.

Of course, at that moment, I had not reasoned it all together and was only panicked at the paralyzed condition I found my parents in and at my awareness of being virtually alone in the house with the thing that was still stomping furiously on the ceiling above me. I was panicked but knew, too, exactly what I needed to do, and that was to telephone the police. My parents have taught me well (oh, mother, if you ever read this, know that you have taught me well and that I love you for it!) and cautioned me a thousand times to rush to a telephone and dial "zero" if ever I was in trouble. And I could think of no greater trouble than what I was confronting at that moment.

And so, though I knew what I had to do—get to the telephone quickly—I took a moment to encourage myself to do it, for I knew that to call the police meant passing through the hallway again, passing the attic door again, and getting to the telephone in the living room..

One look at my mother, paralyzed in time, helped enforce my resolve. "I must rescue her and father, I must" I told myself and, without further hesitation, I moved to the door of their room, which I had closed behind me when I entered. I took a deep breath and tried to think only of my parents as I opened it, cautiously.

Once again, the hallway was empty though I could see the pictures on the walls rattling from the vibrations of the noise and, though I'm sure I imagined this, I thought I saw the door to the attic fairly bursting as if it were being kicked from the inside.

The time was now, I knew, for if something were coming from the attic, in a moment, it would burst into the hallway, and I would be trapped in my parents' bedroom with no means of escape, except through their second-story window.

I took a deep breath and darted out of the room. It was a moment that seemed like an hour for, in my haste, I practically fell out of the room and stumbled forward into the hall, tripping, landing on the floor, catching myself with my hands RIGHT IN FRONT OF THE ATTIC DOOR.!

Something inside of me told me I was doomed, and trying to lift myself off the floor felt like the lifting of a hundred-pound weight. As I rose, I couldn't take my eyes off the attic door, as if I were being compelled by some force within to watch and wait for my destruction.

Slowly, I dragged myself up, expecting at any moment that the door would fly open and reveal its mystery and the origins of the horrifying noises.

And, then, just when it seemed I could bear it no longer, when I felt an involuntary scream working its way up from the depths of my throat . . .the vibrations stopped.

They stopped altogether—dead silence. I paused, still expectant, as if the thing stomping above me had stepped down from the attic and stopped at the bottom step, paused at the door and was waiting for me to make the next move.

Every nerve in my body told me to run—back to my parents' room, to my own room and lock the door, or even out into the street. And yet, the quiet that fell suddenly over the house, was not the purgative silence of a building that had just experience a tumultuous storm, but the calming peace of the sort that made me doubt what had just happened.

In fact, suddenly, everything seemed absolutely normal. The house, which had only a moment ago been a center of cacophonous terror for me, was now absolutely itself again—the house I had lived in, known, been comforted by for thirteen years.

This pleasant feeling of sudden calmness was only disturbed by my own sense that, only moments ago, I had been wholly terrified. It felt so odd to go from a feeling of intense terror to a sensation of calmness and normalcy in an instant.

I cannot remember fully what happened in the next moments. I recall thinking to look back in my parents' room, for, in addition to the earthquake's end, I noted that the light from the lamp my father had been reading under had gone out, throwing the hallway in greater darkness, though the light from my room still dimly lit the passage.

And then, I recall watching my hand reach out for the knob to the attic door. I say "watching my hand" because I hadn't made a conscious decision to inspect behind the attic door. I had made no conscious decision at all and yet, the next thing I remember, I was reaching for the knob, turning it, pulling the door open without plan or desire.

Something inexplicable had come over me—was compelling me to look beyond the door with the assurance that it would be all right. And, indeed, when I opened the door there was nothing to be afraid of, nothing at all, in fact, save the ordinary stairway to the attic. Whomever had been up there last must have left the light at the top of the stairway on, because it shined with intense brightness as if beckoning me to reassure myself further by climbing attic steps.

I do not recall deciding to ascend. I only remember moving before making a rational decision to do so. I climbed the steps, more observing myself in the act than willing myself to it. I recognized that I should be frightened, I should be cautious, and yet the bright light drew me on. I felt myself without willpower, like one of those zombie figures in the Saturday matinees who doesn't seem to have a mind of his own.

At the top of the stairs, I looked around thoroughly to the far corners of the attic. There was nothing unusual or frightening about the attic: no signs of an unknown creature having stomped furiously about the room, nothing in disarray to suggest the presence of any alien agent. Just the boxes and trunks and ancient furniture that had occupied this attic since as long as I can remember—all coated with a thin layer of dust and accented by the many cobwebs that lined the corners of the room.

I was tempted to laugh at myself and what I felt certain were my imaginings. Could I have become a sleepwalker, dreaming up these terrifying sounds and the frozen scene in my parents' room through nightmares and then only fully waking when I was there in the attic? That is the immediate explanation that made the most sense and I felt inexplicably certain that that was the best understanding of events.

Tomorrow, I determined, I would alert my mother to the situation and she and Doctor Randall might find some medicine to cure me of this miserable somnambulism. That was the course I had determined and I turned to descend the attic steps when something caused me to stop and take one last look around the room.

That's when I saw the light coming from underneath mother's old closet in the corner of the room.

I know what is in there. I have seen it a million times and gone through it with mother at least half a dozen. It contains only some of her favorite old fashions—beautiful coats, dresses and blouses from better days that were terribly fancy and totally inappropriate for the life she is leading in these times of Depression. They were clothes from her much happier youth.

More importantly, I knew there was no light in the closet. No switch, no bulb—there never had been. But clearly, now a light was distinctly showing along all the cracks of the door, as if someone were inside, shining a bright spotlight against the interior door.

I do not at all remember walking to the closet. I only recall that, a moment later, I was standing before it, studying the light around the door for any hint of shadow that might suggest someone was inside. But, in truth, the warm light emanating around the door felt more welcoming than frightening, as if I might open it to find a friendly family of well-intentioned sprites inside, anxious to make my acquaintance and develop happy ties.

It was then that I noticed the placard. It had never been there before, I am certain of that, for, as I have said, I have played around and in this cabinet for years and would surely *have noticed it. And yet it was not new, for the placard was weathered and worn. The etchings upon it were old and chipping away as if they'd been painted, but it wasn't quite paint for it seemed to glow like phosphorus as I approached it.*

Oh, what did the placard depict? Was it a scene? a row of cartoon figures? I wish I could tell you, dear diary, but I have sat here for these several minutes trying by every means I know to bring the strange symbols back to my mind. I recall thinking at first they were just doodles but then, after staring at them for several minutes, recognizing them as patterns or figures I had seen before . . .

"It's a cipher," Walt blurted out.

"A what?"

"A cipher, a secret code," Walt explained to Celia. "Like what Dad does at work—looks for symbols and patterns in seemingly random markings. They're a code with secret information if you know how to decipher them."

"It's creepy, if you ask me," Celia decided. "I wonder if she figures out what it means?"

Walt and Celia turned their attention back to the diary to find out.

. . . and as I stood, contemplating this strange but familiar set of symbols, I found that I had, unconsciously, placed my hand on the cabinet door. I was alerted to the fact by an incredible sensation that rushed through my body, racing through the hand that grasped the knob, up my arm and through my limbs to my heart and brain. It was a feeling of safety and compulsion, of pleasure and desire all at the same time, as if, were I to open this

door, I would be fulfilled and overwhelmingly satisfied. If only I were to open this door.

"Don't open it, you crazy girl," Celia shouted at the diary, absorbed in and impassioned by the adventures of Alice Shaworth. She shouted so loudly that Walt jumped and said, "Shhhh," because it was getting late and he was worried that, if his father were reminded that they were in the living room reading at ten o'clock at night, he'd send Celia home. Walt wanted to get through the rest of the diary entry tonight, and he didn't want to do it alone.

"Sorry," Celia whispered.

But just as I was about to open the closet door, a caution ran through my mind. Perhaps I had been feeling it all along, but had been overwhelmed by the reassuring warmth emanating from inside the cabinet. I stood for a moment, torn between what was gradually become an almost irresistible desire (coming from where, I do not know) to open the closet and this dreadful warning (coming from my heart, or so it felt) to turn and walk away.

All the while, my eyes were trained on the placard, and in a moment more, I knew I had to see what was beyond the door— that, even if this were only a dream—something was compelling me, calling me to open the closet and discover whatever waited beyond.

But a sense—good? bad? common?—was warning me at the same time to take precautions and so I determined to return to my room, to write my intentions in this diary and to return to the closet armed in some fashion in case what lies beyond the door is sinister.

70

And so, that is where I am, dear diary, as I write these final words before I return upstairs to try the door of the cabinet. In all likelihood, I shall return in five minutes' time and, feeling foolish, write that there was nothing inside and have some sensible explanation for the light that burst around its seams. I am a sensible girl and have never believed in the supernatural, and so I know there is a logical explanation. Or perhaps, in taking this next step, I will awake from this terrible nightmare and find myself, as always and usual, safe and sound, within my house, within my room, feeling the welcoming sunshine of a new day.

Or perhaps I will discover in the cabinet above my answers to the mysteries surrounding me. I know they are all connected together—the sounds from the attic, the light from my mother's closet, the paralyzed condition of my parents. All of them, I feel certain, are connected—pieces of a mystery I must solve quickly or awaken from soon.

In either case, I must act now. I know it would be wise to throw on my coat, and run to the nearest neighbor's home to call the Lexington Police Station. And yet, the solution seems urgent and up to me.

And so, my dear, dear diary, I bring this narrative to an end, once again in hopes that even you are a part of my prolonged nightmare and that I will wake momentarily to discover my mother at my bedside, moping my fevered brow with a comforting cold cloth. But, if you are real, if all of this real, I hope that you will survive whatever the next moments bring and live to alert the world of my fate and the action that I took this day.

I go now to test the closet in the attic that seems a key to all of the wondrous events I have recorded—and I go not utterly in trepidation for, as I have said, whatever is emanating from the cabinet may have the antidote that frees my paralyzed parents.

But, whether to face good or ill, I close now, hoping to write in you once again soon and bidding you and the world all the best until my return.

Alice Shaworth

Walt Walters gulped audibly as he read Alice's last words. Experience had taught him to look ahead carefully through the diary for further entries and never to assume that a final entry was final in Alice Shaworth's diary.

But there was a definite sense of closure in these last words. Some anticipation, too, in the promise to write again after investigating the cabinet in the attic but, it seemed, limited hope of returning.

"What do you think happened?" Celia asked him. Walt had almost forgotten she was there, he had been so lost in the world of 1934.

"I don't know…"

"We should go to the library—look up old copies of the *Lexington Dispatch*," Celia launched into a plan immediately. That's the kind of girl she was. "See if there's anything about her."

Walt had trouble catching up. He could not stop thinking about Alice Shaworth, writing the final words of her diary and then going up to the attic to confront the unknown.

"She's brave."

"What?"

"She's a brave one."

"It's probably a hoax," Celia said, perhaps trying to change the tone of the conversation.

"I should find that street where I got the portfolio. See if I can find that old man."

Walt and Celia had been reading under the light of two floor lamps on either side of the couch. Suddenly, the brighter overhead light in the center of the room snapped on, startling them both.

"Walt?" It was Mr. Walters at the entrance to the living room. "Celia?"

"Hello, Mr. Walters."

"What are you guys doing in here? It's almost ten-thirty."

"Dad," Walt said, holding up Alice Shaworth diary. "Do you remember that street where I got this?"

"What is it?"

"It's a journal," Celia answered for Walt.

"It was inside a portfolio brief case," Walt added. "I got it last year. At a garage sale."

"Gee, I don't know, Walt," Mr. Walters said scratching his head with indifference—it was too late to raise questions. "We've been to a lot of garage sales. Celia, I'll bet your uncle is worried about you being out so late on a school night."

"I was just leaving."

"And, Walt, you should be getting to bed, too. Did you have any homework tonight?"

"It was a big, old house. I think it was on Mill Street."

Pressing the issue did nothing to improve Mr. Walters' disposition. "I honestly don't remember, guys, but I'll help you find it maybe this weekend. Right now it's late and time for bed. C'mon, Celia, I'll drive you home."

"Okay, Dad," Walt said as Celia turned to him and silently mouthed the words "I'll talk to you tomorrow" then stood to get her jacket. Moments later she and Mr. Walters were gone and Walt climbed the stairs from the living room to go to bed.

While he was brushing his teeth he heard a rumble of thunder outside and a wave of alarm washed over him because the thunder reminded him of the thumping tremors from his own attic that he had heard the night before. He had almost forgotten about them.

A clap of lightning sounded as Walt finished brushing and scrambled down the hall and to bed.

"Sounds like a big storm," he said when his father returned home and checked in on him on his way to bed.

"A lot of noise," his father agreed. "Goodnight, Walt."

"Goodnight, Dad."

Walt fell asleep, grateful for the thunder and lightning, knowing it would help drown out any sounds that might come from the attic.

SEVEN

Walt woke up the next morning feeling groggy. He always woke up on school mornings feeling groggy, but today he felt groggier than usual. When he got out of bed, he stumbled over his comforter that had somehow gotten tossed off the bed onto the floor. He must have had a restless night. Maybe that was why he was so groggy.

From down the hall and down the stairs, he could hear Zelda's voice echoing up to his room. It was her voice that had been next to his ear a few moments ago and had whispered, very loudly, "Wake up, ya bum, time for school. I'm not going to warn you again." And it was primarily her voice he could hear now, wrapped in conversation with Acey's voice, which he could barely distinguish.

Walt made his way down to the kitchen where he found the two of them at the kitchen counter. Acey was doing most of the talking. Zelda's part of the discussion consisted mainly of exclamations like, "You did not!" "You lie!" and "You've been dreaming, Sister."

"Where's Dad?" Walt asked as he entered.

"Had to go to work early," Zelda said in a clipped manner. "I'm responsible for getting you two to school, so don't give me any grief."

"I can get myself to school," Walt replied, not wanting to give Zelda any power over him.

"I didn't tell him, Walt. He was gone when I woke up," Acey explained with urgency even though Walt had no idea what she was talking about.

"Good for you, Ace," Walt commended.

"It's just a dream," Zelda explained to Acey.

"It's not a dream. Tell her Walt."

"It's not a dream," Walt said to Zelda, emphatically. Then he turned to Acey, "What's not a dream?"

"Acey had a nightmare last night. She ended up in your room this morning."

"She did?"

"See?" Zelda told Acey as if the question proved everything. "He was sleeping so soundly, he didn't know you were there."

"It wasn't a nightmare," Acey protested. "It really happened. Tell her Walt."

Walt poured himself a bowl of cereal, not really wanting to debate the dream/non-dream issue, but also not wanting Zelda to win a battle of wills. "It really happened."

"You don't even know what you're talking about," Zelda laughed.

"I do. Whatever Acey said really happened really happened." He ate a spoonful of cereal.

"She said you just kept going on about how much you adore me," Zelda tested.

"Except that part. That's not true."

"Do you think we should call Dad at work?" Acey asked Walt, ignoring the sparring with Zelda.

"It's just a nightmare," Zelda repeated. "That's all he's going to say."

"What was the nightmare?" Walt asked.

76

"It wasn't a nightmare," Acey protested. "You should know, Walt. You were there. Don't you remember the earthquake?"

The word "earthquake" made Walt pause in mid-bite. "What earthquake?"

"The tremors from the attic," Acey pleaded. "Don't you remember? We tried to wake Dad and Zelda."

"We did?" Walt remembered nothing.

"You said they were frozen."

For a moment, Walt was dumbfounded. On the one hand, he had no recollection whatsoever of Acey being in his room the night before. On the other hand, "tremors" and "frozen" were the very same words Alice Shaworth had used in her diary to describe her terrifying experiences. And Alice, too, claimed to have forgotten the horrifying events the next day until she re-read her diary.

"Wait, Acey, wait," Walt said, taking her seriously now. "Tell me exactly what happened."

"It was just a nightmare," Zelda reminded them.

"First there was the banging. Don't you remember?"

"I don't remember, Acey, I'm sorry. Can you tell me again?"

"It really happened."

"I believe you, Ace. Just tell me about it."

Acey hesitated, not sure if Walt really believed her or was teasing. Finally, she began to narrate the events. "First there was the banging on the ceiling that got louder and louder."

"The tremors?"

"You said they were tremors. To me, it just sounded like banging. And it kept getting louder and louder until the whole house was shaking. And when I ran into the hall, you were already there trying to figure out where the noise was coming from."

"Was he wearing a chicken suit?" Zelda asked.

Walt and Acey stared at her.

"People do that in nightmares," Zelda explained.

"Go on, Ace, don't pay any attention to her," Walt coaxed.

"All right," Zelda warned. "But the Zelda school-shuttle departs in 15 minutes, so make it snappy."

"Go on, Acey," Walt prompted again as Zelda left the room to get ready for school.

"You were in the hall and when you saw me, you said 'You go get Zelda, I'll wake Dad.' So I ran into Zelda's room and she was sleeping, so I shook her shoulder and she didn't wake up. She didn't even move. Or breathe. I thought she was dead and then I screamed and ran into the hall. And then you came out of Dad's room and I said 'Zelda is dead,' but you said she was just frozen in time and Dad was frozen, too."

Walt shook his head. He remembered none of this, not even vaguely. "Then what happened?" he asked.

"Then we... I..." Acey paused as if she were searching for the right words. Then, a sudden surprised look came over her face. "I don't remember," she said finally. "It was horrible. The noise and everything."

"Try to remember, Acey," Walt encouraged.

"I ... I ... remember you said we should try something. Maybe call the police."

"Did we call the police?"

"I think we tried. Or maybe we tried to call Grandma. Oh, Walt, I can't remember all of a sudden."

"That's okay. It's okay. Just tell me what you do remember."

"We ...we decided to go into your room and wait."

"Wait for what?"

"The police to show up," Acey said, definitively, but then hesitated. "No, wait, you said the banging would stop soon, and I was crying so we went into your room and closed the door and covered our heads with a blanket."

"Did we call the police?"

"I . . . I don't remember. Walt, it's all flying out of my head." Acey began to cry in frustration at her inability to remember.

Walt circled the breakfast counter and gave her a hug.

"Maybe it was just a dream," Acey admitted, between sobs.

"Maybe," Walt tried to sound reassuring. It might be better if Acey only remembered the events as a bad dream. "It was probably just a dream."

Surprisingly, Acey immediately began to accept that it was a nightmare, even though, moments earlier she had argued vehemently that it was not. Her mood brightened dramatically. "It was just a silly dream."

Just then, Zelda walked back into the room in her school clothes. "Ten minutes," she said, announcing the time until she left for school.

"You were right, Zelda," Acey announced. "It was just a dream."

"Oh, Sweetie," Zelda began, "don't you know I'm always right?"

Acey was so relieved to believe her fading memories were just a dream that she hopped off her stool at the breakfast counter and gave Zelda a hug.

"All right, Kiddo," Zelda said, hugging her tightly. "Go get dressed now."

Acey bounded down the hall, much happier now. Zelda turned to Walt. "And you better get moving, too, Pokie-puppy. I'm leaving in ten minutes. Make that eight."

"I'll just walk," Walt told her. Their route to school was always the same when Zelda drove. First, Acey was dropped off at the elementary school, and then Walt was dropped off at the Middle School. He really could walk straight to school more quickly than riding with Zelda. And this morning, he felt like he needed some time to himself to think through Acey's strange dream and decide what it had to do with Alice Shaworth's diary, if anything.

"Suit yourself," Zelda told him and then went to find her backpack.

After Zelda and Acey left, Walt finished up his cereal, got ready for school, and, making sure to lock the door behind him, started off on his walk to Lexington Middle School with plenty to think about: like what was real and what was dreamed, what was remembered and what forgotten. Like how Acey's story so closely mirrored Alice Shaworth's diary. Like what exactly was happening and what it all meant.

EIGHT

Walt Walters waited as patiently as he could at the Lexington Courthouse. The clock built into the old courthouse cupola was about to chime five o'clock and he would have to be getting home soon. His father would be home from work about 5:30 and the evening rituals of preparing dinner, doing homework, reviewing the day would begin. Walt was supposed to have practiced his violin lesson by the time his father got home. There would be no time for that and he'd have to suffer the consequences. But maybe if Celia came up with something good, he would be forgiven.

"Where is she?" he whispered to himself and walked to the street to see if he could see her coming.

Lexington was an old town, once very rural, and was built on the model of the town square with the giant, red-brick courthouse in the center and several old shops and offices surrounding the courthouse in concentric blocks. This was the oldest part of Lexington and no longer the center as new shopping plazas and medical parks had sprawled out from the center to be closer to the highway. But it was a good rendezvous point for Walt and Celia because it was between their two homes. His house was west of the square. Hers was two blocks to the east.

Finally, after several minutes, Walt saw Celia's bike in the distance. She was pedaling furiously and panting heavily when she finally pulled up to the curb in front of him.

"Did you find anything?" she asked, catching her breath.

"What took you?" Walt asked at the same moment. "I was starting to worry."

"You're not going to believe this," Celia said, pulling off her backpack and reaching inside. "This stuff is so old, they didn't even have it on a database. It was on microfiche." She pulled out several sheets of paper that looked to be poor photocopies, with heavy dark lines streaking through them and around the edge. "Did you find Mill Street?"

After school, Walt and Celia had decided to split up—divide and conquer. Walt went to the county clerk's office to find out if any official county maps listed Mill Street, where Walt bought the portfolio that contained Alice Shaworth's diary. Celia had gone to the newspaper offices of the *Lexington Dispatch*—the oldest newspaper in the area, to see if there was any information in old news stories either about Mill Street or Alice Shaworth. They had agreed to meet up again at four-thirty.

"I found it," Walt told her. "But it's not where I remembered it. It's way out by Carlyle Pond."

"You're not going to believe what I found," Celia repeated. She was arranging the photocopies in order. "It took me forever, because there was no index or way to search for a name. I just had to pick a date and start reading through newspapers."

"October 11, 1934," Walt said. It was the date of the last entry on Alice Shaworth's diary.

"Exactly," Celia responded. "That's where I started, which was stupid because if she were writing on October 11, it wouldn't have made it into the news that same day. But I looked anyway." She handed Walt one of the photocopies. It was a newspaper clipping from October 11, 1934 but it was just an advertisement. "Apparently the Shaworth's owned a hardware store."

Walt looked more closely and saw that the ad was for hardware and general merchandise from "Shaworth's Hardware, Tack and Tackle."

"There was nothing on October 12, either," Celia went on. "Maybe they didn't report it at first, or maybe they didn't even realize what was going on."

"Or maybe the news didn't make it into the newspaper as quickly back then," Walt suggested.

"But then, on the 13th, there was a story." Celia thrust a photocopy of a page from the October 13, 1934 *Dispatch* into his hands. "It was just a little notice. I don't think they took it seriously at first."

Walt read the article she put in his hands:

LOCAL GIRL REPORTED MISSING

Lexington – Julius and Josephine Shaworth reported to police that their daughter, Alice, age eight, had gone missing and have asked for the community's help in locating her. Alice, who is approximately five feet tall and was wearing a red and yellow nightgown with a blue ribbon at the neckline, was last seen Tuesday evening, October 10, when she retired to bed around 10 p.m. The child has no history of running away and is said to be quite stable. Lexington Police and the Wray County Sheriff's Office ask that anyone with any information about the missing juvenile contact them at their offices. Mrs. Shaworth is reported to have a sister in nearby Harrison county, and, as of this afternoon, the Sheriff's office has dispatched a deputy to determine whether the girl may have traveled to her aunt's home.

Walt finished reading the article and then looked at Celia. "It doesn't say anything about her diary."

"I know," Celia replied. "It doesn't say anything about a lot of things." She still had other photocopies in her hand and Walt was anxious to read them.

"So, the news must have spread quickly," Celia summarized, "because there wasn't anything in the papers for a couple of more days until the sixteenth, when it was a front-page headline. She held up a photocopy with a headline Walt could read from two feet away...

Shaworth Girl Still Missing!
Police Investigating Possible Kidnapping

Walt took the photocopy from Celia and quickly read through the article. It restated the basic facts from the first article and then went on to describe the investigation, which had revealed no new leads.

"It keeps saying she's only eight years old," Walt pointed out. "Maybe it's not the same girl." The Alice Shaworth who wrote the diary was older, Walt assumed—his own age or older.

"How many Alice Shaworths could there be living in Lexington in 1934?" Celia asked, doubtfully.

"And they still don't mention the diary," Walt said.

Celia nodded and handed him the remaining photocopies except one. Each contained a follow-up story on Alice Shaworth from later editions of the Lexington Dispatch. "They never mention it. There's, like, fifteen more articles all about the police trying to find her, and none of them mentions the diary. It's like it disappeared, too."

"So, the parents never knew about the mysterious noises and the light in the attic?"

"There's no mention of them anywhere. All the parents knew is that they woke up on October 11th and everything was normal except their daughter was gone."

Walt stared at the photocopies, blinking. He did not want to look up at Celia because he didn't want her to see how the newspaper stories about Alice Shaworth were affecting him. Until now, he wasn't sure what to make of Alice's diary or even whether to believe she had actually existed. But now, these newspaper confirmations made what Walt had read of her in the diary feel so personal and important. Suddenly, he felt close to and protective of her. He felt as if he somehow shared in her destiny and responsibility for her fate because he had found and read her journal.

Or, more accurately, the journal had been placed in his hand by someone who had seemed very anxious for him to have it. Walt suddenly remembered the old man at the yard sale with great vividness: his smile, his benevolence, and, most significantly, his insistence that Walt take the portfolio. Had the old man at the yard sale known something about Walt? Was it some sort of plan? Had he intended for Walt to discover the diary inside the portfolio, to discover its meaning and somehow to connect himself with Alice? Did the old man know that, sooner or later, Walt would read the diary, find out about Alice and feel these sympathetic pangs of regret and responsibility?

"You okay?" Celia asked. She put her hand on his shoulder.

"So, what happened?" Walt asked, ignoring her question. He leafed through the rest of the photocopies to see if they revealed the outcome of the Alice's disappearance.

Celia handed him the final photocopy. And as she handed it to him he read the headline about Alice in the center of the page. "I searched ahead to one year after she disappeared, thinking they might have a one-year anniversary story and they did."

The headline read:

One Year Later: Missing Local Girl's Disappearance Remains a Mystery

"I guess they never found her," Celia explained quietly.

Walt felt as if a weight had been lowered on his shoulder as he read the ancient article. Although he had never met Alice Shaworth, never even lived during her life-time, and certainly could never have done anything to shed light on her disappearance, he felt as if he had let her down.

"Did they ever check the attic," Walt asked, scanning the article, hoping to contribute something to solving the mystery. "Did they ever check the cabinet?"

"They checked the house from top to bottom," Celia assured him, sensing his despondency. A moment later she added, "I'm sorry, Walt. I'm . . . sorry."

"He gave it to me for a reason," Walt said out loud before realizing exactly what he was saying.

"Who?"

"The old man at the yard sale. He wanted me to have it." Walt suddenly found himself revealing to Celia a suspicion that had only half-formed in his mind before he spoke it—an inkling from the back of his mind. "Because, after I read it, I started hearing the same thumping noises from **our** attic. That can't be a coincidence."

"You were probably just imagining that, Walt," Celia tried to talk common sense, even though not many things about this mystery were making sense. "The diary put the idea in your head. Power of suggestion."

"But Acey, heard it, too," Walt replied, "And she never read the diary."

Celia looked suddenly alarmed. "What? Acey?"

"She said she heard it, too," Walt explained, remembering for the first time since that morning how Acey had awoken and claimed to have heard the noises in the attic of their house and, with Walt, discovered Zelda and Mr. Walters frozen in their rooms. It was as if the morning breakfast conversation had never taken place until he mentioned it. It had been so important to him that morning and yet, through the course of the day, it had just slipped out of his mind altogether. Now, suddenly, Acey's report came back to him fully.

"I forgot to tell you," he told Celia. "I forgot the whole thing."

"When did she hear them?"

"Last night, I guess," Walt explained, trying to piece back the recollection from his spotty memory. "This morning she said she heard the noises and came to my room. I couldn't remember any of it, but she said…"

As he described Acey's story, he watched Celia's eyes drift down slowly to the photocopy page in his hand and the newspaper headline that he had read a moment ago:

**One Year Later: Missing Local Girl's
Disappearance Remains a Mystery**

Walt never finished telling Celia the story, for when he looked at her face he saw the same panic that was now racing swiftly through his brain.

"Acey!" he blurted out.

"We better get to your house!" Celia advised turning toward her bike.

Before she had finished the sentence, Walt was on his own bicycle, letting the photocopied newspaper stories scatter to the wind and pedaling, as fast as he was able, toward home.

NINE

Walt had never ridden so quickly or recklessly in his life. His house was only four blocks and two minutes away, and yet those blocks and moments seemed to go on forever. He darted through the light traffic along the square, eliciting honks from cars that had to stop or swerve as he cut across the sidewalk and straight through the lane of traffic paused near the stoplight. He knew he was making good time, because when he turned to check if Celia was still with him, he saw that he was a hundred yards ahead of her even though she was as strong a rider as he.

In his anxiety to get home, he broke all the rules. At the Jimenez's corner lot, he skipped his bike up the curb and cut his time riding across their front yard. And when he was halfway down the block, he cut through the Watson's yard, knowing they had no fence behind the house to keep him from riding straight across to Blithedale St. and cutting half a block off his route. As he dashed across the Watson's yard, he heard Celia's voice in the distance, shouting. It sounded as if she were shouting, "Remember, be careful, Walters," but he was too far ahead and too eager to get home to listen.

And then he noticed the Watson's dog, Bruiser, a small black terrier, incapable of catching or scaring anyone on a bike, but who was famous in the neighborhood for his bravery in chasing anything that moved. But, Bruiser did not chase Walt this time, as Walt shot across the Watson's backyard, where he was chained up. Bruiser only stood, rigid, and stared at Walt as if dumbfounded by his audacity on Bruiser's turf.

From the Watson's backyard, Walt jumped the little gully that brought him into the Baugher's yard. He knew that if Mr. Baugher caught him riding his bike across his carefully tended lawn, he would yell something furious and be on the phone to Walt's father within moments. But when Walt pedaled around the side of the house to the front yard, he saw Mr. Baugher, standing in the driveway, as if he had just gotten out of his car, home from work. Surprisingly, he did not yell at him.

In fact, he did not move. At all.

And that is when Walt began to notice the change in the world around him. It wasn't moving!

Mr. Baugher was the only living human being in sight, and he was standing motionless in his driveway, in mid-step as if walking into his garage.

Nothing else on the street was moving either. No cars were traveling down the road. No pets were in the yards, no birds were singing, no breeze rustled through the tree branches or the fallen leaves that covered many lawns. Everything was frozen.

Walt jammed on his brakes and came to a dead stop. He looked all around him for signs of movement. There was none. Thirty yards down the road, he saw a squirrel frozen in the middle of the street as if it had stopped in a mad dash across the road. He looked back to where he had come from in hopes of seeing Celia, but she was not riding up behind him.

"Oh, no!" Walt shouted and shot off down the street again, more desperate than ever to get home. "Acey!"

He pedaled furiously and in a moment turned the corner onto his own street and zipped passed the houses of his neighbors—all lifeless from what he could tell from the outside, and no one on the street. Down the road, he could see the Contis' car, in the middle of the road, as if it had frozen just moments before its driveway.

When he got to his own house, Walt jumped off his bicycle before it had come to a stop and it coasted on for several yards before clattering into the garage. Meanwhile, Walt was dashing up the front steps. His home, too, seemed totally quiet and lifeless as he bounded to the door.

But as soon as he was inside, the entire house was alive with thumping and clattering so loud Walt had to pause and set his hands in the doorframe to steady himself against the earthquake-like vibrations.

But unlike an earthquake, the vibrations caused nothing to fall or break within the house. Everything remained exactly where it was although the crashing seemed to make every object jump in its place.

"Acey," Walt shouted as he began to move through the house again, past the empty living room and down the short hall toward the kitchen.

"Acey! Dad! Zelda!"

In a moment, he was at the stairs to the second story, for he knew as soon as he walked in the door where he would have to go. Where the deafening noise was coming from. Where Acey would be if he were to find her at all.

He bounded up the stairs, two at a time, knowing he had to get to the attic as quickly as possible. He looked back only briefly when he thought he heard his name being called and saw his sister, Zelda, frozen, too, in a position so typical of her. Her hands were on her hips in the middle of the room, and she appeared to have been frozen at an instant when she was yelling loudly up the stairs, perhaps to Acey. It ran through Walt's mind that if there were ever anyone he wouldn't mind seeing frozen for a moment, it was Zelda in mid-yell.

"Walt," he heard again over the roar, and though the voice seemed to come from behind him, he leapt up the stairs, certain it was Acey's call and coming from the attic. He raced down the hall and into his room where his guess was confirmed as he saw his desk chair propped precariously in his closet doorway and another chair, from his father's room, propped even more precariously on top of the first one. They were stacked just high enough and temporarily sturdy enough for someone of Acey's size and height to climb to the garment rack where she could put her foot and boost herself up to the panel over the attic entrance.

This is what Acey must have done, because Walt could see that the clothes rack inside had been unable to hold her additional weight and one side of the rack had snapped down and was angled sideways in his recently tidied closet, with his clothes fallen upon the closet floor.

"Acey," Walt shouted again over the roar.

"Walt!" he heard. It seemed to be coming from the attic and from behind him at the same moment. He turned to look back and was surprised to see, across the hall, his father standing there, as calm as could be.

"Dad!" Walt shouted before realizing his father's face was calm because it had been frozen in that position. He must have been standing patiently before his dresser, emptying his pockets of change and keys and wallet as he always did when he got home from work. And, at that instant, the noises must have started and he was suddenly frozen. His head was tilted toward the floor and his mouth was open as if he had been talking to someone just in front of him at the moment—someone of Acey's height.

"Acey," Walt shouted and rushed over to his closet door. Above him, the panel to the attic had been lifted and pushed aside and a bright light, like a floodlight was streaming from inside.

He leapt on the desk chair and then placed a foot upon the broken garment rack, searching for footing amid the hangers. He slipped several times before his foot finally found a sturdy hold between several hangers wedged against the back wall of the closet.

The hangers only held for a moment, however, as he hoisted himself up and then they slipped down away from the wall and crashed to the closet floor. But the moment was enough for Walt to thrust himself upward, high enough that he could reach inside the attic opening and grasp wildly at the two-by-four studs that framed the opening.

His right hand missed, but his left hand caught hold. With great effort, he was able to hold on, and swing his right hand up and get a grip on the frame.

He paused for a second to catch his breath, knowing his next move would take all of his strength. At school, in gym, he had never been good at pull-ups. In fact, he'd always been one of the weakest in the class. But now was not time for weakness and he swung his legs once for momentum before kicking them furiously to thrust himself up from this dead hang.

"Acey," he grunted as he let out his breath.

His arms pulled taut and strained and for a moment, he thought he wouldn't be able to do it. But something told him he couldn't fail and so he gave more than he thought he was capable of.

Finally, his head pulled above the attic opening and his arms locked in place holding him, dangling in a chin-up position.

"Walt!" he heard again. He knew exactly where to look: the mysterious panel in the roof that he had noticed earlier with his dad, in the far corner of the attic.

That was the source of the light and the place where the room was brightest. It was like coming out of a dark movie theater into a bright sunny day. It took Walt's eyes a moment to adjust, and then the form near the panel began to take shape.

"Acey!" he shouted. For it was Acey, standing before the panel, facing it, not calling to him at all, but entranced by whatever she was looking at through the mysterious panel. She did not turn when he called her name. She did not move except to take one small step forward.

"No," Walt shouted and suddenly found the strength to hoist himself all the way into the attic and up onto his feet. "No," he yelled again to stop Acey from stepping into the light.

The attic was covered in a thick layer of insulation under which, he remembered his father telling him, were two-by-four rafters he couldn't see and the ceiling panels that couldn't possibly hold his weight. To take a wrong step would mean crashing through the ceiling.

"Acey, don't!" he called out in warning as he felt with his foot through the insulation for the next rafter. He knew they were spaced evenly across the attic floor, and after hesitating on the first two, he figured out the pattern and was able to make better time. How had Acey made her way over without falling through?

In the corner of the attic, Acey was taking another small step toward the light, as if being slowly dragged into it by an unseen force. Her eyes were trained directly in front of her and she reached out with her hand as if feeling her way.

"Acey!" Walt called. He was within a few feet of her now, almost close enough to grab her.

94

"Walt!"

He was close enough, too, to see it was not Acey calling back to him. The voice seemed to come from somewhere else—from everywhere else, all around him. He did not take a moment to look around, but jumped to Acey's side.

"Acey!" he cried at the top of his lungs. The noise and vibrations were so loud here that he wasn't sure she could hear him even when he was so close. It was like a locomotive passing on a track two feet in front of him.

He pivoted behind her and grabbed her around the waist, then dug in his feet along the rafters to pull her back. Normally, he could easily lift her, but now she seemed heavier, being pulled in the opposite direction by the bright light that was blasting from where the mysterious panel in the attic ceiling had been.

The panel was gone and Walt could see around the edges of the light what seemed like a corridor or chute leading out of the attic …to WHERE? Under normal circumstances, Walt knew that beyond the attic ceiling were the shingles and the roof and… the sky? But now, clearly, there was something leading away from the attic and blazing with a light so intense, Walt could not look at it directly.

Acey, he noticed, too, was not looking directly into it as she had appeared to from across the room. Her eyes were trained, unblinking, on a spot just to the side of where the mysterious panel had been. Walt followed her gaze and saw what she was looking at.

It was an ancient placard of wood with gilded edges, worn and battered, like an old wooden mile marker on a centuries-old trail. And in the middle of the placard something was written but barely legible as its painted letters had faded and the brightness of the light made it difficult to study for long.

That was what Acey was staring at. That was what her hand was reaching for, as if she intended to understand it by touching it.

The etchings on the plaque seemed familiar and yet not quite. Walt peered at them as long as he could, trying to make them out.

"Walt…Remember!" he heard someone call, but could not take his eyes away from the symbols which he felt on the verge of understanding:

εσαχέξςομσόκοάνχεοςξομσόκο

And then, Acey took another step forward and Walt was shaken from his fixation on the placard as she almost slipped out of his grip and into the light that was drawing her on.

"No, Acey," he cried and pulled her back toward him. But the force dragging her away, toward the light, seemed to be gaining strength and Walt felt his foot slip against the rafter and inch closer toward Acey.

"No," he shouted again, realizing that not only was he losing the battle against the light beam that was pulling his sister into this unknown, but he was in risk of being dragged in himself if he held on to her.

"Acey! Acey!" he screamed with his lips near her ear. "Wake up, Acey! Wake up! It's Walt! Wake up!"

But Acey continued to stare straight ahead of her and slide inches closer to the light without moving her feet. There was only one possibility left, Walt could see, and he didn't even know if he could pull it off. But he knew he could get more leverage if he pushed rather than pulled. He thought if he could manage to swing around in front of her—between Acey and the blast of light, he might be able to push her with enough force to break the grip that was dragging her away.

It was a reckless plan, Walt knew, but there wasn't any time to think of an alternative. So, he clung to her waist and swung himself, pivoting on one of the rafters with one foot while swinging the other around as quickly as he could before Acey could slip any further into the blazing opening.

In a flash that seemed an eternity, he had managed it, but the move took his balance away for a moment, and while he tried to regain his footing he felt himself being dragged backward toward the light.

Now, he was in front of Acey, leaning and pushing her with all of his strength against a force that was sucking them both into an unknown that, though brighter than anything he had ever encountered, Walt knew, somehow, meant them both harm.

By swinging around in front of her, Walt managed to block some of the light blasting against Acey's face, and the moment the shadow of his body shielded her eyes, she blinked and began to come out of the trance that had been holding her.

He saw a flash of recognition cross her face as he struggled to maintain his footing and push her away from the corridor of light. And in another moment, he saw her lips were moving as she tried to communicate.

"Walt!" he could see her saying though he could not hear her over the deafening roar.

"Acey!" he screamed. "Acey! You've got to help me!"

"Walt!" Acey yelled, and this time he did hear as her voice amplified with the intensity of her fear as she awakened, as from a deep sleep, to the situation they were in.

"Acey!" Walt called back, wanting to calm her, but knowing there was no time for anything but action. "You've got to help me!"

"Walt!"

"I'm going to push you!" Walt tried to explain over the thundering noise. He couldn't tell if Acey was hearing or understanding him. She only stared back with panic-stricken eyes. "I'm going to push you as hard as I can. And you have to pull back as hard as you can. Do you understand me?"

"Walt!" she pleaded. "It's so cold."

"Do you understand me, Acey? You have to pull back!"

For a moment, Acey did not respond as if she had fallen again into a trance, but when Walt yelled again, "ACEY!" she slowly nodded her head in comprehension.

"All right, Sweetie," he yelled, calling her by the name his father always used. "On the count of three, okay? On the count of three."

He waited for her nod which came after a long hesitation.

Walt felt Acey's shoulder tighten and saw the look of determination wash across her face as she forced her fear away and tried to concentrate.

"ONE!" Walt paused to see if she understood him.

"TWO," he called, setting the pace for the third number.

"THREE!" he shouted and at the same moment he pushed her with every bit of energy in his body, pushed her hard and violently, thinking that, however she fell, she could not be harmed more than by whatever was dragging her into the light.

It worked! Between Walt's push and Acey's own thrust backward, the pull of the force dragging her was broken and she hopped, and then stumbled, crashing into the soft insulation, falling on her back, several feet away. She looked surprised as if she hadn't expected to win, hadn't expected to fall.

And then, a look of triumph and relief came to her eyes as she sat up from where she had fallen unto her back and looked around in disbelief at her deliverance.

Walt only saw the look for a split second, because the force he had used to push Acey backward had an equal but opposite reaction on him, causing him to slide several inches toward the lighted corridor, which came to more vibrant life as if in anger at having its victim rescued away.

Walt felt something wrap around his ankles and looked down to see that both feet had slid into the tunnel of light. He couldn't see what had a hold of him, for the light was too bright, obscuring everything below his knee.

"Oh, no!" he yelled, though he couldn't hear himself within this tunnel which whooshed like a vacuum at decibel levels that made his ears hurt.

"Ahh," he screamed as the ropes or tentacles around his legs pulled him with a jerk and made him fall flat on his stomach.

"Walt!" he saw Acey, still, across the attic floor, calling to him with her outstretched hands.

"Stay back, Ace!" he tried to call back, but he was sure she couldn't hear him.

The tentacles at his ankles pulled again, another violent jerk, and suddenly Walt's head was immersed in the light, as well. He could hear Acey shout his name again, but it came to him as if from a hundred yards away.

And he could no longer see her clearly now that his head was inside the tunnel of light. Everything outside the tunnel went into black relief—like an X-ray. He could still see the outlines of

Acey and other things in the attic, but they were black and featureless.

He tried to scramble to his knees and crawl back out of the corridor, but as he did, he felt the tentacles around his ankles tighten, as if preparing for the final pull that would completely submerged him in this ocean of light. He reached forward, hoping to grab something within the attic to pull himself back.

But instead, something grabbed him—grabbed both of his wrists. Still lying on his stomach, he looked up toward his outstretched hands trying to determine what had caught him. Was it something benevolent? Was it Acey? Was it someone to help him or harm him? He could not see into the x-ray movie that seemed to be playing as if on a screen in front of him, a movie that only his hands were a part of.

"Acey!" he cried. He hoped it was not his sister pulling him back. He didn't want her to risk being dragged in again by the light.

"Walt," he heard back, from a voice that seemed to call from miles away. It was a familiar voice, but he couldn't quite place it. And then, the shadowy x-ray figure pulling him must have taken a step closer to the corridor, because he could make out a vague outline of its body.

"Celia," he cried out desperately. "Help me."

"Walt," he heard come back in reply—but he could not be sure it was Celia's voice. "Be careful!"

"Help me!"

"I can't hold on, Walt."

"Help me," he yelled again, but less intensely as he realized that whoever was trying to pull him back was risking being sucked in, too, with every step closer to the tunnel that was taken.

The tentacles around his legs slackened, preparing to yank him backwards.

"Ahh."

"Walt," came the voice from the attic again, "Walt… Remember…Remember!"

And, as the tentacles snapped him forcefully backward into the tunnel, he felt the hands grasping his wrist helplessly let go.

TEN

The morning sun streamed through the open doorway of Walt Walters' room from the windows across the hall, in his father's room. His first waking thought was "School today—uggh!" And when he saw the sunlight creeping across the room, his second thought was, "I must be late," because it was usually still dark outside when he got up for school.

If he **was** late, it wasn't his fault, he immediately thought, defending himself. Nobody woke him up to get ready. So, rather than jump out of bed and hurry to get dressed, he lay with his head on the pillow thinking of ways to blame everything on Zelda. When he finally did look at the clock, it read "8:15."

He sat up. It was later than he thought. School was starting already. He was not just tardy; he was very tardy. He threw off the covers and went to the window. His father's car was not in the driveway, nor was the van that Zelda drove to school.

They've left without me, Walt thought, and then remembered Zelda's many past threats to leave him if he didn't wake up the first time she called, but Walt had never taken her seriously knowing, if she ever did leave him behind, she would be in big trouble. But, perhaps today, she had finally gotten fed up enough to carry through with it. Walt smiled. He admired her bravery and delighted in the thought of the punishment she would get when their father got home.

Pleased at the thought, he left his room to see if she really left him behind and walked straight into the wall at the end of the hallway. "Ow," he whispered to himself, rubbing his nose, and then turned around and headed down the hall the other way. He had taken a wrong turn out of his bedroom and was momentarily dazed at his forgetfulness.

The Walters' house was completely quiet and he poked his head in Acey's and Zelda's rooms before heading downstairs. None of the clocks in the Walters' house were ever synchronized with any of the others and the clock in the kitchen read only "8:08," which helped a little. By the kitchen clock, school had not started, but would in seven minutes and he didn't have nearly enough time to get dressed and get there before the late bell.

His eyes immediately found the piece of paper on the kitchen counter, set out in an obvious position, with a note written on it, for him to find:

Walt:
Had to leave early.
You're on your own for school.

Walt read the note three times trying to figure out who wrote it. The handwriting did not look like his father's—too legible—and it wasn't feminine enough or young enough to belong to Zelda or . . . his other sister.

Walt put the note down, suddenly realizing how hungry he was. He would puzzle out the note later. He felt as if he hadn't eaten for days and he went to the refrigerator, but the refrigerator was as empty as his stomach—even more so—there was literally nothing inside. It was as empty and spotless as if it were new.

The pantry, too, was all but empty, except for an unopened box of Cheerios and a bottle of canola oil.

103

"Geez-louise," Walt muttered to himself. "I'm going to starve to death at this rate."

But there was nothing else to do, so he washed down several handfuls of Cheerios with some cold water and then went back upstairs to get ready for school.

Maybe Zelda had tried to wake him, Walt thought, as he was brushing his teeth. He remembered someone shining a bright flashlight in his face, and a voice admonishing him to wake up. Or was it "wake up?" Well, he remembered a voice admonishing him, but what exactly it was admonishing him to do was fading back into his unconscious. Wake up? Get going? Do what's right? Remember? Look both ways before crossing the street?

He couldn't recall and a moment later the entire memory of the flashlight faded and Walt finished getting ready for school.

It was a warm Indian-summer October day and, as Walt rode his bike to Lexington Middle School, he was surprised to discover he was in a good mood. Normally, the trek to school depressed him and, if he rode with his father or Zelda, he used the time to complain about the injustice of the educational system and question the need for institutionalized learning of any sort. But, today, he was actually excited about school, though he had no idea why. As far as he could remember, it was not a special day: a field trip or pizza day in the cafeteria. But something was different…better.

Something was different, too, about the neighborhood, he realized as he pedaled down the street. First of all, he had taken a wrong turn out of his driveway, heading east instead of west— though he'd made the trek to school a million times. Then, after he turned around and headed back the other way, he noticed, as he drove past the houses on his street that, overnight, almost everyone seemed to have bought an old car. And not just old as in a "beat-up old clunker," but old as in "classic" or "antique." He didn't recognize the names of any of them, but he could see that their styles were fifty and sixty years old. The streets were empty of any neighbors, or Walt would have stopped to ask someone what was up with the old cars.

And then he realized that the streets were **very** empty.

There were old cars in driveways and along the curb, but not a single vehicle was moving along the street in either direction, and not a single human being was outside of their house, in their lawns or driveways.

He passed the Baugher's house and vaguely recalled that he had ridden across their yard recently and Mr. Baugher had gotten mad and threatened to call Walt's father. Or had he? Now the recollection was becoming confused in his mind with a time when Mrs. Baugher had complained that Walt had run his bicycle into a bush in their front lawn.

And then, he saw, standing in the Baugher's front window, the first human being he'd encountered all day, but it was no one he recognized from that family. Not Mr. or Mrs. Baugher. Not their college-aged daughter, Mercy, or their older son, Liivel, but a boy, perhaps ten years old, staring out, watching the world and wearing a very big grin on his face. Walt waved and the boy waved back, very happy to be noticed.

There were several other strange things about the bike ride to school, though Walt could not quite put his finger on many specifics. Things just seemed different, and going from Blithedale St. onto Second Avenue, he made another wrong turn and had to reverse directions. When he did, he did not know where he was until he saw the courthouse cupola rising above the turning fall trees and suddenly everything was familiar again.

Inside Lexington Middle School, the hallways were deathly quiet. For a moment, Walt wondered if the strangeness of the day so far was because somehow he had gotten confused and it was Saturday. Perhaps his father and Zelda and ...--perhaps they were out garage sale-ing, perhaps the streets were empty because everyone was sleeping in on the weekend, perhaps the school was empty because there was no school today.

Walt had almost convinced himself he'd mixed up the days when he heard someone speaking behind him.

"You must be Mr. Whitman," a pleasant voice said.

Walt spun around to face a kindly-looking man in a tweed coat with patches at the elbow and a friendly smile on his face.

"What?" Walt responded. There was no one else in the hallway.

"Mr. Whitman, I presume."

"I'm Walt Walters," Walt Walters told him, uncertain about whether the man had mistaken him for someone else, or simply had his name wrong.

"That's it," the man replied, pleased at the correction, "Walters. Glad you made it. Did you have any trouble finding the place?"

"Ah . . . no," Walt said, still unsure he was who the man was expecting. He was an elderly man, in his seventies, Walt guessed, with thin white hair atop a ruddy, lined face and a white, neatly trimmed mustache shading his upper lip. He spoke with a vaguely English accent and was full of nervous energy. He bounced from foot to foot and swung his arms like a little child.

"Some do the first day, you know."

"This isn't my first day," Walt reported and suddenly the man's face went very gray as if he had forgotten something important and Walt had reminded him.

"No, of course not," he said quickly. "You've been going to…" Again the old man seemed momentarily lost and his eyes roamed the walls searchingly, until he found the name of the school painted high up near the ceiling in big letters at the entrance. " . . . to Lexington Middle School for years. I meant it was **my** first day. Not yours, of course. I'm Professor Fitzmer, the new headmaster."

"Headmaster…?"

"Or whatever you birds call it…Principal…yes, that's it. I'm the new principal of this fine institution, the Lexington Middle Academy."

"Middle school," Walt corrected.

"Exactly," Professor Fitzmer said, pleasantly. "And what a middle school it is, too. We're going to get along famously, Mr. Wilters, I can feel it."

"Walters," Walt corrected again.

"What?" the professor asked, lost in thought.

"My name is Walt **Walters**."

"Pleased to meet you, Mr. Walters," Professor Fitzmer extended his hand to shake Walt's. "I'm Professor Fitzmer of Leeds and I will be your new instructor."

"I thought you were the principal?"

"As, indeed, I am: principal, instructor, janitor, chief cook and bottle washer. You name it, and I'm your man."

"What do you teach?"

"Everything, all things," Professor Fitzmer professed as if his expertise were boundless and unremarkable at the same time.

"What about the other teachers?"

107

"What other teachers?"

"You know…" Walt started, intending to name his other teachers, but realizing he couldn't remember a single one. "The other teachers," he repeated, certain that there had been others.

"Well, if they show up," Professor Fitzmer declared, "I'll put them to work, you can be sure of that. In the meantime, we better get down to studies, I should think. The term is not getting any longer. Please take out your Latin grammar and turn to page thirteen."

Walt looked around, uncertain. Did Professor Fitzmer really intend to teach a class here in the hallway? And if so, what was a Latin grammar?

"Professor Fitzmer…?" Walt began.

"Hands, please," the professor prompted gently.

Feeling somewhat silly, Walt raised his hand.

"Yes, Mr. Watson?"

"Walters?"

"I beg your pardon?"

"I'm WALT WALTERS," Walt reminded him.

Professor Fitzmer extended his hand and shook Walt's. "How do you do, Sir. Fitzroy Fitzmer, at your service. You must be the new boy."

"I . . . guess . . . what?" Walt was thoroughly confused now as Professor Fitzmer seemed to forget having just met him every minute or two.

"Exactly," the professor commended. "Very good. Well, no time for dilly-dallying. The term is not getting any longer. Off to class now. This way."

And then Professor Fitzmer turned on his heels and headed down the hallway toward the classrooms, stopping briefly to look inside the janitor's closet and nurse's office to see what they might contain. Walt was unsure of what to do, and so he followed the Professor down the hall.

Professor Fitzmer was delighted when he found the first open classroom and he immediately entered, turned on the lights and sat at a student's desk in the front row. Walt followed behind but when he entered the room the professor studied him as if he expected Walt to teach him something. Uncertain, Walt stared back.

"Professor Fitzmer?" Walt said cautiously after several moments of silence.

"That's right," Professor Fitzmer said as if happy to be recognized. He stood and offered Walt his hand. "Fitzroy Fitzmer. Here for the symposium."

Walt shook the professor's hand for the third time and explained once again, "I'm Walt Walters—a student."

Professor Fitzmer's face went gray with worry once again. "Oh, good lord, yes. I forgot. The new boy. How horrible. Still, 'forgetting is bliss,' as they say. Come, come, sit down." The professor stepped out of the way and gestured toward the desk he'd just been sitting in. When Walt didn't move for a moment, he swept his hand more emphatically at the chair, and Walt sat down.

Still flustered, Professor Fitzmer went to the front of the class and tucked himself behind the teacher's desk with his hands folded neatly in front of him.

He looked at Walt: "Now then, what would you like to know?"

Walt hesitated and then asked, "About what?"

"Yes, indeed, about what," Professor Fitzmer replied. "But that is a question we will have to save for another day, children, for, as you see, we are out of time for today."

109

Walt looked at the clock above the teacher's desk. It read seven-forty five and he had to look out the window to assure himself that it was morning and not evening—everything was so confused today. He could see the morning sun just rising over the horizon to the west.

"Out of time? I just got here."

"Oh," Mr. Fitzmer waved a finger at Walt, "but I've been here for minutes and you would do well to remember—that is, if anyone were ever to do well to remember—that haste makes waste, Mr. Nathers, and we can't be caught with our knickers down…"

"Walters," Walt muttered hopelessly.

"What?"

"The name is WALTERS."

"Oh, good god, it is? I could have sworn it was Fitzmer—they usually let you keep the name. No, wait, it is Fitzmer." He opened his jacket to find his name written on the inside pocket. "See?" he said triumphantly.

"MY name is Walters," Walt tried again.

"I'm pleased to meet you, Mr. Walters. My name is Fitzmer. But my friends call me 'Fizzy.'"

"Is school really over for today?"

"Why, yes, unless you have questions."

Walt had many questions, but they were so jumbled that he couldn't formulate a specific one before Fitzmer went on, "Then it's all over but the pledge and then we're off."

"The pledge?"

"…the Pledge of Parallelladise. The most important thing you'll learn today or any day, I should venture, is our pledge." Professor Fitzmer suddenly stood very erect and placed his left hand over the right half of his chest and took a deep breath, "I

110

pledge my undying fealty to the cause of Parallelladise…" he began to recite.

Walt stared at the professor in his pledge posture and listened to the recitation.

"Come, come, man," the professor interrupted his pledge to prompt Walt. "Repeat after me. Time and tide wait for nomads, now." He resumed his rigid posture and began again, "I pledge my undying fealty to the cause …"

"What's the cause?" Walt asked before joining in.

"The cause of what?"

"The cause of whatever you're pledging your undying fealty to."

"You'll find out a little later in the pledge," Fitzmer said, dismissing the interruption. "Now where was I?"

"We had just finished the pledge," Walt said, testing to see if Professor Fitzmer would notice. "But I still don't understand the cause."

"Against the hippos. Weren't you listening?

"Why are we against the hippos?"

"What?"

"Why are we against the hippos?"

"They want to take over our world, take over Parallelladise and control our minds and souls with their evil plan for free will, mnemonics, human feeling."

Walt was confused. "What do we have against those things?"

Professor Fitzmer prepared to explode with indignation to the very question, but in the preparation seemed to forget what he was upset about. "I . . . I . . .I'm not sure."

"Aren't they good things—free will, human feeling?"

The professor was puzzled and brought his hand to his forehead as if rubbing away a headache. "I think . . . I suppose they are from a certain perspective… Oh, now I'm confused. Please, no …."

Before he could finish his sentence, a violent shock—like an earthquake—shook the building and Walt and the professor both leaned forward and clung to their desks. The shock wave lasted for several seconds, then stopped, and then started again.

"Earthquake!" Walt shouted to be heard over the roar that accompanied the shaking. He'd never been in an earthquake before, that he recalled, but he could think of nothing else it could be. He remembered—vaguely, somewhere in the back of his brain—that he should run outside. "We've got to get out of here," he warned.

But as soon as the words were out of his mouth, the shaking ceased altogether and Walt and Professor Fitzmer found themselves clinging to their perfectly still desks.

"What did I say?" Professor Fitzmer pleaded. He was looking at the ceiling. "What did I say?"

"We were talking about free will and human feeling," Walt reminded him. "And then the earthquake hit."

"Sheron is angry. What did I say?"

"Let me try to remember," Walt said, wanting to help the Professor who was suddenly terrified about something he might have said.

"NOOoooooo!" the professor shouted at the top of his lung, demonstrating a much more powerful voice than Walt would have ever given him credit for. "Good lord, boy, don't add insult to injury. Sheron is already angry."

"Who's Sheron?" Walt asked. The question was clearly not a good one, for suddenly the room began to shake again and the professor cried out for mercy.

This time, however, the shaking only lasted a second and went on and then off sharply—as if a switch were being flipped somewhere.

"Listen, Winters, you mustn't ask any more questions," Professor Fitzmer half commanded and half pleaded when the room was quiet. "Sheron is listening and somehow I've provoked him, though I have no idea how and have no intention" and here, he looked up at the ceiling again, as if addressing the heavens ". . . and have no intention of trying to recall."

"Who is Sheron?"

"You'll find out at the meeting tomorrow night," Professor Fitzmer explained quickly.

"What meeting?"

"The one where you'll find out," Fitzmer answered and then held up a finger to his lips and added, "Now, no more questions. The school day is over. Excellent work! It's time to go."

And with that Professor Fitzmer stood up and walked out the classroom door.

"Wait," Walt shouted, jumping up from his desk. He hurried out into the hall. "Professor . . ." he called to Fitzmer who was already halfway down the main corridor.

The professor turned and looked at Walt expectantly. "Yes?" Walt could see in his eyes that he'd forgotten who Walt was again.

"What am I supposed to do?"

"About what?" The professor was genuinely puzzled.

"About . . . about the rest of the school day," Walt explained.

"Oh, the school day has been over for days, young man," the professor told him, smiling, "You may go home."

"But...but...isn't it usually longer?"

The professor cocked his head to one side as if trying, literally, to see the question from a different angle: "Is it?"

"Well . . . yes, I . . ." Walt began, but suddenly he could not remember how the school day normally went. A moment earlier, he had been sure the class sessions and the day were hours longer, but now that Professor Fitzmer had raised the question, he was uncertain.

"I think so . . ." Walt started and then was filled with self-doubt. "I'm not sure. . . Maybe not. . . Maybe you're right."

"Thank goodness for that," said the professor, relieved. He walked back down the hall to Walt and put a kindly hand on his shoulder. "I know academics can be challenging sometimes, McGullicuddy, but by tomorrow you'll have forgotten all about it and can stop coming altogether if you wish."

"I can?" Walt was sure that couldn't be right. Or could it?

"And by the next day," the professor smiled, "it will all be gravy as you Americans like to say."

Walt felt very reassured by Professor Fitzmer's forecast, but even though he'd never said anything about gravy, that he could recall, the reference reminded him of how hungry he was. "Well, can I at least stop in the cafeteria on my way out for lunch?"

"That's a splendid idea, Mr. Weevil. I'm a little hungry myself. **Do** stop by the cafeteria and, by all means, discover it's closed. It could be like a learning experience for you."

"It's closed?"

"If we even have one."

"We used to," Walt said but then began to doubt that, too. "At least I think I remember."

"Good lord, don't do that," Fitzmer advised. He drew himself up in his recitation stance again and declared what sounded like more of the pledge, "Forget to remember and don't remember to forget and never the twain confuse." He resumed his normal posture and added, "The market on the square is what you want. Mention my name, they may give you something nice."

"They will?"

"Highly doubtful," Professor waved the suggestion away. "Still, it never hurts, does it? It just never hurts..." and then the professor's face slumped into confused despair. "It doesn't ever hurt at all."

A faraway look appeared in Fitzmer's eyes.

"Professor?" Walt said, trying to call him back to attention.

Fitzmer snapped back. "Whitmore, a jolly good performance today. Now keep up the good work and don't take any wooden halfpence."

"Sir?"

But with that Professor Fitmer turned on his heels and walked with surprising speed down the corridor, leaving Walt with a hundred questions and the certainty that if he asked them of Professor Fitzmer, he would only become more confused.

ELEVEN

Outside the school, Walt stood at the bike rack wondering what to do. He'd walked around inside searching for other students or teachers, but the building was empty and he was not even able to locate Professor Fitzmer again.

It was just as quiet outside, not a human soul in sight and, Walt noticed for the first time, no other animal souls either. This, he knew, was different—perhaps it was what had seemed strange to him on the ride to school—the absence of squirrels or birds or dogs barking behind fences. It was definitely unusual, he thought, but then he couldn't remember if animals were always supposed to be in the neighborhood or if they were only there on certain days. Perhaps they had migrated south for the fall.

Walt's stomach growled reminding him of his hunger, and he remembered Professor Fitzmer's advice to go to the square if he needed something to eat. And so, even though he had no money, his empty stomach prompted him to hop on his bike purposefully and head directly to the square, after first inadvertently starting off in the wrong direction.

Like the neighborhoods he'd ridden through on the way to school, the Town square was quiet. Even the courthouse where, on most days, there were many officious people bustling in and out, was still. Here, too, the streets were lined by makes and models of cars Walt didn't recognize, that seemed to have been transported from a bygone era.

Walt parked his bicycle in front of the courthouse and looked around for a street vendor or store selling food. None of the storefronts looked familiar, though the buildings were as they had always been. Most of them were darkened inside, as if closed, though a cobbler's shop had a light on toward the back of the store and the barber pole outside "Sam's Snip 'N Go" was spinning relentlessly.

At the corner Walt spotted what he was looking for—a small shop with a green and white awning above its front window on which was written in unassuming lettering "Market on the square." He couldn't recall ever seeing a grocer on the square before, but shops changed frequently here, so he wasn't surprised.

Walt dashed across the street and down the sidewalk to the small grocery shop. The sign out front read "OPEN" and Walt went in with a little bell above the doorframe announcing his arrival.

It was an old-fashioned grocery market with only six or eight short aisles that were sparsely stocked with cans and boxes. Some of the brands and labels were familiar and others were not and some were lettered in foreign languages he didn't recognize. There was only one checkout lane and that was a counter at the front of the store behind which a middle-aged man was reading an old magazine through reading glasses perched at the very tip of his nose. He didn't look up and so Walt walked up to the counter to broker a deal.

"Hello."

The man may have glanced up from his magazine, but, if so, it was fleeting.

117

"Um…you probably don't know me or anything," Walt began, working up to his request for store credit. "But my name is Walt Walters."

He gave the man a moment to respond. When he didn't, Walt went on: "I live just a couple of blocks away and my dad left for work without any food in the house. We've lived here my whole life," Walt explained, trying to build credibility. "Ask anybody. We're the Walters. My dad ran for the town council once."

Finally, the man behind the counter paused to look at Walt with an expression more bored than curious about Walt's dilemma. He folded the magazine, keeping his thumb inside at the page he'd been reading, and Walt saw the cover. It was a photography magazine from 1949.

"What can I do for you?" the man asked after studying Walt for a moment.

"I need … uh, I was wondering. . . We've lived here forever. I could bring the money as soon as my dad gets home."

The man stared, waiting.

"I was wondering if I could get a few things on credit," Walt blurted out.

The man did not react for a full minute.

"We're good for it, really," Walt assured him.

"Take what you need," he said, finally, waving his hand in a broad gesture as if the store were an endless warehouse of supplies. Then, he opened his magazine and began reading again.

"We're good for it," Walt repeated, but the man did not look up. "I'll bring the cash by when my dad gets home."

Walt turned away from the counter toward the aisles of food. Quickly, he discovered that the sparsely stocked shelves were even more sparse than they appeared. Several boxes and cans were empty, occupying shelf space among a few genuine and unopened packages.

Not wanting to test the man's generosity, Walt chose only a few items—enough to satiate him until his father got home. He carried his armload of cans and boxes to the checkout counter and laid them out. The man did not look up until Walt cleared his throat.

"What can I do for you?" he asked after studying Walt for a moment.

"I'm ready to check out."

The man stared at the goods Walt had placed on the counter and then looked at Walt as if he expected direction. "Take them," he said.

"But . . . but don't you want to ring them up or write them down or something?" Walt asked. Was it possible the man was going to let him have the groceries for free?

The man shook his head. "I'd just lose whatever I wrote it on."

"I can bring the money this evening," Walt promised, uncertain if the store clerk was angry or indifferent or happy to be charitable.

"I'm not worried about it," the man told him. He looked back at his magazine. Walt could see that he was still on the same page he'd been reading earlier.

"Oh…uh … OK." Walt looked at the cans and boxes he'd placed on the counter wondering if he should ask for a sack to carry them, but the man seemed engrossed in his reading and Walt decided he'd better not disturb him in case he changed his mind. He scooped the items into his arms and walked to the door.

Just as he was about to push the door open the man at the counter called him back.

119

"Hey, wait," he said, suddenly. "Come back here."

Walt turned around reluctantly and walked back to the counter. He was certain the man would now ask for some kind of identification or collateral, but, instead, he ducked behind the countertop for a moment and then stood up holding a large book, which he plopped heavily on the counter causing a small puff of dust to spring up from the book's cover.

"What did you say your name was?" he asked, taking his first genuine interest in anything Walt had to say.

"Walt," Walt said. "Walters."

The clerk began thumbing through the giant volume. Most of the pages were empty, but Walt could see a bit of writing here and there.

"I forgot about you," the man explained. "No harm in that, I guess."

Walt smiled, thinking the man was joking, but he continued turning pages intently until he came to one with a short list of six or eight names on it.

"Winters . . . Winters," the man muttered, searching the names. Walt could see the names were listed in reverse alphabetical order, and his was at the very top.

"Walters," Walt corrected, pointing. "Walt Walters."

"Ah, there you are," the man announced with satisfaction. "I always forget about these things. You're in luck." And then he ducked down below the counter again and came up with a large cardboard box, opened at the top and filled with groceries. "You're new. You get the fresh box, too. Usually, I forget to ask."

He pushed the plain, brown box across the counter toward Walt with a smile.

Walt thought it was some sort of mistake. He wasn't "new" unless by that the man meant it was his first visit to this grocery. Maybe it was a promotional gift for new customers?

"I . . . uh . . ."

"Take it," the man encouraged him. "There's some great stuff in there." And then he turned back to the magazine and read as if Walt had already picked up the box and left.

So, Walt picked up the box and left.

He examined the contents as he walked out into the October sunshine. The box held an odd assortment of foods and beverages: some fruits rolling around loosely at the bottom, some cereal and oatmeal, a can of powdered milk, an egg carton with only two eggs in it, a loaf of bread, three candy bars, two bags of chips, and three soda cans. Walt tore open the chips immediately and began eating them. Among the jars he'd collected off the shelves was a peanut butter container and he looked forward to a peanut butter and chips sandwich when he got home.

And by the time he got home, after turning in the wrong direction several times, he had finished most of one bag of chips and his hunger was finally starting to subside.

Back inside his house he called out Zelda's name, thinking perhaps she had had a short day at school, too. He went upstairs and checked all the rooms and found them empty and somehow different than he expected—though he couldn't say exactly how. Then he returned to the kitchen and finished the bag of chips and a chocolate bar.

Despite being home in the middle of a school day, Walt felt very at ease. In fact, he wasn't sure why this was different than other days, though it seemed much earlier than when he usually got home. Most importantly, he was having fun.

121

Full of chips and chocolate, he went up to his room to lay down on his bed and plan out the rest of his afternoon. Staring at the ceiling above his bed, he thought about riding his bike out to the Lexington quarry, about calling a friend and inviting him over to hang out for a while, about watching TV and playing video games, but none of the ideas motivated him, and in a few minutes he got up and wandered the house.

In his father's room, he examined the items on Mr. Walter's dresser: a comb, a wallet (new), a picture frame with nothing in it. The bedroom right next door was obviously a little girl's room—there were ballerina posters on the wall and Barbie books in the bookcase, but Walt could not remember any little girl ever staying there.

Zelda's room was spare and unadorned: there was a bed with no sheets, a dresser and nightstand and a small rug at the foot of the bed. Beyond that, it was empty, except for an old-fashioned dial telephone on her nightstand. That had not been there before that Walt could remember and he was momentarily jealous that she got to have a phone in her room and he did not. But when he went to pick up the phone to call his dad at work, he found the line was dead and decided it wasn't a working phone after all.

Downstairs, Walt wandered around without purpose. The house, though clearly his, felt unfamiliar and he found himself discovering closets and cabinets he'd forgotten or never knew existed. Inside one of them he found a pair of roller skates and a set of keys and a TV Guide in a language he didn't recognize. Inside another he found a guitar that he took out and tried to play, though the few chords that he knew and strummed sounded exceptionally sour.

Finally, he found his way into the family room where he turned on the television and plopped himself on the couch, weary without any good reason.

He watched a show in black and white about a peaceful and loving community of citizens that was invaded by a group of faceless aliens who came up from their basements and took over their world, forcing them into slavery and taking away their voices.

Either it was a very long TV show or it replayed several times—Walt could not remember—but by the time he looked up from the screen, the day had passed and it was dark, outside and in, except for the light from the TV screen that illuminated the family room. Walt stood up and stretched. He could not recall if he had napped during the show, but he felt very tired.

In the kitchen, he opened the second bag of chips from the box he'd gotten at the grocery, and he took a bite from an apple that was mushy and no good any more. He tried to remember what his family did on most school nights, but could only recall brushing his teeth and wearing pajamas. So, after drinking half a soda pop from a can in the box, he went upstairs feeling as if he hadn't slept for days.

He brushed his teeth and changed into his pajamas. Then he crawled into bed. It didn't take him long to drift off to sleep and, as he did, a thought popped into his head and made him smile. The thought was this: *this has been the best day of my entire life.*

TWELVE

Walt woke up just as happy the next day. Again, the sun was shining brightly. And the house was warm and cozy. His clock read six forty-five and he had a momentary sensation that he was late for something but couldn't imagine what it was.

He got up and went into his father's room but it was empty. He called out "Dad," to see if he were anywhere in the house. His voice echoed in the empty bedroom, but wasn't answered. Walt thought he recalled there once being a bed and dresser in here, but perhaps he was remembering another house he'd been in.

The next room was obviously a little girl's room—there were ballerina posters on the wall and Barbie books in the bookcase, but Walt could not remember any little girl ever staying there. He went and sat on the bed for a moment, testing the springs. The bed sagged and Walt couldn't imagine anyone sleeping comfortably in it.

Down the hall was a third bedroom with a bed (no sheets), a dresser, a nightstand and an old-fashioned phone. Walt went over to try it since he'd never operated a rotary phone before, but when he picked up the receiver, he couldn't think of anyone to call, so he placed it back in its cradle.

Downstairs, Walt found that someone, probably his mom or dad, had left a box of groceries for him on the counter. It contained an odd assortment of foods and beverages: there were some fruits rolling around loosely at the bottom, some cereal and oatmeal, a can of powdered milk, an egg carton with two eggs in it, a loaf of bread, two candy bars and two bags of chips (one empty and one almost full) and a soda can. Walt guessed his father was responsible for eating and emptying one bag of chips. Walt opened the other bag and took a handful of "Munchettos" in his mouth.

Next to the box on the counter were two notes. One read:

Important Meeting at Courthouse Tonight—7:30.

The second note read:

Walt:
Had to leave early.
You're on your own for school.

Only when Walt read this did he remember he was supposed to go to school. He looked at the clock. It read six-thirty. He still had plenty of time, so he finished his breakfast of chips and water and went upstairs to get ready.

The bike ride to school was delightful and took almost two hours as Walt kept taking wrong turns and discovering side streets and dead ends he'd never ridden before. Walt loved discovering new directions and seeing parts of Lexington he had never seen.

Most of it, in fact, he'd never seen before, he realized, because every new road and turn brought unexpected vistas and quaint streets.

Walt found Lexington Middle School mostly by accident. He'd been admiring some of the big old houses on a street named

Concord, when he made a turn and found himself right in front of his school, though it took him a moment to recognize it.

He parked his bike in the rack and went inside, and it wasn't until he walked through the front doors that he remembered his encounter the previous day with a kindly old man who had taught him something and, most importantly, had said he didn't have to come to school at all if he didn't want, which Walt had taken to heart.

But Walt was there now, and so he decided to find the old man, if only for a little human contact. He checked the Principal's Office first, but it was dark and empty. And then he wandered down the hallways of the school, poking his head in rooms and searching, though, by the third room he'd forgotten what he was searching for and only knew that he hadn't found it yet. The search for something he couldn't remember made him giddy and he began laughing every time he entered a classroom and didn't find whatever it was he was looking for.

Most of the classrooms were empty—even of desks and chairs, but some had chalkboards and some had pull-down maps. On every chalkboard a message was written in large letters that covered the entire board:

Important Meeting at Courthouse Tonight—7:30.

After reading that same message on several boards, Walt wondered if the message was intended for him and then got a fun idea to add his own message to it.

So in the very next classroom, he added the words, "Important if you have webbed feet, that is." And in the next classroom, he erased some of the letters in the original message and added his own until it read,

"Import Meet at house night *if you dare*."

By the third classroom, Walt was letting his giddiness get the better of him and he wrote on the board, "This is chalk. This is chalk on a chalkboard. Any questions?"

And in the fourth classroom he wrote, "Learning is for dummies."

He was trying to think of something exceptionally witty to top his previous effort as he went into another classroom. He went to the chalkboard immediately and picked up the chalk, prepared to write, "Just say 'No' to dummies," when he saw the repeated message, "Important Meeting at Courthouse Tonight—7:30" had been erased and replaced with a message, scrawled apparently very quickly and barely legibly. It read:

Your name is Walt Walters.
Your father's name is Benjamin Walters.
Your older sister's name is Zelda.
Your younger sister's name is Acey.
They all love you.

Walt stared at the words on the chalkboard for a full minute as a wave of memories flooded his brain, making him dizzy and his body feel heavy. Tears welled up in his eyes when he read and now, suddenly, he burst out crying as images of his father and sisters flashed in his mind.

"Acey," he whispered, realizing that he had not thought of her once in the last twenty-four hours. It was as if she hadn't existed for a full day within his consciousness until he saw her name on the board and then it felt as if he was reuniting with a long lost twin—as if he was suddenly reconnecting with the world.

Zelda, too, he had forgotten about, though more recently, and he suddenly remembered that the bedroom he discovered at home with the phone in it had been hers but had not looked like that until only a day or two before.

And his father, though he had remained in his memory, had faded and the features of his face, his unique character, his qualities as a human being had dulled in his mind to a shapeless "Dad" until he read the name "Benjamin Walters" and then an image of his true father, as Walt had always known and loved him, emerged from the back of his mind and leapt into the foreground.

"Dad," Walt cried out, as if his father were suddenly before him. The kindly, befuddled look Walt most readily associated with his father dominated Walt's mind's eye and he cried out, uncontrollably, "Dad!"

He had felt so happy only moments ago, but now, with the memories of his family filling his head, he felt very lonely and longed for face-to-face contact.

And then his head started to hurt—to throb, as if he had stepped in front of a huge amplifier pounding out loud music. His ears rang and his temples thudded as if they were being smashed by heavy fists on either side.

"Acey," he cried out. "Zelda… Dad!"

The pain and pressure on his head were becoming unbearable, and now he couldn't stop the images of his family from bombarding his mind, though, the more they did, the more his head hurt.

And in a moment, the room started to spin, slowly at first, like a carousel just getting started, but then more rapidly, until it was turning with dizzying speed. Walt tried to focus on the chalkboard, on the teacher's desk, on the door, all to stop the whirling momentum, but his memories, having been brought back to life by the message on the board, dominated his brain and he only saw his dad and sisters before him, until, at last, his mind went blank and suddenly all was dark.

THIRTEEN

"Pssst."

Walt heard the whispered call of someone trying to get his attention before he opened his eyes. His head hurt severely and he didn't want to open his eyes for fear that light would make it worse.

"Pssst," he heard again, but still could not bring himself to open his eyes until he heard his name called, "Walters. Pssssst."

It was the first time he'd heard his name spoken in two days, he realized, except by Professor Fitzmer who had gotten it wrong most of the time.

But Walt still hesitated to open his eyes, unsure of where he would find himself. Maybe he would awaken to his own bedroom with his father sitting by his bedside explaining he'd been sick with a high fever and delirious for days—that it had all been a nightmare caused by an elevated temperature. Maybe Acey would be there, wrapped in a heavy coat and smiling sympathetically, and even Zelda might be keeping vigil.

But Walt knew, even when his eyes were still closed, that he wasn't in a soft bed anywhere. Whatever he was lying on was cold and hard and whoever kept saying "Pssssst, Walters," was not someone he knew.

Slowly he opened his eyes anticipating harsh light, but instead he found he was in a darkened room. Hours must have past while he was unconscious, because it was night time and, looking up, Walt saw first the ceiling and then the chalkboard he'd read only moments before losing consciousness.

He was still in the classroom at his school where he had fainted.

Except the message—the reminder of who he was and who his father and sisters were—had been erased from the chalkboard. Now it was blank.

Walt rolled his head around to see what else had changed. Only a faint light from a streetlamp outside was illuminating the floor and the chalkboard of the dark room.

"Psssst. Walters. You've got to wake up now, c'mon."

The wake-up message reminded Walt of the many he'd heard from his father and Zelda trying to get him up for school every morning—curt, impatient. But the voice was new—masculine and raspy and laced with urgency.

Gingerly, Walt rolled onto his side from his back. He turned in the direction of the whisper but saw only the big teacher's desk a couple of feet away. The room was empty otherwise and Walt craned his neck around, surprised to find no one behind the voice. He looked to see if it might have come from some other direction. He could see no one, and he pushed himself up on his elbow to survey more closely.

"Hello," Walt whispered.

"Pssst."

The sound had come from the teacher's desk. Walt looked at it cautiously and saw, from between the legs and drawers of the desk, in the space where the teacher would put his legs, someone was poking a hand out and using a crooked index finger to signal that Walt should come over.

Walt got onto his hands and knees and crawled in the direction of the beckoning finger. Even these small movements made his head throb.

131

"Dad?" he whispered, though he had no hope that it was his father under the desk. "Zelda?"

Walt reached the finger and carefully peered around the corner of the desk drawers to look into the cubby.

"You okay?"

At first, Walt mistook the person asking for another kid, like himself, but younger, smaller anyway. He was curled up comfortably in the small space and his eyes darted around constantly as if expecting, at any moment, to be discovered and interrupted.

And then, as Walt's eyes adjusted to darkness of the shadowy cubby, he realized the person there had a mustache and goatee. It was not another kid at all, but a very small man—no taller, Walt guessed, when unraveled to standing position, than three and a half feet.

"My head hurts," Walt said.

"Yeah," the man sympathized. "Sorry about that. If I could, I'd let you sleep it off. But we've got to get going."

"Get going where?"

"I've been trying to wake you for over an hour."

"Sleep what off?"

"The lethemine," the little man explained, poking his head out of the cubby and checking around the room as if readying for a mad dash. Walt could see in the fleeting glimpse that the man was Asian, though he had no distinguishable accent. "That's what's causing the headache. Or actually, it's the memories fighting the lethemine, but let's not quibble now, for Pete's sake."

Walt asked. "Who are you?"

"Sprat. Just call me Sprat," the man stuck out his hand and Walt shook it. "At least until we get underground. We're glad you're here Walters, but we haven't much time. You were a booger to wake up and it's already quarter past eight. Community starts at 7:30."

"Much time for what?"

"Debrief. You still know who you are?"

"Walt Walters."

"What's your dad's middle name?"

"Walt."

"What's your sister's favorite flavor of ice cream?"

"Which sister?" Walt asked, but he didn't really want the man to answer for he found that his headache was becoming more intense the more he talked.

"Perfect," the man declared. "Now let's get going."

With that, he squeezed past Walt and out from under the desk, and, staying on his hands and knees he crawled toward the door of the room. "Stay low."

Walt watched the man crawl to the door. He and the situation seemed more ludicrous than frightening, but the message on the chalkboard—the reminders of who he was and where he came from—made him cautious because, regardless of how familiar some things seemed, Walt knew now he was not in his own world and he didn't know who he could trust.

The small man was at the classroom door when he realized Walt was not following him. He sighed heavily and crawled back to where Walt waited.

"C'mon, it's okay," he assured him, looking at his watch. "I'm one of the good guys. Really."

Still, Walt hesitated. He looked up at the blackboard where the personal information about him had once been written. Now that he had recovered some memories of himself, he didn't want to lose them, and he felt, somehow, the more he remembered who he was, the easier it would be to figure out whom to believe.

"The stuff on the board?" the man questioned, watching Walt's eyes. "About your name and your dad's name and everything?"

Walt didn't answer. He studied the little man's eyes trying to gauge him.

"Who do you think wrote that?" the man asked, and then pointed a finger at his own chest. "I had to snap you out of your lethe-haze. It was risky."

"How . . . how did you know about me?" Walt asked.

"A friend of yours," the man told him but seemed reluctant to elaborate. "And a friend of yours sent me to get you."

Walt studied the man's face for trustworthiness.

"C'mon," he encouraged. "Time's a wasting. We've **got** to go."

The Asian man checked his watch and looked concerned. Walt didn't know whether to trust him, but he knew that, whatever was going on, he was not going to figure it out by staying here.

So when the man crawled off again with another warning to "stay low," Walt followed, cautiously.

They crawled all the way out of school on their hands and knees and when, in the very dark school hallway Walt had tried to stand up, the Asian man warned him with a whispered shout, "What are you doing? Get down! Get down!" and Walt dropped to his hands and knees again.

Outside, the man stood but remained perceptibly crouched as he canvassed the area around the school entrance, so Walt stayed on his knees until the man gave him the "thumbs up" sign.

"Now let's move. We don't have much time! Kind of zig-zag back and forth as we go and they won't be able to detect you so easily."

"Who won't be able to . . . ?"

"And if we run into anyone, remember to call me 'Sprat.'"

"Sprat," Walt repeated. But the man who wanted to be called "Sprat" had darted off into the darkness along the wall of the school zig-zagging like a spy infiltrating enemy headquarters. Walt followed, hunched over for a moment, but then he felt silly and stood to his full height. "Mr. Sprat!" he called softly.

The man had gotten far ahead of Walt and dashed around the side of the school building. By the time Walt turned the corner, he was far enough ahead that Walt could only see him in fleeting glimpses in the darkness. It didn't help that the man was dressed completely in a dark brown robe and pulled a hood over his head like a ninja. Soon, he was out of sight altogether and Walt had to rely on the sounds of the man's scurrying feet to lead him.

And then, even the sounds of the scurrying feet began to fade and Walt looked up to the sky, hoping the moon would come out to help light his way.

But there was no moon. In fact, there was no night sky at all—no stars, no reflections of street and house lights against clouds. It was as if there were a black ceiling overhead, as if Walt were running inside a huge gymnasium that somehow encompassed his school and the whole neighborhood.

For Walt was no longer next to the school building. He wasn't quite sure when he had left it behind, but, in following the Asian man's footsteps, he had headed out into the school yard and soccer fields and was now . . . He wasn't quite sure where he was!

135

"Mr. Sprat!" he called, more frustrated than frightened, but concerned he wouldn't find his way back without some light. Way off behind him he saw a single streetlight shining across an empty field. The school must be near there, he thought, but he couldn't see its outline.

"Mr. Sprat!" Walt called again and walked on a few more steps, determined to turn around if the little man did not respond this time.

"Mr. Spr...!" Walt started as he walked, but suddenly felt himself falling when the ground disappeared beneath his feet.

For a moment, he thought he was plummeting through thin air, but then realized he was not falling, but sliding, very quickly. He had gone over the side of a hill or slipped into a huge hole. He felt himself sliding smoothly as if down a well-trod mud trail on his back with his feet out in front of him.

Walt couldn't say how far or long he slid, but it seemed like a long time before he finally came to a thudding stop on a hard brick surface.

"Ow," he said aloud, not seriously hurt, but bruised.

"Walters!" he heard the little man's voice a few feet away and then saw him approach. "You okay?"

Walt moved around slowly to test. "I think so."

"Good. Now quit goofing around. We're almost there."

"I wasn't goof . . ." Walt began, but the man had scurried off into the darkness again, calling "zig-zag and stay low." Not wanting to get lost, Walt hurriedly jumped to his feet and followed.

They did not run long or far this time until Walt saw a light ahead and the outline of Sprat's back as he approached the light. As he got closer, Walt realized the light was from a wooden torch, like those he had seen in movies about castles and medieval times.

He ran to where the little man was waiting for him near the torch and saw that they were standing in front of a thick metal door.

The man's eyes scanned the area as if searching for enemy scouts.

"Nice work, Walters," he said when Walt was at his side. "I think we lost them."

"Lost who?"

"Whoever was tracking us."

"Someone was tracking us?"

"Someone is always tracking us."

"Where are we?" Walt asked, examining his surrounding in the light from the torch. He saw the ground beneath their feet was actually a floor made of huge blocks of granite. Smaller blocks curved up from the floor and seemed to be forming the beginnings of a wall on either side of them. How high the wall continued Walt couldn't tell in the dim light.

The Asian man looked around, too, as if he were noticing for the first time that their surroundings were unusual.

"Catacombs...underground. From back when this whole area was ancient Rome."

The "underground" explanation helped Walt understand the falling slide he had taken to get there, but the "ancient Rome" reference was puzzling. He began to wonder if this man was as confused as Professor Fitzmer.

"This used to be ancient Rome?" Walt asked.

"Maybe," the man nodded. He looked around again at the walls and floor, assessing the possibility. "Or the medieval Paris sewer system," he suggested and then suddenly shouted, "Look out!" and ducked his head.

Walt ducked his head and fell to his knees, but nothing happened—no noise, no sound or sensation.

"What?"

The little man stood up slowly. "Thought I saw a gnome probe," he explained and then added, without much confidence, "Guess I was mistaken."

"Well, it's a . . . an easy mistake to make," Walt replied, hoping to sound reassuring. "Let's get inside before one of them spots us." The man knocked on the door with the bottom of his fist.

There was no answer for several moments and the little man was preparing to knock again when a small panel in the door opened and a shadowy face appeared on the other side.

"Who are you?" the face asked, suspiciously.

The panel in the door had slid open at Walt's eye level, and so the first thing the person inside saw was Walt's confused look. The Asian man's face was several inches below, unnoticed.

"It's Mr. Sprat," Walt said, assuming the man inside would want to know who knocked.

At that same moment, however, the little man called out, "Ling!"

"Ling?" echoed the voice inside. "Who's this Sprat fellow you got with you?"

"His name's not 'Sprat,'" the man clarified.

"Why did he say he was?"

The man said, impatiently, "You can ask him after you let us in."

"What's the password?" the face inside inquired.

"I forget," the little man who now called himself "Ling" barked back.

"What about you, Sprat?"

The man inside was looking at Walt who realized, after a moment, that the man had decided his name was "Sprat."

"I'm not Sprat," Walt tried to explain, "I'm . . ."

"Wrong," the face replied, "Two more tries."

"But . . . I . . ." Walt started.

"Psst, Walters," the Asian man cut in. "Just tell him 'I forget.'"

"He forgot," Walt said quickly, happy with the simplicity of the solution.

"Wrong!" the man inside declared again. "One more try." He was obviously taking some pleasure in thwarting their entry.

The little man kicked Walt's shoe to get his attention. "'I FORGET!'" he repeated emphatically.

"I forget?"

"Ahh, you got it," the voice beyond the door announced, disappointed. Then the small panel slid shut loudly and Walt could hear the unbolting of the door from inside.

"'*I forget,*'" the little man repeated, "'*I forget*!' And don't forget it…just in case you ever want to get in on your own."

"'I forget' is the password?"

The man rolled his eyes. "I know, I know. I argued for something a little more obscure . . . protect-able. But we found that so many hippos forgot the password if they were out in the lethemosphere for any length of time that we just decided to make it '*I forget*' since, if you ask them for the password and they've forgotten that it's '*I forget,*' they just say, '*I forget*' and you let them in."

"What if someone who isn't supposed to come in pretends to have forgotten, not knowing it's the password and just says '*I forget*?'"

"Oh, they're way too clever for that. They'd come up with something a lot trickier."

The door swung halfway open and the little man hurried Walt inside. Then he and the man who had let them in closed the door quickly behind them and bolted several latches to lock it. The room they'd entered was also lit only by torchlight, but there were several torches and Walt could see clearly for the first time since he'd awakened to consciousness back at the school.

The two men turned toward Walt. The Asian man, by this light, was pretty much as he had seemed in the semi-darkness of the classroom and the outdoors: about four feet tall, wearing a hooded cloak, like that of a monk with a simple rope tie around the middle. His features were vaguely Asian and the look was enhanced by a long mustache that drooped on either side of his mouth and a small, pointed goatee on his chin.

The other man was a little taller than Walt. He had a rounded belly and was bald. His face was reddish and friendly— like Santa Claus without the beard. He, too, wore a hooded cloak though his large, pleasant face was not at all obscured by its shadows.

The man stuck out his hand, "Mr. Sprat? I'm William."

"I'm not Mr. Sprat," Walt explained. He pointed to the man at his side. "That's Mr. Sprat."

"Ling is Mr. Sprat?"

"I didn't know his real name."

"I'm Ling," Ling announced.

"You said your name was Sprat," Walt reminded him, "back at the school."

William laughed. "Still fussing with the phony names? You know they don't help."

"I'm still here," Ling countered.

"But who are ye then?" William asked Walt again.

"It's Walt Walters," Ling cut in.

William raised one eyebrow in a questioning expression.

"Walt Walters, Walt Walters," Ling repeated, exasperated. "Don't you remember a thing, man? Walt Walters? The mission? 'Operation *I Forget*?'"

William stared at Ling. "I'm drawing a blank."

"For Pete's sake, what kind of hippo are you?

"Apparently the third-rate kind," William retorted and then laughed.

Ling shook his head. "Well, at least you can keep your sense of humor about it."

"Yes, yes," William laughed. "That I can, that I can." He paused a moment, thinking about his sense of humor and then, suddenly, he burst out crying.

"Now, now," Ling consoled, patting William's arm. "Don't be like that."

"I'm going to miss you," William blubbered and he turned to hug Ling.

"It's not so bad, now." Ling spoke soothingly. "You're fine. You are. Keep doing your mnemonics. You'll be fine."

"Of course," William rationalized, " I won't even remember that I miss you, so it won't be so bad."

"You're not going to miss anyone. You're going to be fine."

"I will," William protested. "I'll miss you terribly," he sobbed and then turned to Walt again, "I'll miss you, too . . ." and then after a moment, he asked, "Who are you again?"

'It's Walt Walters, man."

"Ah, yes," William nodded. "Mr. Walters who claims to be Mr. Sprat. Rather suspicious, don't you think?"

"No, no. It's just Walters. Forget about Sprat. This is Walt Walters--THE Walt Walters." Ling was clearly trying to clue William into an important revelation by repeating Walt's name, but William remained unenlightened.

Finally, Ling crooked his finger so William would bend over, and when he did, Ling whispered something in his ear. Walt could not hear clearly what he said, but it sounded as if he had said a single word, "Rememberer."

William stood erect again, his eyes now wide with recollection. "Good Lord, yes, Walt Walters! Of course. The mission!"

"There you go," Ling said proudly, "The lights are back on, power's restored."

"Graciousness, you're late!" William called, suddenly becoming alert, as if he had been awakened from a nap and asked to steer an airplane to a safe landing. "You were to have been here an hour ago."

William put his hand on Walt's back and steered him ahead, through the room they had entered from outdoors, and toward a dark hallway across the floor.

"Couldn't wake the boy up," Ling explained.

"Surely, it's almost 7:30 by now," William worried.

"It's just now eight," Ling reassured. "We've got a half an hour."

William hustled in front of Walt to lead the way when they reached the hallway. "But we still have to get him to the courthouse."

"We'll have to hurry, that's all."

A door made of heavy wooden split logs sat at the other end of the hall, and Walt was certain they would never make it to wherever they were going if another password and another William waited beyond the door to slow them down. But it was eight o'clock and the meeting started at seven-thirty, he deduced from the conversation.

"Haven't we missed by half an hour?" Walt ventured to ask.

"Time runs backwards to what you know, son," Ling explained. "You'll get used to it—after a while."

Now they were at the door, but rather than knock and wait for permission to enter, William burst through the door and announced, "They're here! They made it" and for a moment Walt expected his family and friends to all jump out from hiding places and yell "Surprise!" as if the last two days had been a birthday-party hoax.

But the room was empty except for three figures at the far side. It was a large room with a high ceiling, like the central station of a metropolitan train line.

The three figures at the other end of the room did not acknowledge their entrance. They were huddled in earnest conversation. Two were tall men, facing in the direction of Walt, William and Ling. The other was a smaller figure, wearing a long brown robe with a dark hood over the head.

Walt could not hear what they'd been talking about, but he heard the cloaked figure give out instructions as he and others entered: "Make sure, if anything happens, that you get him out of there as quickly as possible. Now, go, get into positions."

With that, the two tall men nodded, turned and hurried out a door at the other end of the room.

The cloaked figure turned, too, and began walking briskly across the long, stone floor toward Walt, William and Ling. Walt

143

could not see the figure's face because of the shadow cast by the hood. This room, too, was lit only by torchlight. The pace at which the figure clicked across the stone floor made Walt apprehensive—this was a person with a purpose that would not be stopped or slowed.

"I got him," Ling was saying proudly to the approaching figure. "It took some doing, but I got him."

"It's nearly seven-thirty," William warned. "We'll never make it."

The cloaked figure was only feet away and walking straight toward Walt with deliberate intent. He braced himself for whatever might happen.

And then, when the figure was within a few feet, the hood was thrown back and Walt had only a fleeting glimpse of a beautifully familiar face before he was pulled in closely for an embrace and felt a warm kiss on his cheek.

"Celia," he whispered.

FOURTEEN

"Stay with me, Walters," Celia said, drawing her face away from his cheek and looking intently in his eyes. "You have to stay with me. We're running out of time."

But the moment he saw Celia's face his head began to ache and the room began to swim, just as it had back in the Lexington Middle School classroom when he read the message left by Ling reminding him of his father's and sister's names. At the sight of Celia, memories began flooding into his brain, as if the dam that held them in a hidden corner of his mind had burst and released a torrent of recollections across the landscape of his consciousness.

There were many past memories—detailed and full of color—of he and Celia, riding bikes through Lexington, sitting next to one another in fifth grade, eating pizza with his father and sisters at the *Mama Lisa's* pizzeria. There were recent memories as well—more hazy and rough—but they reminded him, all at once, of where he was and how he had gotten there.

He'd been on the square with Celia. At the courthouse, they had discovered something about a little girl in his house—this part was still murky—and he had gone to rescue her. Celia had been with him at the square and . . . and, yes—now he remembered—and chased the memory through his mind, trying to hold on to it. Celia had been with him at the square and she had ridden after him on her bike as he rushed home.

And at home, it was Celia's voice calling him as he rushed upstairs to his closet.

145

No! It wasn't his closet—it was above his closet. That was it! Above his closet was an attic and he climbed into the attic. And in the attic was a light—a bright, bright, blinding light that drew him in, pulled him across the floor. He'd resisted—he'd resisted with all his strength but couldn't stop from being drawn in.

And Zelda was there, calling to him. Warning him to remember something.

No, it wasn't Zelda . . . It was . . .

"Celia," Walt whispered through the heavy fog that was clouding his brain. He felt certain he was going to faint. "You were there."

"Don't think about it, Walt," Celia's voice called through the fog. "Don't remember just now. You've got to focus. You've got to stay with me."

"Celia," Walt repeated, feeling his knees weaken and droop. Someone caught him from behind. His head throbbed as if something wild were trying to get out.

"Walt—listen to me," he heard someone say. "Listen to me."

"I'm . . ."

"What is the name of the man who answered the door and let you in here?"

In where? Walt wondered. Where was he? The last thing he could remember was that he was in his attic with Zelda, watching television.

"How is this room lit?"

"Poorly," Walt heard someone say with a chuckle.

"This is no time for levity," someone else answered.

146

Someone named Sprat. The name popped into Walt's head out of nowhere. Sprat! There was someone named Sprat in the room—with Celia! He was in a room with Celia.

"Sprat!" Walt cried out.

"Who's Sprat?" a female voice—Celia's?—responded. Slowly, the room came back into focus and the bright spots before Walt's eyes began to take the shape of torches.

"Torches," Walt whispered. "The room is lit with torches."

"What was I wearing on my head when you came in?"

Walt tried to think. He realized this had happened only moments ago, though it seemed like days. His eyes began to focus once again and he recognized a face, inches from his, staring at him with concern.

"A hood," he said, seeing Celia before him.

"Boy claims to be someone named Sprat," a male voice was saying.

"No, I'm Sprat. You've got it all confused," another voice answered.

"Ling!" Walt called. "William."

"There you go," he heard happiness in Ling's voice. "The gas is on now. The heat's coming up."

And now the room came into sharp view and the clouds cleared from Walt's brain.

"Celia!" Walt hugged her again, happy to be seeing clearly. "Celia."

Celia smiled and tears welled in her eyes. "I've missed you."

"You followed me. You got pulled in by the light, too."

Celia touched his cheek with her hand. "I couldn't let you go off adventuring without me."

"Where are we?"

"I can't explain it all now," Celia told him. "But they call it 'Paralleladise.'"

"Some of the hippos call it 'Parallelysis'" William added with a laugh. "It's a kind of sad joke."

"They have talking hippos?"

"Not like the animal hippos. Not hippopotamuses."

"Hippos are individuals with a highly developed hippocampus region of their brains," Ling explained.

"Like us," William added tapping an index finger against his temple.

"The hippocampus," Ling went on, "is the part of the brain that does memory work."

"The hippos," Celia explained, "are the resistance fighters of Paralleladise."

"Resistance fighters?" Walt repeated. This was going too fast for him. "What are they resisting?"

"Why, Paralleladise, of course" William told him, as if the answer should have been obvious. "NyXus, lethemine, Sheron, the portals, the gnome probes, all of it."

"What . . .?" Walt started. It was all very confusing and he wasn't quite sure whom to ask what. William seemed full of information, but unable to present it in an orderly way. Ling appeared to have a better grasp of starting at the beginning. And, yet Celia, who had been in Paralleladise only as long as Walt had, looked as if she bore the most authority. "How long have we been here? What is Paralleladise?"

"It's hard to explain," Celia tried to explain, "The easiest way to think of it is as a kind of alternative universe—a lot like the one we came from, but sort of backwards and opposite. Have you noticed yourself turning in the wrong direction a lot?"

"Yes," Walt said, grateful that the confusion was happening to someone else.

"They get a lot of things backwards or wrong."

"Who does?"

"But most people have forgotten the right way after a day or two, so they don't notice," Ling told him.

"If they notice at all," William added.

"Exactly."

"How do you know so much?" Walt asked Celia.

"I . . ." Celia began, but then hesitated as if she didn't quite know the answer or wasn't ready to share it.

"They weren't expecting two of you," William jumped in. "Just the one." He pointed at Walt. "Just you."

"She came in under the radar, so to speak," Ling explained. "And we were able to get to her before Sheron picked her up."

"She's been down here out of the lethemine, recovering."

"What's lethemine?"

"It's in the air here."

"It's everywhere."

"It makes you forget."

"And keeps you from remembering."

Finally, Celia spoke again: "We can explain all of this later. Right now, we have to get you to the assembly."

"If you're not there," William added, worriedly, "They'll come looking for you. They'll know something's wrong."

"Something IS wrong," Walt pointed out looking at Celia. "We've . . . We've been transported to . . . to an alternative universe, people are talking nonsense. I have no idea about how to get out. Can't we go to the police?"

"You're in Paralleladise, boy," William replied. "Sheron is the police."

"Walt," Celia spoke pointedly now, grasping Walt by his shoulders. "I know this is all disturbing and confusing and frustrating. But you have to trust me. I can't explain it all now, but I will after the assembly."

"Which starts in eight minutes," Ling said through gritted teeth.

"The important thing," Celia went on, "is that we not arouse suspicions. That you not let on that you've been here or met us. You have to pretend that you're exactly as you were a few hours ago."

"Dopey and confused and happy," Ling clarified.

"Why didn't you just leave me that way," Walt wondered, "until after the meeting?"

"Because they're going to ask you to drink from he cauldron, and you don't want that," William warned.

"The cauldron?"

"The Cauldron of Forgetfulness," Ling elaborated. "It'll pretty much do you in memory-wise, if the lethemine hasn't already mashed your hippocampus to smithereens."

"There's no turning back after that," William went on. "Least not that we've figured. It's kind of new technology."

"So, whatever you do, Walt," Celia insisted, "don't drink from the cauldron. Put the ladle to your lips. Tilt your head back. Do whatever you can to make it look like you've taken a drink."

"But don't drink," Ling instructed. "We need you."

"Just go along with the assembly. It will seem odd to you," Celia elaborated. "But just go along. Do what the others do. Say what the others say."

"And when they call for new initiates," Ling told Walt, "go up with the rest. Don't resist. They'll know something if you resist and they'll put you under again."

"Have you got that?" William asked.

"No!" Walt cried out, frustrated. "I don't have anything. I have no idea what you're talking about. Why can't I just stay here? Why can't I just run away?"

"Walt," Celia spoke in a pleading tone and again cupped his cheek in her hand. "I know this is confusing and crazy and unreal."

"Celia," Walt tried to be rationale, "Do we even know these people?" He motioned toward William and Ling and lowered his voice. "Do we know what we're doing? How do we know they're not the bad guys here and whatever is in the cauldron would help us and send us back home?"

Celia looked intently into Walt's eyes, her furrowed eyebrows expressing all the concern and compassion humanly possible.

"I trust them, Walt. Now you have to trust me. You have to."

The sadness in Celia's face made Walt's frustration melt away. It was the familiar sadness he'd known since the moment he'd met her, from the moment she approached him on the school playground, four years earlier, and asked him about his mother. It was the familiar face of a friend he had relied on and confided in for so long.

"All right," he said with a heavy sigh. "Where do I need to go?"

Ling sprang into action at Walt's words of acquiescence. He drew his cloak firmly around his head so his face was in shadows. He took Walt by the arm and began walking across the great room toward the door at the other side where Walt had seen the two men exit when he and the others came in.

"We've no time to waste," Ling said. "Assembly starts in five minutes."

Walt looked back at Celia as Ling pulled him away. She smiled at him. "Trust Ling," she said. "Do as he says. He'll keep you safe."

"Aren't you coming?" Walt cried back.

They were at the door now. "She can't come," Ling explained. "They don't know she's here. If a gnome probe picks up her mnemonic signature, they'll be all over us. She'll be taken in."

Ling opened the door to darkness. "She's got to stay below. The lethemine is less intense here. It's like hot air. It rises."

Still holding Walt's arm, Ling led him through the door. It took a moment for Walt's eyes to adjust and then he realized they were outdoors again, or at least what passed for outdoors in Paralleladise. For, again, he noticed there were no stars, no moon, no celestial lights at all—just a blank, black ceiling extending beyond sight, hovering over them.

"That's why we should stay low," Ling went on. "Protect yourself as much as possible."

"Ling thinks it's his stature that's preserved his mind for so long," a voice in the darkness said, and Walt realized that William had followed them into the night. William laughed at Ling's theory. "He thinks aliases and crawling around will keep you safe."

"It's worked for four hundred years," Ling shot back.

"There's no science to it, of course," William told Walt, ignoring Ling's evidence.

"And, remember, zig-zag, zig-zag." With that, Ling darted off into the darkness, zig-zagging as he went.

"Thinks zig-zagging helps, too," William chuckled.

"Does it?" Walt asked.

"No telling," William admitted, "but I do know this. By the time he zig-zags to the courthouse, he'll have traveled a clear mile further than us if we stick to the straight and narrow path." He laughed again at Ling's extra effort. "Let him work up a sweat," he said and then walked ahead leading Walt.

FIFTEEN

It took Walt a moment to orient himself in the darkness. They had come out of the torch-lit cavern by a different door than the one they entered, and they climbed a steep embankment until they were in the middle of a field. In the distance Walt could see scattered lights and trees and, further on, a greater concentration of lights and buildings that illuminated the sky in a dingy grayness.

He followed William who, unlike Ling, walked straight and purposefully toward the lights. After several minutes, Walt realized they were headed for the square—that the buildings and illumination ahead of them were from the town center or what passed for it in Paralleladise.

He had been disoriented, because the topography was not precise at all. Now that he'd recovered some memory, he realized that the field they started off from would have been Liberty Bell Estates—an old established subdivision in his real neighborhood. Here, Liberty Bell Estates was only an undeveloped field. After another minute or two, Walt could make out the clock tower of the courthouse on the square.

"Everything is so . . . different," Walt said out loud, looking at the ancient cars along the road as they made their way along the blocks leading to the town center.

"Different and the same," William expanded. "It all depends on how much you remember. When the hippocampus is clicking each clog, it's all different because you remember how it was.

But most people in Paralleladise barely remember how yesterday went, and it's all new to them all the time."

"Like a goldfish," Walt whispered to himself. He remembered reading one time that the goldfish—which had no memory at all—never got bored in his bowl because each circle around the perimeter was a fresh experience.

"Me," William went on, "I've been here so long with my clogs clickin' that now I can barely remember what the real world looks like. Of course, my real world was much different than this one."

"How long have you been here?"

"Since the year of our Lord 1318."

"You're seven hundred years old?" Walt was astonished.

" In your time I suppose I would be," William calculated. "But..." he said, and his eyes lit up with the idea, "But . . . if I could find my portal and my key...Ha, ha! I wouldn't be a minute older than the forty-eight years I was when I left."

"I don't understand."

"I'd walk right in," William continued in a reverie of possibilities, "and my little bairn would be cooking over the fireplace again, and she'd say, 'Where have you been father?' and I would say, 'I've been out fishing,' and I'd throw the fish on the table and we'd feast this very night." William chuckled to himself at the possibility.

"So," Walt clarified, "if you escape Paralleladise, you go right back to where you were?"

"That's the theory," William said with a shrug. "But only if you find your own portal and your own key. If you went through **my** portal with **my** key . . ." William paused, trying to reason out the science, "you could have dinner with me and my little girl."

They were just two blocks from the courthouse now, and Walt was beginning to piece together what had happened to him and the nature of the place he found himself in. And he was beginning, too, to feel some trust for William who seemed simple and good-natured and incapable of doing harm on purpose.

"In the year 1318?"

"Or thereabouts," William clarified. "Some say the more you remember in Paralleladise, the older you'll be when you return. But so few have returned and hardly any through their own portal and none have reported back—almost. So it's all conjecture."

"And you're a hippo, so you've remembered a lot, and so you'd be older?"

"In theory," William nodded. "In theory. But it gets harder to remember every century. Sometimes, I lose hope."

"But you'd return to where you left off. You'd see your daughter again."

William stopped walking and faced Walt. "That's why I keep hanging on all these years. The only thing that keeps me going is the possibility that I'll one day be reunited with . . ." William's voice trailed off, and suddenly a look of panic flashed across his face, a look that quickly turned to despair.

"Psst." Walt heard behind them. "Psst."

The whispered call was coming from behind a tree a few yards behind them. Walt peered into the darkness and saw Ling crouched there.

"Is it you?"

"It's us," Walt reported. Ling came out from behind the tree and approached them. And at that moment, William burst loudly into tears.

"What happened, what happened?" Ling asked, concerned. William could not stop sobbing and Ling looked at Walt. "What happened?"

"I don't know," Walt told him. "We were talking about portals and time and then he . . . he just started crying."

"My girl," William cried out. "My little precious girl!"

"Oh, William," Ling sympathized. "It's okay. She'll be fine. You'll be together again."

"You don't understand," William sobbed. "I . . . I . . ." William's looked as if he couldn't even believe what he was about to say. "I've . . . forgotten her face . . . Oh, Ling, I've forgotten . . . her name."

Ling hugged William. "Now, now," he said, "you're mistaken. It's okay."

"I've forgotten!" William cried. "Forgive me, forgive me. I've forgotten."

"William," Ling said sharply. "Look at me. Look me in the eyes."

William looked, his own eyes full of tears.

"What is your name?" Ling asked.

"Oh, it's no use," William said, shaking his head.

"WHAT is your name?" Ling said, forcefully.

"William . . ." William said in a half-hearted effort.

"William who?"

"William of Chelsney."

"What is your trade?"

William shook his head as if he didn't want to continue, but eventually sighed, "Tinker."

"Where do you live?"

"The North Road past the milestones.... Chelsney," William had a sad, faraway look in his eye, as if staring at his home in the distance.

"How did your wife die?"

"Giving birth to my little girl."

"What is her name?" Ling asked.

"Mar . . ." Suddenly William's face brightened dramatically as he spoke the name. "Mary . . . it's Mary! My little girl's name is Mary. Ha-ha!" William laughed and did a little jig. "Her name is Mary."

Ling smiled at him and clapped him on the arm. "You've still got it, old man."

"Her name is Mary," William sang out. "Oh, thank you, Ling, thank you."

"You're still good for another half century, you old crybaby."

William gave Ling a long hug and repeated, "Thank you, thank you, thank you."

"All right, all right," Ling responded, smothered by William's joy. "There's no time for this now. We've got to get to the service. It's seven-thirty already."

Up the street in the next block, Walt could see the courthouse, lit up brightly. People were filing in steadily and, even from this distance, Walt could hear singing from inside the building.

"All right, all right," William said, still beaming.

Ling directed, "Let's get a move on, then. You go ahead. The boy next. Then me."

William looked at Walt, "And when we get inside, pretend you don't know us. Pretend you don't know anyone. Just act like any normal person who couldn't remember anything."

158

"All right," Walt said, suddenly feeling as if there were a lot riding on his behavior at the assembly.

"You'll do fine," William said, still too happy from his recovered memories to worry. Then he turned and walked quickly and jauntily up the street toward the courthouse, repeating to himself, "My name is William, I live on the North Road past the milestones, my little girl's name is Mary . . ."

Once he was out of earshot, Ling began walking after him with Walt at his side.

"The poor man is losing it," Ling said. "Too much time in the lethemosphere."

"Why doesn't he stay underground?"

"Too brave, too good. Whenever there's a mission, he's the first to volunteer. Spends too much time out in the open. Stands too tall. Never zig-zags."

"What will happen to him?"

Ling shrugged. "Hard to say. If he keeps doing memory exercises he should be good for a while. But he's always too busy, doing for others. Hard to believe he once had one of the most highly developed hippocampuses in Paralleladise."

"What happens if he doesn't do the exercises?"

"He'll become just like one of the others."

"What others?"

They were at the steps leading up to the courthouse now and Ling stopped to face Walt. "Like the people inside," Ling clarified, nodding toward the building. "Now just remember three things—act like they act, pretend you don't know us, and, no matter what you do, don't drink from the cauldron."

"All right," Walt said, nervous about what he would encounter.

159

"It'll be fine," Ling assured him. "Just remember what I told you... Try not to do anything to call attention to yourself and we'll be on our way in an hour."

"All right," Walt repeated. "You're coming in after me?"

"I'll be in there."

Walt turned and slowly climbed the steps of the courthouse, wondering what might be waiting inside. He heard singers singing an upbeat but confused song, as if no one were singing the same words. When he turned around for a reassuring look at Ling, the cautious little man was gone.

Walt sighed and tried to think of Celia's plea to trust as he mounted the last step and walked through the front doors into the courthouse.

SIXTEEN

As soon as Walt walked through the door, he knew this was not the real courthouse on the Lexington town square. Gone were the marble entry ways and the heavy, gilded-metal-and-glass doors, gone were the imposing, mahogany clerks' counters and windows with the black signs that directed separate lines to be formed for paying taxes, for registering new property, for filing deeds.

The giant room Walt walked into looked more like a 19th-century meeting hall than a modern courthouse. It had a high ceiling with wooden chandeliers hanging down, some with electric lights, others with candles. A balcony lined one wall above the first floor and was crowded with people who had climbed a ladder to get to the balcony. Large canvas paintings decorated the walls, some wonderful copies of famous masterpieces, some indistinct historical murals, and some poorly drawn cartoons.

The main floor was filled, in makeshift, meeting-hall fashion, with rows of benches and some wooden folding chairs, all facing the opposite side of the room from which Walt entered. These seats were packed with men, women and children of all ages most of whom were singing, accompanied by organ music piped through two huge speakers on either side of the room.

The tune was one Walt knew well from Christmas and New Year's celebrations. But the lyrics were unfamiliar and most of the congregation was not singing together anyway. Many were belting out whatever words popped into their heads. Walt heard parts of "Row, Row, Row Your Boat," "Cats in the Cradle," "I Can't Give You Anything But Love," and "Heigh Nonny, Nonny" as well as other lyrics he didn't recognize, some sung in languages he'd never heard. And some singers appeared to be just opening and closing their mouths in time with the others. The few that were singing in unison were performing a version of the original words and Walt could make out a few lines amid the cacophony of other voices:

> *Let old acquaintance be forgot*
> *Forget eve-rything else, too!*
> *And think of all the awful things*
> *Remembering can do!*

At the opposite end of the room were a wooden riser and a podium. There were several chairs set up on the platform as if for the elders of the community or the town council, though no one sitting there appeared to have an official function. Members of the larger audience appeared to be taking turns wandering up onto the stage, sitting in one of the chairs, looking around, smiling at the new vantage point and waving to the crowd, and then, a few moments later, wandering back down off the riser.

Behind this inauspicious stage was a stained glass window, extending several feet above the stage and designed with incongruous scenes of people and trees and engine parts as well as symbols Walt did not recognize. Words were also designed into the glass, creating inspirational phrases: "Forgetfulness is Bliss," "Ex Memoriam," "Remember Not, Lest Ye Be Remembered."

At the podium on stage, a tall, gaunt man with long, gray hair was trying to lead the crowd's singing, waving his hands in conducting motions and, while some paid attention, most looked around vacantly, in awe of their surroundings.

Walt stood near the entrance and watched until he felt a gentle hand grasp at his elbow. He turned to see a large woman in a floral print dress and a bonnet smiling at him. She nodded toward a pair of empty seats along one of the walls in the middle of the room.

"There's a couple of seats left," she said, helpfully. "He'll be starting up any minute." She gave Walt a coaxing nudge in the direction of the empty chairs.

Walt's inclination was to remain near an exit, but he remembered Celia's and Ling's admonitions to remain inconspicuous, so, following the woman's advice, he made his way through a crooked aisle toward the empty seats. He watched the faces of the attendees as he went. Many nationalities, races and traditions were represented, and every single face was jubilant, happy and festive. It was as if an entire global village of peasants had gathered to celebrate the triumph of a returning heroic prince over a meddlesome, tyrannical usurper. Some in the crowd pointed several rows away and laughed as if they had seen someone they knew but the gesture was always met by a pleasant but confused look of non-recognition.

Walt, too, thought he'd had a fleeting glimpse of a familiar face as he made his way through the crowd and when he looked again, he recognized Professor Fitzmer who had met him at Lexington Middle School the previous day. The professor was enthusiastically singing the words to "Patty Cake" to the *Auld Lang Syne* tune and wrapping his arms indiscriminately around the people on either side of him, swaying back and forth. Walt gave a wave of recognition, but he could tell from the overly enthusiastic smile and return salute that Fitzmer had no memory of him whatsoever.

It seemed a long time before Walt finally made his way to the empty seat, halfway across the room. As he sat down, the piped-in music ceased and, a half a minute later, most of the crowd realized the song was over and gradually stopped singing.

Walt looked around cautiously, trying not to stand out but noticing that many others were looking around the room, too, as if this were their first time here. Goldfish, he thought to himself, remembering the fishbowl creatures for whom all experiences were always new.

The members of the crowd who'd been standing began to settle in their seats. Out of the corner of his eye, Walt saw William sitting a dozen yards away, smiling and swaying like many of the others, fitting in perfectly as Walt was supposed to be doing. But Walt could see William's lips moving—barely perceptibly—and imagined he was repeating to himself, "My name is William of Chelsney. I live on the north road, past the milestones. My daughter's name is Mary."

As soon as the crowd was quiet, bright spotlights bounced against the large stain glass window at the front of the room, and the gaunt man at the podium, with the voice of one who is used to un-amplified oratory, began speaking.

"Good citizens of Paralleladise . . . Welcome," he called out in a powerful but warm voice.

"Welcome!" many in the crowd called back in unison, though some called "You're welcome!" and some said "Happy Holidays!" and others "Gesundheit!"

"Some of you may recall," the man continued, "though, let's hope not—that we begin with our creed."

A murmur of delighted recognition ran through the crowd.

"All rise!" a woman at a seat on the stage cried out, as she rose to her feet.

The congregation rose with her and waited until the man at the podium started them off: "We believe…"

And now, the entire congregation spoke as one, in perfect synchronization, as if they'd been drilling and practicing for years.

". . . in the here and now and in the power and possibility of the future. And we revile what has passed and vow never to recall a single instance of life before these moments in which we exist. We reject the horrors of recollection and the affections and regrets they inflict upon souls too wretched to forget. We believe in the goodness of NyXus and benevolent healing powers of this paradise—a haven for those who forget, a bane to the remembering hoards…"

Walt looked around as the crowd chanted, with mechanized precision but also with obvious conviction and emotion. Congregants of every age sang out the creed as if the beliefs were close to their hearts. Even William, several yards away, was chanting with seeming fervor, and when Walt craned his head to look behind him, he spotted Ling, only a few chairs away, reciting the words in total seriousness.

Walt was the only member of the crowd, that he could see, who did not know the words, and so he listened patiently as the creed wound down with a rousing list of convictions:

"We believe in the rehabilitation of the hippos and the ultimate conquest of our people over the multitudes of remembering infidels. We believe in our salvation on that day when, unencumbered by stifling memories, we will rise up and triumph over the weakened world of recollection and bring its

165

people into the full happiness of forgetfulness and the comforting protection of our one true leader. We believe in these principles and in our collective power to make them immutable, invincible, incontrovertible and the principles of all, forever and ever."

"May you never remember," the man at the podium called out.

"May you always forget," the congregation responded and then broke out into feverish applause at the successful conclusion of the creed. Walt noticed several in the crowd weeping with the powerful emotions the recitation evoked. A woman in a seat next to Walt turned to him and said, "I've never heard anything so beautiful..." and added a moment later, "Not that I remember, leastwise."

The man at the podium held his hands up to quiet the crowd. "Please be seated," he called out, and everyone dutifully sat. "Thank you all for coming and welcome to our first Community of the new season. We have a full agenda this evening: first, Dr. Coubert from Tactical will give us a numbers and weapons update and we ask that each of you commit to forgetting it as you walk out the door. Next, Madame Vlatsky will talk about upcoming re-Creation projects. Those of you with familiarity or pertinent information will be asked to report as needed..."

A collective groan went up from the congregation and Walt guessed "report as needed" meant some kind of unpleasant work.

The man continued, "Many of you will have forgotten the NyXus Corp. filmstrip from last time and we will be watching that again, and finally, Professor Zaharwi will present his recent paper entitled "Memory Tips and How to Forget Them."

"That should be good," the man seated in front of Walt said to the woman at his side.

"What should be good?" the woman asked.

The man looked at her, confused. "I beg your pardon...have we met?"

"But first," the man at the podium reminded them, "we will welcome the new initiates and perform the Rite of the Cauldron."

A ripple of anticipation went through the crowd. Again, bright spotlights from some hidden source scanned over the stained glass window bouncing colors across the walls of the room.

"So at this time, I would ask that the Ministers bring forth the cauldron and that all new initiates please rise."

Again, a ripple went through the crowd, but this time it seemed less anticipatory and more confused.

Sensing the confusion, the leader on stage clarified, "You're only a new initiate if you didn't know the Creed when we recited it a few moments ago."

The clarification satisfied most of the congregants, but many continued to look about them, uncertain.

"If you know the Creed now," the man explained further, "then you knew it a few minutes ago when we recited it."

That quelled the remaining confusion, and the crowd settled in for further instructions.

"And now I would like to invite anyone who does not now nor ever has known the Paralleladise Creed to please come forward to share in our Rite of Forgetting and be welcomed into our community!"

The significance of the ritual was obvious in the crowd's reaction. Everyone turned in their seats to scan the room and see who might step forward as a new initiate. Speculations were whispered about who would be honored. The woman next to Walt closed her eyes and crossed her fingers as if praying she would somehow qualify despite her knowledge and recitation of the Paralleladise Creed. When Walt rose up next to her, she gasped, privileged to be seated so close to someone about to undergo the Rite of Forgetting.

Walt stood, ambivalent. The warnings of Celia and Ling about drinking from the cauldron echoed in his mind. He knew and worried about the extreme and irreversible consequences if he did and yet he wasn't sure he could fool everyone in such a large crowd by faking a sip. What if someone noticed that he hadn't really drank and he was caught, or worse, forced to drink? Wasn't he safer to run away now? Involuntarily, he looked at Ling, hoping for a sign. But Ling was gone from the seat he'd occupied moments earlier.

Walt looked for William, but he too was gone.

"Come forward, oh lucky ones!" the man at the podium beckoned, "Come forward and drink from the Cauldron of Happiness, the Cauldron of Clean Conscience, the Cauldron of Destiny."

A gong sounded loudly and all eyes shifted from the speaker to the back of the room. The door by which Walt had entered the assembly hall swung open slowly and two burly men in white robes entered, carrying a large dark, black cauldron between them. Steam rose from it in wispy, sinister tentacles.

While the attention of the room was on the cauldron procession, Walt glanced around, looking for an alternative escape route. There was an exit twenty yards ahead of him and along the same wall, but blocked by several rows of congregants. Still, if they would remain distracted, he might be able to slip by them before they realized he was making an escape.

And then Walt noticed movement across the room near a parallel exit on the opposite side and realized that someone else had stood up, too, another new initiate. It was a girl, a few years older than Walt. She had spiked, multi-colored hair and wore jeans and a denim jacket. She watched the progress of the two men with the cauldron and when they passed close to her, she moved along the aisle of chairs to follow them.

"Go on," the woman next to Walt encouraged him. "Go on, pet. You won't believe the beauty." Walt looked at her and saw a tear of joy roll down her cheek. "Soon you'll forget all about that nastiness. Soon it will all be over," she reassured him.

Walt was about to ask "what nastiness?" when he felt the hands of other congregants upon his arms and shoulders, leading and guiding him toward the aisle behind the bearers of the cauldron, leading to the stage at the front of the assembly.

He heard words of support and encouragement and he felt himself being swept through the crowd: "Good show" and "Welcome" and "It's so beautiful" and "You're going to be so happy."

Walt found himself coaxed into the main aisle, behind the bearers of the cauldron as they passed and at the exact moment that the other initiate reached the aisle. Closer, he could see that she was perhaps fifteen or sixteen—Zelda's age—and made up heavily with eye shadow and lipstick. Her hair was dyed orange and red and blue and she wore several small hooped earrings in one ear and none in the other.

Her eyes met Walt's and she smiled dreamily. "I've never won anything before in my life," she told him in a heavy French accent.

Walt could see that, in contrast to him, she was very excited about the ritual she was about to undergo. Congregants on her side of the room had been encouraging her, as well, and she was moving to the front of the room in happy anticipation of a wondrous experience.

Ahead of them, the two men bearing the cauldron were struggling to make their way through the increasingly excited assembly. The congregants thronged around them, reaching out to lay a hand on the cauldron as it passed. Finally, with great effort, the two hoisted it above their heads to make their way through the crowd more easily.

Walt looked over at his companion. Her face was radiant with all of the attention. He realized that she was as he had been just that morning—before going to his school, before he had read Ling's reminders of who he was and where he'd come from on the chalkboard, before he'd met William and found Celia. She was in the dopey haze of diminished memory caused by the lethemine in the atmosphere of Paralleladise. It was a dopey haze of well-being and the feeling that all was right with the world.

But she had not been rescued. She had not been warned and so she was prepared and even anxious and happy to follow the Rite of the Cauldron to its conclusion.

Walt leaned toward her and whispered beneath the noise of the crowd, "Don't drink from the cauldron."

"What?" the girl shouted back, above the din.

Walt cringed at her loud reply and he looked away. He wanted to help her, but he did not want to give himself away.

The cauldron bearers had reached the front of the room and as they mounted the stage with their prize, a roar of approval went up from the assembly.

Walt used the distraction to warn the girl again, "Don't drink from the cauldron," he whispered emphatically, leaning toward her. "It will destroy your memory forever."

But the girl was too caught up in the jubilance of the crowd and the blissful promise of the man at the podium. Walt could not tell if she heard him, for she turned her head and said, "Can you believe? Finally!"

They were nearing the stage now. The cauldron bearers had set the steaming pot into a metal frame in the middle of the riser and the man who had been leading the assembly walked over and stood beside it while the bearers stepped toward the back of the stage and stood at attention, like sentries guarding museum treasures.

As Walt and his fellow initiate reached the riser, he saw, squeezed in like a child among adults, Ling standing with his arms crossed, waiting, huddled and discreet. Almost imperceptibly, when he caught Walt's eye, he shook his head, looking dour. Was it a stern reminder not to drink from the cauldron? Or had he seen Walt trying to warn the girl?

Walt and the happy French girl climbed up on the riser with the helping hands of several congregants and they, too, received a roar of approval as they approached the cauldron and, at the direction of the assembly leader, circled it to face the crowd.

"Don't drink," Walt tried one last time as he let the girl pass in front of him and take the place next to leader.

"What?" she asked again, oblivious to Walt's attempt at secrecy.

Her question caught the attention of the leader who looked at Walt expectantly.

"I beg your pardon . . ." Walt said quickly, looking at the girl and trying to appear nonchalant, "Have we met?"

"I don't know," she replied, smiling.

She reminded him a lot of his older sister. Despite her current giddiness, she had sharp features and narrow eyes, like Zelda's. She looked smart and world-wise and Walt could imagine that, in the place from which she'd come, she was capable of torturing a younger brother mercilessly with sarcasm and teasing.

Soon, Walt realized, if she had a younger brother, she would forget him forever, once she drank from the cauldron. And Walt, too, would forget Zelda . . . and Acey and his father and Celia and William and everyone he'd ever met, if he didn't manage to fool the assembly leader and the rest of the crowd into believing that he'd drank deeply from the brew steaming before them in the black pot.

Suddenly, he was overwhelmingly sad at the thought of everything and everyone he'd known being erased from his memory. He realized the despair and sense of mourning William must have felt when he couldn't remember his little girl's name and the horror of never remembering he had been so closely connected with the family members who meant so much to him. Who would he be, Walt wondered, if he were not Zelda's brother, if he were not his father's son?

He was tempted to cry out, but caught himself as tears welled up in his eyes. He tried to blink them away inconspicuously, for the leader of the assembly was now silencing the crowd and preparing to address Walt and his fellow initiate.

Gradually, the room fell silent as the man with the white hair began the Rite of Forgetfulness.

"My friends," he said, his voice booming over the room. "Tonight, we welcome into our paradise these beautiful young people who have suffered for so long with the burden of memory and the horror of conscience."

He turned to the girl and asked, "What is your name and how old are you, dear?"

The girl laughed self-consciously and blushed. "My name is Lisette Deavereaux," she said in her distinctly French accent. "I am sixteen."

"My friends," the leader addressed the crowd again. "For sixteen years Lisette has lived in a world of remembering, has grown up in a universe of recollection, suffering the insufferable affections of familiarity, knowing love as only those who remember can know it—cheaply, poorly, grotesquely—as a thing built by time and grown through shared experience, lodged pathetically and inexactly within a deformed consciousness riddled with the disease of recall."

The speaker's words were having a powerful effect on the crowd. Walt saw several men and women close to the stage weeping uncontrollably, staring at Lisette and imagining the horrors of the sixteen years of her existence.

"Until . . ." the man continued, "Until our merciful deliverer chose her. Found her and chose her—just like this young man." The man moved to stand between Walt and Lisette and put one hand on Walt's shoulder as he continued, "Found them both and chose them both, saved them both, redeemed them both and brought them back from the wayward pernicious journey humanity has taken since first the seeds of recollection began to sprout in the consciousness."

Walt stood rigidly under the hand of the leader. With each passing moment, the possibility of escaping from this assembly with his life and memory intact seemed more remote. Only minutes ago he'd been part of a crowd, anonymous and with a ready means of escape. Now, he was the center of attention in a large crowd that blocked his way to an easy exit and watched expectantly for him to drink from a cauldron that would wipe

173

away his family, friends, and past, forever. He felt his heart race as the crowd seemed to close in around him.

"And now," the leader was saying, "their return journey…their journey home is about to be completed. Mercifully, our deliverer has created for them and within this cauldron the antidote of freedom that will track and obliterate that virus, memory, that has condemned them—until this day—to the tortured life of the soul that each of us has been spared, thanks to the benevolence and wisdom of our savior."

No, no, no! Walt thought to himself. The crowd was responding joyously to the salvation the leader promised. They couldn't understand what they had lost in their turn against memory.

"Lisette!" the leader called out, lifting his hand from Walt's shoulder and moving to stand next to the cauldron from which he pulled a long, black ladle, careful so as not to spill any. "Lisette, are you ready to renounce all memories, to return home to the here and now where humanity began and has always been meant to dwell."

Lisette had stopped smiling and was staring in awe at the ladle the man was holding up with both hands before the crowd so that all could see.

"Yes," Lisette whispered, a note of longing in her voice.

"She is ready," the congregation chanted in unison

"Lisette!" the man went on, "are you ready for the deliverance from affections and the ties recollection binds us to?"

"Yes!" Lisette called out emphatically.

"She is ready," the crowd chanted.

"Drink then, now, from the Cauldron of Forgetfulness!" the leader cried out pleadingly, commandingly. He passed the ladle to Lisette who took it with both hands, reverently. "Drink and leave behind the horror of images and ties of emotions locked in your memory. Destroy that memory and join in our happiness, in our oblivion, in our supremacy."

"She is ready!" the assembled shouted once more, and Lisette raised the ladle to her lips.

"NOOOOOOO!" Walt Walters screamed at the top of his lungs as he swung his hand at the ladle, knocking it away from Lisette's lips and hands. It sailed over the cauldron in front of them and clattered upon the stage floor, just inches from the edge of the riser.

The room fell deathly silent.

Walt froze. He had not intended to shout out. It was an involuntary reaction to the fear that Lisette would lose her memories. Even though he didn't know her—had seen her for the first time only minutes earlier—the idea that she would forget every important moment of her sixteen years of life alarmed and saddened him and he shouted before he even knew what he was doing.

And now, the entire congregation stared at him, awed and confused. Obviously, no one had ever disrupted the Rite of Forgetting, for the assembly was momentarily paralyzed with uncertainty about how to respond. A child near the stage stared at the ladle, a few feet away from him as if it were an amazing artifact from outer space.

Walt felt the sinking feeling of being discovered—of being caught in a lie—but this discovery had more serious consequences than any minor fibs and half-truths he'd been found guilty of. He was surrounded by an unsympathetic crowd—only momentarily stunned into inaction—but with no ready means of escape and no compatriots anywhere that he could see. Where was William? What had happened to Ling?

175

Lisette was gawking at him in slack-jawed amazement, like a socialite whose cocktail party is suddenly disrupted by stampeding rhinos.

Walt turned to her to plead, explain and maybe, he hoped, to gain an ally. "Don't you have a little sister who pesters you?" he asked, hoping to spark a memory and bring her to full consciousness about all she would have lost in drinking from the cauldron. "A brother you love to annoy? A mother who adores you, a father who calls you his 'little baby girl?'"

Walt turned to face the larger crowd.

"Can't any of you remember your families, your friends, all the people who were so important to you before you got here?" Walt asked them, plaintively. He thought he saw a blink of vague recognition in the eyes of one or two. Perhaps the power of the Cauldron of Forgetfulness was not as absolute as Ling and William believed. "Maybe you had a cat that curled up in your lap when you read a book," Walt continued, thinking, perhaps he could win the crowd over, "or an aunt who sent the same awful fruitcake every year for Christmas. Can't you remember?"

Walt saw a woman looking down at the floor, contemplative, puzzled, as if trying to recall a name. Further into the crowd, Walt saw several congregants bring their hands to their heads and he wondered if they were suffering the headaches that came in Paralleladise with sudden remembering.

"They are still there," Walt shouted. "They still love you."

He heard the gasp of a sob released and he turned to see Lisette, crying uncontrollably. "Pietra," she whispered, staring at the invoked the image of this loved one in her mind's eye.

"She's still there," Walt whispered. "She hasn't forgotten you."

176

The gaunt man with the white hair who had been leading the ceremony took in a deep breath as if a recollection had sneaked up on his sleeping memory and startled it awake.

And then the room shook violently—more powerfully than any of the earthquakes Walt had felt until then and so forcefully that many in the audience lost their footing and fell against one another like dominoes knocking one another to the floor. Others grabbed onto their seats and leaned on the walls to steady themselves against the vibrations. The podium and stand with the cauldron rocked back and forth as if they might tip over. And one of the cauldron bearers stumbled backwards and fell off the stage into the small aisle between the riser and the stained glass window behind it.

The quake lasted for several moments and seemed to jolt the assembly from its paralysis of amazement at Walt's defiance.

When the room stopped shaking, the face of the leader shuttered with terror and, pointing at Walt Walters, he gasped, "It's a hippo!" as if Walt were a mythical beast. "He's a hippo!"

Suddenly, lights flashed everywhere—red and yellow and white, against the stained glass window and the walls, and accompanied by a blaring alarm that honked in rhythm to the flashing lights. The noise and lights, as well as the leader's cry, spurred the crowd to action as several shouted out in fear and amazement, "A hippo! A hippo!" From the huge speakers at the sides of the room a mechanized voice began repeating the alarm, "Hippo intruder! Hippo intruder!"

And then the crowd's terror turned to action with several cries of "Seize him!" and a massive surge toward the stage.

Walt looked to Lisette as his only possible aid and accomplice. But she was still staring, dazed, and repeating the name, "Pietra."

He looked about him for escape just as one of the cauldron bearers rushed to pounce.

But before he got to Walt, someone in a brown robe came leaping from the side of the stage tackling the cauldron bearer. Walt heard their grunts as they fell against the wooden stage, but did not take a moment to look at his rescuer as he instinctively turned away from the leader who was pushing Lisette aside to grab Walt.

But again, Walt saw the flash of a rescuer and felt someone prod him toward the back of the stage and throw himself into the leader. Walt turned when he reached the back of the stage—there was nowhere else to go—and saw that it was Ling who had intervened and was pushing the congregation leader back, plowing into his mid-section with his head and growling out a furious yelp.

The man in brown robes who had tackled the cauldron bearer stood up now and Walt recognized him as one of the two cloaked figures Celia had been talking to at the hippos' underground sanctuary. Had he been at the assembly the whole time, waiting to jump in if things went wrong?

He was a good man to have on your side, Walt could see, as the man picked up the heavy podium on the stage and threw it at the charging crowd. The other man from the sanctuary, too, was there and had leapt on stage. He was holding a wooden bench, swinging it forcefully from side to side, knocking off anyone who tried to climb up the riser. For the moment, they were holding the crowd at bay, but Walt realized that, with no clear means of escape, it wouldn't be long before the mob overwhelmed his few allies and seized them all.

"They're all hippos!" the leader cried out, spurring the congregants. "Take them! Take them all!" He managed to grab the back of Ling's shirt and shovel him to the side, making a clear path toward Walt. Ling used the momentum to swing his body into the crowd, knocking down several on-rushers and then recovering quickly enough to jump back on stage before they could get a hold on him.

"Get the boy out of here!" Ling shouted as he turned to take on the mob again.

Walt tried to dash off the back of the stage—though there was nowhere to run—but as he did, the leader of the congregation seized him from behind with a triumphant cry of success. "Ahaa!"

"Let me go!" Walt yelled and turned to face the man, pummeling at his arms with his fists, hoping to break free.

But the leader held tight, and Walt could see out of the corner of his eye that the crowd was starting to overtake Ling and the other men, mounting the riser by pairs and threes, pushing them further back on the stage toward where Walt and the leader struggled.

"I've got you!" the leader shouted at Walt. "Give up, and you won't be hurt!"

But Walt pushed and swung at the man, frightened that if he and Ling and the others were overpowered, they would be forced to drink from the cauldron.

"Lisette!" Walt cried. "Lisette! The cauldron!"

Lisette, who had been standing, dumbfounded and unmoving since Walt had knocked the ladle from her hand, turned her head now to look at him.

"Knock it over!"

Walt could not see if she heard him, because the leader now had him by the shoulders and was trying to secure him in a tighter hold. His face was only inches away from Walt's. He wore an impassioned look of determination as he grunted out, "You can't win, Hippo. Give up now before I have to hurt you."

Suddenly, the leader's eyes sprung open wide as he dropped to his knees, felled from behind by a blow to the back of his legs.

"Celia!" Walt shouted, for it was Celia's face revealed behind the leader as he fell to the floor. She had brought him down with the playground trick of a blow to the back of the knees, causing them to buckle and drop.

"Ooopf," the man grunted as Celia stepped over his back and grabbed Walt's arm.

"We've got to get you out of here!"

But Celia's goals seemed much bigger than their possibilities, for even now, Ling and the other two allies were only feet away, being pushed back further and further on the stage by the crowd which was becoming bolder and bolder, realizing the overwhelming superiority of their numbers and sensing victory. Walt and Celia turned to the left and then the right, looking for an escape route, but the crowd was closing in on all sides.

"What do we do now?" one of the men in brown robes shouted to Celia. He was still swinging the wooden bench at the crowd—the only thing keeping them from overpowering him.

Celia looked about her for any means of escape.

And then, there came a thundering crash upon the stage and the mob stopped its onslaught abruptly to locate its origin.

It was Lisette. She had pushed the cauldron over and it crashed through the floor of the riser and onto the concrete floor beneath making a splintered hole in the middle of the wooden stage. The contents, still steaming, splattered upon the floor and the shoes and legs of congregants near it.

"Thank you," Walt whispered. If anyone were forced to drink from the cauldron tonight it would have to be refilled first.

Lisette's diversion, however, only delayed the mob for a moment as they turned back toward Walt and Celia and their cornered allies, warily preparing to seize them.

"YEEEEEEEEE!"

The powerful yell of a lone voice suddenly echoed through the room and Walt and the others looked up to see William, with his stocky build and bald head, swing joyfully across the ceiling of the room as if he were on a carnival ride. He had managed to unleash one of the chandeliers from its mooring on the wall, lowering it to allow him to swing halfway across the room. He must have started atop the balcony, Walt decided, calculating his trajectory as he swooped in suddenly very low, approaching the stage and prompting everyone in his path to duck their heads or suffer the blow. There was no stopping him.

"YEEEEEEEEEE!" William screamed again as he came in over the stage.

Too low! Walt panicked, thinking William would crash against the riser. But he cleared the floor by a few inches causing everyone in his path to jump out of the way.

Walt had only a moment to wonder how much help having one more ally on stage could be when he realized that fighting off the congregants was not what William had in mind. For he did not slow down or aim to take out the mob, but kept coming straight across the stage, full speed, barreling with tremendous momentum and yelling at the top of his lungs.

"Look out!" Celia cried, leaping to one side, out of the way. Walt ducked the other way and the chandelier swung between them. He thought, surely, William would be killed when he crashed into…

And then William was on top of him, dropping onto the stage and allowing the chandelier to continue its trajectory—straight into the stain-glassed window behind them.

Walt heard the crash as the heavy wooden chandelier shattered the stained glass window. The impact and the clattering of glass echoed through the room but Walt could not see what was happening because William was lying on top of him.

"Stay down," Walt heard someone say as the chandelier, on its return arc, swung back through the window and across the stage, striking several congregants and barreling them off the stage.

"All right, are you?" William asked.

Walt gasped, "I can't breathe" and William rolled off of him.

William's daring acrobatics and the flying glass it created had sent the crowd scurrying, but now, as the chandelier swung out and to rest in the middle of the room, the congregants prepared to remount their attack on the outlawed hippos.

William stood and helped Walt to his feet.

"We've got to get out of here!" Celia shouted, turning toward the dark night outside beyond where the stained glass window had been.

Walt looked out. There was a twelve foot drop off behind this part of the building and at the bottom was the broken glass from the shattered window. And beyond that, all was darkness.

"What are we going to . . .?" Walt began, but then Ling dashed by him, leaping through the window frame and out into the night.

The crowd of congregants was nearly upon them. Walt heard Ling land with a thud and the tinkle of glass and saw one of the men in the brown robe throw his bench at the oncoming mob and leap out after him, followed quickly by the other.

The leader of the congregants grabbed William from behind, but William turned quickly and shoved him back into the on-rushing crowd. Then he looked at Walt and Celia expectantly.

Celia shrugged. "Geronimo," she called as she leapt out into the darkness.

Walt took a breath to work up his nerve, but by then, William had grabbed him by the arm and jumped from the window, pulling Walt out into the dark night air.

SEVENTEEN

Walt crashed to the ground outside the courthouse building, landing on his feet, then falling forward onto his hands and knees. Had any of the broken glass been jutting up, he might have been seriously hurt, but the shards lay flat and he stood up quickly, without a scratch.

"Everybody okay?" he heard Celia call and saw her a few yards away—a shadow in the dark night.

"Okay!" several voices called back and then Walt added his own, "I'm all right."

"Let's get out of here!" It was Ling's voice and Walt saw the outline of the little man to his right.

Behind him, Walt heard the calls of the angry crowd and he turned to see many of the assembly mob perched at the window frame, ten feet above them, peering into the night to spot the escaping criminals. "The hippos!" someone cried. "They're getting away."

"Let's get them," another voice called, but no one in the mob seemed willing to risk the jump.

"Stay low," Ling advised, "Zigzag," and Walt watched his shadowy figure dash off into the night. Two taller figures—the men in the brown robes—followed him.

Then Celia was at Walt's side, grabbing his arm. "Anything broken?"

Walt shook his head. "Celia, I'm sorry I…"

"It's okay. Let's go," and Celia ran off as Ling had done.

"It's not your fault," Walt heard a voice at his ear. It was William. "We didn't prepare you."

"I should have . . ."

"No time for regrets," William said, giving Walt a directing push from behind and Walt started off running in the direction of the others with William at his elbow.

"What about Lisette?"

"She's fine for the moment," William assured.

"But she'll never . . .?"

"We can't save everyone," William said, sadly. "We can't save everyone."

Walt slowed his pace at the thought of leaving Lisette behind. Surely, she would be held and, even though she had temporarily forestalled the ritual by tipping over the cauldron, eventually she'd be initiated through the Rite of Forgetting. But when Walt turned his head back toward the courthouse, he saw that many from the crowd had run out of the building and were in pursuit. William saw it, too.

"We must hurry," William warned, and they picked up the pace.

It wasn't hard to catch up to the others. They ran cautiously because of the darkness and Ling's insistence on zigzagging slowed their forward progress even more.

Walt and William drew abreast of them. Celia was ahead by a few yards, having abandoned the zigzag strategy.

"Where are we going?" Walt called.

"We can't go back to The Combs, now," one of the men in the brown robes pointed out. "Unless we circle back."

"They'll catch us if we do," Walt huffed out, struggling to run and talk at the same time.

"I'm not worried about them so much," Celia called back.

"They'll forget who they're chasing in a minute or two and go back," William panted.

"It's the gnome probes we have to watch out for," Ling warned.

Walt had heard the term several times. "What **are** gnome probes?" he asked.

As if in answer, a buzzing sound, like the whine of a dozen mechanical toy airplanes, blared out of the night sky behind them. He turned to see where it came from but the darkness obscured the source.

Then, as he turned around, right in front of his face was a startling surprise. Walt skidded to a halt, afraid he might run into it.

"Gnome probes!" one of the men in the brown robes yelled out.

The figure in front of him, indeed, resembled a garden gnome, a ceramic leprechaun. It was a foot and a half long cast in the shape of a gnome, complete with pointed hat and shoes, a thin pointed beard with no mustache, bright red hair, and a green vest over a flannel shirt, and mischievous smile on his face. At first, Walt thought it was a living gnome, but then realized it wasn't moving—its expression didn't change, its eyes didn't blink.

It was borne through the air by wings on its back that flapped so rapidly as to look like a blur of motion and it hovered right in front of Walt's face. As Walt stared at it, a tiny panel in its chest opened and a nozzle extended from it.

"Run, Walt." It was Celia, yelling to him from several yards ahead. She and the others had continued to run when he stopped.

They batted away at the air, knocking aside the gnome probes that were clustering around their heads in twos and threes.

"Watch out!" Ling yelled.

Walt dashed off after the others and as he did, a tiny spurt of red florescent paste shot from the nozzle of the gnome probe, just missing him.

Walt ran as fast as he could to catch the others, who were slowed by the probes that darted in front of their eyes and head, weaving in and out, like huge pesky flies. Celia and the others continued to swing their arms at the probes, but rarely made contact.

As soon as Walt caught up to them, he was descended upon by his own set of probes. They circled his head rapidly, diving before his eyes.

"Don't let them slime you!" Ling warned.

"What should I do?" Walt shouted, ducking his head to get below them, but unable to shake them off.

"We've got to get out of here!"

"Prairie Dog Flats!" Celia called out, veering off in another direction. The others followed her with Walt just behind them.

It was difficult enough to see where they were going in the darkness, and even more so with the gnome probes circling their heads. The wings of each probe glowed with a bright, white light—like a fairy's wings—making it harder to focus on the darkness beyond them.

And now, they were leaving the streets and sidewalks in the neighborhood near the courthouse, and swerving into an open field. Walt did not recognize the locale at all. It was as if he had left the real world of Lexington behind and was now leaving the Paralleladise version behind, as well. William had been right about the pursuing congregants who appeared to have given up the chase altogether when the gnome probes descended.

Walt increased his speed to pass William, thinking he might run his gnome into William's, if he ran close enough. But the probes were prepared and darted between and among their heads without crashing, until Walt was ahead of William and then his own probes centered around him once more.

"We're not going to make it with this many probes," Ling warned.

"It's not far," Celia panted. They had been running vigorously for several minutes.

Walt saw one of the men in brown robes bat at a gnome near his head, making contact and sending the probe squealing in a tumultuous spin to the ground where it broke into several pieces. Walt did not have time to study the inner workings as he leapt over the broken fragments when he passed.

"Stay with us, Walt," Celia called. "Don't let them slime you."

"I'm trying!" Walt shouted back. He wondered how Celia knew so much. She was leading them to their destination, and now she seemed to know all about the gnome probes and being slimed.

He had no time to reason it out, however, for the gnome probe directly before him was hovering and the panel in its chest had opened and the nozzle was extending.

With instinctive alarm, Walt swung hard at the probe, slapping it with his open hand and sending it crashing into another circling probe, inches away. They both were damaged by the impact and went squealing to the ground.

"A two-fer," Celia shouted. She'd been watching his struggle while trying to ward off her own pesky gnomes. "Good shot!"

Walt's momentary triumph lasted only for a moment, however, as two more gnomes descended around his head from out of the darkness.

And then the ground started shaking.

"When it rains it pours," William reminded them, in a tone used to disaster.

The quake started slowly, rattling the ground beneath their feet, but increased dramatically with each running step.

"Sheron!"

"Almost there!" Celia cheered them on, her voice filled with doubt.

"Ahhh!"

Walt heard the cry from off to his left and looked to see one of the men in the brown robes. He was slowing his pace dramatically and slapping at his cheek as if trying to kill a mosquito there.

"Franz has been hit!" William called out.

Walt slowed to help, but felt a solid push from behind. It was Ling, whom he had somehow passed in the darkness. "Keep moving or we're all done for."

The man William had called Franz had slowed when he was hit with the florescent spray of the gnome probe, but now accelerated furiously, as if a new terror were spurring him on.

The intensity of the earthquake increased, too, and suddenly, from behind them, a bright light snapped on to illuminate the night. It shone like a powerful spotlight and pierced the darkness, centering on Walt and his allies.

The sudden brightness and the shaking of the earth made it hard for Walt to maintain his footing and he peered ahead, squinting, while swatting the gnome probes, in hopes of seeing anything that might clue him into their proximity to Prairie Dog Flats. There was a billboard ahead, anchored nonsensically in the middle of this open field, but when Walt passed, it gave no hint of how close they were to their destination. It read:

NyXus Corporation
Forget Everything and
Leave It to Us!

Before they reached the billboard, the man called Franz fell to the ground, letting out a panicked holler. Walt thought he had tripped on the uneven ground. But then he saw the gnome probes abandon him to buzz off in the pursuit of the others and saw Franz being dragged, on his stomach and by his feet, back toward the light that blasted from behind them. The light itself appeared to have a hold of him, though, for nothing was touching him but the bright ray of illumination and the ground he was being dragged across.

"Ling!" Walt shouted and pointed, trying to draw attention to Franz's plight.

"Watch out!" Ling yelled and Walt looked in front of him to see the nozzle of gnome probe taking aim. He ducked just in time to avoid the splatter of slime that fired at his face.

"Stay alert," Ling warned. "There's nothing we can do for him now."

Walt could not help but glance back, quickly, and saw that Franz had disappeared completely into the light.

What had happened to him? The possibilities terrified and angered Walt, and when another gnome opened its firing nozzle in front of his face, his hand darted up with lightning intensity to clench it around the neck and fling it violently off into the night. He heard it squeal and shatter in the distant darkness.

"There!" Celia shouted, several yards ahead. She adjusted her course slightly and Walt and the others followed. Wherever they were running, Walt hoped they would be there soon. They could not avoid Franz's fate forever. His legs were weary and his lungs were bursting. He had picked up an extra gnome probe, too, and now had four of them circling his head, positioning themselves for an opening to fire.

If their destination was close, however, Walt did not see it. It was open field for as far as he could see, except behind them, where the bright light blared with hot intensity.

Then Celia changed course again and the others followed, but still Walt could not see anything ahead of him. A gnome probe near his ear took aim and Walt ducked as it fired, its discharge flying over his head and striking another circling probe.

The illumination of the slimed gnome's wings blinked out. It floated momentarily and then dropped toward the ground but was sucked with intense velocity into the light behind them before it hit the ground. The slime, Walt determined, must be used to mark the target for the pursuing light—to give it something to hone in on.

Celia changed course again—and in the same direction as before—and Walt realized they were now running in a big, irregular circle. Perhaps the lights and gnome probes were distracting her and she didn't realize they weren't getting anywhere.

"Celia" he called out, hoping to alert her.

But then Celia disappeared.

She did not get drawn into the pursuing light, like Franz. She simply disappeared into the night. One moment she was there and the next she was not.

"CELIA!" Walt screamed in a panic. He could not lose her—his only contact with his own world.

"She's fine," Ling called back to him. "Just keep circling."

And then Ling disappeared.

"Ling!" Walt shouted just before he saw a gnome probe, its nozzle readied. He shot his arm out at another gnome bearing down from the other side and drew it in front of his face and blocked the discharge of slime. Then he threw the probe he had seized at the one that had fired and they both smashed together to the ground.

"Ling," Walt shouted once again, looking around and realizing that the other man in the brown robe had disappeared, too. He craned his head quickly in a panic.

There was William, still at his side.

"Keep circling," William shouted. Suddenly, the gnome probes around William's head stopped pursuing him and hovered in the air as William ran on. An instant later, they darted off, buzzing into the darkness as quickly as they had appeared.

And then the ground stopped quaking, the incredible vibrations, switching off in a flash.

The sudden stillness caused Walt to lose his footing. He stumbled forward, throwing his hands and arms out in front of him, in reflex, to break his fall.

But, he didn't hit the ground as he expected, for the ground opened up underneath him and he fell and fell into a yawning blackness.

EIGHTEEN

Walt Walters awoke to the murmur of voices and the gentle touch of a soft hand upon his forehead. And he awoke, for the second time that day with a reverberating headache that overwhelmed every other feeling in his body.

He groaned, opening his eyes cautiously to find that the hand stroking his face belonged to Celia, whose own face hovered above his, smiling—concerned and sympathetic.

"You really should watch where you're going, Walt Walters," she said, her expression gleaming with relief that he was waking up.

"Where...?"

"You're safe," she said, "with me."

"My head . . ."

"You kind of landed on it."

"I had a horrible dream I was being chased by gnomes with wings."

Celia laughed. "I have bad news for you, Walters."

Walt blinked his eyes fully opened and looked about. It hadn't been a dream at all, he saw, for he and Celia were in some sort of cave or underground cavern, lit only by a small campfire a few feet away. Walt lay on his back on the floor and Celia kneeled over him.

On the other side of the cave, he saw Ling and William. It was their voices he'd heard as he awoke. Ling had his hands on William's shoulders and was attempting to prompt his memories.

"What is your name?" Ling quizzed him. "Where are you from?"

"I don't remember," William muttered. "I tell you, I don't remember."

Walt propped himself up on his elbows, his mind murky. "What happened?" he asked Celia.

"You fell in a prairie dog hole," Celia gestured toward the ceiling. It was a very low ceiling, perhaps six feet above the cave floor. Carved into it were several holes, approximately five feet in diameter spaced irregularly and covered with what looked to be retractable sliding panels.

That was why Celia and the others had been running in circles in Prairie Dog Flats—Walt realized—they'd been searching for the holes, waiting for them to open up. But who had opened them and how?

"Must be an awfully big prairie dog," Walt observed.

"According to Ling, the Flats were designed by some of the earliest hippo resistance fighters in the third century. The mechanical parts are made of wooden pulleys and cogs."

"How do they open?"

Celia shrugged. "It's a mystery. One of those things nobody remembers. There are a lot of things nobody remembers—even hippos."

Unfortunately, Walt was remembering things—many things, mostly his mistakes.

"I'm sorry about what happened at the courthouse."

Celia smiled and stroked his cheek. "You couldn't have known."

"You warned me. I should have . . ."

"Ling says, 'Remembering is the province of the wise man, but dwelling not so much.' We have too much work to do."

"But the girl, Lisette," Walt mourned, "And that guy. . ." He'd forgotten the name and his heart skipped a beat. Every forgotten detail felt like a harbinger of greater losses. "Franz!" Walt said emphatically when the name came back to him.

"Franz is strong. He'll resist them."

"Resist who? Where are we? Who's in charge?"

"Better do your mnemonics first or your head will hurt even more than it does already."

Walt didn't think that was possible.

Across the room William cried out loudly, "I tell you, I've got nothing. It's all gone."

"Are you telling me, *William*," Ling asked, impatiently, "you don't even remember your name? Because I just gave you a clue, and if you say you don't, I'll know you're not trying your hardest."

"What are mnemonics?" Walt asked Celia.

"Memory exercises," Celia explained and then jumped right into them, "What is your name?"

"I don't think we need to start so basic."

"It's like practicing scales to warm up on the piano. It gets your brain limbered up. Now, what is your name?"

Walt sighed. He sat up fully. "Walt Walters."

"What is your father's name?"

"Benjamin."

"What are your sisters' names?"

"I think I'm limber."

"What are your sisters' names?" Celia repeated.

"Acey and the Wicked Witch."

"Who is the prettiest girl in Lexington Middle School?"

Walt hesitated. "I forget," he said, after a moment, "Must be the lethemine."

"Chicken."

"Wait. It's coming back to me" Walt said, rubbing his temples, "Yes, it's…it's Felicity Kleinschmidt."

"You're worse off than I thought," Celia said, shaking her head. "I see months of rehabilitation ahead for you."

They heard shuffling nearby and turned to see Ling approaching. William remained at the other side of the small cave, seated and rocking and repeating to himself, "My name is William. I live in Chelsney… My name is William. I live in Chelsney."

"How is he?" Ling asked Celia as he approached, studying Walt carefully.

"His head seems okay," Celia told him, "But he's developed a severe case of bad taste. How's William?"

Ling shrugged, but his concern was obvious. "Hard to tell how much of it is genuine memory loss and how much is temporary hysteria." Ling looked at Walt. "All that running around in the lethemine…gets in the lungs, affects the hippocampus."

"Is he going to be okay?" Walt asked. If William suffered, he thought guiltily, that would make three victims of his outburst at the courthouse.

"Most likely," Ling replied and then turned to Celia. "Why don't you work with him a bit. See if you can bring him around. He's just resisting me now."

Celia nodded, standing up. "I'll see what I can do," she said, and started over toward William.

Ling squatted down and gave Walt's knee a friendly slap. "You took quite a spill. She was worried. No time to warn you, however."

"I'm all right." Walt rubbed his neck.

"Think you can travel? As soon as MacGruder gets back, we should get moving. After all these years, the gnomes are still fooled by the Flats, but Sheron will send minions soon enough to search the area."

"Where are we?" Walt looked around the cave. Across the room, Celia was kneeling before the seated William and asking him memory questions in a low voice. William had stopped crying, but wasn't responding well to her prompts.

Ling studied the cave and pointed to a pair of large stone blocks in one corner. "Probably built to replicate the Roman viaduct system. That's my guess."

"What do you mean?"

Ling glanced at Celia and William to judge whether he was needed and then, seeing William more subdued, he sat down next to Walt: "One theory is that all of Paralleladise is no bigger than the region in your country called 'Texas.' There are eight known portals throughout the world, but they all empty into Paralleladise and so anyone who comes through must be made to think they are back at home until the Rite of the Cauldron or the lethemine obliterates their memory of what home looks like. In the times you know as the Roman era, this part of Paralleladise was dug out and re-Created to look like the viaducts—to fool a newcomer into thinking he or she was home in Rome."

"And they just let it fill in after all that work?"

"Well," Ling explained with a sigh, "you hardly need Roman viaducts in twenty-first century Lexington. They fill in. They pave over. They tear down and reconstruct."

"Seems like a lot of time and energy."

"Time is one thing there is plenty of in Paralleladise," Ling told him. "And in the Roman era they didn't have the Rite of The Cauldron. That's a new technique—only a hundred years old or so. Before that, they had to wait for the lethemine in the atmosphere to have its full effect, to eat away enough memory so that the newcomer no longer remembered what his home looked like."

"What's in the cauldron?"

Ling shrugged. "We don't know . . . yet. There's a liquid form of lethemine in it. And an activating agent. And we don't know what else. There are chemists—hippos in the resistance—working on it. But access to microscopes and oscillators and other equipment is non-existent. We must fashion everything out of something we find discarded."

"And there's no antidote," Walt guessed.

"Ah," Ling said, nodding and smiling for the first time since Walt met him. "But perhaps there is a human agent that can minimize its effects."

"What do you mean?"

Ling slapped Walt's knee again. "Did you see what happened at Community when you spoke. People were thinking. People were remembering."

"I didn't do anything," Walt reminded Ling quickly. "I just asked questions."

Ling held up his index finger, as if he were about to make a singular, important point. Then he leaned forward and rested the finger on Walt's forehead. "Perhaps, you have a gift."

"But . . ." Walt started, and then they heard scuffling from a darkened corner of the cave and looked over to see the second man with the brown robe from the assembly enter, crawling in through a tunnel Walt hadn't noticed before.

"MacGruder," Ling announced. He turned to Walt. "I'll bet you're hungry. Let's see if he brought back anything good."

Ling rose and helped Walt to his feet. They hurried over to where MacGruder had entered.

"Mac," William called. "Mac is back." He rose to his feet with Celia to join them.

"See!" Ling pointed out. "You remembered MacGruder."

"It's going, Mac," William sobbed to MacGruder. "I can't remember the basics."

"Perhaps a bit of food will help," MacGruder offered. He swung from over his shoulder a pillowcase, half filled with food, opening it in front of William.

"May not help my brain," William said, cheering. "But it'll certainly help my belly."

"Bring it over by the fire," Ling suggested, "and we'll have a look."

MacGruder was a tall man and had to stoop to stand in the cave. He carried the pillowcase to the campfire and spilled out its contents, scattering cans and packages and bottles.

"I'm starving," Celia announced.

They all sat like happy campers around the small fire, taking to eat whatever was in reach. There were crackers and beef jerky and dried fruits in plastic packages. There were cans of meats and vegetables and soda, and tiny jars of fake-cheese dip, relish and jam.

"It's a feast," William exclaimed, taking up a can of anchovies and peeling the lid back.

Walt had not realized how hungry he was until he saw the unappetizing collection of processed goods and felt ravenous. He opened cellophane-wrapped crackers and ate half of the package before looking around for jam to spread on them.

"Any luck with our Chelsney boy?" Ling asked Celia after he'd eaten for several minutes and begun to feel his hunger pangs subside.

Celia patted William on the back. "Well, he did remember the North Road."

"You gave me a hint," William responded quickly, not ready to believe that his memory loss was less than catastrophic.

"A tiny hint."

"No matter. It was a hint and so it doesn't count."

"Come now, Willie," MacGruder put in, "are you sure you're trying?"

"I tell you it's a blank," William assured them, ripping open a cellophane package of dry cereal. "Everything past the last five years or so is a blank."

"Usually works the other way around," Ling chided. "You forget the most recent things first."

"All I know," William defended himself, "is that it's all a blank."

"The old boy's set on being as forgetful as he likes," MacGruder observed.

Walt and Celia listened to the banter while they devoured their food, without concern for manners. The conversation sounded lighthearted to Walt, but he could hear a note of genuine concern in Ling's voice.

"William," Walt said when the conversation momentarily lulled, "what is a tinker?"

"Ah," William responded, shaking a breadstick at Walt, "it doesn't work that way, my boy. Don't try any of your little tricks on me."

"You don't lose your common knowledge," MacGruder explained to Walt.

"You lose your memory born of circumstances," Ling went on.

"So," Celia tried to clarify, "We won't forget what a middle school is. We'll just forget that we went to one in Lexington and what went on there."

"And who your teachers were and what classes you liked and who your friends were," William continued.

"And what Lexington is, for that matter," MacGruder added.

"So I can tell you, proudly, without a moment's hesitation," William told Walt proudly, "that a tinker is a man who repairs things—mostly small items around the house—your plates, your cups and saucers, flatware. But I have no idea why you asked."

"That's the kind of hint that doesn't count, anyway," MacGruder elaborated.

Walt considered the new information carefully. Celia, sitting next to him, nodded. The more he learned about Paralleladise, the more he was confused. There was too much to know. And yet Celia seemed to be taking it all in stride—understanding, making the connections, seeing how it all fit together. She had always been quicker than him.

"It will come to you, William," she said to the tinker in a reassuring tone. "I'm certain of it."

"I wish I could believe that, girl," William said, his lips starting to tremble again. "But I'm afraid by tomorrow, you'll all be strangers." And then William began to sob, quietly.

Walt expected Ling or MacGruder to tease him again with a playful reminder of his exaggerations. But MacGruder was looking thoughtfully at the floor, and Ling was staring at his old friend, tearfully. Celia, too, looked sympathetic but clueless about how to help.

Walt thought long and hard before speaking. His last efforts to help, at the courthouse, had been disastrous and there was so much about Paralleladise and its effects on the mind and the memory that he did not understand. And yet, the possibility of losing William, of seeing him suffer the fear of forgetting, was excruciating to watch silently.

"Were you a good tinker?" he asked finally, breaking the silence. Everyone looked at him as if to say, "You don't get it, Walters. Leave it alone."

"Was I a tinker?" William asked after several moments—more in a polite attempt to take Walt off the spot than any hope that the questioning might help.

"That's what you told me," Walt assured him. "That you were a tinker, and you lived on the North Road, past the milestones."

William shrugged. "Could be true. I don't recall."

"And that you had a daughter named Mary."

"Tch!" Ling scolded. "You can't *give* him the information. He has to *remember* it. Otherwise, there's no telling what he remembers and what he knows as facts you told him."

"And that when you came back to the house," Walt went on, ignoring Ling, "on a rainy day, you'd walk through the mud to the front door because the path was so worn it could only become mud when it rained."

"I don't remember!" William cried out.

"Leave him alone," MacGruder said. "You can't push it. You're doing it all wrong."

"And your daughter made fish every night it rained and you'd have to scrape the mud off your feet coming in."

"Fish, yes," William nodded, not really listening. But then he shook his head violently. "No, no . . . no fish. You're trying to trick me. No one fishes when it rains hard enough to muddy the lane. That's a common fact. That's not memory."

"…fish your wife had caught at the stream behind your house."

William's face drew up in puzzlement, as if he'd just seen the impossible but wasn't quite sure his eyes hadn't tricked him.

"You'd clean your boots off with a stick by the front porch . . ."

"Porch?" William scoffed. "What porch? You're making everything up now."

"Poor tinkers don't have porches in William's day," Ling explained. "You're taking the wrong tack."

"That's it," William agreed, "You don't know what you're talking about, my boy. I appreciate the effort, but . . ."

"You just need to rest your mind a little," Celia suggested to William. "Just don't think about anything for a bit."

Walt stared at William for a long moment, anxious to continue his interrogation, feeling certain he was on to something. But he was only making matters more confused for William and making the others frustrated with him.

"And no one would leave a muddy walkway to their door," William went on definitively. "That's common knowledge, too. We don't have your running water and if you muddied the floor inside, it was a hundred and fifty paces to the well and a hundred and fifty paces back again to clean it up."

Walt looked at the others. He knew that if his strategy could work, one more question could bring William around. But Ling and MacGruder might think he was only making mischief.

"So what did you do?" Walt asked, unable to resist.

"We built walkways to the door from the lane. Out of stone."

203

"You built it yourself?"

"No," William squawked, exasperated with Walt's ignorance of medieval life. "Big stones, heavy stones. Took me and me brother and a mule and a cart to move them."

"Your brother's mule?"

"He never had an extra pence in his life. It's the neighbor's and the neighbor's cart."

Ling, MacGruder and Celia all sat straight up, realizing what was happening before William, in his exasperation, understood.

"How many stones in the front walk?" Walt asked quickly, not wanting to lose William now.

"How many stones?" William asked, still not seeing the point, "Fourteen. Fourteen of the heaviest boulders the neighborhood had seen."

"Fourteen stones from the front gate to the door of the house."

"Gate?" William scoffed, "You're thinking of a rich man's villa. We have no front gate. Fourteen stones from the lane to the house."

"You said it was fifteen before?" Walt challenged.

"What?" William bellowed in frustration. "Fourteen! Fourteen! That's how I taught Mary to count—marking the stones and ..."

William stopped in the middle of his sentence. Ling and MacGruder smiled at him in amazement and Celia beamed with pride.

"Marking . . ." William stumbled on, stunned at the memories coming back, "Marking each stone, counting them off. That's . . . that's how I taught Mary to count."

A grin burst across William's face as the memories flooded his mind and the relief of remembering—of not losing every recollection—poured across his heart.

"The switch is flipped," Ling called. "Power's restored."

"What is your brother's name?"

William looked into Walt's eyes and said, calmly, "Richard." He let out a laugh of recognition and Walt could almost see the images of Richard washing across William's brain. "Richard . . . Richard . . . Richard the Ox, people call him. Lazy and big as an ox."

And then William started to cry again, but this time they were tears of joy at the returning memories rather than regret at recollections lost. Walt watched with great satisfaction as Celia moved closer to William, put an arm around his shoulder and hugged him to her.

"I have a brother," William said, looking into Celia's eyes. "I have a brother."

"He's called 'Richard,' I understand," Celia replied, "'Richard the Ox.'"

"His wife's name is Christina," William told them, marveling at each recollection as they paraded before his brain. "They have a little boy. They named him William."

"After his favorite uncle," Celia said.

"Ha-ha!"

Walt felt a surge of warm pride and happiness—the first good feeling he'd had since finding Celia here, lost, too, in this land of forgetting. He looked over at Ling to find the little man staring at him, a newfound gleam of respect shone in his eyes.

"You will be a great Rememberer," Ling whispered.

And then the earth began to shake with fury.

NINETEEN

"It's Sheron!"

"Douse the fire!" William cried. He and the others jumped up and kicked dust on the campfire to extinguish the flames.

Walt tried to stand, but the tremors came in quick waves and he was knocked to the floor again. Finally, he struggled to his feet and swayed with the quaking earth.

"They must have followed you back to the cave," Ling said to MacGruder.

"I wasn't followed," MacGruder insisted. "It's the kid. His mnemonic signature is probably off the scale. It's like a lighthouse beacon!"

MacGruder gave a final kick at the loose dirt on the cave floor and brought up a cloud of dust that completely snuffed out the small fire. The cave was plunged into total darkness.

"We've got to get Walt out of here." It was Celia's voice. Her tone was commanding and, once again, Walt wondered how she'd earned such authority in such a short time while he remained so confused and helpless.

Walt felt Celia grasp his arm and direct him through the cave in the direction of the tunnel MacGruder had entered with the sack of food.

"We haven't much time." Celia told him. "Focus on the moment."

In total darkness, they moved toward the tunnel, stumbling over the campfire logs and stones and rocks and debris from their makeshift meal. Walt heard the others following close behind.

"Try not to bring up any memories," Celia warned him. "Sheron's honing in on them."

Walt, reaching out with his hands before him, felt the wall of the cave. They were at the tunnel. "What does he want?"

"You."

An especially powerful tremor quaked just above them nearly knocking them to the ground. Walt steadied himself against the cave with one hand and held Celia with the other.

"You've got a highly-developed hippocampus." Celia spoke hurriedly. "NyXus has to destroy it—to destroy all the hippos— to make his plan work."

"What plan?'

"I'll go first with MacGruder…" This was Ling's voice, right beside them. "Just in case Sheron's waiting at the other end. Then the boy and then you and William."

"All right," Celia acknowledged.

"But we're all in danger!" Walt protested. He did not know what would happen if Sheron were waiting at the other end of the tunnel, but he did not want Ling and MacGruder in front, protecting him. He did not want them in harm's way for his sake.

"Sheron knows about you now!" Ling spoke with hoarse intensity. The tremors were coming in rocking waves, fading momentarily but then coming on strong again, as if a giant, stomping on the earth above them, was pacing back and forth, sniffing them out. "He knows your power."

My power? Walt thought. What power? He'd never felt so powerless in his life, groping frantically in the dark, taking direction from everyone else, uncertain of what was happening and why.

"Put all memories from your mind, Walt," William urged, gravely.

"If it's me he's after, then leave me behind!" Walt cried. He turned to Celia, reaching out in the darkness to grasp her shoulders. "Celia! I don't want him to get you! I couldn't stand it if he got you. Leave me here and get away!"

Celia sighed deeply. He wished he could see her face.

"Walt," she said. "We've got to get you out of here."

"You're much too valuable," Ling added.

The source of the tremors was right above them once again, keeping them off balance.

"Sheron's fishing now!" Ling called out. "Just shaking the world to see what will fall out. MacGruder!"

"I'm already in the tunnel."

"Let's move, then!"

Walt felt Ling swish past him, ducking and entering the tunnel. Then he felt William's hand upon his shoulder, encouraging him in after Ling.

"Concentrate on the moment," Celia urged. "Try not to use your memory right now. It sends out mnemes that Sheron can detect and follow."

Walt peered to see her but the darkness was total. "How do you know so much?"

"They're zeroing in on you. You have to focus on the moment!" she responded.

Walt hesitated but then allowed William and Celia to guide him. He crouched to his hands and knees and crawled forward into the tunnel, hearing Ling just ahead of him.

"Move out!" Ling cried.

Ling and MacGruder scuffled off and as soon as Walt felt Celia crouched behind him, he followed them, slowly, cautiously, unable to see where he was putting his hands and knees, uncertain of what lay even six inches ahead. It was like the pitch-black funhouse he'd gone in at the carnival in Lexington, except this was even more disorienting and not fun at all.

Now the earth shook with such violence that Walt sprawled forward, his chin crashing into the cave floor. The others, in front and behind, let out grunts and groans as they, too, were tossed inside the tunnel by the tremor.

"Don't remember! Concentrate on now!" Ling called.

Had the brief recollection of the funhouse signaled their position to Sheron? Concern crowded Walt's mind as he realized that he was totally responsible for the fate of the others who were risking so much for him. Focus, he chided himself, focus! He pushed himself back to his hands and knees and hurried after Ling, who was up again and crawling forward.

It was almost impossible, Walt realized, not to remember and even harder in this total darkness—there was nothing he could look at for distraction. But the quaking seemed to recede as Walt forced himself to think only about the feel of the hard uneven, rock surface he crawled upon, about the sounds of knees and hands thudding along this narrow tunnel.

"I think they're moving away," MacGruder shouted back from the head of the pack.

William called out. "Stay focused lads and lassies!"

"Duck!" Ling warned, but too late. The tunnel narrowed and dipped and Walt bumped his head against a rock protruding down from the ceiling. It stung bitterly and disoriented him. He wondered if Ling had warned him late on purpose—so he would have a sore head to concentrate on. If so, the strategy worked. Walt's head rang with pain as he moved forward more cautiously.

The earthquake continued to recede. It was now a distant tremor—like a jackhammer breaking up concrete several blocks away.

"He is," William cried with delight. "He's moving away!"

The entire group stopped crawling to listen.

"The depth and thickness of the tunnel muffles the mnemonic signatures," Ling speculated.

Soon the earthquake was a mild vibration, barely distinguishable under their hands and knees. They listened in silence to see if Sheron might swing back around in their direction. But after a full minute of quiet, Ling announced, "He must be gone."

"We should stay here for a bit," MacGruder suggested. "Make sure."

"Sheron was just fishing," Ling repeated his theory.

"I don't know," MacGruder said. Walt could hear the relief in his voice. "I think we should hole up for a few seconds."

"It couldn't hurt," Celia agreed. "To give him a little distance."

"Do we know where we're going?" William asked.

William's question brought only silence in response. Walt heard Ling adjusting his body into the space of the tunnel so he could sit with his back against one wall. His small stature made this possible, but when Walt tried to relax, too, he found he could only sit scrunched up on one leg and an elbow.

"The rendezvous is not for three days," William went on, when no one answered his question.

"The plan will have to change," Ling responded. There was tension and concern in Ling's and William's voices. "We can't afford to hide and run for three days. We'll end up giving away The Ruins, The Flats and every hideout and sanctuary we have left."

"And we'll starve to death in the process," MacGruder added.

"We could hole up with the weepers," Ling suggested. "Might disguise Walt's signature."

"No weepers," MacGruder said quickly. "Too dangerous. Plus, they scare me."

"And how would we get to them?" William asked. He was not enthusiastic about the idea, either. "After what happened at Assembly, there'll be gnome probes at every street corner until Sheron catches him."

Walt flushed and was glad it was too dark for anyone to see. He was beginning to feel like a heavy burden to this hapless band of resisters, though he had no idea about why he might be of special interest to Sheron or anyone in Paralleladise. He should, he realized, convince the others to leave him behind—to take Celia with them and get her back home. It was a risk, but it might keep them all from danger. And then Walt would find a way back on his own. The idea of going it alone frightened him—he wouldn't even know where to begin. But the possibility of Celia getting caught because of him worried him even more.

"We'll have to find one of the Protectors to tell us where Romannie is," Ling was saying. "And move up the timetable."

"Achebe is a protector. He's not far from here."

"But getting him there without alerting the gnomes . . ."

"You should leave me," Walt said, abruptly. "Save yourselves…"

"We can't . . ." Ling started.

"If it's me they're after," Walt interrupted, "then you should leave me. I will find the way back. Don't worry about me."

"Find your way back where?" MacGruder asked, a note of incredulity in his question.

"Back home...back to the real world," Walt said. This world of Paralleladise was "real" enough, of course, and full of terribly real dangers, but he didn't know how else to describe the world where his father and Zelda and Acey were, where he longed to be, safe and secure. He wouldn't even mind being back in boring, old school if it meant escaping this universe where constant peril or eternal forgetfulness were the only two options.

No one replied to Walt's suggestion. He wished he could see the look in their eyes or their body language. Were they astonished at his boldness or stymied by his ignorance? Their silence was worrisome.

Finally, he felt Celia's hand cover his. "Walt," she said with sympathetic sorrow in her voice.

"You won't be going back any time soon, Walters," Ling said. "We need you."

"What?" Walt was stunned. Not going back? What did that mean? He had assumed his rescue by these hippos, their fleeing from the gnomes and Sheron, their hiding in this tunnel were all part of an escape plan—an effort to return him home. He couldn't speak for a moment. Suddenly, the blackness of the tunnel was more frightening than disorienting.

"We need you, Walters," MacGruder echoed. "Besides, it's almost impossible to get back."

"Only a handful have done it," William explained, "and always through another portal, always with someone else's key. Getting back to your own time . . . it just doesn't happen."

212

"But you said . . ." Walt began, looking in the direction of William's voice. His mind was flooded with images of his family, of his father's befuddled demeanor, of Acey's shivering sweetness, of Zelda's wicked grin. He couldn't imagine that he would never see them again. He couldn't imagine living like William and Ling for hundreds of years in this bizarre universe. "I have to get back," he told them, determined. "I have to."

"You'd have to get to your portal," Ling said. "You'd have to know your key."

"What key? What is the key?"

"Exactly," Ling replied quickly in a knowing tone, as if Walt had just fallen for a trap under cross-examination. "No one remembers their key. That's just the point. We don't even know if the key is the same for everyone or is changed each time. We don't even know if it's a thing or an idea."

William picked up the explanation. "The key is something we all knew only briefly when we came through the portal. But it is the first thing wiped from our brains when we arrived—totally wiped clean from all recollection. Only a few are ever able to recall what opened the portal. I've been trying for almost a millennium."

"But you said some have gone back through," Walt protested. He could not believe what he was hearing. Was he really trapped in Paralleladise forever?

"Two or three times in all the recorded history," Ling told him. "Though there are plenty of stories and legends of others. But we only know for sure of a handful of hippos that made it back. Four or five escaped about a thousand years ago. Not through their own portal, mind you. Somehow they got a hold of someone else's key and went through a portal into . . . who-knows-where. Two of the four were recaptured almost immediately by Sheron and made an example of."

"Ling's great, great, great, great grandmother may have made it back," William reported.

"We don't know that for sure," Ling corrected. "We only know that's where she was headed the last time she was seen."

"Eleven escaped into the year 1743," William went on with the list.

"All were recaptured by spring 1744," Ling reminded him.

"And once, more recently," MacGruder added to round out the list of known escapees from Paralleladise. "Four hippos squeezed out a portal that was opened by a weeper, but they didn't go back to their own time. One was recaptured within a few hours and had every shred of her memory wiped clean. She can't even recall her name or how to tie her shoe. Sheron made sure she would never try to escape again. Another was recaptured only a few days later."

"So you see," Ling said, "We all want to get back, but it's nothing to pin your hopes on, and certainly nothing you can accomplish on your own without a good deal of training."

"NyXus would pick you up within an hour if you went out on your own," MacGruder speculated. "He'd fry up your hippocampus and have it for lunch."

"And even if you made it back," Ling continued, "your chances of recapture are better than fifty-fifty."

"Especially with a mnemonic signature like yours."

"Once Sheron has your signature," Ling said ominously, "he can easily track you in the real world and bring you back. We're not sure quite how he does it."

Walt listened to all the warnings and speculations in this tunnel of darkness. It felt as if the world were closing in on him, taking away his options, denying him any chances. It was true that he needed Ling and the others to get him out of this upside-down universe—to point him in the right direction—and he knew he owed them something for getting him this far. And yet, he could not accept the fate they described.

"Walt." It was Celia's voice. She had moved closer, only inches away, "I wanted to tell you earlier but I hoped . . . I hoped when they brought you to me . . . when your memories started to come back . . . that you'd know your key. That you'd remember how we got here, where the portal was . . ."

"I do! It was in the attic . . ." Walt blurted out. He did remember. Perhaps others couldn't remember their portals, but he could! He was not doomed to stay in Paralleladise. "It was in the attic of my house."

"Yes," Celia prompted him, "the attic of your house. But do you remember a key? A . . . something about the portal that opened it up?"

"Yes!" Walt said definitively, thinking he remembered everything about the terrible events that brought him to Paralleladise. "I was in the attic. There was a panel in the roof. Zelda was there." Walt poured out everything he could recall as quickly as he could, knowing his memory would stumble across a key at any moment. "And then the panel opened up and a bright light . . . Sheron!" Walt was beginning to put the pieces together. "That was Sheron, wasn't it? The light . . . He was drawing me in."

"How did you open the panel?" Celia prompted. "Can you remember?"

Walt wracked his memory, trying to bring back the details. It was more difficult than he imagined and as he tried to bring

215

back the moment, his head began to vibrate with excruciating pain. "Ahh!"

"Don't try to bring it all back so quickly," Ling advised. "You'll only hurt yourself."

"Zelda was there," Walt continued, ignoring Ling's advice. "She had opened the panel. She had warned me. . ." Pain crashed through his brain, like a bomb detonating inside his head. He was desperate to remember quickly, so he could stop the explosions. "No! No! Not Zelda. Someone else. Someone else had opened the panel when I got there." Walt closed his eyes and tried to visualize the scene. The pounding in his head was making him dizzy. "Someone else was there . . . someone else."

And then a single word appeared before him in the darkness. A single word—a name—and with it came a powerful blow inside his brain.

"Alice!" Walt gasped before losing consciousness.

TWENTY

Walt Walters awoke to the sight of a blurry face, a few inches above his and repeating his name.

"Walters...Walters."

Walt blinked to clear his eyes and the face came into focus. It was a dark-haired Asian man with a long mustache and a thin goatee. He looked like someone Walt knew, but Walt could not quite place the face. The man studied Walt with concern.

"Walters?"

There was something familiar about this scene. Walt remembered awaking once to the call of his name from another Asian-looking man. Or was it this same one? Where was that? When was that?

The memory made his head throb and he closed his eyes and groaned.

"No, no, don't drift off on me again," the Asian man was saying. "We need to get going."

Walt felt something cool on his cheeks and forehead and realized that the man was pressing a damp, cold cloth to his face.

"Where?" Walt asked. Was it time for school already? Where was Dad? Why was he letting this stranger wake him up? He opened his eyes again to study the face. Yes, he definitely recognized it from somewhere. Was he a friend of his father's?

Walt tried to sit up. A searing pain ran up his spine and into his head. He groaned.

"Take it easy," the man was saying. "Take it slow."

And then Walt remembered that the last time he was awakened by this man calling his name, he'd had a terrible headache, too. Was he a doctor? Was he trying to cure him of some rare headache disease?

"What is your name?" the man was asking.

Walt moaned.

"Where do you live?"

The pain screeched through his brain as his address came to the front of his mind: 511 Lauren . . .

"Please," Walt pleaded, "no mnemonics."

Mnemonics! Walt opened his eyes fully. Where had that word come from? It was a word he'd never heard until . . .

And then it all came rushing back to him in a fury of recollections accompanied by increasing pain: Paralleladise, Sheron, hippos, the resistance, Celia...

"What is your sister's name?"

The man's face was now crystal clear.

"Who am I?"

The last time he'd been awakened by this man was in a building that looked a lot like Lexington Middle School, but was really a re-creation of it, built in Paralleladise to fool Walt into thinking he was in his own world—to fool him until he drank from the Cauldron of Forgetfulness.

"Who am I?" the man repeated.

"You're the guy who keeps waking me up and giving me headaches," Walt said finally.

"Ha," Ling laughed. "The valve's open. Steam's coming up." Ling pulled his face back, rocking on his feet. He was squatting next to Walt who was lying on the floor.

"My head," Walt whined. Now, without any effort, full recollection of where he was poured into his consciousness: the rescue by Ling from the school, Celia, the Assembly, the flight from gnome probes, the cave and the tunnel.

"It's your own fault," Ling chided, lightheartedly. "I warned you not to remember everything at once. Trying to bring back the portal and the key has battered the brains of bigger men than you. Lesser hippos have cauterized thousands of memory cells trying to draw up the key. But the headaches get less severe the longer you're here, if that's any consolation."

Ling stood up and walked out of view. Ignoring his throbbing head, Walt forced himself up to a sitting position.

He and Ling were in a room, Walt saw—the small, single room of a wooden shack that was filled with wheels and cogs and pulleys, all inter-connected and attached to the walls and the ceiling. It was as if they were inside a huge watch with all its parts and gears at the ready to keep time, though none were moving. The room was dimly illuminated by tiny rays of sunlight that pierced the cracks in the ancient planks of the wall. Ling was at one of the larger gaps now, peering out through it.

"It's the engine of Prairie Dog Flats," he explained, when he saw Walt marvel at the complexity of design and the primitive materials of this machine room. "It's a wonder," he added. "Been here longer than I have."

"How did I get here?"

Ling nodded toward the floor near his feet, and Walt looked to see a hole in the floorboards, large enough to crawl through. He guessed it was the opening at the other end of the tunnel they'd been in when he lost consciousness.

"We had to drag you out." Ling turned his head to look through the crack in the wall again. "Here they come."

Before Walt could ask "who?" there was a knock on the door near Ling.

Ling crossed to the door. "What's the password?" he called.

"I forget," a voice replied, and Ling unlatched the door.

Celia was the first to come in and the furrowed concern of her face immediately brightened to a big smile when she saw Walt sitting up and alert.

"Walt!" she said, crossing the room and coming to kneel beside him. MacGruder and William followed her into the shack. All three were wearing long, brown, hooded robes. Ling quickly closed the door behind him. Celia pulled her hood back.

"Our hero's awake," William cried jovially.

"I'll bet his head's ringing," MacGruder laughed.

Celia rubbed her knuckles across Walt's head. "How was the nap?" she asked. "Refreshed?"

Walt sighed, his headache throbbing in waves. Standing, Celia took his arm to help him to his feet. "Think you can travel?"

"Don't forget his armor," MacGruder called and tossed two brown robes he'd been carrying under his own robe to Celia. She unfolded one and held it opened for Walt to put on.

"We rendezvous in an hour," Celia explained.

"You've found one of the protectors?" Ling asked.

"He's gone ahead to arrange the meeting," William reported. "We rendezvous at the Summit at midday."

"That doesn't give us much time."

Walt only half paid attention to what the others were saying. His head thudded when he stood up and he felt off balance. The edges of his vision were blurring again, and so he focused on Celia's face as he slipped into the brown cloak she held out for him. It was a very kind and pretty face, he decided.

Celia held out the second cloak, shaking it and Walt realized he was to put this on, too, over the other one.

"Here's the drill," Celia explained, helping him fasten the drawstrings of the cloak. "If we run into gnome probes, put your hood up, and if you get slimed, throw the top cloak off as quickly as you can, before Sheron can track you."

"What's the second cloak for?"

"In case you get slimed again. It only takes a second for Sheron to lock in once you're slimed, so you have to be quick."

"What if I get slimed a third time?"

Celia put her hands on Walt cheeks and looked him in the eye. "Don't get slimed a third time," she said.

Ling, too, was shrugging on a brown cloak. He surveyed the group for readiness and then gave the command, "Let's go. We haven't much time." He went to the door, listened carefully and then opened it cautiously, peering out in all directions before turning back to the group and instructing them in a whisper: "Stay low. Zig-zag." And Ling stepped briskly out into the bright daylight.

William called after him, "Enough with the zig-zagging! It doesn't help," then followed Ling out the door, shaking his head.

MacGruder nodded at Walt and Celia, indicating they should go next and so they trailed William out of the machine shack and MacGruder followed them.

They were in a valley, Walt saw, emerging into sunshine for the first time in what seemed like days. Huge barren hills, some rolling, and some running almost vertically toward the sky in places, like the cliffs of a bluff, stretched before them on either side of a trail that ran as far as Walt could see into the distance. It was like a re-creation of the beautiful desert landscapes of Arizona that Walt's father had taken the family to last summer. But the ground beneath Walt's feet echoed like a wooden floor, and the brush along the path looked to be made of lint and wire spray painted to look like desert tumbleweeds. Walt realized that this was the first time he had seen Paralleladise in the daylight since he'd been shocked out of his lethemine forgetfulness by Ling at the Lexington Middle School. The artificiality of the re-creations in this alternative world was so obvious now that his memory had been restored.

But this was the world he and Celia were trapped in for . . . how long? All at once, the conversation in the tunnel before he passed out came back to him. Ling and the others had been telling them to plan on being in this poor imitation of a world for a long time. Walt's shoulders slumped and he felt the energy in his body evaporate with the prospect of the many years before he would see his father and sisters again.

Ahead of them by a couple of yards, Ling and William walked and argued about the merits of zig-zagging. Perhaps they had been having this same argument for centuries as they worked with the other hippos in their never-ending resistance to Paralleladise. How could they keep going, Walt wondered? Would he and Celia be here five hundred years in the future, trading tips on how to avoid gnome probes and worrying every moment about their memories being slowly eaten away?

The path ahead of them began to tread upward in a slow, steady incline. Behind him, Walt could hear MacGruder doing his mnemonic exercises while, at his side, Celia hiked purposefully, her eyes steadied on the uneven trail. She was deep in thought and Walt wondered if she, too, were trying to come to grips with their potentially long sentence in this prison of forgetting.

"I have a brother-in-law," William called back to them. "Simon is his name—lives just up the lane from me and Mary. Bachelor man. Always too shy with the lasses."

222

"Your wife's brother, then?" MacGruder clarified.

"Exactly," William replied. "And I only remember him because of you, Walt."

William had turned and was walking backwards as he spoke. He looked at Walt, smiling. Perhaps he had sensed Walt's despair and was trying to cheer him up. "Ever since your little memory game in the cave, a lot of things have started coming back. Things and people I haven't thought of in hundreds of years."

"I'm glad," Walt said, softly. And he was glad, but William's returning memories did nothing to alleviate his apprehensions about the future.

"Oh!" William barked suddenly as if he had just been pinched from behind. "And my wife's cousin, Catherine, lives along the lane, too. I just remembered."

MacGruder laughed and tapped his head. "He's got a regular family reunion going on in there."

"Less talking and more zig-zagging will keep the gnome probes off our backs," Ling cautioned. "You'll give yourself a headache."

"Just a little innocent recollection," William responded, but he turned around again and walked silently behind Ling.

Walt thought about William's life in the fourteenth-century—extended families living close together, rarely travelling more than twenty miles away. So long ago, it was amazing William could remember anything. Walt wondered if the simple memory of a distant relative would be a thrill for him when he had been here so long.

"Why do you resist?" Walt wondered, thinking out loud.

"What?" William asked, unsure he'd heard the question correctly.

223

"If you can't escape," Walt asked again, "why do you resist? Why do we even try to keep our memories?"

"Now you can't be talking that way, my boy," William scolded. "Not so soon. Give us a decade or two before we have to start worrying about your first crisis of purpose."

The others were silent, as if the point of Walt's question had never occurred to them. Finally, Ling spoke, "We can't escape individually. But, working together, we'll defeat Sheron and NyXus one day. We'll figure out how all the portals work. We'll find the master key that opens every one of them."

"And we'll all return home," MacGruder added. "To the world we came from and the ones we love."

"Working together," Ling went on, as if reciting an inspiring pledge to keep the resistance movement motivated. "With the help of the Rememberer."

The Rememberer. There was that word again. An image popped into Walt's mind of a huge contraption with dials and switches and a helmet that attached to your head and made you remember whether you wanted to or not. But Ling had called Walt a great Rememberer at the campfire in the cave. And he had whispered it to William when he was first introducing Walt.

"What is the Rememberer?" Walt asked.

"The Rememberer?" William responded. "The Rememberer is the most revered of all hippo resisters."

"Your leader?"

Ling, MacGruder and William chuckled.

"We're not exactly organized enough to have a leader," MacGruder explained.

"The Rememberer's job is to remember," William went on.

"And help others remember," Ling added.

"Especially about portals and escapes."

"And how to fight Sheron."

"I don't understand," Walt said. Things were more complicated with each new piece of information. Did Celia understand all this? Had they explained it all to her while Walt was lost in the phony world of Lexington that had been recreated for him? Had she struggled as much as he to make sense of it? She was listening quietly now, taking it all in.

"The best thing for you," MacGruder went on, "is that the Rememberer is protected—as much as possible—from NyXus. We've haven't lost one in centuries."

"NyXus controls Paralleladise. He created it," William added to dispel Walt's confusion.

Walt was very confused. "If NyXus controls Paralleladise, what does Sheron control?"

"Pah!" MacGruder spat out. "Sheron isn't smart enough to control his own feet and chew gum at the same time. He's just a thug. NyXus controls him."

Walt tried to organize the information in his mind. First there was NyXus, and then Sheron and gnome probes and then all of the others—ordinary people—who had been kidnapped from their homes around the world and throughout history and brought here, through portals with mysterious keys, to have their memories all but wiped away and who worshipped NyXus as their savior. On the other side were the hippos and the Rememberer who had come through a portal and had managed to retain their ability to remember and had established a resistance movement against NyXus and Sheron.

"Ling, why did you say I would make a great Rememberer?"

There was no immediate response, and Walt realized that the answer to the question required careful wording.

At last, William spoke. "We need you, Walt."

"You have the most powerful mnemonic signature of any hippo to come to Paralleladise in a long, long time," Ling told him. "We picked up your signature as you came through the portal. Your mnemes ratio was incredible." After a pause, Ling added, "You have the power to do a lot of good here."

"But I've got a lousy memory," Walt protested.

MacGruder laughed. "That's what every Rememberer says."

"It's more than just memory," William explained. "It's an intuition about mnemonics. It's an ability to use that power of memory to help someone else."

"Just look what you did for William. And what you accomplished at the Assembly."

"But I didn't do anything!" Walt insisted. "I just asked questions."

Ling stopped in his tracks and turned to look at Walt. "Then, if you prefer, you have a gift for asking questions." He smiled.

Walt studied Ling. He was certain they were wrong about his memory. In school, he was often getting in trouble for forgetting his homework and leaving his coat and books behind. At home, his father was always chiding him about forgetting his chores and losing his shoes and gloves. Surely, they had mistaken him for someone else.

"What about Celia? "

Ling shook his head, "She was sucked in when Sheron was trying to get you."

"Why would he want me? If I've got such a great signature-whatever, I'd be a threat to him." Walt struggled to make sense of the reasoning. He was sure Ling and the others were wrong—there was nothing special about him. And once they discovered their error, they would let him and Celia go back home.

"That's how he used to think, too," William explained. "And then, a few centuries ago, he realized he had to seek out the hippos first."

"That's when he came up with the cauldron."

"Bring them all in, destroy their memories and obliterate any hope of real resistance. Only then could he really implement his plan."

"That's when Sheron started to go after the most powerful signatures he could find."

"She," Ling finished, nodding at Celia, "was never to be brought back."

Walt felt a wave of heavy guilt. He had gotten Celia into this horrible situation. He couldn't remember how she managed to be in the portal with him—or how he'd gotten in for that matter. But now he knew he was responsible for her being trapped, too.

As if she knew what he was thinking, Celia touched his arm and said, "We're in this together, Walters. Don't get any of your big hippocampus ideas."

"I've got to get you out of here," Walt told her. Where had she come from when he was pulled into the portal's shaft of light? Was she trying to save him? To pull him out? He tried to remember, but his head began to swoon with pain and dizziness.

"Whoa, whoa," MacGruder said, catching Walt from behind as he swayed unsteadily on his feet.

"Let's have none of that," Ling warned. "No time for portal memories now. We're nearly at the drop off and time is flying."

"The drop-off . . .?" Walt echoed as MacGruder steadied him. "What are we dropping off?"

Ling raised one eyebrow. "Hopefully nothing." And then he turned and hurried up ahead of them and then into a clump of brush to the side of the path.

Walt and Celia looked at William, who only shrugged resignedly. He took a deep breath and then followed Ling in quick steps, as if hoping to get it all over with as quickly as possible.

"It's not as bad as it used to be," MacGruder assured them, as he followed William. "Just try not to look down."

Walt didn't like the sound of MacGruder's warning, but he could hear the urgency in everyone's voice and see the hurry in their steps, and so, with Celia, he waded into the clump of weeds where the others had just disappeared.

They had walked just a few feet off the pathway, and, suddenly, it was as if they stepped from a desert trail into tropical jungle. Flora and fauna were everywhere in thick reeds and palm leaves. The undergrowth, too, was dense and hard to walk as it twisted about at their feet. The weeds Ling and the others had trampled before them told them which direction to take, but the three men were several yards ahead and could only be seen in glimpses through the surrounding growth. Above them, tall palm trees blocked the sunlight.

Walt led the way for Celia. He peered ahead intently and so, when she reached out to take his hand, he was startled.

"So, we don't get separated," Celia said when he jumped. "Don't worry—I've been cootie-free since fourth grade."

"I thought you were some jungle creature."

"You're a charmer."

Walt clasped her hand and turned back to the trail being made ahead of them, but the thick growth was springing back so quickly it was hard to tell where the others had gone. He peered into the tall weeds, trying to catch sight of their backs.

"Do you see them?" he asked Celia, hoping to keep panic from his voice.

"No, don't you?"

"I'm looking," Walt said, quickening his pace. He was about to shout out for the three men when, all at once, the jungle growth cleared and they were on solid stone rock with Ling, MacGruder and William just a few yards ahead, waiting.

Walt breathed a sigh of relief.

"Come along," William called back to them.

"We can't be late," Ling added. "They won't wait for us."

Walt and Celia trotted to where the others had stopped and Walt saw very clearly now why Ling had called this "the drop off."

The rock surface they were on ended abruptly at a cliff that dropped off steeply. The cavern was so deep that Walt could not see the bottom. Several hundred feet below, the crevasse fell dark and smoky with wisps of vapors, like a thick fog that obscured the view beneath it.

"How do we get down?"

"We don't," William replied. "We get across."

"It's the only way," Ling said, pointing to a distant log, no more than eight inches wide, split in half to form a crude walkway, that was laid across the cavern at its narrowest point. The other side was less than twenty yards away, Walt estimated, eyeing where the log walkway ended. But one false step would end the journey for good.

And then, Walt heard a distant humming noise like the sound of a chain saw, but so faint and faraway that Walt couldn't be sure he heard anything at all.

"At least you can take your time now," MacGruder told him about crossing the log. "Back in the days of the banders, you had to get across so quickly, it's a wonder we didn't lose everyone who tried."

229

A rustling shook the jungle brush behind them and Walt look back to see the palm leaves and tall grasses swaying as if giant, invisible feet were walking through them.

"Don't remind me," William replied to MacGruder. "Let's just get across." He walked purposefully toward the log.

The chainsaw noise was increasing, getting closer, and now the others noticed it, too.

"What's that?" Celia asked.

"Sounds like . . ." Ling started, but then paused to listen, as if he couldn't believe his ears.

"It can't be . . ." MacGruder added. He and Ling turned to look into the jungle. They saw the leaves and grasses moving as if being shaken by a strong wind.

"You had to mention it," Ling said sharply to MacGruder.

"Run!" MacGruder shouted and dashed off after William who had already scurried off toward the walkway.

Ling put his hands on Celia's and Walt's shoulders and urged them along. "Get moving!"

Walt and Celia ran after MacGruder and William. Ling looked back into the jungle and then sprinted behind them.

"What is it?" Walt shouted.

"Banders!" Ling, William and MacGruder all yelled at once.

Walt looked back and saw a metal sphere the size of a large beach ball suddenly burst out of the jungle and onto the rocks they now ran upon. The sphere rolled on bands of steel that, when compressed made a smooth round exterior. But, as it rolled, the set of bands at the front of the ball opened several inches wide and bore saw-tooth ridges that snapped closed, allowing the next pair of bands to open and snap as it moved forward. It looked like a huge silver marble with snipping razor-sharp teeth that opened and closed as it moved.

230

We can outrun it, Walt thought confidently, or stop it somehow.

And then, dozens more rolled out from the jungle behind it.

TWENTY-ONE

"Where did they come from?" MacGruder shouted the question as he ran toward the log walkway. "I thought for sure they'd all expired by now."

"There's not many of them," Ling shouted back.

MacGruder was ahead of Ling, Walt and Celia, but now he paused and picked up a weapon—a limb the size of a baseball bat that had fallen from one of the trees. William, further ahead, stopped, too, and hunted for a similar club.

"You three get across," he hollered.

"Can you hold them?" Ling asked.

"Just like cricket practice," MacGruder called back, taking a swing with the stick as he turned to run backward and keep the oncoming banders in view.

Walt looked over his shoulder. There were sixty to seventy of the chomping metal spheres rolling after them with incredible speed, their circulating jaws snapping open and closed in a menacing rhythm. Most were the diameter of a basketball, but a few were half Walt's size, and others were as small as a softball. They glinted as if made of heavy metal, but bounced along like loosed tires rolling over the uneven surface, some propelling themselves several feet into the air as they formed a pattern of pursuit.

William finally found a suitable weapon among the brush. "Haven't played bander ball in centuries," he called out. As he stooped to pick up the limb, Ling, Walt and Celia ran past him and straight to the log walkway across the cavern.

Ling skidded to a halt as MacGruder and William took up positions behind them, pulling their crude weapons back, ready to take on the banders who were coming on fast.

"Crawl on your stomach," Ling advised. "It's the safest option. Like this." The Asian man took a bold step onto the log, kneeled and then laid flat on his stomach. He began pulling with his arms and pushing with his feet, scootching himself across the cavern.

"And try not to look down!" he added.

But it was too late. Walt was already staring down into the seemingly bottomless gulf. Its sides were sheer rock, with nothing to grab onto and nothing to break a fall. His head swirled with momentary vertigo.

"You're not supposed to look down," Celia reminded him.

Ling looked back when he was halfway across and called with consternation. "Come on! They can't hold them off all day."

"You first," Walt said, protectively.

"Age before beauty," Celia responded, putting her hand on Walt's shoulder and nudging him forward. "Let me know how it goes."

Walt looked at Celia. She did not seem frightened, but then, she never seemed frightened. Perhaps she needed him to be courageous and cross first—to show her the way. "See you on the other side?"

"Assuming I don't get a better offer."

Walt stepped forward, placing one foot gingerly on the log footbridge. Ling was almost across now.

SMACK! SMACK!

The loud noise startled Walt and he nearly tumbled forward onto the bridge. He looked back to see the first of the banders reaching William and MacGruder. MacGruder had just slapped one with his club and sent it flying over the cliff. The whirring motors of the others filled the air with a steady buzzing.

"Hurry!" Ling called, seeing that Walt and Celia had not started across.

Walt steadied his foot and leaned forward until he was lying on the log bridge. Don't look down he reminded himself sternly.

SMACK! SMACK!

Now, several banders had reached William and MacGruder and both men were slugging away at them, knocking many of the spheres over the cliff. Others they simply batted off into the jungle brush and, moments later, they would re-emerge, battered and dented, but ready to renew the assault.

"Go, Walt!" Celia cried.

Walt scootched himself across the log slowly. It was more difficult than Ling had made it look. The rough surface of the log inhibited sliding and Walt had to lift himself an inch off the surface with each push in order to move forward.

SMACK! SMACK! SMACK!

He heard a bander, batted by MacGruder or William, sail by him, only a few feet away and watched it whiz past on its trajectory before plummeting down into the cavernous gulf. Seeing it fall set off a wave of dizziness. He laid flat and hugged the log.

"Don't look down," Ling called again. "Get behind him!"

This last command, Walt guessed, was directed at Celia. He wanted to turn and see if she obeyed but he didn't dare look until his dizzy spell passed.

"Behind you," Walt heard William cry out followed by a SMACK, SMACK, SMACK as MacGruder thwarted the rear assault.

Keep crawling, Walt whispered to himself. Don't look down. He scootched forward another foot and was now, he guessed, halfway across.

"AAAHHH!" It was Celia this time, and it was a cry of alarm.

Without thinking, Walt rose to his knees, looking back to see what had happened.

A grapefruit-sized bander had somehow scooted passed William and MacGruder and attacked Celia. It had missed her arms and legs but champed into the fabric of the brown robe she wore to protect against the slime of the gnome probes. It rolled along the garment, releasing and champing again with lightning speed as it made its way up her cloak, searching for something solid to sink its teeth into.

"Celia!" Walt cried out.

Frantically, Celia worked to tear off the outer robe, trying to fling it away before the bander found an arm or leg to snap at. Her shaking slowed its progress and, for a moment, it looked as if she might jar it loose, but it chomped in hard, clinging on with determination.

SMACK! SMACK!

William and MacGruder continued to swing at the army of banders surrounding them, the loud buzzing deafening them to what was happening to Celia behind them.

Without taking a moment to consider, Walt was on his feet and running across the slender walkway back toward Celia.

"No!" Ling cried. "Come back!"

The log walkway vibrated with the impact of Walt's running steps, but he did not look down. He concentrated on Celia, who shook her robe furiously as she tried to undo the tie that held it and, at the same time, bat at the bander without getting snapped by its jaws.

Ling's cry alerted MacGruder and William. They had succeeded in knocking many of the banders into the cavern, but at least twenty of the larger mechanical monsters remained, circled around, gnashing ferociously. MacGruder spotted Celia, fighting off the bander that was inching up her gown. With a kick and a blow from his club, he sent two of the larger snapping balls sailing straight past her and over the edge of the crevasse, and then MacGruder dashed to her rescue.

Despite her efforts to dislodge it, the relentless bander was now at Celia's waist, and when she swung her arm to knock it back its jaw opened at her wrist.

Walt Walters dove off of the slender footbridge before the determined bander could snap into Celia's forearm. With his own arms outstretched before him, he snatched at her robe with his hands, pulling it off and away from her as he sailed over the rocky surface and landed with a thud on the ground.

"Ooomphf," he cried.

In his hands, the brown cloak shook violently and he realized that he had somehow managed to wrap the assaulting bander inside it when he tore it from Celia.

SMACK! SMACK!

The sound of William's battle with the other banders resounded.

"Walt!" Celia shouted. "Look out!"

236

One of the large banders William batted came flying through the air, straight at Walt. He rolled to the side just as it soared past him and then he jumped to his feet.

SMACK! SMACK!

Quickly, Walt bundled Celia's robe once more around the relentless jawed sphere in his hands and prepared to fling it off the cliff.

But it was too late.

The bander had already chomped its way through the layers of the garment and Walt was looking straight into the widening jaws of the next snap, inches away.

And then there was an arm where the snapping jaws had been.

And then there was a cry—part pain, part anger—as MacGruder flashed before Walt's eyes. He had thrust his fist between Walt and the champing jaws, just as it was about to sink its teeth into Walt. Instead, it sunk its metal clamps into MacGruder's hand and latched on like a vise.

"ARRRGGHHH!" MacGruder cried. He'd run to save Celia and Walt and now, with his momentum, was unable to stop. He skidded across the loose gravel near the cliff and slid to the edge, swinging his hand wildly, trying to shake the vicious bander loose.

"MacGruder!" Ling called, watching the action unfold from the other side of the cavern. He was about to step unto the log walkway—to run across and help his comrade, when MacGruder, still off balance, slipped on the gravel at the cliff's edge, and fell forward landing on the narrow footbridge.

It cracked under the big man's weight.

SMACK! SMACK!

William was now battling the last of the larger banders surrounding him and with one roundhouse swing he sent the final two sphere troopers swooshing through the air and smashing against a palm tree at edge of the jungle. They thudded to the ground, broken and unmoving.

For a fleeting moment, it looked as if the log footbridge might not break in half—that it might hold long enough for MacGruder to stand up and crawl back to the edge where Walt and Celia now hurried to help him. But, with a final loud crack, it shattered, and MacGruder, still struggling to shake loose the bander, plummeted down into the cavern.

"MacGruder!" Ling cried out from the other side of the canyon.

"Mac!" William echoed.

Walt and Celia dove simultaneously to the edge of the cliff, their arms outstretched, hoping to catch MacGruder's leg or a piece of his robe, but they were too late. MacGruder plunged into the deep abyss.

"MacGruder!" Celia yelled hopelessly, watching him fall.

And then everything went dark. It was as if the sun had been switched off, plunging the entire planet into darkness. As if nightfall had fallen instantaneously like a black curtain thrown over all of Paralleladise.

And with the darkness, the earth began to shake.

"Sheron!" Walt heard Ling cry from the other side. "Run for cover!"

Walt jumped to his feet as a bright shaft of light from the far side of the cavern suddenly cut the darkness. The ground quaked violently and Walt struggled to stay on his feet, knowing the bottomless cliff was only inches in front of him.

"Celia" he cried out, knowing she was somewhere close, but unable to see her because it was pitch dark except for this narrow shaft of light, directed like a spotlight into the cavern.

Walt felt a hand on his arm, grasping firmly, tightly. He tried to shake it loose.

"He's going for MacGruder," Ling was shouting from the other side of the canyon. "Get away while you can!"

"Ling?" This was William's voice coming from behind Walt.

"Get him to safety," Ling called back. "I'll find you."

Walt was far too disoriented in the sudden darkness and earthquake to move anywhere. He focused his eyes on the light to keep from losing his balance.

And then, below him in the canyon, he saw a figure in the illuminated shaft rising, as if riding an elevator of light toward its source.

"Sheron," Walt whispered, his first thought being that this is what it meant to be caught by Sheron—you were plunged into sudden darkness and Sheron came to you in a shaft of light and took you to have your memory erased.

"Get going!" Ling's voice called to him, sounding further away now, and coming with a reverberation. Ling was moving on the other side of the cavern, Walt realized. Who was he talking to? Were Celia and William safe in the daylight somewhere?

Walt felt the hand around his arm pull at him. "I'm right here." It was Celia.

And then, he realized that the figure ascending through the shaft of light was not Sheron at all, but MacGruder. He was being pulled up from the depths of the bottomless canyon by Sheron's tractor light. The bander, still attached to his hand, led the way, held above MacGruder's head acting like a magnet attracted upward by the illumination. And MacGruder, in bitter resistance, was still shaking his arm violently, trying to free himself from the metal sphere.

"Let me go, you thick-brained flunky," Walt heard MacGruder shouting as he rose higher. He couldn't tell if MacGruder was yelling at the bander or at Sheron who was up there somewhere along the bluffs on the other side of the cavern, reeling MacGruder in. "Let me go, you fat-headed gopher!"

"Mac!" It was William's voice. He, too, must have been watching MacGruder's ascension somewhere close by, in the dark.

It caught MacGruder's attention, for he stopped struggling for a moment and looked ahead, squinting as if caught in an onstage spotlight and trying to see who might be out in the audience.

And as he was pulled up even with the cliff edge, MacGruder seemed to see the rest of them through the light, for he smiled a snarling smile and shouted defiantly, "I'll be back. Don't you worry. They ain't got the best of me, yet." Then he turned his face upward again, toward the source of the light and yelled at the top of his lungs, "You hear that—you two-bit thug! You ain't got the best of me."

"We've got to get out of here," Celia said, at Walt's side.

"He'll get MacGruder stowed away and be back after us." Somehow, in the rolling earthquake, William had managed to make it over to Walt and Celia. He was at their side now.

Walt could not take his eyes off MacGruder, shouting defiance as he was pulled away.

"We'd better move!" Celia tugged at Walt's arm and William's hand found Walt's shoulder.

240

"We'll be sitting ducks out here when the daylight comes back on," William was saying. "And who knows if there are more banders regrouping."

Walt felt the insistent pull of Celia and William and saw MacGruder rise faster and faster and then, suddenly, disappear altogether as the shaft of light snapped off along with the quaking of the earth and Paralleladise fell again into total darkness.

TWENTY-TWO

"Run!" Celia shouted pulling at Walt's arm. He felt her moving away and followed as best he could. They were on uneven rocky ground near the cliff and they both stumbled along in the darkness. Just ahead they heard William scrape and tumble on the rock, too.

"Where are we going?" Walt called out. "We'll kill ourselves in this darkness."

"Back into the jungle," Celia told him. "Sheron knows where we are now. We have to get as far away as we can before the sun comes back."

"We should be getting close," William called from up ahead.

Walt and Celia slowed and, with their hands out in front of them, felt for brush and foliage that would indicate they were near the jungle.

And then the sun came on, bold and bright, jumping from total darkness to midday in an instant. The sudden illumination was blinding and Walt, Celia and William squinted against the light.

"Get going!" a distant voice called. They turned together and looked up in the direction of the call. On the other side of the cavern, Ling had climbed further up the bluffs and was now on a steep rock-face twenty yards above them. He was waving his hands, motioning for them to move away, into the jungle. "I'll find you!"

The jungle brush, they saw now, was just ahead. William pushed his way into the thick overgrowth, forging a path for Walt and Celia to follow.

Letting go of Walt's arm, Celia stepped quickly into the jungle. Walt followed, looking back once more to Ling, but he had disappeared from the cliff.

Ling had acted as the leader of this tiny platoon of hippos. Who would lead them now? Walt wondered. And where would they go? They were obviously not going to make their rendezvous. Who were they supposed to rendezvous with? How important was it? When would they stop running? His mind could not shake the image of MacGruder being dragged up and away into the light, struggling and cursing. Would they see him again?

"Look out!" Celia cried, grabbing Walt's arm, pulling him forward.

"What is . . .?" Walt jumped and ducked at the same time, not knowing where the newest threat was coming from and then saw a bander at his feet—one that William or MacGruder had batted away. It was dented and disabled, incapable of moving forward, but it's metal jaws still opened and clamped shut in reflex, determined to catch an unaware passerby. Walt had almost been its victim.

William heard Celia's warning and saw Walt avoid the immobile bander. "Didn't even see that," he admitted. "We have to be mindful."

"What are they?" Walt asked. "What do they do?"

"Before the gnome probes," William explained. "There were the banders." He turned and began walking again, into the thickest jungle ahead. "When they latch onto something solid—a leg or hand—it activates a homing signal that alerts Sheron. Sheron triangulates the location and reels you in."

"Does it hurt?"

"Probably," William speculated. "The nice thing about Paralleladise is that nobody ever remembers the pain."

"What will happen to MacGruder?"

William was still holding the club he'd used to beat off the banders. Now, he was swinging at the brush ahead of him, clearing the way. "Don't worry about Big Mac. It won't be the first time Sheron's tried to purge his memory. Mac's too stubborn."

Walt felt a pang of guilt and responsibility. MacGruder was the second hippo taken while trying to help Walt and Celia. And all because they believed Walt had a special ability—a power of memory Walt was pretty sure he didn't have. "Should we," Walt started. "Shouldn't we . . . try to rescue him, or something?"

"That'd be a grand idea, son," William agreed, "if we knew where to rescue him from."

"From Sheron," Walt blurted out. There was so much about this strange world he didn't understand. "From NyXus."

"They zap all that clean, my boy—clean and away, and the short-term memories are the hardest to bring back. Nearly impossible," William explained in short breathy sentences as he swatted at brush in front of him. "That's why no one remembers the key to their portal. That's why no one remembers where they are taken when Sheron sucks them away. That's why, if anyone's ever seen him, no one remembers what NyXus looks like, or how to find him."

Walt listened with increasing despair. Every new piece of information only made matters seem worse. Not only was it virtually impossible to escape Paralleladise, but somehow he and

Celia had aligned themselves with freedom fighters who had no idea about how to locate the enemy who was holding them.

"What are we going to do?" Walt wondered aloud, hopelessly.

"We'll have to find Romannie on our own," William said, sounding skeptical. "We've missed the rendezvous. He'll have moved on by now."

"Who is Romannie?"

"Max Romannie," William replied, as if Walt should have guessed the answer already. "The Rememberer. That's where we're taking you. You'll become his protégé. And someday . . ." William paused and smiled at Walt. "Someday, you will lead us, my boy. You will lead us to destroy Sheron and NyXus and we'll all be heading home singing your praises."

There was so much hope in William's eyes, so much assurance that Walt truly could lead a successful revolution against their captors, that Walt was destined to save all the victims of Paralleladise. It made Walt immeasurably sad.

"I can't," he said, pleadingly. "You don't understand. I don't have any . . . I don't know how."

William winked and laughed off Walt's concern and went back to pummeling a path through the jungle. "You do. You do. You'll discover it. Don't worry. You'll discover it."

"How will we find Romannie?" Celia asked. She hadn't spoken in several moments, and now there was a tone of revived purpose in her voice. She quickened her step until she was abreast with William.

"Now that," William responded, "we'll have to figure out. But the first step is to get as far away from this jungle as possible. They'll be sending out the gnome probes soon enough. And who knows that there aren't other banders about."

"We'll have to use the weepers," Celia suggested.

William considered the option as he walked. Finally, he said, "Maybe."

Walt had heard them talk of the weepers before. MacGruder, he remembered, had called them "creepy," and anything that a resident in this world of creepy banders and even creepier gnome probes found "creepy" had to be pretty strange.

"What are weepers?"

"It's the only way," Celia said to William. "We can't stay out in the open like this. They'll find us."

"What are weepers?" Walt repeated. And how does Celia know about them?

"You're right, my girl," William admitted, ignoring Walt's question. "But the weepers are over in the Tuscany valley and we're here . . ." William looked around to double check. "In the jungles of mid-America. It would take us three days to walk around the Andes and the Sahara."

"We could use the maze," Celia suggested.

"Ha! Yes, the maze," William repeated, as if it were a joke. But when he saw that Celia was serious, he said it again, his eyes wide with incredulity. "The maze?"

"It's the only way."

"What's the maze?" Walt asked.

"I haven't done the maze in . . . a hundred years!" William calculated. "And I've never done it successfully. Not once! No one has."

"How do you know about the maze?" Walt asked Celia.

But she was intent on her debate with William. "The weepers are our only option. And the only way to the weepers is through the maze."

246

William shook his head. "It's too risky," he declared. "No one will know where we are. And if we get lost, we'll starve to death in there."

"We won't get lost," Celia argued.

"I suppose you've made it through?"

Celia hesitated. "Not . . . all the way."

"You've been through the maze?" Walt asked. When did she have time to go through the maze? "What is the maze?"

"But I almost made it through," Celia went on.

"What makes you think you'll have better luck this time?"

"I won't," Celia said. "But Walt will."

William stopped walking and turned to Celia, who returned his stare. "If he fails, we're sunk," William warned.

"What are you talking about!?" Walt yelled with obvious frustration as he came to a halt where they had stopped.

Celia and William turned to acknowledge him. "Sorry," William said softly. "What were you saying?"

"Who are the weepers?" Walt asked again. "What is this maze?" He looked at Celia. "What makes you think I could make it through?"

"You will, Walt," Celia replied confidently.

"There are actually two regions of the human brain responsible for memory," William explained, taking up Walt's first question. "One is the hippocampus—you know about that. The other is the amygdala. The weepers have a deformed amygdala. It makes them weep."

"It's not really deformed," Celia corrected. "It's just overactive—like a highly developed hippocampus except it's a highly developed amygdala."

"The point is," William went on, "when Sheron goes on a hunt for victims with a strong mnemonic signature, he can't tell

247

the difference between the ones with a powerful hippocampus and the ones with an overactive amygdala. He catches both in the net, and then he is stuck with the weepers."

"Stuck? Why? What do they do?"

"They weep," William explained. "All the time. They weep and weep and weep."

"Not all the time," Celia said.

"All the time," William said, nodding confidentially to Walt. "Some hippos believe the weepers hold the key to our deliverance. But they just can't quit weeping long enough to be useful."

"Why do they weep?"

"Because they can't forget," William went on. "The hippocampus is the center of normal memory functions, but the amygdala is the seat of emotional memory."

"You remember the feeling more so than events," Celia clarified.

"When they get to Paralleladise, all the lethemine you can give them without frying their brains can't make them forget the loved ones and the life they left behind. And, after a century or two, when their actual recollections diminish, they still feel the sense of loss as intensely as ever. So they weep. They weep so much that they are completely useless to us."

"Then, why are we going there?" Walt asked.

"Shhh!" Celia said suddenly, holding up her hand to halt the conversation. "Listen!"

At first, Walt heard nothing. But after a moment a faint, steady buzz reached his ears.

"More banders?"

"Or gnome probes, more likely," William responded. "Either way, we better move on."

"Come on," Celia cried.

They dashed forward again with William leading the way, trotting as fast as they could through the jungle brush. The giant fern leaves and fronds snapped back, slapping them in the arms and legs as they ran.

"We'll never make it to the maze!" William shouted back to them.

"Keep running!" Celia advised.

Walt ran as quickly as he could. But something was bothering him, making him hesitate—it was an intuition that William and Celia were not telling him everything. It was something in their tone, something in Celia's voice, something about the weepers they weren't saying.

"I'm getting turned around," William called, slowing a bit and looking for landmarks.

"Left," Celia panted, passing William to lead the way. "Keep your memory clear. Concentrate on the moment!"

The buzzing drone that had been almost indistinct was now much louder and seemed to be coming from all directions. Walt could not tell the difference between the buzz of the banders and the drone of the gnome probes, but whatever was pursuing them was coming on fast.

How did Celia know to turn left? The question popped into his head as he watched her running ahead of him. She was now leading William—as if she were in charge. Why did William trust her judgment so? Had they been in Paralleladise much longer than Walt knew? Perhaps they had been there for years and Walt had forgotten much of it, while Celia had become a leader among the hippos. *How else could she know so much?*

All around, the buzzing intensified. Walt looked around but did not see anything.

"Almost there," Celia called back. She and William were running furiously, twenty yards ahead. And then they disappeared. First Celia and then William.

Walt slowed to a stop, looking around in every direction. Where had they gone? The buzzing drone seemed to blanket the jungle from the treetops like the sound of a helicopter descending on top of him. He was alone. Had they been captured somehow? Without Sheron's light?

"Celia? William?" he called over the noise.

He walked forward.

"Psst. Down here!" It was William's voice and Walt was overwhelmed with relief. Three more quick steps and he found himself at the edge of a trench, six feet deep and camouflaged by a cover made of leaves and grasses fashioned to a thin rope netting.

"Down here!" William repeated and Walt saw the bald man's head peeking out from under the camouflage near his feet. "Hurry!" William pulled back the netting and Walt jumped into the trench, just as the first of the gnome probes dropped into view from above the trees. William pulled the camouflage back over the trench.

"It will only confuse them for a minute or two," Celia whispered. She was standing next to William in the trench. "Come on!"

She turned and hurried along the gully with William and Walt behind.

The trench was no more than two feet wide, but precisely dug on either side with smooth mud walls. The floor, however, was uneven so, in spots, they had to duck down to keep their heads from striking the camouflage cover.

Now, dozens of gnome probes descended and hovered above the trench like bloodhounds that have lost the scent. They circled, looking for a clue to the direction of their prey. The camouflage was sparse in places, letting in plenty of light and making it possible to keep the probes in view.

"Look at this!" Celia called. William and Walt stopped beside her.

At first, Walt was not sure what they were supposed to look at, but then he saw a stone tablet embedded into the dirt, halfway up the wall of the trench. They all squatted down to examine it.

The gnome probes continued to circle above the trench.

"They're catching on," William warned.

"What is it?" Walt asked. A diagram was chiseled into the tablet—a diagram consisting exclusively of lines that formed incomplete, irregular boxes.

"It's the maze," Celia told him. "Memorize it."

"What?" Walt looked at the diagram again and realized that it was the drawing of a maze like the sort in puzzle books—a series of lines with breaks in them, leading in many directions, but only one direction led from beginning to end. And now, he saw a "T" followed by a star at one end of the diagram, and a "WV" and another star at the other end of the diagram—the beginning and end of the maze, he guessed—though which was the beginning and which was the end was impossible to tell.

"Memorize it!" Celia repeated without taking her eyes off the maze. Walt realized that she, too, was trying to commit the diagram to memory.

"You've got to be kidding!" Walt said, looking at her. Though it was the kind of maze they put on the back of children's menus, this was much more complicated than any he had ever seen. There were so many turns and dead-ends, and the lines creating the maze were so dense and complex, Walt wasn't even sure he could draw a line from beginning to end, much less memorize the puzzle.

"They're closing in!" William called out in a panicked whisper. A cluster of gnomes was hovering beyond the camouflage just above them. It would only be a matter of moments before they figured out that the mnemonic signatures they were hunting were disguised beneath the netting.

"We've got to get out of here!" Walt cried out.

Celia put her hands on Walt's face and looked into his eyes. "Memorize the maze, Walt," she said. "You can do it."

Walt looked at the maze one more time. It was incredibly complex. He could never memorize it. Not in a million years.

"I can't!"

"All right," Celia announced. "Let's go!" And she ran off down the trench.

Walt and William hustled after her.

Within moments they came to a rock wall at the end of the trench. The gnome probes above the netting were confused again by their movement, but quickly recovered and were hovering their way along the trench, trying to get another lock on the fugitives.

"We're trapped," Walt said, seeing nowhere else to run, with this boulder at the end of the trench.

But Celia pushed with all her strength against the boulder and William shouldered his way past Walt to help. With both of their efforts, the huge rock began to slide, as if on a hinge, creating a small gap.

As soon as there was enough room, Celia squeezed through the opening and disappeared.

"Go on," William prompted, putting his hand on Walt's shoulder and guiding him through the narrow space.

Walt stepped forward and pushed his way through. It was dark inside with only the light from the opening to illuminate the space they had entered.

"Over here," Celia whispered. Her voice was just ahead to guide him.

William managed to squeeze through the small opening, as well, and then Walt heard him sliding the boulder back into place, sealing them into this darkness.

TWENTY-THREE

"There's a switch around here somewhere," William called.
Sealing the boulder back in place blocked all the light and noise
from the outside. It was impossible to tell what the gnome probes
were up to, but William's voice sounded calmer, relieved. Walt
heard him scratching his way along the wall looking for the
switch. Celia was close by, too. Walt could hear her breathing.

Suddenly, tiny bulbs, like Christmas lights, illuminated the
space.

"Let there be light," William announced.

Walt looked around. They were in a long, narrow room. The
walls were painted white and unadorned. Strings of light ran
along the base of the wall at the floor and along the ceiling,
providing modest illumination—enough to see by but just barely.
The room was shaped like a hallway that simply ended, thirty
yards away at a blank wall. William was standing at a large
switch with a handle that cranked near the boulder where they
had come in.

And right before Walt was the girl who had been his best
friend for the last four years.

"How do you know so much?" Walt asked her.

Celia held his gaze for a moment, but then started, "There's
no time now, but…"

"Celia," Walt interrupted. She'd been evading his questions
for too long. "How do you know so much?"

254

She lowered her eyes to the floor. "I'm sorry, Walt," she whispered.

"She wasn't supposed to come back, you know," William interjected. He walked over and put a hand on Walt's shoulder.

"What do you mean?"

"She took a big risk. She may not get another opportunity for millennia."

"An opportunity for what?"

"To escape again."

She's been here before! Walt realized, suddenly. That's how she knew all about the gnome probes and weepers and the crazy escape routes and secret passages!

Celia raised her eyes to meet Walt's gaze once again. They were filled with guilt and pleading and kindness and empathy. "I'm sorry. I wanted to tell you," she said finally. "I've been wanting to tell you for a long time."

"She couldn't say anything before you came through the portal, you understand, before you got here," William defended her. "Sheron would have picked up that signal in an instant and she'd have been dragged back and had her memories scrubbed before you could say 'jack robinson.'"

Walt studied Celia's face. His eyes burned with tears. He wanted to run away from her as far and as fast as he could, for suddenly she was not the Celia he had known for these four years. But he also wanted to hug her, to hold her tightly because, now, the familiarity of her face was the only thing connecting him to the world he'd come from, the world where Walt's father and sisters were. The only world he'd ever known. Walt was overwhelmed with loneliness.

"She risked herself coming back, you know?" William went on. "All she had to do was let you go through the portal and then escape into the world again. She was running a risk everyday she stayed close to you, every day she remained in Sheron's range."

"You knew the portal was there?" Walt asked, just beginning to understand the ramifications of this revelation. "You knew they were coming for me?"

Celia shook her head. "Not exactly."

"We knew that the next person to come through that portal **could** be a powerful hippo," William explained, "perhaps the most powerful memory ever to be trapped in Paralleladise. We knew how important that power would be if we got to you first, before NyXus knew what he'd snared."

"If NyXus didn't know, how did you know?" Walt demanded. Finally, he took his eyes from Celia's to look at William. What don't I know about William, he wondered? Is he who he seems to be? "How did you know the next one through would be so powerful?"

"It's very complicated . . ."

"Sheron's tractor beacon is designed to identify any powerful mnemonic signature within its reach and bring it in," Celia cut in. "It usually takes several tries. But anyone with a highly developed hippocampus will be attracted. And we knew, as William said at the Lexington portal, that would mean a very phenomenal memory might be the next victim."

"But I don't have a highly developed hippocampus!"

"Oh, you've got a powerful memory, all right," William corrected. "Very powerful. Incredibly powerful."

Walt turned to Celia, "Then what did you mean? Who were they after?"

Celia hesitated. She was trying to decide how much to tell him. "It's better if you remember some things for yourself," she said, finally. "But if you hadn't come through the portal . . . well, someone else would have and you wouldn't have liked that either."

"What does that mean?" Walt snapped at her. He was frustrated now with the games and rules of Paralleladise—he just wanted answers.

"Remember," Celia coaxed him, plaintively. "Remember and it might bring back your portal. It might bring back your key."

"You let me go through the portal, knowing I could be stuck here forever."

"She risked everything," William pleaded.

"Walt," Celia shook her head. "You don't understand…"

"Then explain it!" He shook his head. "You're my best friend, Celia. And you didn't tell me for four years where you came from, who was after me."

Celia opened her lips to speak, but then looked to William for help. He shrugged his shoulders, "Let's walk as we talk."

"I want to know the truth," Walt said, not moving.

"Believe me, son," William sighed as he continued down the hallway-like room toward the wall at the end, "you'll have plenty of time to ask all your questions."

Walt thought William was going to step straight into the wall, but at the last moment, he turned to his left and disappeared.

"Where did he go?"

"Come on," Celia told him, and walked down the hall after William.

Walt followed her and, when they got to wall, he realized it was not a dead end at all, for another corridor branched off to the left. The angle of the walls and dim lighting obscured the turn until they were right in front of it.

William was now several steps down this next corridor and Walt and Celia turned after him. "Do you remember what MacGruder said about a handful of hippos who escaped Paralleladise?" he asked.

Walt thought back to the conversation they had when they were in the tunnel beneath Prairie Dog Flats. What had MacGruder said? "That four hippos escaped," Walt reported, as the memory came back to him. "They were helped by a weeper."

William stopped and smiled at Walt. "See, you have a better memory than you thought."

They were at the end of the second corridor now. This one, too, branched off at what had seemed to be a dead end. But it branched off in two directions, opposite directions, both looking exactly the same. William turned and headed down the corridor to the right. "Do you remember the fate of the four escapees?"

Again, Walt tried to recall the conversation. Several hippos had escaped over the centuries, he remembered. But most had been recaptured.

"Two were recaptured immediately," he recalled.

Now Celia jumped in. "They went to the police immediately after they escaped," she explained. "They wanted to warn the world about the portals and Paralleladise. They wanted to save humanity from NyXus and his plan."

"But, of course," William went on, "you can't talk about Paralleladise if you escape. Every mention, every memory, gives away your location to Sheron—gives him something to lock in on. Something to drag back."

William stopped walking suddenly. They hadn't reached the end of this third corridor yet. It continued on for as far as Walt could see in the dim light. But now, two other hallways branched off on either side. William looked down each. He turned to the right, then checked with Celia who nodded her head before he headed off in the new direction.

We're in the maze! Walt realized. When they pushed aside the boulder in the trench and entered the first hallway, they stepped into a life-sized construction of the maze that replicated the one diagrammed on the stone tablet outside! The diagram had been incredibly complex, Walt remembered, and now William and Celia were trying to find their way through it by memory alone.

We'll be lost forever, he thought in a panic. He tried to remember the way back to the boulder before they got too far along.

"So you see," William was talking again as they walked. "She couldn't warn you about what was going to happen. To even speak the name of Paralleladise in the real world is to guarantee recapture."

Walt tried to piece together William's explanation: four hippos had escaped; two were recaptured when they went to the police. He turned to Celia, "You were one of the others who escaped?"

Celia nodded. "I tried to tell you, Walt, a million times and in a million ways without giving away my position to Sheron."

"And the other one who escaped . . ." Walt said, understanding more as he spoke, "That was your uncle."

She nodded again. "The man you knew as my uncle, yes. His real name is Adonis Chikidas. He had been in Paralleladise for three centuries. We looked out for one another . . . protected one another. He helped me find you."

"Helped you find me? Why?"

William led them on another turn into a corridor that looked exactly like all the rest. Walt tried to memorize the turns: left, right, right again and now a third time.

"When Sheron tracks a specific mnemonic signature," William explained, "he's deadly accurate. That's how he recaptures escapees so quickly."

"But when he's fishing for new victims, he drops in his line and doesn't know what he'll reel in," Celia continued. "We knew the next one through the portal could be very powerful, and we had to make sure Sheron caught the right fish."

William turned down another corridor, this one to the left. Left, right, right, right, left, Walt repeated to himself. It was difficult to concentrate on the conversation and memorize the turns of the maze, too.

"And so," Celia went on, "when they saw an opportunity with the Lexington portal to bring back a powerful hippo, they sent me back to make sure it was you that Sheron caught."

"I'm not the right fish," Walt protested. "I have a terrible memory. Celia, you've got the wrong person!"

"I didn't want you to go through, Walt." There was regret and sadness in Celia's voice. "At the last minute, I tried to stop you."

An image flashed in Walt's mind—a memory of the portal. He was facing it, the bright light dragging him in and someone was trying to pull him back.

No! The recollection was becoming clearer. His head started to throb but he ignored the pain as he tried to bring the mental image up. He wasn't facing the portal—he was turned away from it? Running from it? The portal was near the courthouse somewhere and it had opened as he was riding his bike away from it. Zelda was calling to him, and someone grabbed his hand. He couldn't see the face. Someone was trying to pull him back. Celia! It was Celia! She was holding on tightly trying to pull him away from the light.

No! No! That wasn't right. Walt shook his head.

"I wanted to help the hippos," Celia went on. "I wanted to help everyone in Paralleladise and stop NyXus. But when I saw you being dragged into the portal, I couldn't watch." Celia paused. A tear fell down her cheek. "You had become my best friend. I couldn't do it. I couldn't let you go."

Walt studied Celia's face. He was glad she had called him his "best friend." Perhaps everything about their last four years had not been a deception.

"Celia," he said, reaching out to squeeze her arm for comfort.

Suddenly, William came to a stop in front of them and Walt and Celia stopped, too. They had come to another turn in the maze. There were three different corridors stretching in three different directions. William started to step to the left, but stopped, uncertain.

"That's it," he announced after a moment's more deliberation. "That's my limit. I don't know where to turn next." He looked at Celia. "It's up to you, now, my dear."

"You did well," Celia told him. Though her eyes were still teary, she smiled a reassuring smile. Then, she squeezed past him to lead. She stood in the middle of the corridor for several moments with her eyes closed, concentrating and, when she opened them, she stepped confidently down the hallway on the right.

Left, right, right, right, left, and now right again, Walt reminded himself. Was that it? No. Had they made another turn while they were talking? He couldn't remember.

261

"You've gotten through this maze before?" Walt asked, looking for reassurance. It seemed impossible to remember all the twists and turns of the maze diagrammed on the stone tablet. And, inside the maze, each corridor was the same as the one before it. Each choice looked exactly like the other.

"Sort of," Celia replied. Her concentration was intense now.

"What does that mean—'sort of'?"

"I've made it about seventy-five percent of the way," Celia reported calmly.

"Seventy-five percent?" Only seventy-five percent! They would never make it out of here.

"A lot of people don't even make it that far. Now let me think." Celia closed her eyes again and then turned down another corridor to the left.

"We had no other choice," William whispered. "It was our only hope."

"What happens if you lose your way?" Walt spoke softly, too, not wanting to break Celia's concentration.

"There used to be escape hatches along the way for anyone who couldn't remember the maze."

"Used to be?"

"No one can remember where they are."

Celia took a quick right and then another right. Walt and William trailed her, a few steps behind. It felt as if they were walking in a circle.

"What's it for—this maze? A prison?" Walt asked. "A torture?"

William laughed. "It would make a good one—that's for sure. Many a hippo have been driven mad trying to make their way through."

"It was made by hippos?"

262

"It was built in the time of the fourth Rememberer," William informed him. "Built as a mnemonic exercise for the resistance. They thought it would help with short-term memory."

"Does it?"

William shrugged. "Hard to say. No one has ever made it through. In the beginning, several hippos were lost when they went in and never came out. So they built the escape hatches, but no one could find those either. Eventually, they gave up using it altogether."

"That was wise," Walt agreed.

Celia continued to lead them. Her eyes were half-closed and Walt could tell that she was trying to visualize the map of the maze they had seen in the trench—trying to lead them by memory rather than sight.

They continued on in silence now, making several turns and Walt gave up trying to recall the way back. He lost track, too, of how much time they had been in the maze. It seemed like hours, but in the absence of any external light, wandering through dozens of hallways that looked exactly the same, it could have been less. Or more. One thing was certain: if Celia's memory failed, they would be in here a lot longer.

The possibility of wandering for days in these dark, enclosed corridors frightened Walt. He thought about his family and longed to return to his everyday world—to squabbles with Zelda, to Garage Sale Saturdays with his father, to incessant whining about the cold from Acey. What he wouldn't give to find his way out of these suffocating hallways and step into his own world. He would never complain again, he told himself, about waking up for school, about cleaning out his closet, about babysitting Acey when his father worked late. He would never ask for more than the safe and happy life he enjoyed, if he could just get out of here. All the mundane and pestering facets of his life at home felt precious to him now as he searched with Celia and William for a way out of this endless maze.

But would they let him out, he wondered? NyXus and Sheron—who were mere specters in Walt's mind since he had never seen either—were determined to keep all prisoners of Paralleladise trapped until they could launch a plan Walt did not understand. And the resistance fighters—the hippos—were convinced Walt had a special power of memory he didn't have. They would not let him escape. He looked ahead at Celia. She had said she regretted leading him to the portal. Would she help him escape if he could remember his portal? Would she help him find his key?

Celia stopped. They were at a wall with no corridors on either side to lead them on. They had reached a dead end.

She turned to face Walt and William with a grave expression. "I must have made a wrong turn."

The look on her face told Walt she was worried.

"No, no," William said. He grabbed her shoulders, looking in her eyes. "It's all right. We're all right. It was the last turn. It must have been. We just have to go back a little." Despite his reassurances, William's voice betrayed alarm.

Celia shook her head. "I don't know."

"That must be it," William said, "you were so certain," and he turned and began walking back down the corridor the way they had come.

"Let's not panic," Celia called to him. "That's how people get stuck. We just have to think. We just have to remember."

Her warning not to panic made Walt panic. If Celia couldn't get them out, no one could. She had seemed confident. Now, all the blood had drained from her face and she studied the hallway as if she expected a new corridor to appear. The walls of the hall felt suddenly narrower.

William stopped and came back to them. "That must be it. It must be the last turn we made. You were fine until then."

"Maybe," Celia responded. "Or maybe I've been off the last several turns or dozens of turns."

"Who's panicked?" William asked, his voice cracking with obvious nervousness. "What are we going to do?"

Celia studied the walls again, searching for inspiration. Walt watched her eyes to discover just how dire their situation was.

Suddenly, she turned to him and grabbed his hands in hers.

"Walt!" she said, looking determinedly in his face. "You can get us out of here."

"What?"

"You can get us out of here," she repeated. "You're our only hope."

"I can't . . ." Walt protested.

"No!" Celia interrupted sharply. "You can. You really can."

"How?"

"Remember the maze—the diagram we saw outside. Remember it and lead us through."

"You're crazy!" Walt told her. He pulled his hands from hers. If this was her best idea about how to get out of this trap, they were in big trouble. "I can't remember... I only saw it for a second."

"You can remember, Walt," Celia encouraged. "You just think you can't. But you have a very powerful memory. You have a nearly photographic mind."

Walt laughed at the absurdity of the claim. "Me? Me? I can't remember to bring my lunch to school. I haven't got a photographic . . ."

265

"You do!" William jumped in. "You really do, my boy. You don't know it, but you do. Your mnemonic signature is incredible."

"You've got the wrong guy!" Walt argued. "I keep telling you."

"We don't have the wrong guy, Walt," Celia said, a pleading tone in her voice. "It's you. You can get us out."

"I can't . . ."

"You just need to concentrate." Celia put her hands on either side of Walt's face and held his gaze. "Concentrate."

"Celia," Walt pleaded, "I can't . . ."

"Close your eyes," she coached him.

"You've got the wrong guy . . ."

"Please, Walt," William coaxed him. "Please try. What can it hurt?"

Walt studied Celia's face. The look of expectation in her eyes broke his heart. He could only disappoint her, but he closed his eyes. "All right, they're closed."

"Clear your mind."

"We should try to find our way back," he suggested. "We should have left bread crumbs or something."

"Clear your mind!"

Clear your mind. He wasn't quite sure what that meant, but he tried anyway, focusing on a brown-gray nothingness streaked with light that he saw when he closed his eyes.

"Clear your mind," Celia repeated, this time in a softer, reassuring voice, as if she were trying to hypnotize him.

"It's clear," Walt reported, impatiently. "All clear."

"It's not clear," she replied, "or you wouldn't be talking."

"I'm not talking," Walt said. "I'm telling you it's clear."

"Clear?"

266

"Yes, clear," he assured her, "and this is a waste of . . ."

"MAZE!" Celia suddenly shouted out.

Walt opened his eyes with a start. "What was that for?"

"What did you see?"

"What? Nothing. You scared me and I opened my eyes."

"What did you see the instant before you opened your eyes."

"Nothing," Walt reported, but then realized he had seen something for a fleeting second when Celia shouted "maze." "I .
. ."

"MAZE!" Celia yelled again, even louder.

"Ow! Stop that! You hurt my ears."

"What did you see?"

Walt had seen it again when she yelled. And this time, he recognized it. It was an image of the diagram they had studied right before they entered the maze. "I saw . . . just for a second."

"Close your eyes," Celia said, excited. "You can do this, Walt. You've just never known. You've never tried."

Walt looked at Celia doubtfully and then at William who nodded. Slowly, Walt closed his eyes.

"The maze," Celia said, but this time in a measured, steady voice.

An image of the maze diagram floated before Walt's closed eyes as if it were suspended in space. It hovered there, indistinct.

"I guess I see it, but not clearly."

"There are two sets of letters on either end," Celia prompted. "What are they?"

Walt focused on the hazy diagram taking shape in his memory. It was definitely the diagram, he knew, but he could not see its features.

"I don't see them."

267

"One set of letters is 'Q' and 'R'," Celia told him. "I'll give you that much, but you tell me if they're at the beginning of the maze or the end."

Walt concentrated, trying to bring the hazy vision into focus. "Q" and "R." He tried to locate them on the diagram but it remained a blur. "Q" and "R," he thought, "Q" and "R." "They're not there..." he told Celia, but then, two letters suddenly appeared on the vision of the tablet he was holding in his mind's eye. They were not "Q" and "R."

"Hey! You tricked me."

"It was for your own good," Celia reassured him. "What are the letters?"

The letters jumped out at him now. "There's a 'WV' at the end of the maze," he announced. "And a 'T' and a star at the beginning."

"The 'T' is for 'trench,'" William explained, "and the star marks the start of the maze. You're getting it now."

"It will come all of a sudden if you let it," Celia added.

"The 'WV' indicates Weeper Village, where the maze ends."

"That's all I can see," Walt said. "I can't read any more."

"Don't force it," William advised. "Let it come to you."

Walt tried not to force it, though he didn't know how.

"Maze!!" Celia yelled once again.

Walt startled, but the shout had its effect. Suddenly, the image of the diagram in all its detail popped to the front of his mind and this time he did not open his eyes to chase it away. "I see it!"

"I knew you could do it!"

"Hold on to it," William cautioned. "Hold on!"

268

It was incredible! Walt was actually seeing the diagram before his closed eyes. And it was not the murky and fleeting, half-formed visual he normally retained when he remembered images. This was a crystal-clear picture of the maze diagram, floating in front of his mind as if it were actually there, less like a memory and more like a … photograph!

A sensation of awe ran through Walt's body. Could it be? Did he really have a photographic memory? Was it possible that Ling and William and Celia did not have the wrong guy? Could he truly be what they believed him to be?

"Don't lose it," Celia was saying. "Keep it there."

Walt concentrated on the image, letting it rest in front of him. For the moment, it seemed to have no inclination to fade away.

"I've got it!" he reported. "I've really got it."

"Can you use it to get us out of here?" This was William's voice.

"What?" Walt asked. He was seeing the diagram clearly, but he had no idea where they were on it. "How?" Without knowing their location, the image in his mind was useless.

Worry ran through Walt's mind, and as it did, the diagram began to fade. "I'm losing it!" he cried out.

"MAZE! MAZE!" William shouted desperately.

But it was no help, the visual faded into the blankness of his mind. Walt opened his eyes, defeated. "I lost it."

"It's okay," Celia said calmly. "We'll get it back."

"But what use is it if I don't know where we are?"

"I know where we are," Celia told him. "Come on."

Quickly, Celia started down the corridor in the direction they had come. Walt and William exchanged confused glances and then followed her. She trotted back several yards to where

269

they had last made a turn, into the corridor that had become a dead end. There, she stopped and faced Walt once again.

"This was our last turn," she explained. "It might be where I went wrong or it may have happened earlier." She took Walt's hands in hers once again. "Now close your eyes, Walt, and bring back the diagram."

"What if I can't?"

Celia smiled. "You have to," she said. Her smile and words conveyed so much confidence that it seemed inevitable. "Close your eyes."

Walt closed his eyes and tried to clear his mind. "Maze" he whispered to himself, trying not to force the image but let it come naturally. "Diagram."

Slowly, as if being dredged from the depths of a murky pond, the tablet with the maze emerged. But this time, the details were clear almost immediately, as if he had pulled photographic film from its developing solution and brought it before his eyes.

"I've got it!" he said, surprised at the ease with which it had come back.

"Excellent!" William commended.

"I knew you could do it!" Celia told him. "Now listen and follow me, if you can."

Walt held himself still, hoping it would keep the visual of the diagram steady before his mind.

"We came in at the star," Celia began.

Walt's studied the maze and found the star at the beginning. "I've got it."

"Very good," Celia encouraged him. "We followed the first corridor to the end and turned left."

As she spoke, Walt followed the beginning corridor on the diagram to the first left. He saw clearly that it was the only direction to take.

"At the next corridor," Celia continued, "there was a passage to the right and a passage to the left and we turned right."

Walt traced the steps in his mind around the right turn. The other direction, he could see, would have quickly led them to a dead end. "That was right," he reported.

"And then we took two more right turns."

"That's good."

"And then a left . . . and then another left."

Walt followed along the image in his mind, moving along the diagram as Celia described each of the turns they had taken. With each new corridor, he could see that she had made the right choice, avoided the dead ends, and moved in the shortest direction toward the end of the maze, until ...

"Wait!"

"What is it?"

"That last one—the left." On the diagram in his head, Walt could see the turn Celia was describing led off in several directions, all of which ultimately ended at a solid wall. "That's it! That's where we went the wrong way."

"Ha-ha!" William exclaimed. "We're going to make it out of here, after all."

"That was just two turns back!" Celia announced. "Let's go!"

Walt opened his eyes to see Celia and William hurrying away down the corridor, back in the direction they had come. He hustled after them as they took two quick turns and were at the point in the maze where they had taken the wrong corridor.

The hallway they were in had three other passages branching off of it. One was the false corridor they had mistakenly taken. One of the other two must be the correct direction. But which one?

Walt looked down both passages. They were exactly the same.

"Close your eyes," Celia told him. He could feel the anticipation in her voice. "Which way?"

Walt closed his eyes to bring the diagram to the front of his mind again.

"Can you see it?" William asked anxiously.

The excitement made concentration difficult. Walt tried to clear his mind. "Maze," he whispered to himself, "diagram."

"I'm not getting anything."

He felt Celia's hand on his arm, squeezing gently. "It's okay," she said, calmly. "You'll do it."

Slowly, the image of the tablet began to form once again. "Maze," Walt whispered again to coax it along. Finally, he could see it all clearly.

"Straight ahead," he said, "and then right."

He didn't want to open his eyes, afraid he would lose the mental picture and not get it back. Celia's hand was still on his arm and now he felt William take his other arm. They were going to lead him through the maze, so he wouldn't have to open his eyes.

"Steady," William cautioned, "steady."

They moved along the passageways, Walt calling out the turns coming up and Celia and William repeating the call as they went.

"Right."

"Turning right."

"There's a turn to the left, but it leads to a dead end."

"Passing the hallway now."

Walt was very excited now. He could see they were close to the exit marked "WV." Only a few more turns to go.

"Right, again," he called out, seeing so clearly the path to completion in his mind.

"Right," Celia cried.

"Left and then right," Walt told them, wanting to get the final steps out as quickly as possible. "And then left."

He opened his eyes. Celia was beaming at him. "You did it!"

"Come on, now," William shouted, letting go of Walt's arm and trotting down the corridor.

Celia and Walt hurried after him. They turned left and then right and then left again, bursting into a full out run at the last corridor, unable to contain their relief and elation.

And there, at the end of the corridor, was another huge boulder, like the one Celia and William had pushed aside to enter the maze. It had a stone tablet fastened to it with a wooden frame around it.

Walt, Celia and William stopped when they reached it and read the simple inscription chiseled upon it. "WV," it read, and underneath the word "Fini."

"I can't believe it," William cried.

"No one has ever made it through the maze before," Celia said. She kissed Walt on the cheek. "But you did it, Walt."

Walt felt a flush of pride, but told her, "We all did it together. Come on. Let's get out of here."

Walt, William and Celia put their hands against the giant boulder and pushed. At first, it didn't budge, but then, gradually, it began to swing on its hidden hinge and opened to the side.

Sunlight streamed into the maze corridor, blinding them, but looking and feeling so good in contrast to the claustrophobic hallways they'd been travelling.

"Ha-ha!" William laughed when they'd opened the passageway large enough for all three of them to step out into the sunshine. They walked together, feeling the warm light on their faces.

"We made it!" Celia sighed, beaming with satisfaction.

William pushed the boulder behind them back into place to hide the exit to the maze. Then he threw his arm around Walt's shoulder and let out a hearty laugh. "Do you still think we got the wrong guy?" he asked.

Walt looked at him, proud of the accomplishment, feeling for the first time since he'd come to Paralleladise that he had done something right.

TWENTY-FOUR

"What's that noise?" Walt Walters asked.

He, Celia and William had emerged from the maze into a green valley surrounded by squat, grassy hills. No breeze blew and yet Walt heard a low whistling that crescendo-ed to a wail and then softened again, like an air-raid siren.

"Weeping," Celia answered.

Walt listened closely. It was, he realized, the blending of dozens of human voices, all moaning at different pitches and intervals, creating a hum that rose and faded.

"Are we close to the Weeper Village?"

"Come on," Celia responded, climbing the hill in front of them. Walt and William followed her.

Now Walt could see why MacGruder had called the weepers "creepy." Even the sound of their cries at a distance was haunting, like eerie organ music in a scary movie or the howl of a pack of prowling wolves. But it was reverently melancholy, too, like a funeral dirge. Walt felt a chill tingle up his spine.

"How long does the weeping last?" he asked William, hoping it would stop soon.

"Forever."

They crested the hill to find the other side was steeper and overlooked a wide valley. Walt could see for miles from this view. At the bottom of the hill was a small village with dozens of huts and lean-tos across several acres of land. Campfires outside the huts sent strands of smoke into the air. The pathways around the huts and the roads leading into the village were wet and muddied. It looked to Walt like an impoverished, medieval hamlet.

"Weeper Village," Celia announced.

From the top of this hill, the haunting cries of the weepers were louder and sadder, like the bitter moaning of a widow at the grave of her husband or a mother who has lost a child. And the cries had the power to call up memories, for Walt's mind turned, in the presence of this melancholy aria, to those he missed. An image of his father, fumbling with some simple mechanical device he could not understand flashed before his mind. It dissolved into another image of Zelda rocking a feverish Acey while their father went to get medicine.

"My goodness!" William exclaimed. "Look at the patrols."

He pointed to the numerous groups of three and four men and women circling and walking through the village. They marched with precision in their small groups, but wandered aimlessly as if they couldn't remember which direction they were supposed to be going. They carried black tubes, a yard long, strapped to their shoulders and looped under their arms.

"Sheron must have figured we'd go to the weepers sooner or later," Celia guessed.

"But so many! He must have deputized a hundred new troops."

"He's getting desperate." Celia looked at Walt. "By now, he's had the chance to study your mnemonic signature. He probably knows how dangerous you are to him."

"They're humans," Walt said, studying the patrols. He had grown used to evading mechanical pursuers. These flesh and blood guards surprised him.

"Gnome probes don't work around weepers," Celia explained. "They give off so much mnemonic energy, it just confuses probes and they go haywire. So Sheron has to use human patrols."

"Are those weapons?" Walt was looking at the black tubes the guards carried.

"Slime shooters," William answered. "But the guards march around in the lethemine all day. We shouldn't have any problem."

"Still," Celia warned, "every once in a while, they get lucky. You can't take them too lightly."

She started down the hill and Walt and William followed.

Celia was clearly in charge now of their little group and William seemed content to let her lead. How long had she been in Paralleladise before she escaped to bring Walt back? It must have been many years, Walt guessed, because she had won so much influence over a long-time detainee like William.

She was a different person here in Paralleladise. In their own world of Lexington and the Middle School, Celia had always been a watcher, a follower, an outsider with a witty and ironic perspective on classes and teachers and the popular kids. Here, she was an important hippo in the resistance and, while she retained the wit and skepticism of his old friend, she was a leader, too, commanding and authoritative, and with a purpose and mission.

Which was the real Celia, Walt wondered? Or, how much of the real Celia had he known back in Lexington? They'd been friends for four years—which was almost a third of Walt's life, but she may have already lived a dozen lifetimes or more before she came through the portal to find him. What he didn't know about her was far greater than what he knew. And yet, he couldn't help but believe that their friendship was based on something true. Surely, he had not been totally fooled about that.

They were at the bottom of the hill now. Walt could hear the leader of a nearby patrol shouting out orders. "Left! Left! Your OTHER left!"

"If we get stopped," Celia said to Walt, "better let one of us do the talking."

They walked to the muddy path that led into the tiny village. The wail of the weepers was like a chanted chorus amplified through a loud speaker. It permeated the air. Up ahead, a patrol of five guards marched onto the path and approached them, their slime-shooting tubes leveled to fire.

"Hold on there!" said a stout woman with a white armband. She was apparently the leader of this patrol. "Halt. Stop. Freeze."

Celia, Walt and William stopped before the patrol. Walt saw Celia's and William's faces go blank with false naiveté and he, too, tried to adopt the guileless expression of the citizens of Paralleladise.

The woman poked at William with her slime-shooter and looked as if she were about to speak. But, apparently she forgot what she was going to say for she paused to take a laminated note card from her shirt pocket. She poked William again as she read from the card:

"What is your name?" she demanded.

"State your business!" another patrolman called out.

"Who are you?" another asked.

"What are you doing in Weeper Valley?" a fourth wanted to know.

"This area is restricted," the woman informed them, reading from the card.

"Weepers only," the second man explained.

"You have to have a pass," the third elaborated.

The woman turned in frustration to face the other guards. "Pipe down, now. I'll ask the questions."

"You'll ask what questions?" a confused guard wondered.

"Who died and made you queen?" another guard challenge.

"The king?" a third patrolman offered.

Walt looked at William who seemed confused and totally innocent. "I'm sorry," he sputtered. "We must have gotten turned around. Is this the way to *Le Mont Saint-Michel*?"

The woman and the men looked at each other, uncertain.

"Le Mont Saint-Michel?" they all said at once and pointed in different directions.

"It's over there," the woman announced.

"You have to take the Holland Tunnel," the second added.

"Oh, you can't get there from here," the third assured them, shaking his head.

"Except on the bus," the second man retorted.

"Pah! The buses," the woman spat out. "Do they ever run on time?"

"I think they use petrol," the second offered. "Or coal."

A third man wondered, "What are buses?"

"That's very helpful," William told them, shaking each guard's hand in turn. "Thank you very much. That's very kind. We can find our way from there."

"Happy to be of service," the woman replied with a smile.

"That's what we're here for," the second reminded them.

"Write if you get work," a third requested. And then the small patrol waved a salute and marched away.

"She's good," William commented, when they were out of earshot.

"They've trained her well," Celia agreed, starting up the road again.

Suddenly, the patrol leader stopped, twenty yards away. Her squad halted with her as she wheeled on her heels to face Walt, Celia and William again.

"Watch for brown robes," the woman read from the index card she was holding. "Watch for brown robes, especially wearing more than one."

Now every guard in the patrol wheeled around, alarmed. Walt, Celia and William still wore the brown robes they'd donned at the machine room of Prairie Dog Flats. The guards leveled their slime shooters, suddenly suspicious. The patrol marched back to Walt, Celia and William. They were too close to make a run for it.

"How many robes have you got on there?" the patrol leader asked William.

"Why I don't recall exact..." William started, but the woman stepped forward and pulled the top brown robe off his shoulder to reveal one just like it underneath.

"Why are you wearing two robes?" she demanded.

"Chilly," William replied.

The woman raised one eyebrow in a look of disbelief then, quickly, turned to Walt and barked out, "Where did you get the robes?"

Walt was surprised by her sudden turn to him and unprepared. He hemmed for a moment before sputtering out, "I can't remember."

"You got two robes, too?" the patrol leader asked, then pushed aside the top layer of his robes without waiting for an answer. She saw the second robe underneath.

"Very suspicious, I should say," one of the other patrolmen commented. "Very suspicious, indeed."

The other members of the patrol huddled in, forming a loose circle around Walt, Celia and William. The leader took a whistle out of her pocket and blew three sharp toots bringing several other patrol squads hustling over. Within moments, they were surrounded by a dozen men and women with menacing slime shooters leveled to fire.

"What's going on?" one of the patrol leaders called out.

"We caught us some renegades," someone answered.

"We're looking for *Le Mont Saint-Michel*," Celia protested.

"We're not renegades," William answered. "We just got turned around."

"They've got multiple brown robes," the patrol leader argued. She referred to her index card again, "The bulletin says 'watch for brown robes, especially wearing more than one.'"

"We were chilly. We're looking for *Le Mont Saint-Michel*."

"Slime 'em first, ask questions later!" another patrolmen cried out, as if reciting official policy.

"Starve a cold, feed a fever," another chimed in.

"What's this *Le Mont* thing they keep talking about?" One of the leaders of another patrol asked the woman with the armband. "Maybe it's a test to see if we'll slime them."

"It's a secret code word, I'll bet," someone suggested.

"They've got more than one robe on," the woman replied. "That's all I know."

"I say, 'slime 'em,'" a voice called out.

"Yay!" other voices agreed.

More patrolmen were joining the crowd. There was no way to escape them all now, Walt realized, as they closed in, filling gaps, creating a solid ring of bodies around them.

281

"It's a little obvious," the woman said, eyeing William suspiciously, "them walking straight into the village like that."

"It's a trick, I tell you," the other patrol leader said. "Sheron's trying to trip us up."

"Slime them! Let Sheron deal with them."

"It's a secret code! They're working for the resistance, I tell you."

"I'm hungry!" someone called out.

"PIPE DOWN!" the stern patrol leader yelled fiercely. The crowd of guards quieted all at once. The leader glared around the circled patrols and then announced. "We'll test them first and then slime them—just to be sure."

"Bring them along!" a second leader called.

"We're only looking for *Le Mont . . ."* *William* started, but suddenly the entire circle of men and women moved at once with Walt, Celia and William in the center of it. They shuffled along the muddied path like a lynch mob with its victims surrounded. William looked to Celia expectantly, wondering what to do.

Walt felt himself being jostled along by the guards behind him who shoved him in the back repeatedly to prompt him to keep up.

"Renegades!" someone in the crowd called out. "We've caught renegades!"

"Slime 'em!" others chanted as they moved along the muddied trail.

Celia searched about her for some means of escape or distraction, but there was nothing on either side of the path to help them—only open fields and the hills behind them. Ahead was Weeper Village, but the huts and outbuildings were too sparsely spaced to provide cover if they could manage to break free from the surrounding patrols.

"What are they going to do to us?" Walt asked Celia. The wail of the weepers and the chants of "Slime 'em" from the patrols were loud enough to drown out his voice for anyone except Celia.

"They've probably got a signature-gauge in the village. They'll test to see if we're hippos."

"What do we do?"

Celia looked about, concerned, "I'm thinking... I'm thinking."

"Send them to Sheron!" someone called out.

"Slime 'em back to where they came from!"

They were approaching one of the first huts of the Weeper Village now. At a small campfire, two women with dirty, stringy hair and tattered clothes were sobbing inconsolably, rocking before the fire. They paid no attention to the mob of guards marching into their hamlet.

"Weepers," William indicated to Walt, seeing him study the women who looked like homeless derelicts he had seen in movies, usually standing around steaming metal trash cans in the city alleys.

"We can't let them test you!" Celia said urgently, apparently giving up on finding a means of escape. "We've got to get you free."

"I'll make my mind a blank."

"That won't work on the gauges."

"I'm not going without you two!" Walt protested.

They were quickly in the center of the village and Walt could see where they were headed now. Amid the grass and mud huts of the village was one more permanent structure, a wood building with a long porch that looked like a general merchandise store of the Old West. They passed three other weepers who had come from the building carrying cloth sacks over their backs. Despite the noise of the many patrols, the weepers, two women and a boy, seemed oblivious as they sobbed and wailed.

"We've got to get you out of here!" Celia shouted over the chants of the guards, which grew louder as they neared the wood building.

Walt looked around. He saw no means of escape. They were surrounded by dozens of men and women. He might be able to wrestle a slime shooter from one of the guards, but he would be slimed himself before he figured out how to fire it. The situation seemed hopeless, and the fear of never seeing his family leapt into his mind.

And then he heard a loud whistle and voice shouting above all the other noise, cutting through the unceasing wail of the weepers and the chanting of the patrol mob.

The guards heard it, too, and, one by one they quieted until Walt could make out what the voice was shouting.

"Hippos! Hippos! Hippos attack! All W-V guards to their stations!"

The cry was followed by another loud whistle and then a repeat of the warning.

"Hippos! All guards to their stations."

The mob of guards fell silent.

"Attention! Hippos attack! Hippos attack! Attention!"

The patrols surrounding Walt, Celia and William took a moment to process the alert. There was a pause. And then panic set in.

"Hippos! Hippos!" they cried, as if powerful aliens had landed and were destroying everything in sight. "To your stations!"

The guards shrieked and scurried in confusion—unsure where to turn. Finally, each seemed to find a direction and they hustled off, bumping into each other, knocking one another into the muddy path.

"Hippos!"

"To your stations!"

"Man the pumps!"

"Send up the alarm!"

It was a full two minutes before the patrols each figured out what they were supposed to do and managed to break out of the pack to escape. In the meantime, the whistling continued followed by the announcement of the attack. "All W-V guards to their stations."

Finally, Walt, Celia and William found themselves all alone on the path in front of the General Store, abandoned by all the guards who had fled to ward off the assault.

William looked at Celia, confused: "Hippo attack?" he asked. "Hippos don't attack."

Celia searched above their heads to the roof of the General Store and the surrounding huts, for the alarm seemed to come from a speaker somewhere above them.

"There!" she shouted when she spotted the source.

"Ling!" William cried out with happiness.

Ling stood atop one of the hippo huts, a bullhorn in one hand, a whistle in the other. He continued to sound the alarm: "Hippos attack! Warning! Hippos attack!"

Celia sighed relief. "I don't believe it."

She sprinted to the hut Ling was standing on. William stood admiring his old friend in amazement and then followed her, and Walt hurried behind him.

"All guards to your stations!" Ling was calling through the bullhorn when they reached the hut. "All guards to their stations." When he saw them gathered below, Ling set the bullhorn on top of the grass roof and, laying on his stomach, slid off the hut, dropping the short distance to the ground and springing to his feet.

"Ling!" Celia and William exclaimed at once.

"Now let's get out of here," Ling said urgently, "before they realize they don't have stations."

Ling ran off around the weeper hut and Walt, Celia and William followed him. They dashed along the dirt and mud pathways passing guards, frantically trying to find their stations, and weepers who sat or walked, unconscious or unconcerned about what was happening around them. They darted around a young man, just a few years older than Walt who was kneeling in the middle of the path, writing something with a stick in the mud and sobbing intensely. As Walt passed he saw he was writing the name "Cordelia" again and again.

Quickly they were nearing the outskirts of the village at the opposite end from where they had entered, escorted by the patrols. There were only a few more buildings before Weeper Village ended in open field and Ling stopped at the very last hut. It was a taller structure than many of the surrounding buildings and set off from the others.

Ling checked to see if any patrols were watching and then rapped on the door of the hut. When there was no response, he knocked again and then entered cautiously. "All clear," he announced once he was inside.

It was some kind of storage building, Walt saw as they entered, filled with tools and maintenance equipment for the village. It was cluttered and disorganized and in the center of the room was a ladder that ascended into a loft, ten feet above them, that circled the ceiling. It, too, looked cluttered and overstuffed.

Ling quickly shut the door behind them. The roof and walls of the structure were poorly thatched so that sunlight streaked in, illuminating the single, large room. "We should be safe here," Ling told them.

Celia ran to Ling and hugged him. "You saved our skins, for sure."

Ling smiled at her. "Precious skins to save."

"How did you know we would be here?"

Ling shrugged. "That's where I would have gone."

"You've taught me well," Celia told him.

Ling looked at Walt. "So he knows then?"

"Yes, I told him."

"Better that you should know," Ling assured Walt, seriously. Walt did not answer. Better I should not be deceived in the first place, he thought.

"But how did you get here so quickly?" Ling asked, his tone becoming more lighthearted, "I thought I would be waiting for days. And then, the minute I get here, you're already being carted off by the patrols."

William threw his arm around Walt's shoulders, like a proud father. "We came through the maze. Walt led us through."

Ling's eyes glistened as he turned to Walt. "Ha! I knew you had it in you," Ling laughed, clapping Walt's arm. "You'll be our salvation."

Walt did not want to be anyone's salvation. "We helped each other through," he replied.

"He's being modest,"

"But how did **you** get here so fast?" Celia asked Ling. "The mountain pass takes at least a full day, too."

Ling studied Celia for a moment and then looked away. "I can't tell you all my secrets." His words were playful, but his demeanor was suddenly very serious.

"Oh, Ling," Celia said, her face shadowing over with concern. "You came through the mines."

"I'm fine," Ling said, shaking his head. "I took shallow breaths."

"Oh, Ling," Celia repeated.

"What are the mines?" Walt asked.

"They run through the mountains," William told him, though he was staring at Ling. His face, too, was furrowed in worry. "It's where they mine lethemine. The toxic levels are extremely high."

"Well," Ling said, trying to sound nonchalant. "I couldn't leave you to fend for yourselves."

"What will happen?" Walt asked. Celia was looking at Ling as if he had just announced he was heading to the front lines of a brutal war zone.

"Time will tell," William replied.

"That's right," Ling said, to change the mood and topic. "Only time will tell, so we shouldn't dwell on the possibilities." He looked at Walt. "We've got to get you to Romannie."

"One of the weepers is bound to know," Celia replied, though her face still registered sadness. "We just have to find the right one."

"And as quickly as possible," William added. "I don't like all the patrols."

"It will be getting dark soon." Ling was devising a plan. "One of us should stay with Walt while the others question the weepers."

For a moment, no one spoke. And then Celia volunteered. "I'll stay," she said, looking at Walt. "If you're okay with that."

"You should be safe here," Ling told her, not waiting for Walt to respond. "You might want to hide in the loft."

"Talking to weepers." William shivered at the thought.

"You better get going," Celia said. She looked at Ling, "Your tour of the mines is going to give you a headache, at the very least."

"I took shallow breaths," he reminded her.

Celia placed her hands on Ling's cheeks and kissed him on the forehead. "You're a brave man Ling Chou Fei. We won't forget you."

"I won't forget you either," Ling told her. "I promise."

William sniffled and Walt saw a tear trickle down his cheek. Ling's shortcut through the mines obviously had serious consequences, but Walt could not guess what they were. He seemed fine for the moment.

"Come on," Ling said to William, trying to avoid further discussion of his situation. "We'd better be going."

He hugged Celia and then walked to the door with William following, still sniffling. As he opened the door he pointed at Walt. "Stay hidden. We'll be back as soon as we can." Then Ling looked in Walt's eyes. "You'll be our salvation," he said and then added with a civility that was not characteristic of him, "Goodbye, Walt." He turned to William. "Remember," he advised his old friend, "zig-zag."

TWENTY-FIVE

When Ling and William were gone, Walt was alone with Celia for the first time since he'd arrived in Paralleladise. How long had he been here? Only a few days? It seemed much longer. The first two had flown by because he was loopy from the lethemine. And then he'd met Ling and William and learned to resist the memory loss. The time since he'd reunited with Celia in the underground hippo sanctuary seemed like ages. The melee he'd started at the Paralleladise community service seemed weeks ago, though he could only remember the sun rising once since then.

Ling had said that time ran differently here. Perhaps one day was a lifetime in Walt's real world. Perhaps his father was now a grandfather. Perhaps Acey was an old woman in Lexington.

Or perhaps time didn't matter in Paralleladise, since no one ever aged and, if you found your way back through your portal, you went back to the moment when you left your own world.

I've got to get back! Walt thought. Ling believed Walt would be the salvation of all hippos and everyone trapped in Paralleladise. And Walt surprised himself with the abilities of recall in the maze. He wondered if it were perhaps possible that he could be a Rememberer. But, even if he were capable, it would take thousands of years to help everyone trapped in Paralleladise remember their individual portals and keys. And there were more being kidnapped and trapped here every day.

Walt could not fathom the possibility of life without his family for thousands of years.

He looked at Celia, standing near the door where William and Ling had just departed. How long had she been in Paralleladise, he wondered? Had she been so desperate to escape after hundreds of years that she was willing to leave through a portal that was not her own—to live in the real world, though it was not the time or place she'd come from? And had her desperation made her agree to trap Walt in the portal in exchange for her freedom?

Walt could tell the evening sun was preparing to set by the suffusion of warm, orange light streaking through the crevices of thatching around this maintenance shed. A shaft lit Celia's face and he saw tears cascading on her cheeks. She was worried about Ling.

"What will happen to him?"

She shook her head. "I don't know. Some have come out of the mines with little damage. Others . . . Most . . ." She paused to collect herself. "There's always some memory loss."

Walt thought back to the moment he'd first met Ling at the Paralleladise replica of Lexington Middle School—how he'd mistaken him for a child, crouched underneath the teacher's desk in the classroom. Ling had been very focussed from the beginning—keeping them all moving, avoiding the pitfalls and finding solutions. He was resourceful and devoted to the idea of saving the captives of Sheron and NyXus.

"Why do you think he did it?" Walt asked. "Went through the mines."

Celia wiped tears from her cheeks and turned to Walt. "He believes in you. We all do. He's willing to sacrifice himself, because he hopes, one day, you'll be able to help us destroy NyXus."

Walt shook his head. The expectations of Ling and Celia and the others were overwhelming. He didn't want to live up to them. He wanted to go home.

"Celia," Walt whispered, "I can't. I just want to get back."

Celia studied him for a long moment, considering, and then nodded, sympathetically, "I know," she replied. "I was wrong to get you into this. I'm sorry." She walked to where Walt stood and gazed into his eyes, searchingly. "And I promise, if you can remember your portal and your key, I'll do everything I can to help you escape."

The sadness in her voice and the penitence of her response made Walt feel guilty. After all, she had come back to Paralleladise when she could have escaped forever. She had sacrificed her freedom to help Walt and the resistance fighters in their cause. And if he were to remember his portal and his key, if they were to escape together back to Lexington, she would be forever cut off from her own history.

"What about the Rememberer?" Walt asked.

"Romannie would tell you to go, too," Celia said, "if that's what you wanted. We are all here because we can't remember our key. But none of us wants any hippo to remain if they can find their way out. That is what we're fighting for. It's just that no one . . ." Celia paused, ". . . hardly anyone has ever remembered their key. But with your memory, you may just do it."

She walked to the ladder in the middle of the room that ascended to the loft and she started up. "Come on. We'll be safer up here if one of the patrols thinks to check."

Walt began to climb after her. He looked beyond her to the opening of the loft and an image flashed before his mind so fleetingly he could not grasp it except to see a figure climbing a ladder with Walt below, looking up. Was it Celia in the vision?

Walt closed his eyes to focus and bring back the image.

It was his father. Climbing the stepladder. Climbing it where? Then, Walt saw an image of his father hanging Christmas lights outside the house, standing on the old wooden stepladder he'd bought at a garage sale. But that wasn't it. Walt opened his eyes. Celia had reached the loft and was climbing in.

The attic! Walt suddenly remembered. His father had climbed up the ladder to show him the attic of their home. When was that? Why was he showing Walt the attic? What was in the attic to see?

Walt reached the loft now, too, and scooted in after Celia. The ceiling was low and they could not stand up, so they remained on their knees. Like the floor below, the loft was cluttered with maintenance equipment. There were tools and parts of tools, dusty crates and unmarked grain sacks.

Celia pulled a sack to her and smoothed it out like an oversized pillow. "Might as well make ourselves comfortable," she said, leaning against it. "It may take Ling and William a while to find a weeper who can lead us to Romannie."

Walt found several sacks piled in the corner and pulled them out, laying them next to each other and forming a soft mat to lie on.

"Why do the weepers know so much about Romannie," Walt asked. "I thought they weren't hippos."

"They track him daily. There's always one or two of them tailing him wherever he goes. We don't try to stop them. And one or two weepers try each day to get in to see him, to get help finding their way to their portal. They've got incredible memories and usually they can recall their portals but not their key. They think Romannie can help them."

"Can he?"

"Sometimes," Celia admitted. "But their emotional memories cloud the effects of their hippocampus and when they get close to their portals, they break down completely. There are weepers who have been here since the time of the first Rememberer, trying to see him . . . or her, daily or weekly for hundreds of years but never quite putting it all together."

Walt thought about the intensity of grief he'd seen in the boy who was carving "Cordelia" into the mud in the pathways of the village. Who was Cordelia, he wondered? And how many years had he been pining after her? How many visits had he made to the Rememberer, hoping to find his way back to her?

"How long have you been here?" Walt asked Celia.

Celia smiled. "Not so long as many."

"A hundred years? Two hundred?"

"Do I look that old?" she laughed, patting her hair as if primping. But she could see that Walt was intent on understanding, so she added, "You know how long I've been here, Walt."

"I do?"

"Think about it. It might help you remember your portal."

What did that mean? Celia gave cryptic answers to so many of his questions.

"Do you know my key?" Walt asked.

Celia shook her head. "No. Everything about your portal and key was wiped from my memory when I was sucked back into Paralleladise, just as it was from yours. I tried to remember. I knew what would happen when I went through the portal, so I tried to hang on to it. But when I awoke here, I couldn't remember anything.

The image of Walt's father climbing a stepladder to the attic flashed again in Walt's mind. His father was talking about how empty and uninteresting the attic was. And then an image of the attic itself replaced the image of his father and Walt could see the attic space as he had viewed it the day his father let him poke his head in to satisfy Walt's curiosity. Why was he curious about the attic?

"I do remember," Celia went on, "what happened before we went through the portal. I do remember that we were best friends, and I do remember trying to warn you of what was coming."

Walt studied Celia closely. She was hoping to assure him of their friendship in spite of her deception. Walt did not know what to think. She had deceived him before. Could he be sure she was not deceiving him now?

"How did you try to warn me?"

Celia put her fingertips to her forehead. "Try to remember," she whispered.

The loft was quickly becoming dark as the sun set in the Weeper Village. Celia features were obscured in shadows and dreamy, dusty rays retreated slowly in the thatching.

"Maybe we should get some sleep," Celia suggested, "while we have the chance. When Ling and William come back, we may have to move quickly."

Walt did not answer but gazed, instead, at the enigma that was Celia. How had she tried to warn him? He wracked his memory for an instance in which she may have hinted, ever so vaguely so that Sheron could not trace her mnemonic signature, at the world of Paralleladise. He could not think of one.

"The attic," he said to her, after several moments.

295

"What?"

"The portal is in the attic of my house."

The memory had come upon Walt all of sudden. He'd flashed on his father, showing him the attic entrance, and then fast-forwarded to a memory of a mysterious panel in the attic that his father had thought was a construction error. And then his mind had flashed forward again to a moment when he was standing in front of the portal, Sheron's tractor beam of light pulling him into it while he pushed Zelda—no, not Zelda! Walt closed his eyes and focussed on the remembered images. It was Acey!—She was the one he was trying to free from the force drawing her toward the portal.

"Acey was there," Walt told Celia without opening his eyes. "She was being pulled in. It was Acey they were after."

"Acey is like you," Celia said. "She has a very powerful memory. She gives off a very strong mnemonic signature. I didn't know. I didn't realize."

"And you were there," Walt went on, the recollection coming to him as he spoke. "You were trying to save Acey."

"I had no way of knowing Acey had such a strong mnemonic signature," Celia replied. "And when I saw you being pulled into the portal, I decided not to go through with the plan of sending you—or Acey—into the portal. I was trying to pull you back, but Sheron's grip was too strong. I couldn't do it. I tried. I do remember that."

"I remember, too," Walt said. His eyes were still closed, and he could almost feel Celia holding first his wrists and then his hands as he was dragged into the blinding shaft of light. He remembered thinking, at that moment, it was Celia trying to save him.

Walt opened his eyes to the darkened loft. Celia was just a shadow now. The rest of the room swirled as the effects of remembering so many details caused his head to throb. He groaned at the sensation that ran through his body.

"Easy," Celia said. "Not too much at once. It will come back to you eventually."

Walt concentrated on Celia's outline against the roof of the maintenance hut, to steady himself. Slowly, he lay down on the grain sack to let the feeling of vertigo pass.

"That's a good idea," Celia said. She was moving toward him. He felt her hand on his forehead, stroking his hair away from his face. "Lay back, Walt Walters. Relax. It will come back to you. It will. But you can't force it."

Walt closed his eyes again, and it helped to settle his throbbing brain. He'd been close to seeing it all, he realized, and he didn't want to stop now. But the headache was too strong and closing his eyes felt too good.

While he slept, Walt dreamed fitful and erratic dreams that shifted constantly between one scene and another.

He dreamt he was being chased by Sheron down a stark white corridor, like those in the maze. Sheron was not a bright light in his dream, but an actual monster—though more silly looking than frightening. He had the body of a gorilla and the head of Professor Fitzmer and Walt only realized he was Sheron because he kept roaring, "I am Sheron. You cannot escape."

And then, the scene shifted and Walt was being pursued by Sheron, only now they were running in front of the courthouse on Lexington square and Sheron was shouting, "Those who forget history are doomed to repeat it." Sheron chased him, never gaining or losing ground, around the square and along the streets of Lexington. They were running in the direction of Walt's house, but suddenly, the scene shifted and they were out in farm country running along a quiet, asphalt road.

Walt kept checking behind him on Sheron's progress when suddenly, Sheron disappeared altogether. Walt stopped and turned around and found himself standing in front of an old, white farmhouse, and after a moment, Celia walked out of the front door and off the porch. She was holding a small, white terrier puppy.

"Hi, it's me," she said. "And this is my dog."

"We need to get out of here," Walt said, in his dream. "There's a monster chasing me."

Suddenly, Celia became horrified and yelled, "Run!"

So Walt turned to run down the country road, but found he was on his own street and he was not running but riding his bicycle as fast as he was able to his house. He jumped off and let the bike clamor to the ground as he dashed in the front door. "Mom! Dad!" he yelled. "Acey's in danger!"

When no one answered, he knew to go straight to the attic, but when he climbed the stairs, Walt realized he was not in his own house at all. He was on the second floor of a home that seemed vaguely familiar, but that he knew he'd never been in before. He was walking down the hall, and a tremendous thumping was shaking the house, like an earthquake.

At the end of the hall was a door and Walt saw the knob turning as he approached. The door swung open on its own. Walt entered a bedroom where a woman in overalls was lying on the bed. She looked at Walt and then at a man who was sitting under a reading lamp in a chair at the opposite end of the room. He was smoking a pipe and holding a book.

"Who are you?" Walt asked them.

"Why, we're Alice's parents," the man said. "You must be the Withers boy."

"Walters," Walt corrected. "Who is Alice?"

Neither the man nor woman answered, and Walt was about to ask again when he realized they were suddenly frozen, like statues. Walt turned back into the hallway, and Celia was there in front of him, with the little white dog.

"Celia," Walt said, relieved to see her. "Who is Alice?"

"She's a very mixed up girl," Celia replied, sternly. And then the dog turned into a book and Celia handed it to Walt, saying, "Here. This ought to be confusing."

Walt opened the book and saw on the first page the words:

Property of Alice Shaworth.
DO NOT FOLD, SPINDLE
OR EXPECT A REWARD FOR YOUR EFFORTS.

But as Walt flipped through the pages, he found them all blank.

"What is this?" he asked Celia. But Celia was now Acey.

"It's a map," Acey explained. From under her arm Acey pulled a map, rolled up like a scroll, and handed it to Walt.

Walt unrolled it and found that, while it looked like the parchment of an ancient treasure map, there was only a square drawn on it and in the middle of the square was a single word: "Attic."

"We have to get to the attic," Walt told Acey.

"That's what I've been trying to tell you, but would you listen!" Acey replied. "Let's go." But when she turned around, she seemed lost.

"I think that's it," Walt told her, pointing to a door in the middle of the hallway, next to the bathroom. They went to the door and opened it to find a stairway, leading to the attic. "We're in Alice Shaworth's house!" Walt realized.

"She's a mixed-up girl," Acey responded. "You should help un-mix her."

"How?"

"I don't know," Acey shrugged. "I'm not a hippo."

Acey started up the stairs and Walt followed her, but when they got to the landing where the attic should have been they found another staircase, leading up another flight. And when they followed that staircase, they found another that looked exactly the same as the previous two.

"This is ridiculous," Walt complained.

"Maybe we should just jump," Acey suggested, pointing up to a rectangular hole in the ceiling. And then she leapt into the air and was swooshed through the opening as if by an enormous vacuum. Walt did the same and soon they were inside the attic, which looked exactly like the attic in their own house—filled with insulation and rafters and nothing else—except in the corner was a closet.

Walt carefully stepped from one two-by-four rafter to the next, making his way over to the closet. Acey followed him complaining the attic was too drafty for kindergartners.

When they got to the closet, Walt pulled on the handle.

"It's locked," he told Acey. But Acey had turned into Zelda.

"You need a key, knucklehead," Zelda explained, and from under her arm she pulled a piece of wood, etched with symbols.

"What is this?" Walt asked, taking the board from Zelda.

"It's a warning," Zelda told him. "Don't lose it or I'll have to give you another one." From under her arm she pulled a worn, black, leather portfolio and undid its clasp. "Put it in here for safe keeping."

Walt took the portfolio and opened it. At first, the wood looked too big for the open flap, but as he slid it in, it shrank to a perfect fit.

Suddenly, the closet door flew open and Zelda was instantly pulled through it by a gorilla arm that reached out from a beam of light and dragged her in.

"This is so stupid!" Zelda protested as she flew past Walt into the closet.

The door slammed shut and the scene shifted and now Walt was outside standing at the edge of the canyon where the banders had attacked and MacGruder was spirited away by Sheron. But now MacGruder was at his side, looking into the canyon.

"That sister of yours," he said. "She's a firecracker."

"I suppose I have to get her," Walt muttered. Then he crawled out onto the thin log footbridge that spanned the canyon. He leaned over and maneuvered himself until he was hanging upside down by his knees from the log. Then he stretched his hands out, reaching into the foggy depths below him.

A pair of hands reached out of the fog and grabbed Walt's. He pulled as hard as he could until Celia's face emerged from the mist.

And then Walt Walters awoke.

The loft of the Weeper Village maintenance hut was totally dark now, but Walt could make out the form of Celia, a few feet away. He smiled and crawled over to where she slept, her head propped up against a grain sack.

"Wake up," he said softly, brushing her hair from her forehead. "I've figured out the portal. I know the key."

301

Celia breathed deep-sleep breaths.

"Wake up," Walt repeated gently. "I've got it figured out."

She stirred and murmured.

"Wake up," Walt whispered. "Wake up, Alice."

TWENTY-SIX

Celia woke, smiling at the call of her real name.

"You're a smart boy, Walt Walters," she said.

"Alice Shaworth, Celia Washroth." Walt shook his head at the simple anagram. "I should have unscrambled it when I first saw the name on the diary."

"You were probably too dazzled by my beauty to think straight."

Walt pulled Celia up to a sitting position. "I've figured out the portal," he told her. "And the key."

"What . . .?"

"It's a placard," Walt said.

Celia's watched his eyes. "What do you remember?" she whispered.

"There's some gibberish on it," Walt told her. "They look like an alphabet but aren't really." Suddenly, Walt was very excited. "We need to get back to the portal, which is in the attic of my house. That's how we'll get out of here."

"How did you remember the placard?"

"I dreamt," Walt explained. "I dreamt about you and the diary you left and the portfolio and then I saw the plaque."

"You remembered the diary?" Celia asked. "So you did see that I tried to warn you."

"What do you mean?"

"I wrote the diary for you. To let you know what was happening . . . what was going to happen, so that when you were summoned by Sheron, you'd know it was dangerous."

Walt was confused. He had not reasoned it all out, yet. "I thought you wrote the diary in 1934?"

"No, no," Celia shook her head. "I was only nine years old in 1934. And that's how old I was when I came back through the portal and met you. Remember? Third grade. Mrs. Dickinson's class."

"So, you wrote the diary after you came back?"

"To warn you," Celia explained. "I had to let you know what was happening without giving too much away. I didn't want Sheron to be able to locate me. It was the only way I could think of."

"But . . ." Walt started. "I don't understand. The diary wasn't real?"

Celia put her hands on Walt's shoulders as if to hold him steady against all the new information bombarding him. "It was real. It was true. I am Alice Shaworth and I lived on Mill Street, in Lexington before I was captured and taken to Paralleladise. Mill Street used to be one of the major county roads leading all the way into town. But then the town grew and new subdivisions were added and streets renamed. Mill Street became just a little road and then picked up again at the county line. Where I lived . . . where Mill Street used to be . . ."

Walt nodded, starting to catch on. "Is where the portal is," he finished her sentence.

"And where your house is now," Celia went on. "You live on what used to be Mill Street—where my house was in 1934."

"But what about the garage sale where I got the portfolio?"

"That house is still on a part of the original Mill Street—not too far from your house."

"The old man who gave me the portfolio?"

"He's one of the four hippos who escaped with me through the portal. He's the man you knew as my uncle, but you didn't recognize him when he gave you the portfolio."

Walt had never had a good look at Celia's uncle in the four years that he knew her—he'd only seen the man from a distance or when his face was in shadows or turned away. And now, an image of the old man who had given Walt the diary and the portfolio flashed in front of his mind. He could have been the same man.

Celia went on, "I wrote the diary so I could give you bits of information about what was happening, what was going to happen, so you could understand. And remember. I wrote the entries and then put the diary in the portfolio for you to read when you discovered it." Suddenly a fresh memory came back to Celia as she retold the story. "We read them together, actually. Remember—that day in your room."

"You must have been frustrated when I let the portfolio sit in my closet for such a long time" Walt said, understanding now the efforts Celia made to alert him.

"I learned a lot about patience in Paralleladise," Celia responded. "And I wasn't too concerned until you told me you were hearing noises from the attic. That's when I knew Sheron was starting to lure you in."

"But how did you get more writing to appear in the diary. There were entries and then blank pages and then more entries appeared."

Celia smiled at her own cleverness. "That night, after we cleaned out your closet," she explained, "your family went out for pizza."

Walt tried to remember. It seemed like a long time ago.

"And while you were out, I went to your house and wrote more diary entries. I really wasn't trying to be mysterious—I was just trying to get you to search the attic and find the portal before Sheron trapped you—so you could prepare yourself."

Walt nodded. Celia had been very careful with the diary entries, he realized—giving as little information as she thought she needed to make Walt aware of what was happening. But he had been slow to understand or to believe it was real.

"And the third time," Celia reminded him, "I added the new entries when you loaned the diary to me at school."

Walt thought through the chain of events. He recalled now that he had taken the diary to school to show Celia and she had kept it until late that evening when she called to tell him new entries had appeared.

"Do you remember," Celia continued, "that I wrote about the placard in the diary?" She paused letting Walt digest the information. He thought he'd been on to something when he remembered the plaque. Now he was learning that other hippos had recalled the same key. "Many of us have remembered the plaque—or something like it. Some carving in stone or wood at each portal. But hardly anyone has been able to figure out what to do with it."

"We'll figure it out. I know we can. We'll figure it out when we get there," Walt assured her, not wanting to waste time. He was sure if he saw the placard again he would understand how to use it to return to his own world.

"The Rememberer can help us," Celia said. "If we could get to him."

Walt shook his head. "No. Let's go to the portal . . . try to figure it out ourselves."

"Oh, Walt," Celia said, "I know I got you into this, and I have never regretted anything more. But we can't go back. We'll be caught for sure. So many have tried to return to their portals to decipher the key, but Sheron finds them first. He knows the moment you touch the plaque."

"No . . ." Walt started. He did not want to wait.

"And if the Rememberer can help you recall how your key works, it may help others figure out how their keys work. We could help others escape."

As soon as Celia spoke the words he knew she was right. If a placard was the key to everyone's portal, they had to let someone know before they escaped. But now that he'd remembered it, he was afraid to wait, afraid he would be captured and have his memory scrubbed before he could get to the portal and decipher the key.

Below the loft, the door to the maintenance hut suddenly opened. Celia put her finger to Walt's lips in a signal to remain quiet. They listened to footsteps below and then heard William's whispered voice:

"Halloa! Are you here? Hello?"

"They're back," Celia whispered, scrambling to the ladder. "Up here," she called softly as she descended.

Walt followed her to the ladder. He saw William and Ling as shadowy forms in the darkness below.

"I was beginning to worry," Celia called softly to them as she descended.

"We ran into … a spot of trouble," William whispered confidentially.

"What happened?"

At the bottom of the ladder Walt jumped to the floor next to Celia. He saw William gesture to Ling with a nod of his head and realized Ling had not said anything since they'd entered.

"Ling?" Celia said, concern in her voice. She placed her hand on his shoulder.

Ling looked at her blankly. "Hello," he said, mildly. He studied her face as if trying to remember it. "Hello . . . Alice?"

"Oh, Ling," Celia gasped out sadly.

At Ling's side, William began to sob, softly. "It came on all of a sudden. It was that short-cut through the mine. He had to be a bloody hero."

"What's happening?" Walt asked anxiously. "What's wrong?"

Celia was stroking Ling's face as if the gentle gesture could bring back her old friend. "He's losing his memories. The lethemine he breathed in the mines is destroying his hippocampus."

Anxiety rushed over Walt. Ling and his power of memory had seemed so strong, so invincible. Of the hippos Walt had met, Ling had seemed the most invulnerable. "Shouldn't he do mnemonics? Shouldn't we jog his memory?"

"I've been trying," William answered tearfully. "It's going so fast. He's losing everything so fast."

Ling was coherent enough to realize what was happening for he tried to show them that he could still perform his mnemonic exercises, "My name is Ling Chou Fei. I live in Xiang Lin Province. My father was a . . ." Ling paused. His eyes registered confusion. He began again, "My name is Ling Chou Fei..." but then he fell silent as if he'd forgotten he'd been reciting at all.

"Ling," Celia whispered sadly.

"We've got to do something," Walt said urgently. There had to be some way to restore his memories. Walt stepped between Celia and Ling. He leaned over at the waist to look the Asian man in the eyes. "Your province is in Mongolia," Walt tried, hoping to spur some reaction, any reaction would be fine.

Ling nodded.

"Do you understand that? About your province?" Walt asked.

Ling shook his head.

"Your father was a blacksmith?"

Ling studied Walt, trying to determine whether this was true. Finally, he nodded. "If you say so," he said calmly. "I trust you, young man."

"My name . . ." Walt tested, "is Sprat."

"I trust you . . . Sprat," Ling assured him.

William cried out, "It's going so fast!"

Walt turned to Celia, "What can we do?"

Celia was looking at her friend mournfully. "I don't know..." she said. "I don't know. Maybe . . . maybe Romannie . . ."

"Yes!" William blurted out. "The Rememberer. He can help. He could do something." William looked at Celia. "He could help. Couldn't he? He has tricks for this sort of thing."

"I don't know," Celia said. There was little hope in her voice.

"We've got to try," Walt told her. He turned to William. "Did you find a weeper who knows where Max Romannie is?"

"Yes . . ." William said quickly, as if just remembering their mission. "We found a weeper who knows someone who shares a hut with. . .," he started but then stopped himself. Excited at the possibility of helping Ling, he had obviously almost revealed something he meant to conceal. "No," he corrected himself.

William looked at Celia, like a little boy who'd said too much. At first, Celia was confused. But then recognition washed over her face. Her eyes widened.

"She's here?"

William nodded. "She's still a weeper."

"Did you tell her?"

William shook his head. "I didn't see her. She lives in a hut at the other end of the village."

Walt glanced back and forth from Celia to William, trying to decipher the cryptic conversation. "What?"

Celia looked to the floor, lost in thought. Walt could see she was recollecting some significant event and trying to come up with a plan of action. After several moments, she looked up at William. "Is she . . . all right? Is she . . . coherent?"

"I don't know," William said softly. "All I know is that she's been to see the Rememberer recently."

"What?" Walt asked. "Who is she?"

Slowly, Celia turned to face Walt. She studied his eyes as if trying to gauge what he was capable of understanding. When she spoke, her voice was heavy. "Walt, you know I came back through the portal to Lexington—the very same portal I was abducted through in 1934?" Celia started.

"Yes," Walt nodded "I know . . ." But before he could finish his sentence he realized what she was getting at. He asked, "Why didn't you go back to 1934 if it was your portal and your key?"

Celia searched for the words to respond.

310

"It wasn't your key," Walt said, putting the pieces together. "It was . . ."

Walt paused. Whose key was it? Celia had already told him she was abducted through the Lexington portal. If she returned to a different time, it could only mean she'd come back using the key of someone who'd been abducted from the same portal but at a different time—who had gone through four years ago, when Celia had come back. Someone who...

Celia was watching him, letting him figure it all out.

And suddenly, Walt knew the answer.

"Mom," he whispered.

TWENTY-SEVEN

William led the way with Ling at his side. Walt and Celia followed as they hurried along the paths of the Weeper Village. There were no stars or streetlights, but unattended campfires burned outside the huts around the village to light the way.

This section of the village was eerily quiet and empty, though, in the distance they heard the cries and lamentations of the weepers. By night, Walt thought, the wailing of the weepers was even more tragic and anxious.

As they hustled forward, William reminded Ling of facts about his past to keep his mind focused and his memory engaged.

"Your name is Ling Chou Fei. You are from the village of Mai Laos in the Xiang Din province. Your father was a soldier. Your great, great, great grandmother was the sixth Rememberer." Ling did not respond to William's recitation and Walt couldn't tell if the reminders were helping or only making William feel useful.

"Walt," Celia said. Her voice was heavy with concern. "There are some things you should know about your mother."

"Like what?"

"I'm not sure what condition we'll find her in."

"It doesn't matter," Walt replied.

"I didn't know if she was still…still functioning. I didn't know what happened to her. That's why I didn't tell you. She may . . . She may not remember you. She may not remember anything about her life."

"It doesn't matter," Walt repeated.

He was thinking about the last time he saw his mother, four years earlier. It was a typical school morning. They'd had breakfast. Walt was a third-grader then. Zelda was in fifth grade. Acey, eighteen months old, had only recently started to walk with confidence. She was sitting in her high chair eating Cheerios dipped in peanut butter when Walt and Zelda left for school.

Walt's mother kissed his forehead and handed him his lunchbox as he shrugged his backpack over one shoulder. "I hope you have a good day," she said. And Walt, who had hated school in third grade and every other grade, groused about having to go at all as he walked out the door. He waved to his mother from the street as they joined other neighborhood grade-schoolers at the bus stop.

That was the last glimpsed he'd had of her.

When he came home from school that afternoon, she was gone. Acey was sleeping peacefully in her crib. She had not been awakened from her afternoon nap but otherwise everything was just as it always was except Zelda, who'd come in a few minutes earlier, met him at the front door with the greeting, "I can't find Mom." They made a thorough search of the house and found a load of laundry in the dryer and a message on the notepad near the phone that read, "Zelda, Dentist on Thursday." But this was not Thursday and there was no other sign of their mother. She would not have left the house without Acey—even for a moment. Something was wrong.

When she still had not returned a half hour later, Zelda called Mr. Walters at work. He came home immediately and searched the house again. He phoned their friends and relatives and neighbors, but no one had heard from her all day. Then he called the police.

Now, four years later, Walt finally knew what had happened to his mother that day. He could piece together her disappearance, speculate on the details of her abduction.

Perhaps she had just put Acey in her crib, or perhaps she had made a dentist appointment for Zelda when the house started shaking violently. She would not have remembered the shaking from previous days—if, in fact, like Walt and Celia, the day of her abduction was preceded by other, unremembered attempts to draw her to the portal—because Sheron was blocking her recollection. And only after time would she have thought to check the attic. There, she would have seen the portal, blazing with Sheron's light, attracting and scaring her at the same time. By the time she realized it was a trap—that she was being dragged irresistibly into the corridor of light—she would not have been able to stop herself from being pulled in. Perhaps her last thoughts as Sheron's beam clenched her were of leaving little Acey asleep in her crib, or what Walt and Zelda would do when they came home and found she was gone.

Walt was imagining his mother's fears when, suddenly, from another parallel path a few yards away, a loud cry burst above the steady roar of the weepers. Walt, Celia and the others turned to see a half a dozen or more weepers moving in the shadows, running among the village huts in a line as if they were being chased or hurrying to get somewhere.

"What's going on?" William called back to Celia.

Celia shook her head. "There's no time to find out."

Something was wrong, Walt could tell, seeing the weepers scurrying off into the darkness. They moved with purpose, as if pursuing something so interesting as to momentarily distract them from their usual grief. He could not worry about it. He had to concentrate on finding his mother.

"She may not have any memory at all," Walt heard Celia saying beside him, trying to prepare him for the encounter.

"You came back through the portal with her key," Walt reminded her. "Only she could have known what the key was. She remembered that."

"Yes," Celia admitted, "but when I last saw her, the last thing I saw . . . Sheron had her. And then the portal closed."

Walt was beginning to understand. "She was trying to escape?"

"Yes."

"And she was taking you with her?"

Celia nodded. "She was helping me and three other hippos escape Paralleladise."

"But they weren't going through their own portals."

"They'd given up. They just wanted to get out of any portal they could."

Ahead, William and Ling slowed. A three-person patrol was approaching a few yards away. William glanced around for a place to hide and then led them behind the closest hut.

"This way," he whispered. They huddled in the hut's shadow and a moment later the patrol marched by, not seeing them in the darkness. They heard the patrol leader bark out directions as he passed: ". . . we'll flush them out, so keep a sharp eye…"

In the distance they heard the indistinguishable roar of a crowd of people—a sound different from the wail of the weepers.

Ling, who hadn't spoken at all since they'd left the utility hut, pointed over the roof of one dwelling where a haze of light

315

illuminated the dark sky beyond it, as if one of the small campfires had flamed into a larger conflagration.

"What's going on?" Walt wondered.

Celia shook her head. "I don't know. I don't like it."

"We're almost there," William promised. He stepped back on to the main thoroughfare, but another patrol, hustling from the other direction was nearly on top of them and William ducked behind the hut again.

He let out a sigh of relief when they passed. "The patrols are thick tonight."

Now, all four of the fugitives continued along the paths through the village. Walt thought about the details of his mother's escape attempt with Celia, four years earlier.

"You said you were sent back to get me," Walt reminded Celia as they hurried along.

"There was every reason to believe that we wouldn't make it," Celia explained. "Your mom had demonstrated remarkable powers of memory, but we didn't really believe she would remember her key—it had never been done before. And even if she escaped, we knew Sheron might recapture her."

"Then, why did you go along?"

"We knew if she did recall her key, it meant she had unprecedented powers of recall. And that meant her offspring would most likely have a very powerful memory."

Walt shook his head. "I don't get it. Were you trying to escape or coming to get me?"

"Both," Celia told him. "I didn't want to go through the portal with your mother's key. I wanted to go through my own portal, with my own key--to be with my family again. But your mother, she . . . she wanted to bring me back, to save me from spending eternity in Paralleladise. And . . ." Celia hesitated.

316

"What?" Walt prompted.

"And the Rememberer," Celia went on haltingly. "He asked me to go for the sake of the hippos. If your mother didn't make it, or was recaptured, I was to bring one of her offspring back through the portal—someone who was capable of becoming the next Rememberer."

"Why didn't she make it?"

Celia shook her head. "She made sure everyone else was through the portal first. I was the last to go, just before her, when Sheron caught us."

"He caught you, too?"

"He had us both," Celia narrated, reliving the memory as she spoke. "He caught us and was holding us back as the portal closed. Your mother fought him, fiercely."

"I thought Sheron was a beam of light."

"He can take many forms," Celia told Walt. "He's very powerful and he caught your mother and me, but somehow she managed to free me of his grip and I fell backwards toward the portal, just as it was closing. Then your mother got one hand free—I don't know how. But she freed her hand and pushed me through the portal before it snapped closed. The last thing I saw was Sheron, furiously angry, picking her up and holding her, like a ragdoll, above his head."

Walt tried to envision the scene but he could only imagine a beam of light transforming itself into the shape of a luminescent giant and picking his mother up. And he could only picture her as his mother—as the kind face that smiled to cheer him up when he was discouraged; the soothing voice that calmed his fears or made him laugh, the gentle hands that stroked his cheek to wake him in the morning or that circled to hug him when he came home from school. The woman in his memory was not a fierce warrior against monstrous demons in an alternate universe.

"Walt," Celia said, a pleading tone in her voice "please, just prepare yourself. I can't imagine what Sheron did to her memory after he caught her. But he would have done whatever was necessary to stop her from remembering her key again. Even if it meant totally obliterating her hippocampus."

Walt remembered what MacGruder had said about those who had escaped Paralleladise and been recaptured—that their memories were so totally destroyed afterwards that they could not even recall their names or how to tie their shoes. He pictured his mother, a hopeless vegetable, unable to recollect anything from the past or even think clearly from moment to moment. Worse, she would be a weeper vegetable, sobbing ceaselessly with an overwhelming sense of loss, but unable to remember the source of her mourning.

Walt shook his head. It didn't matter, he told himself. He would get her back through the portal somehow. Doctors, specialists in the real world would help her, would restore her memories. Or even if they could not, it was better that she be with her family than left here in this sad, cold world.

Walt was so lost in planning the rescue of his mother that he didn't see William and Ling stop abruptly in front of him or notice the commotion that brought them to a dead halt as they rounded a turn and came into a small village square.

"No, good lord, no!" William cried out. Walt and Celia stopped short behind him and Ling.

Then Walt saw what was alarming William. Across the square was the source of the dancing light they'd seen from a distance—one of the huts of Weeper Village was on fire and blazed brightly and intensely, shooting flames high into the dark, night sky. The source of the cries and wails was here, too, as several dozen weepers were gathered around the burning building, shocked and confused, calling out indecipherable cries of anguish.

The weepers had formed a loose circle around the blazing hut and they swooned and rocked, contorting their bodies in a wild dance of weeping and screaming at the conflagration before them. It was a frightening sight, as if a mob of witches and warlocks had gathered for a primitive and unholy ritual. Their shadows, lit by the fire of the blazing hut, darted in bizarre shapes across the open ground of the square.

"What's going on?" Celia called to William.

William pointed to the burning hut, "That's it!" His voice was a mix of incredulity and despair.

"What?" Walt asked, feeling panic rise up from his stomach. "My mom?"

But before William could answer, a weeper woman spotted them and broke off from the crowd around the hut. She stumbled toward them, crying violently and waving her hands above her head in horror.

"It's a trap!" she shouted at William. "It's a trap!"

Celia grabbed William's arm. "What is she saying?"

"That's the woman who told me where to find your mother," William said, looking at Walt, wholly confused.

"They took her," the woman was now shouting. "They took her away!"

She was only a few feet from them, now, and Walt could see her clearly. She had long black hair, stringy and uncombed, that obscured her face. She wore a simple brown dress that might have once been a cloth sack, with a rope tied around the middle. She was barefoot, hunched over and shaking from side to side.

She looked like a castaway on a deserted island who has finally seen a ship come ashore only to realize too late it was a pirate vessel. "It's a trap! Run!" she screamed.

Out of the corner of his eye, Walt saw movement to his left. He turned to spot a patrol of six men approaching.

"Look," Celia shouted, pointing in the other direction.

Another patrol was coming at them from the right and when Walt looked behind them to see if they could retreat in the direction they'd come from, he saw yet another patrol of eight determined guards marching briskly in their direction. If setting the hut ablaze was a trap to lure Walt and the others out of hiding, it worked perfectly. There was no place to run.

"This way!" Walt heard a cry from beyond the old woman. He looked over her head and saw a tall man in a brown robe signaling to them from among the circle of weepers surrounding the conflagration. "This way!" He swooped his arm like a hook to draw them on.

"Achebe!" Celia shouted and, without waiting to explain, she pushed Walt ahead and started them both running across the village square toward the man in the robe.

"Come along," Walt heard William cry to Ling, but he did not look back to see if they were following.

Walt and Celia ran to the man she'd called Achebe, who pulled them both to his chest in a hug of protection. He was a big man, seven feet tall, Walt estimated, and his long arm totally surrounded Walt's body. But he was certainly not big enough to protect them from the assault of the twenty or more patrol guards who were approaching.

Walt craned his head to see how close the guards were and realized Achebe had no intention of fighting them off. He'd been waiting for William and Ling to catch up, and now that they joined the group, he turned toward the burning building with purpose.

"It's going to be hot!" he called. "Cover your heads!"

"We're not going to . . ." Walt heard William begin to protest, but Achebe did not wait to hear his complaint. Still holding Walt and Celia in his arms, he ran straight toward the door of the burning hut.

"This is not a good idea!" Walt could hear William calling. But, even over the din of the weeper cries and the shouts "Get them!" from the pursuing patrol guards, he could sense William and Ling following close behind.

In another moment, they were at the entrance of the hut and, without pausing or missing a step, Achebe managed to kick the fiery bamboo and thatched door open with such power that it snapped off its hinges and flew wildly into the burning building.

"We'll be scorched to cinders," William warned helplessly, following them, with Ling, into the blazing inferno.

Walt felt the hairs on his arms stand up against the intense heat as he half-ran and was half-carried by Achebe into the conflagration. He knew, in the back of his mind, that if he'd had time to consider his actions, he would not have so unquestioningly dashed into a death-trap in the arms of a strange giant. But he had no time to think and Celia seemed to trust the man who held them, and even William, who clearly doubted the wisdom of the escape route, trusted this Achebe enough to follow.

The blast of heat inside the hut was overwhelming and the smoke made it almost impossible to breathe or see what was going on. But just as they entered the door on one side of the hut, Walt could see the far wall of the structure collapsing at the opposite end of the floor. The roof would go in a minute, he realized, and they would all be buried beneath the flaming rafters.

Suddenly, he felt the strong arms of the tall, athletic man who had carried them into seeming doom release him and Walt and Celia both fell to the floor.

"Achebe!" Celia shouted. It was impossible to see even a foot ahead in the dense smoke, and Walt only caught a glimpse of Achebe's legs as they hurried ahead.

Behind them, William and Ling shuffled forward, coughing in the overpowering smoke and crying out for direction. "Where did you go? Achebe? Where are you?"

For a moment, Walt worried that Achebe had somehow been part of the trap the old woman had warned them about. That he had led them into this burning building and was leaving them there, blinded by the smoke, with no escape.

"Celia!" Walt cried out, overcome by the smoke and heat and feeling the need to say some final word to his friend.

And then, Achebe's voice rang out over the smoke—not threatening or panicked, but almost sing-song in its nonchalance. "Watch your fingers and toes!" he called out.

And then, once again, Walt felt himself falling.

TWENTY-EIGHT

Walt did not fall far this time. A moment later his hands and knees hit solid earth as he landed in a little tunnel just under the floor of the burning weeper shack.

He heard the grunts of the others as they fell into the tunnel, too. The floor of the hut must have contained a trap door, Walt reasoned, and the man called Achebe had somehow opened the door to drop them through it.

"Mind your head." This was Achebe's voice just ahead. In the darkness and smoke, Walt could see nothing, but, above him, he heard gears grinding and guessed it was the trap door closing.

"Forward!" Achebe called, and Walt felt someone nudge him from behind in the direction of Achebe's voice. He began crawling forward, uncertain of what lay in front of or behind him and trusting to the voice of this stranger who had just led them into a burning building.

"This way," Walt heard William advising Ling.

"It's okay," came the reassuring voice of Celia. "Achebe is one of us. He's a hippo."

In the disorienting darkness, Walt found it hard to be reassured. Just because Achebe was a hippo did not mean he had a good escape plan. Besides, anything Celia knew about Achebe she knew from four years ago and much could have changed since then.

Walt heard the lament of weepers and the confused cries of the village patrols above his head and realized they must be crawling right underneath the wild crowd that had gathered around the burning hut. If they put out the fire and did not find the trap door to the tunnel, the patrols would probably believe that Walt and the others had foolishly thrown themselves into the conflagration and perished rather than be caught.

"Keep your voices down," Achebe called up ahead. "And keep moving."

They crawled forward for several minutes in the darkness, leaving the smoke and the noise of the Weeper Village behind them. No one seemed to be following and in a few more minutes they were crawling in an eerie black silence, as the noise of the crowd died out.

Then, suddenly, Achebe stopped. Now, Walt could sense the order of the crawling fugitives, for he ran into Celia who had stopped behind Achebe and then felt William run into him. The disoriented travelers paused a moment to catch their breath. The air was still and stuffy in this tiny tunnel, a yard tall and a yard wide.

Where were they going? Walt had only a moment to wonder, and then he realized Celia was moving once again in front of him, inching forward. Somehow, she was squeezing by Achebe and Walt heard the tall man say, "Get ready to slide," and then he heard a whispered yelp from Celia as her voice moved off quickly into the distance.

"Celia?" Walt cried out, but instead of Celia, he felt a big hand on his shoulder—Achebe's hand—and it was pulling him forward. The tunnel must have widened slightly here, for Walt felt Achebe guiding him ahead, encouraging him to go pass, to follow Celia.

Again, Achebe warned "Get ready to slide," and Walt had only a split second to wonder what that meant when he felt himself abruptly sliding down a steep decline, steeper and faster than the fastest playground slide.

Down and down he slid, moving much too quickly to stop himself with his arms and legs against the side of the tunnel. He felt the solid floor of the tunnel whooshing beneath him. Behind him he heard a panicked yelp from William and then Ling, and knew that they, too, had just crawled unprepared unto the steep sliding tunnel.

Walt guessed he was descending for a full minute at a speed so fast a whistling wind sounded in his ears. If he did not slow down, he knew, he would hit whatever was at bottom dangerously and painfully fast.

But he did not hit anything at the bottom of the slide. Suddenly, the tunnel ended abruptly at a drop off, like a rain sewer ending at the river, and Walt felt himself sailing through the air, projected out of the tunnel by the speed of his descent and flung several feet forward into the night sky. He had only a moment to realize he was out of the tunnel and soaring through the air, only a moment to worry about the pain he would feel when he struck the ground. Then he crashed with a tremendous splash into a deep pool of water.

Walt had not taken a breath before plunging into the tepid pool of whatever he had fallen into, and, in surprise, he took a little water into his lungs as he splashed down, but then understood what was happening enough to know he should hold his breath. He heard, above him at the surface, another huge splash and guessed it was William falling into the water after him. And a moment later, Walt heard Ling's splash.

Walt knew, as his body's sinking momentum slowed that, in a moment he would cease to descend and start back up again. He looked to the surface and guessed that he was fifteen feet deep or more. He kicked against the descent and, in another moment, felt himself begin to rise.

He broke the surface of the water, gasping for breath, and just in time to see the long muscular body of Achebe sailing above him, just coming out of the tunnel and arcing gracefully and swiftly into a nearly splash-less dive into the water.

"Woo-hoo!" Achebe shouted like a delighted child at a summer water park.

When Achebe was below the surface, Walt looked around, kicking steadily with his feet to stay afloat. The tunnel they had crawled through and that had dumped them in the water was several yards above, its mouth gaping in the face of the rock cliffs that surrounded much of the lake or sea they were in. The tall cliffs ascended fifty feet and were too steep to climb. In the opposite direction the water extended to the horizon and as far as Walt could see in the dim light of what was slowly becoming a Paralleladise dawn.

"Celia," Walt called.

"Right here," his friend replied. Walt saw her ten yards away, treading water and studying their location just as he was.

A moment later, William's and then Ling's heads broke the surface next to Walt, and then, after another moment, Achebe splashed above the water, smiling and exhilarated.

"That was fun!" he shouted to no one in particular.

"Achebe!" Celia cried out. "Thank goodness you came when you did."

"Alice, Alice!" Achebe kicked his way through to throw his arm around her. "My girl."

"I've missed you," Celia told him, kissing his cheek.

"Didn't think I'd ever see you again, girl. You've grown! I barely recognized you." Achebe shifted around. "And this must be Walt."

"Achebe!" William broke in before Walt could respond. "You've got to help! We're losing Ling."

"William! Ling!" Achebe hailed them, his voice losing only a little of its good humor at William's report. "We were worried about you two."

"Do you know where the Rememberer is? Can you get us to him? Ling is fading fast."

William had paddled over to Celia and Achebe as he spoke and now, along with Ling, they were huddled in a small circle of hippos, treading water. Achebe put his hand on William's shoulder.

"First things first," the big man warned, more seriously now. "We should get out of the water. We can't float all day." Then, once again Achebe laughed and looked up at the mouth of the tunnel that seemed to smile above them. "It was a fun ride, though."

And with that Achebe started kicking and stroking with his long arms, swimming in the direction of the towering cliffs. Uncertain, Walt and the others followed, knowing they would not be able to climb the steep rock wall when they got there.

Achebe slowed to let Walt catch up with him. "Your mother dug that tunnel," he reported.

"My mother?" Walt repeated. "You know my mother?"

"She and a whole bunch of other weepers. Don't know how they did it," Achebe went on. "But she organized them, got them to stop weeping enough to start digging tunnels. She's an amazing woman."

"They've taken her," Walt reported. Perhaps Achebe could help find and rescue her. "Do you know where they went?"

"I have some ideas," Achebe replied enigmatically, but then, with a powerful kick of his legs, he shot forward in the water and moved ahead of Walt.

They were approaching the base of the cliffs now and the rising sun was beginning to illuminate their way. Walt could see what Achebe had in mind, where he was leading them.

Just ahead at the bottom of the cliff was a cave, its entrance gaping darkly. It was hard to tell in this half-light how big it was or how far it extended into the rock. But there was clearly enough room for all of them to huddle there and devise a plan.

Celia realized where they were headed, too. She said, "A cave," as if she were surprised by its existence. "Where are we supposed to be?"

"Cliffs of Dover, I think," Achebe replied. "It's pretty new, put up since you've been gone. Not many people know about it." And as he spoke, the waters became shallower, for he stopped swimming and began walking along the bottom of the lake, his shoulders and head and, eventually, his torso emerged above the surface.

In a moment, Walt and the others felt their feet touch bottom, and they, too, stepped slowly on the hard but smooth lake bottom, and made their way out of the water.

Ashore, Walt could see the cave before them was quite deep. Several feet back, it was illuminated by the light of the rising sun, but the cavern trailed off into cliff rock getting narrower and darker as it went. Perhaps this was the way out—through the cave—though Walt had no desire to go back into dark, cramped spaces, especially with Achebe, with his peculiar sense of fun, leading the way.

Walt shivered, dripping wet in the cool dawn air, and he realized that it was the first time since he'd been in Paralleladise that he had been cold or hot. It had always been a perfect temperature. And even as he thought about the chill, he felt himself warm as the sun broke the horizon. Perhaps that was part of the allure of Paralleladise—that you were never too hot or too cold, that you never felt much of anything, unless you were a weeper, and life went on—for centuries, without pleasure or pain, without cold or heat, without ever feeling passionate about anything.

Achebe waited until they were all gathered just inside the cave and then he began helping Ling and William take their wet brown cloaks off.

"I've got other hoods in the cave," he reported.

"Achebe," Celia blurted out as she removed her own wet outer cloak, "What's going on? Do you know? Why did they take Walt's mother?"

Achebe shrugged. "So he would come find her. That's our best guess. They are setting a trap."

"It won't work," Walt said, feeling defiant, though there was no one here among his comrades to defy. "I'll find her."

"That's what they're counting on," Achebe said, knowingly. "And they will be waiting for you. They know who you are, now. They've put two and two together and have realized—as we did—that the offspring of Geneva Walters would be a powerful threat to them."

"They didn't destroy her?" Celia asked. "When she tried to escape, they didn't obliterate her hippocampus?"

Achebe looked less grave momentarily. "Oh, they tried . . . they tried. And we thought she was lost, too, after she was forced to drink from the cauldron. For months, she was like the others who've been memory-purged—listless, stupefied." Achebe turned to Walt as if he had just realized this information would be troubling to him. "Sorry, kid. She's okay, now."

"How?" Celia asked.

Achebe shook his head as if rational answers were inadequate. "She must have one heck of a resilient hippocampus. Never seen anything like it," he said, and then added, "I don't know how. But slowly, over the last two years she started to bring herself back. It was amazing to see." Again, Achebe turned to Walt. "Your mom is pretty remarkable. She must really love you, because she fought off the forgetting. They put her with the weepers to take care of her. And, over time, she fought off the lethemine and whatever else they gave her, and when she was back to normal, when she could think and remember with the best of us, she went right back to looking for an escape. Never been done before."

"Ling will do it!" William interrupted. "I'm sure of it." He looked at Ling, his voice cracking with emotion. "You'll fight back. I know you will."

Ling smiled at William as if he wanted to make him feel better but had no power to do so. He shrugged his shoulders and whispered, "I'll do my best, sir."

"I'm not a sir," William cried out. "I'm not a sir. I'm your old friend, William."

Ling nodded politely. "All right," he agreed.

"Ohhhh!" William cried out. "Ling, Ling." He looked at Achebe. "We've got to get him to the Rememberer. There must be something that can be done. Do you know where he is? Can you take us there?"

Achebe smiled sympathetically. "Maybe," he said, "Wait here."

And then, without further warning, Achebe took two running steps and dove back into the water with a wild yelp of enthusiasm. Walt saw his body plunge under water and then, after several moments, his head broke the surface several yards out as he stroked big swimming strokes that moved him across the calm body of water at an admirable clip.

"But . . . but . . ." William was calling after Achebe. It looked as if he might try to follow Achebe into the water. But then he stopped, realizing he could never catch the tall, athletic man. "There's no time," he sputtered futilely.

They watched Achebe swim for a full minute, his body seeming to grow smaller as he edged his way to the horizon. Walt wondered where he could possibly be going and whether he intended to swim the whole way, for it looked as if he were heading out into a deep wide ocean. And then, an amazing thing happened: just when it looked as if Achebe was about to break out into the open sea, he stood up. He'd found the end to the waters depths and began walking, the water only covering his feet and ankles.

Walt realized then, that he was staring at an illusion. The waters immediately around the cliffs were deep and dark, but further out, only a foot or less covered a blue-bottomed surface making it look like a lake or sea that went on forever, but actually became abruptly shallow enough to walk on. From this distance, Achebe appeared to be walking on water.

"Where does he think he's going?" William cried out hopelessly, his anxiety intensifying with every moment that Ling was left without help. "There's no time."

Ling gently placed his hand on William's arm. "It will be okay," he said.

Celia looked around the cave, searching for the other cloaks Achebe had said were stored there. "It will have to be okay," she echoed. "We don't know where we are or where to go. We'll have to wait and do what we can."

Walt watched these three long-term residents of Paralleladise. There were many other things at stake for them than for him. They were driven to restore the memory of their good friend, to find the Rememberer and bring Walt to them, to reverse the series of defeats and losses they'd had in their numbers since Walt arrived.

And Walt—he had to find his mother and escape.

William was shaking his head, "No, no. We can't wait here. We must get to the Rememberer."

"How?" Celia said.

For a moment, no one answered. And then, they heard a powerful voice from the darkness of the cave behind them:

"If you can't bring yourself to the Rememberer, let the Rememberer come to you."

TWENTY-NINE

Startled, Walt, Celia, William and Ling wheeled around in the direction of the voice. At first, they saw only the blackness at the back of the cave but then three figures emerged, like apparitions, from the dark recess, their shadows cast against the ceiling by the sun that was now streaming into the cave entrance.

They were three men, Walt saw, two large imposing figures, strong and athletic, like Achebe, and a third man of ordinary stature walking between them. They wore the brown robes and hoods of fugitive hippos.

The man in the middle walked two paces in front of the others. His face was framed by a neatly-cropped beard and mustache. His lips were pursed but a hint of a smile played at the edges. He was a stout man, not much taller than Walt and he walked gingerly, as if stiffened with age or pain.

"Max!" Celia cried.

"Romannie!" William shouted out, the dread that was in his voice only moments earlier was chased away by delight.

Celia dashed across the cave and threw herself into the welcoming hug of the round man, who drew off his hood as he returned her embrace and kissed her cheek. William, impatient and full of gratitude, pulled one of the man's hands from around Celia back in order to shake it with obvious and powerful enthusiasm.

The man buried his face into Celia's hair, kissing the top of her head while shaking William's hand. He threw off his hood to reveal a long and wild mane of thick, white hair that cascaded to his shoulders and his forehead and cheeks were creased with lines of age and worry.

"Alice, Alice, Alice," he whispered, and when William shook his hand more deliberately, he drew his face up from Celia's hair and added, "And William of Chelsney, my old friend."

The other two men who had come from the back of the cave remained standing at the older man's side, their arms crossed, their demeanors serious and their eyes looking about warily as if the meeting in the cave were a worrisome risk.

Ling had remained standing next to Walt when the others ran to greet the old man. Now, he leaned toward Walt, smiling, and said, "They seem rather fond of one another."

"Yes," Walt agreed, surprised by the sudden turn of events. "They do."

The brief exchange caught the attention of the old man and he looked across the cave. "And Ling, old man," he said, "aren't you going to shake my hand?"

Ling looked surprised to be recognized but he answered, "I will gladly shake your hand, sir." He moved across the cave. "And call you friend," he added.

"Oh, Max!" William exclaimed. "You've got to help him. He's been through the lethemine mines. He's losing everything!"

The man called "Max" shook Ling's hand with a grave expression. "Always the dutiful soldier, eh, Ling? The good of the many?"

"I suppose," Ling responded. "I don't recall."

The white-haired man put a supportive hand on Ling's shoulder and looked at William. "We will do what we can."

Celia interjected, gesturing, "This is Walt Walters."

"Ah, Walt Walters," the man echoed. "We've heard a lot about you." He reached out a welcoming hand. Despite his age and apparent physical weakness, the man's grip was firm and powerful.

"You're the Rememberer," Walt whispered beginning to understand what was happening, why Achebe brought them to this cave.

The old man waved away the comment. "A title," he said, "but, yes, I am Max Romannie. I am, for now, the Rememberer."

"For now, . . .?"

"We heard about what you accomplished at the Community Assembly the other night," Romannie went on, before Walt could finish his question. "They say you nearly brought the crowd out of their lethe-haze."

"I don't know about that," Walt replied. "I just was trying to keep them from drinking from the cauldron."

"And could it be that you actually made it all the way through the maze? And on your first try, too?"

"How did you hear about that?"

Romannie smiled. "Word travels fast in Paralleladise. It travels fast and is quickly forgotten."

The elderly man turned and gestured to the two other men. They remained standing at attention, watching the reunion, but scanning the cave for dangers at all times. "And these are two of my protectors for today—Von and Jimenez."

The two men nodded, but did not speak.

"You know them, William," Romannie went on.

"Yes," William acknowledged the two men. "Good to see you."

"You know them, too, Ling," Romannie added, "and you'll remember that in time."

"I hope to," Ling responded.

"Max," William interjected. "Can you help him? Can you bring him back?"

"We'll do what we can," Romannie offered cautiously. "We'll see."

"There's more," Celia jumped in. "Sheron knows about Walt now. He's taken Walt's mother—we don't know where. He's not going to let up until he captures Walt. He won't let us rest."

The Rememberer began to pace the small space of cave floor in front of him, watching his feet and thinking carefully. "Yes," he agreed. "Things look grave—but not hopeless. Word is out to every hippo in Paralleladise to set up decoys and distractions for Sheron until we can ensure Walt's safety . . ." Romannie paused abruptly and looked at Celia. "And did I mention how much I have missed you?"

Celia smiled. "I haven't forgotten you for one moment."

"We will get through this little spot we're in," he reassured. "We have to." He looked pointedly at Walt and William as if to emphasize his confidence. "But, first things first," he announced, becoming more focussed. "I must work with Ling. See what we can do. And you . . ." he gestured to Walt, Celia and William "could probably use a moment's rest and something to eat."

"Take care of Ling first," William responded immediately. "Don't worry about us."

"I will let Von and Jamie worry about you, for now," Romannie told William with a nod, resting a reassuring hand on his shoulder. "And I will tend to our friend."

Then, he turned to Ling and put a hand on his back. "Shall we talk, Ling, about old times?"

Ling's eyes were curious but friendly, "I'll do my best."

336

"You always do," Romannie told him and then gestured toward the darkness at the back of the cave, indicating that Ling should walk that way.

"Have some food," Romannie told the others as he guided Ling along. A moment later Romannie's brown robe faded in with the blackness as they disappeared into the dark cavern. Briefly, Walt and the others could hear the two men talking, but their voices became soft and then faded altogether.

"The cave must go back quite a bit," William commented to the two protectors. There was an obvious catch in his voice, like a concerned parent trying to sound nonchalant while sending his child off to school for the first time.

The protectors did not reply. Instead, when Romannie was out of sight, they wordlessly parted and went to opposite ends of the cave. From behind large rocks they pulled out a sack of food and a pile of brown robes to replace the wet ones Walt, William and Celia had removed.

They brought them back to the middle of the cave. The robes they set on a rock nearby and the food was poured out on the cave floor.

"I couldn't possibly eat," William told them. "Not until we hear about Ling."

For the first time, one of the stoic protectors spoke. "You should eat while you can," he suggested. "When the time comes to move, we will move quickly."

Celia put her hand on William's back. "There's nothing we can do now, William. Let's have a bite to eat," she suggested, "and let the Rememberer do what he can for Ling."

William stared at the back of the cave for a long moment before finally conceding. He faced the scattered picnic the protectors had poured from their sacks and, with Celia, sat down on the cave floor in front of the unappetizing feast. The protectors sat, too, forming a semi-circled around the canned goods and cellophane sacks they were offering and the small party ate in silence.

Walt sat cross-legged across from the hippos and tried to make sense of what had happened since he and Celia awoke in the maintenance hut of the Weeper Village.

Sheron and NyXus must have discovered the relationship between Walt and his mother. They must have realized that the rebel-rousing newcomer who had caused a commotion at the Community Assembly meeting and the woman who was famous among hippos for having deciphered her key and almost escaped were related and a threat to their power. They must have reasoned that Walt would try to find her.

Did they know already that his mother's memory was restored? Or had his mother remained hidden among the weepers in the years since her failed escape and slowly brought her mental capacities into shape while avoiding detection of the patrols? In either case, Walt's retreat to the Weeper Village must have helped Sheron and NyXus put two and two together and devise the plan to seize his mother and hold her captive to lure Walt to them.

But the Rememberer and the hippos also had been tracking Walt's movements—how else would Romannie have known about Walt's blunders at the Assembly and his success in the maze? No doubt they realized that Walt and the others were about to fall into Sheron's trap by going to his mother. So they sent Achebe to rescue them using the tunnel Walt's mother had helped to build.

The tunnel fascinated Walt. Mrs. Walters had been good at so many things as a mother: Mr. Walters was a little too absentminded to be an effective handyman and Walt's mother had always stepped in to fix things around the house, to repair plumbing and replace thermostats. And yet, he found it hard to picture her supervising a team of weepers in the secret construction of an underground escape route. Clearly there were many more sides to his mother than he had been aware of as an eight-year-old boy, when she disappeared, and he felt a flush of pride when he thought about how Achebe had praised her. Without her tunnel, they could not have escaped from Weeper Village. And they would not have made it to this unexpected rendezvous with the Rememberer.

Walt looked across the circle of hippos. The two Protectors sat watchfully, alert for any signs of danger from inside or outside the cave. Celia ate quietly, lost in thought, perhaps marveling at the circumstances of their escape. But William, unable to suppress his anxiety about Ling, frequently checked over his shoulder as he ate, as if he expected the Rememberer to emerge at any moment with news of Ling's condition.

Finally, the protector who had advised William to eat and rest spoke, in an attempt to console, "The Rememberer can do many wonderful things."

William turned to him, "Do you think he'll be able to help? Do you think he will be able to restore Ling?"

The protector stared at William for a long time. "The Rememberer can do many wonderful things," he repeated.

The ambiguous reply only heightened William's anxiety. He stopped eating altogether and turned to the back of the cave. "I don't know what I'd do without him," he said. "If Ling is lost..." His voice trailed and he did not finish the thought, but stood up and walked quietly into the cave's recess. Where the cavern veered into impenetrable darkness, he stopped and stood, waiting.

Celia rose to her feet and followed. She put her hand on William's shoulder. "You're a good friend," she whispered.

Walt felt a surge of sympathetic despair watching William. He recalled from the days after his mother disappeared the feeling he knew William was experiencing now—a dawning dread that things might not ever be the way they once were. Walt admired William's devotion, but it also made him feel guilty. For he knew that William's anguish, as well as Ling's loss of memory, was largely because of him: because they had been trying to rescue him, to save him so that, one day, he could help all the hippos by becoming a Rememberer.

But Walt had no intention of becoming a Rememberer. He couldn't! He was not a responsible leader of a rebellion against tyranny in an alternative universe. He was a kid--a seventh grader, an average student, an annoying little brother and a teasing older brother who was always getting in trouble for forgetting his chores and goofing off. He couldn't possibly do the things Max Romannie was capable of.

All he wanted to do was find a way back to the world he knew. To free his mother and return to his family and to the universe of memories.

Yet, watching Celia at the back of the cave, consoling William, Walt realized that what he wanted, what he believed was the right thing for him to do, was not so easy and simple. Supposing he did have the powers of memory they claimed he did? After all, he had surprised himself in the maze. If he did have this powerful memory—even greater than his mother's, even greater than Max Romannie's—did he have an obligation to stay in Paralleladise and use his abilities to help the hippo resistance, to possibly put an end to the tyranny of NyXus and bring this empire of forgetting to a crashing close?

Walt studied William and remembered that, when he'd first met this twelfth–century tinker, the man had broken into tears at the horror of forgetting his daughter's name. William, too, Walt realized, even after so many centuries, felt the furious longings to return home. And yet, he knew, William would not hesitate a moment to sacrifice himself if it meant saving Ling or Celia or any of his hippo comrades.

Suddenly, the meager food in front of Walt was wholly unappetizing. He pushed away the snacks and wrappers and stood up. The rising sun reflected brightly off the waters of the false sea outside the cave and Walt squinted as he walked onto the sand and gravel of the cave entrance. There, he found a large boulder set just inside the shadow of the cave ceiling. He leaned against it and watched the quiet waves that gently pushed their way to the shoreline a few feet away.

The water was clear and the sunlight bright enough to reveal that, just beyond the sand that cascaded into the sea, a rubber surface, like the lining of a backyard pool, continued and dropped off deeply, forming the bottom of the phony lagoon. It seemed so obviously false and unreal now that Walt was studying it, and, yet, if Ling hadn't rescued him from the Lexington Middle School, would he have even enough power of recollection now to recognize the artificiality of this parallel world?

For most hippos this was the reality they'd known for decades and even centuries. How had they managed to keep fighting and clinging to their memories of what the real world was like? How many times had they used some recollection of a real-world detail in their daily mnemonics to connect them with those they loved? How had they resisted the enticements of forgetfulness?

For years and years they had been searching for their portals, trying to recall their keys. But, while fighting incessantly to return to their families, these resisters had formed a bond among themselves. Though they were from different time periods and different parts of the world, they had come together in this fight against NyXus and formed a surrogate family that was obviously very close, as the friendship between the twelfth-century English tinker, William, and the fourteenth- century Chinese scholar, Ling, proved.

Walt imagined that hippos like William and Celia must feel great ambivalence about fighting so hard every Paralleladise day in the resistance, for it took time from their own pursuit of escape. And if they did achieve their freedom, it would separate them from these friends and comrades they had made over centuries.

Walt himself felt a growing feeling of closeness to the resisters who had saved him from eternal forgetfulness and become his protectors. William, Ling, MacGruder and, of course, Celia, whom he'd been close to but felt even more connected to now--these freedom fighters of Paralleladise had quickly become his friends.

What would he do, Walt wondered, if he truly could help the hippos? What did he owe them for saving him? What did he owe them for their friendship and protection? And didn't he owe his family something, too? Walt's father had already suffered the loss of his wife, Zelda and Acey the loss of their mother. Could Walt choose to stay and fight in Paralleladise knowing the heartbreak it would cause when they discovered they'd lost a son and brother, too?

Walt boosted himself upon the boulder he was leaning against and sat, deep in thought. Only a few days ago his biggest worries were homework, chores, bugging Zelda to distraction. Now, suddenly, he had the destiny of a whole other world on his mind.

THIRTY

Walt didn't know how long he sat outside the cave looking out at the calm waters. He was lost in thought and memories. Minutes may have passed, or hours.

Finally, he was roused from his thinking by footsteps and he turned to see the more taciturn of the two protectors at his side.

"Romannie will see you now," the big man said. It was the first time Walt had heard this protector speak. His German accent was thick and hard to understand, but his voice was deep and full as if his will were incontrovertible.

Walt climbed down from the rock and followed the protector through the cave. The food wrappings and other debris from the makeshift meal had been cleared away and someone had crudely swept the area where they'd eaten to hide traces of their stay.

Celia, William and the second protector were nowhere to be seen, but Walt knew they could not have left the cave without passing him at the opening. They must be further inside with the Rememberer.

The protector wordlessly led the way into the darkness at the back of the cave. There, Walt saw, the cave continued for a long way. They wound a path cautiously around rocks along the cave floor and stalactites jutting from the ceiling. As they stepped into complete darkness, Walt stayed inches behind the protector so he wouldn't get lost.

A moment later, though, they turned a corner and were greeted with soft firelight as they walked into a rounded cavern, much like the one Ling had taken Walt to after waking him at the Lexington Middle School. It appeared to be a natural space created within the recesses of the cave, but it was too large and too symmetrical to have been formed by time and nature.

The walls of the cavern were punctuated with torches lighting the space and its inhabitants. Across the rock floor, on the other side of the room, William and Celia huddled over Ling who lay upon an awkward cot. The sound of footsteps caught Celia's attention and, when she saw Walt, her eyes lit up, like someone unexpectedly spotting a friend in a crowd. But she did not come to greet him. Instead, she offered a sad smile and then turned her attention back to Ling.

William did not look up. He was deep in conversation with Ling—or rather, deep in a monologue, for William was the only one speaking with an occasional nod or murmur of acknowledgement from the smaller compatriot. "You were trapped outside the bander guild hall and couldn't get your leg out of the gutter trap..." William was explaining, telling Ling about a past misadventure. Perhaps William and Celia had been advised by the Rememberer to tell Ling about the past to help restore his memories.

This room was not Walt's destination, however, for the protector kept walking, leading Walt through to an opening on the other side. There, they stepped into a tunnel that ended ten yards away where the second protector—the one William had called "Jamie"—stood, cross-armed, on guard in front of the entrance to yet another cavern.

345

Hearing William's voice trail off, Walt followed the protector. At the end of the corridor, the protector moved aside to allow Walt to pass.

"He's expecting you," Jamie reported, and Walt walked through a natural archway into the next cavern.

This space was much smaller than the other cavern—not much bigger than Walt's bedroom at home. It was lit by one, low-burning torch on the opposite wall and its ceiling hung low, giving the overall impression of a storage room or garage, though the space was empty except for the Rememberer who lay upon two rocks of identical height settled next to one another, creating a hard, stony bed.

The Rememberer's eyes were closed peacefully and his chest rose and fell with sleep. But as soon as Walt stepped into the room, he awoke.

"Excuse me," the Rememberer said, softly. "Excuse me, Walt." He sat up and rested his feet on the cave floor, smiling to reassure Walt that the interruption was welcome. "Please come in."

Walt took another measured pace toward the Rememberer.

"I was just resting," the Rememberer went on. "Restoration sessions can be taxing. Rewarding... but draining, too." He chuckled. "Perhaps Achebe is right. Maybe I am getting too old for this job."

Walt was not sure what to say. Max Romannie was the oldest person he had seen since coming to Paralleladise. Or, at least, the oldest-looking person, for now that the subject of age had been raised, Walt realized that even the elderly people here—Professor Fitzmer, the speaker at the Community Assembly—did not seem old. For everyone in Paralleladise was imbued, it appeared, with energy.

"I thought nobody got old in Paralleladise."

The Rememberer nodded. "True," he admitted. "No one—except the Rememberer."

Walt must have looked puzzled for the Rememberer shrugged his shoulders. "No one knows quite why. One theory, proposed by the ninth Rememberer, is that memory and aging are connected, and the lethemine that destroys memories also retards aging."

"But all hippos remember," Walt pointed out.

"Yes," the Rememberer agreed. "They remember as much as they can, when they can. But the Rememberer—his whole existence is about remembering—remembering his own past and everything anyone tells him about theirs."

Walt was confused, but Romannie held up his finger to signal a demonstration. "Your third-grade teacher, Walt, was Mrs. Busch. And your first bicycle was black with blue and yellow stripes. You had your tonsils out when you were three. And you invented a little delicacy as a toddler that involved dipping cereal in peanut butter which you ate with your little finger extended."

Walt was astonished. "How did you …?"

The Rememberer smiled. "Your mother," he replied. "I've had countless conversations with her over the last four years . . . Actually, I've had exactly four hundred and eight . . . and she has told me so many things about you and Zelda and your father and little Acey. She loves you all very much."

"And you remembered it all?"

"I'm the Rememberer," Romannie said with a shrug, as if the title itself explained the remarkable feats of memorization. "That's what I do. I think…I remember… I listen to others and retain as much as I can about them so that when they come back

347

to me with some other key to their portal or some information vital to the survival of the hippo resistance, I have it in my memory, even if they no longer have it in theirs."

"You know my mother," Walt said. It was not a question. He had been told that his mother had seen the Rememberer, but repeating the fact made it more real. It placed her in this world more believably, made it possible for Walt to imagine her here. The details of Walt's history that Romannie had recounted sounded like the sorts of things she would focus on in her daily mnemonics—little things, family things.

"I know her well," Romannie assured him. "Before her battle with Sheron—when she was trying desperately to recall her key—she sought me out almost every day to work on the memory. Then when she nearly escaped and liberated Alice and the others, Sheron knew what a threat she was and took her away and thoroughly scrubbed her mind clean. I thought she was lost to us forever. Then, a few months ago, when she started regaining mnemonic functions, she showed up at one of our sanctuaries, ready to start from scratch, determined to get back to her portal. She is very persistent."

Walt knew that about his mother. She never gave up, whether it was arguing with the school board about a crosswalk or raising money for a needy family at Christmas or getting a nasty stain out of a favorite blouse, his mother persevered in any cause she deemed worthy until she'd accomplished her goal.

"And even though I thought she was lost to us, I remembered the details she'd told me, because that is what the Rememberer does," Romannie went on. "And perhaps because the Rememberer remembers, the Rememberer ages...visibly." Romanie rubbed a hand over his wrinkled cheek to emphasize the point.

"How . . ." Walt stopped himself. He wondered how old the Rememberer was but realized that, even in the mixed-up circumstances of the ageless Paralleladise, it might be a rude question.

Romannie smiled, intuiting Walt's curiosity. "I was fifty-three when I was drawn through the portal into Paralleladise. The year was 1810." A glint of playfulness flashed in Romannie's eyes: "How old do I look now?"

"I . . ." Walt paused, not wanting to offend, "I don't know . . . sixty-five?"

Romannie laughed warmly. "You are a polite, young man. Thank you. But perhaps I truly look twenty years more than that? Fifteen on a good day?"

Walt felt flushed. He shrugged, "It's hard to say in this light."

The Rememberer laughed again. "You see, even if I'm ninety now, it took me two hundred years to get this old. That's not so bad." Romannie paused, thoughtfully.

His expression became graver. "Still, it is a sacrifice— aging. One of the many one makes when one becomes the Rememberer." Romannie studied Walt carefully now, preparing to change the subject. "And still it is a sacrifice every hippo would gladly make if he or she could return to his own world where aging and the march of time are unstoppable."

Walt remembered reading a story in school about a man who traded his soul so that he would not age. What would that character think of agelessness without memory? Would he wish to live forever if he couldn't remember who he was from one minute to the next?

"Sacrifice," the Rememberer said again. "Is that what you were thinking about outside the cave?"

The question surprised Walt, because he wasn't aware he'd been monitored outside the cave, but also because, in his thinking, he had not considered the word "sacrifice." Was that what he was confronting? Walt wondered. He'd been thinking about obligations, actually. Where did he owe his allegiance—to his family, to his own desires, or to the needs of these hippos and the other victims of Paralleladise? If you did not choose a cause—if it was thrust upon you—even if you believed it was a good cause, could you become responsible for it? Was it Walt's obligation to become a part of the hippo resistance? Was it wrong to think only of finding his mother and escaping with her and Celia through their own portal, leaving all the others behind? Did he owe the prisoners of Paralleladise anything now that he understood their fate? Did knowing of their suffering require him to do something to help them? To sacrifice?

"I'm just a kid," Walt said aloud, though he was still arguing with himself as much as he was answering Romannie.

"You're a young man with an extraordinary ability," Romannie responded, "a gift. You must decide what to do with that gift."

Walt looked into the Rememberer's eyes. They were not challenging or demanding, but sympathetic and compassionate. He seemed to be genuinely questioning the value of self-preservation versus sacrifice for the greater good. "What should I do?" Walt whispered.

Romannie stood and walked to Walt. He placed his hand on Walt's shoulder.

"Only you can decide that." Sadness crept into his voice alongside the concern. "In many ways, you are 'just a kid,' Walt, and I regret that. I regret even asking you to work with me, to develop your skills so that you might one day take my place, if necessary." Romannie turned and paced away from Walt, as if what he was about to say were especially difficult. "But, I know, too, what you are capable of. I have heard from many reports and from Celia and William of the remarkable retention you've displayed and, even more importantly, your ability to touch others, to bring back their recollections."

"I haven't done anything, really," Walt responded. He was not being modest. His swaying of the crowd at the assembly, the tricks he'd used to help William remember his family—they were just guesses. Walt didn't know what he was doing. He did not plan to move the crowd—he only spoke what he felt was true. He did not believe he could restore William's memory. He simply tried something the others weren't trying and it happened to work. "I can't do what you do."

"Your intuition tells you what will help others. You follow it, and you succeed in bringing back what they've forgotten." Romannie tried to summarize Walt's gift. "That is a rare quality, a form of empathy that many of the most resilient of hippos don't have. Ling may have one of the strongest memories of any of the hippos, but he does not have your gift of intuition. Your mother has an extraordinarily developed hippocampus and a wonderfully sympathetic nature, but her sadness and sense of loss overwhelm her concentration."

"I wasn't able to help Ling," Walt reminded Romannie. "And what if the Community Assembly was just a fluke?"

Romannie shook his head. "It wasn't a fluke, Walt. It may seem like very little to you, but even that momentary hesitation, that glimmer of recollection you caused in the entire crowd is more than you can possibly imagine until you have been in Paralleladise for years."

"But they turned against us," Walt protested. "They charged us."

"At least half a dozen incidents of returning memory have been reported since the Assembly. What you said is something hippos have been saying for a millennium. But when *you* said it, the *way* you said it . . . the crowd responded. It was truly a phenomenon," the Rememberer assured him. "And, as for helping Ling, well, he is a special case. The damage caused by vapors of the lethemine mines is especially devastating to the hippocampus. He will require special attention and long-term convalescence before returning to himself."

"You see!" Walt argued. "That's what I mean. I don't know how to treat him or what to do in his case. I could never remember all the things you do."

"I will teach you," Romannie said. Then he drew a long breath and continued in calmer tones. "I have some few good years left in me, perhaps many. Enough time to train you, to show you the methods we've developed, to teach you to be the Rememberer." Romannie paused and then spoke deliberately to emphasize his next point: "And I am convinced, Walt, you can become the greatest of all the Rememberers. Perhaps the one who defeats NyXus's evil purpose and delivers us from Paralleladise. The one who sets us free."

Walt could not speak. He was overwhelmed with the weight and responsibility of the Rememberer and still not at all clear about what he could do. How could he defeat NyXus's evil purpose if he didn't even know what NyXus's evil purpose was? The entire alternative universe in which Paralleladise existed was pitted against this rag-tag group of hippos and the Rememberer seemed to be their greatest hope. How could Walt possibly be that person?

Romannie paced the floor of the tiny cave room, his compassionate eyes trained on Walt, letting him absorb a vision of the future that he was painting. Finally, he spoke again, this time in a different tone, as if he were telling a story:

"Some say NyXus has survived since the beginning of time, quarreling with the universe as he found it and arguing with its Creator that the two greatest afflictions humanity has suffered are memory and the affections it brings. That he—NyXus—to thwart and oppose the universe he hated, created this parallel world as a true paradise that would rival and revile the messy world of memory that human beings were heirs to and victims of. That this world…" the Rememberer waved his hand above his head to suggest all of Paralleladise, "is the destiny he would have created for the creatures he loved."

"Others believe that NyXus is not of this world at all, that he is some species from an alien galaxy far advanced of humanity, a species that has learned to control time and memory and that he has founded Paralleladise as a slave colony and when he has the slaves he needs he will return with them to his own galaxy.

"And still others believe that NyXus is a figment—a contrivance, a symbol—for, you see, no one has ever seen him. Stories are told of the third Rememberer, having aged beyond usefulness as Rememberer and determined to destroy Paralleladise, who went to confront NyXus and never returned. But they are only unproven and unprove-able legends from millennia past. And so, there are many who have decided that NyXus is just a word to stand for the negation of our natural world, of the home we all hope to return to but never can. For them, Paralleladise is our hell and our final, timeless destiny."

Max Romannie paused, letting the theories about the origins of NyXus settle in Walt's head. Finally, he went on: "But, regardless of where NyXus came from, the goal he's pursuing is clear. It is repeated every week at Community Assemblies and inscribed in the plaques and monuments throughout Paralleladise."

Romannie looked at Walt as if he expected that Walt might, with those hints, be able to surmise NyXus' goal.

"I don't remember," Walt confessed.

Romannie smiled. "That's what I used to think before I met Malthus Kahn—the Rememberer who mentored me. But he taught me this: everything that has ever happened to us—from the moment of birth to the here and now—every face we've encountered, every word we've heard, every fact, every detail—we remember it all." Romannie tapped his forefinger against his temple to emphasize the point. "It's all in there somewhere, ready to be brought back to life when we need it. We have only to learn how to bring it forward."

Walt shook his head. If everything about the Community Assembly was in his brain somewhere, it was hiding pretty well and very reluctant to show itself. He could remember very little about the wild meeting except his own anxiety—his trepidation about the cauldron, his fear of losing his memories forever, his apprehension for the girl who was called up with him to drink the liquid lethemine—what was her name. Lisa? Libby?

"Lisette." Walt heard himself speak the name.

Romannie nodded. "You see. It's all there waiting. And you can remember it. Your mind holds every word said at the Community Assembly. It contains every impression of sight, sound and smell. You can recollect what NyXus' goal is. 'It is not a skill,' Malthus Kahn used to say to me, 'but an act of will.'"

Once again, Walt thought about the Assembly. What was said about NyXus's goal? Had the leader of the crowd spoken of a final plan? There was a song— "Auld Lang Syne"—and some sort of chant, but nothing about the meaning and purpose of Paralleladise.

"We believe in the here and now," the Rememberer said softly, like a stagehand prompting an actor who has forgotten his lines.

We believe in the here and now… the words echoed with distant familiarity. It took Walt only a moment to recognize them as the beginnings of the chant the Assembly's crowd had recited—what had the Community leader called it…the "creed?"

"We believe in the here and now…" Walt repeated, trying to bring back more of the creed to his mind. What else did they believe?

"… and in the power and possibility of the future," the Rememberer continued, seeing Walt on the verge of recall.

"In the power and possibility of the future," Walt echoed. Yes, it was coming back. Something about the horrors of recollection and the pain of affections. And they hoped to reform the hippos. Was it reform? Something like "reform." Rehabilitate—that was it!

"How did it end, Walt?" Romannie asked calmly.

Walt tried to recall the ending of the creed. He was amazed at having remembered as much as he did, since he had heard the creed only once and in very distracting circumstances. But being with Romannie made it easier somehow. Was that one of the gifts of the Rememberer?

"The ultimate conquest?" Romannie offered.

"The ultimate conquest?" Walt repeated and then, in the back of his mind, he heard the rest of the phrase…*the ultimate conquest of our people over the multitudes of remembering infidels.* Was that it? Was that NyXus' goal? If so, what did it mean? Which people? Who were the remembering infidels?

Walt looked at Romannie, but the old man was not offering any other help. "You can do it, " he whispered.

"The ultimate conquest of our people over the multitudes of remembering infidels," Walt said, repeating the words he'd remembered. And suddenly, other words began attaching themselves, like a magnet sweeping up shards of metal. *We believe in our salvation on that day when, unencumbered by stifling memories, we will rise up and triumph over the weakened world of recollection and bring its people into the full happiness of forgetfulness and the comforting protection of our one true leader.*

"We've got to stop him!" Walt blurted out without thinking. Until now he'd thought of Paralleladise as a prison camp from which to escape and return home. Now, it had become a prototype of a new universe NyXus would rule. It was unthinkable!

The Rememberer could not suppress a smile at the passion in Walt's voice. This, Walt realized, is what Max Romannie had hoped for. He had counted on the fact that once Walt understood the scope of NyXus' plan, he would take up the cause of the hippos as his own, become one of them, and even be motivated to become the next Rememberer.

"I mean . . . I mean," Walt stammered. "That can't happen, can it?"

Romannie shook his head. "I don't know, Walt. I really don't know. When I was brought to Paralleladise, there were six portals—six doors between the real world and this weak replica. I was told there had been six portals for many centuries and before that only five for a millennium. Now there are eight—two have been created to serve NyXus' master plan in the last century and a half. He has accelerated his construction of portals and doubled his abductions. And the Cauldron of Forgetfulness has made it easier to destroy the memories of his prisoners."

Romannie looked suddenly grave and Walt could see he was anxious about the prospect of NyXus' success. "There's time," he went on. "Two centuries? Five centuries? It's hard to say how long." Romannie looked into Walt's eyes. "That is why we must work together now to stop him. And I know that we can. The three of us. We can stop him."

"The three of us?"

"You, me … and your mother."

Of course, Walt thought. His mother would join the resistance, too, if Walt were the Rememberer. She would do whatever she could to help him. To get them both home. He had been so focussed on getting out of Paralleladise, he hadn't considered what would happen if he couldn't escape. But now he realized that whatever future he faced here would include his mother. That is, if he could find her and free her from Sheron before her memory was obliterated.

"The three of us," Romannie continued, "could mount a crippling resistance. We could stop NyXus from erasing the memories of those he abducts. Perhaps, with our combined powers of memory, we could bring an end to Paralleladise altogether."

This, too, Walt understood now, was part of the Rememberer's hope. If he could persuade Walt to become the next Rememberer, he would gain the mnemonic power of Walt's mother, too. Her protective instinct toward Walt would lead her to put the strength of her memory to the service of the hippos.

Could they do it? Walt wondered. Could they destroy Paralleladise? It seemed such a monumental task, beyond the power of the hippo movement, even if Walt and his mother joined them. Would his mother even allow him to become a Rememberer?

"Do you know where she is?" Walt asked.

A glimmer lit Romannie's eyes. "I have a good idea," he said. "And Achebe is working right now on a plan to free her. We will bring her here and the three of us will travel together. With your combined mnemonic abilities, you and your mother will be a true force for NyXus to reckon with. We can bring an end to Paralleladise forever."

"Where is she?" Walt asked. They could settle the question of his work for the resistance later. Now, his concern was stopping Sheron before he could harm his mother's memory irrevocably.

Romannie's eyes widened to suggest the answer was easier than Walt might think. "They've taken your mother as bait to lure you to a trap. They think you'll come to find her."

"And I will," Walt assured him, "if you tell me where she is."

"It would be a daring rescue," Romannie told him, though his enthusiasm for the challenge was evident. "And it may take all of your abilities to accomplish the task. But we have an advantage this time. A little bit of technology and a little bit of intuition." Romannie smiled, obviously delighted to be thinking one step ahead of Sheron.

"This time?"

"Sheron tried this once before to trap Critos Meon, the second Rememberer. He captured one of Meon's proteges and then set a trap."

"Did it work?"

Romannie hesitated but then admitted, "Yes. But we have an advantage."

"What's that?"

"Sheron will think it would take you several days to figure out where to look, as it did Critos Meno. And then, a day or more to get there. He believes he has all that time he needs to set his trap for you."

"But he doesn't?" Walt asked. He could not imagine where to begin searching for his mother. It could easily take him days or weeks to figure it out. As for getting there—he knew of only one way to get anywhere in Paralleladise: by foot.

"Where," the Rememberer responded with a question, "of all the places you've been in Paralleladise, would you think to look for your mother?"

"I don't know," Walt said quickly. The first possibility that came to his mind was the Weeper Village, but that is where she'd been taken from. He did not even have a clear sense of the size of Paralladise, how much of it he'd seen, where he had been.

If not the Weeper Village, then where? Walt had been in the caves under Prairie Dog Flats, which would be a good place to hide, but not necessarily a good place to keep his mother hostage. And, besides, Sheron supposedly did not know about that hippo sanctuary.

There was the Lexington City Hall where Walt had attended the Community Assembly. It was a familiar locale from his real world, but Walt could think of no other reason to search there. Walt looked at Romannie, puzzled.

"Where did you see her last?" Romannie asked.

"I . . ." Walt started to explain that he hadn't yet seen his mother since he'd come to Paralleladise. He'd been to her hut in the Weeper Village as it went up in flames, after she was taken away. But then he recognized what Romannie was truly asking.

"Home!" Walt shouted out, surprised at how obvious the answer was. He'd last seem his mother four years ago at home before he left for school. Of course! That is where she would be now. "Home!" he repeated.

"Exactly," the Rememberer responded. "Home. Even if you didn't know your mother was being held as a trap, eventually your heart would lead you home. Or, in the case of Paralleladise, to the replica of the home you once knew."

"We've got to get her!" Walt urged. He would have dashed out of the cave at that moment, with or without Romannie, if he had any notion of which way to go to get home.

"We will, we will, my boy," Romannie assured, patting Walt on the shoulder to encourage calm. "But we must be cautious. We cannot risk losing you in an attempt to rescue your mother."

"I have to go," Walt insisted, sure that Romannie was about to insist that the protectors retrieve his mother.

To Walt's surprise, however, Romannie agreed. "Yes, yes," he said. "If I could think of an alternate, I would try to keep you with me. But, time is of the essence and you, of course, would know your own home the best. And, if Sheron has started to work already to erase your mother's memories, you would be in the best position to restore them."

"We've got to hurry!"

Romannie hesitated only a moment longer, clearly reluctant about sending Walt on the dangerous rescue. "Yes, we must hurry. But, please, Walt, be careful." Romannie held Walt's gaze. "Be very careful."

"I will," Walt nodded.

Romannie continued to study Walt as if trying to estimate the wisdom of the rescue they were planning. Finally, the doubt on his face turned to resolution. "Let's go see if Achebe has returned."

THIRTY-ONE

In the larger cavern, William and Celia were still attending to Ling when Walt walked in, following the Rememberer. They were heading for the cave entrance to await Achebe, but when William and Celia saw Romannie, they rose to their feet expectantly. Celia's grim expression suggested things were not going well. Ling lay quietly on the cot, his eyes closed.

"He's very tired," William reported. "Perhaps we should let him rest."

Romannie studied Celia's face. Clearly, he expected she would be the best judge of Ling's condition. She did not return the Rememberer's gaze.

"You've run him through his mnemonics?"

"Yes, yes," William responded. "He's still confused, but I think it's just fatigue." Walt could see that William was grasping for hopeful signs. "Maybe after he rests a bit…" His voice trailed off.

"Yes," Romannie agreed. "Rest may do him some good."

An awkward silence hung in the air among these hippos, like the silence of friends politely avoiding a difficult truth. It was broken by the appearance of the protector, Jamie, who entered from the darkness of the corridor leading to the mouth of the cave.

"Achebe has returned," he announced officiously.

Romannie turned to face the big man. "Did he bring the gnomes?"

"Six of them," Jamie reported and then, without further word, he turned and moved back into the dark corridor.

The Rememberer spoke thoughtfully, "Let's hope that is enough."

Gnomes? Walt wondered. Were they the flying gnome probes that had hunted them throughout Paralleladise? What was Achebe doing with gnomes?

Celia, too, seemed puzzled. "What are you planning?"

Romannie eyes glinted. "A little rescue mission," he told her. "But don't worry, my dear, I'm not going along."

"But I am," Walt jumped in before anyone could volunteer ahead of him.

Celia looked at Romannie. "Walt is going?"

"It makes sense, Alice," Romannie explained. "We must act quickly if we are to get to her before Sheron destroys her memory. He will not make a mistake this time. Besides, I think it might be hard to stop a boy from saving his mother."

"I'm going, too," Celia announced, as if there were no room for discussion. She looked at Walt. "Your mom saved me from Sheron once."

"Very well," Romannie replied after a brief pause. If he had hesitations about Celia going, they were clearly outweighed by his sense of urgency. "You, Walt and Achebe will go. We must act quickly. William, you will stay with us and help me with Ling."

William nodded. His thirst for further adventure was quenched in his concern for his friend. "You will be careful," he said looking first at Walt and then at Celia. He blinked away tears. "We need you back. Both of you. We can't afford to lose another."

"Now, now, we haven't lost Ling yet, my friend," Romannie replied. "We will think of something and we will not quit until we do."

William nodded, lowering his eyes to the ground. Celia lay a comforting hand on his arm. "When we bring Walt's mother back, she may be able to tell us something about how she regained her faculties. She may be able to help Ling."

"Yes," William acceded quietly. He did not look up immediately, but then, as if struck by an idea he raised his eyes to look at Walt. "Perhaps you could do something," he said, his voice suddenly full of hope.

"What?" Walt was taken by surprise.

"Perhaps you could say something to him before you go . . . have a few words, get him started again."

Walt's heart sank. The hope in William's eye was depressing because there was nothing he could do. He would only demoralize the good-hearted tinker more if he spoke to Ling with no effect. "William," Walt whispered. "I can't. I don't know what to say."

"No, Walt," William interrupted, clutching Walt's arms in his hands. "You have powers. I have seen them. You helped me. Perhaps you will hit upon just the right thing with Ling."

"I tried earlier—in Weeper Village—remember?"

"You have to try again," William argued. "You have to. It may not help . . ." William shook his head. His voice cracked. "But it may."

Walt looked at Celia and then Romannie. If he failed, William would be only further convinced of the sad prospect of losing his friend forever. Celia only shook her head at the futility of the request. Romannie's expression was full of compassion for William and for Walt. But, finally, he said, "One precious memory can bring back a thousand. And a thousand precious memories can make up a lifetime."

Walt felt a world of responsibility bearing down on him. Here in Paralleladise, people were expecting things of him—things he was not sure he could do, things he wasn't prepared for. And, more and more, Walt wished he could just be a kid—without any expectations. The responsibilities were frightening and the prospects of letting others down heartbreaking. He was certain anything he would try to help Ling would fail.

"Please, Walt," William said, softly. Walt studied the tinker's face. It was a caring and compassionate face that would never shrink from helping others, even in the most futile of endeavors.

"I . . . I'll try," Walt finally managed to say. "I'll just say goodbye and . . . and if I think of anything . . ."

"You'll think of something," William assured him. With a hand on Walt's arm he urged him across the cavern floor.

Suddenly, the sight of Ling was frightening to Walt. He felt himself moving toward the cot, watching the diminutive Asian breathing softly, and feeling as if he didn't know the man at all. Ling's face, with his hair swept back from the forehead and temples, was gaunt and strained. It was not the lively face, always alert with a countenance of quick thinking, Walt had come to know in the last couple of days. But it was a face and a man to whom Walt owed much. Ling had rescued him more than once from threats of eternal forgetting.

Ling's eyes suddenly opened as Walt approached and some of the animation of his features returned. He watched, expectantly, as Walt sat on the stool next to his cot.

"You are . . ." Ling started, but then seemed to lose his train of thought. Finally, he continued, "Don't worry. Everything will be fine." He smiled genuinely, but with the vacant expression of many of the residents of Paralleladise Walt had seen at the Community Assembly. It was a smile that didn't know what it was smiling about.

"We're going now," Walt told him. "To get my mom."

"Your mom," Ling repeated without any sense of its meaning.

"But, we'll be back," Walt added quickly. "I'm sure you'll be better. Max Romannie will work with you."

"Better?" Ling asked. He seemed confused. "Am I ill?"

"Yes . . ." Walt started, but then stopped himself. In Paralleladise, Ling was actually only now quite normal. Being a hippo, having memories in tact, that was the disease in the world NyXus had created. "You've lost a lot of your memories."

Ling nodded, thoughtfully. "I hadn't noticed."

"But we'll get you back. When my mom gets here . . . she can help you get your memories back."

"Is that a good thing?"

"What?" Walt was surprised by the question. It suggested just how much damage Ling had sustained. He no longer understood the role memories had played in his life. "Yes, yes . . . It's a good thing."

"Why is that?"

"Why is that?" Walt echoed, searching for a meaningful reply. "I don't know. I don't . . . I'm not sure who I would be without my memories. "

"Aren't some memories painful?" Ling asked. He nodded his head toward William who was watching from across the cavern. "The fellow over there was telling me some of his memories. They sounded very sad. Like when his wife died . . . or was it his daughter?"

"Some are sad," Walt admitted, quietly. "But even the bad ones can be very valuable because they make you appreciate what you have. And most, I think, are good, especially if you count all the little ones."

Ling seemed puzzled. "Like what?"

Like what? Walt asked himself. An image of his father's winter overcoat had flashed before his mind when he spoke of the little things, and that led him to mention their importance. But to answer Ling with such a trivial detail might cause him to mistake memories as trifles. "I don't know. They kind of give a difference to every life. They make us all not the same."

"Like what?" Ling repeated. He seemed more confused and Walt worried that the confusion might drain his mental energies.

"I don't know . . ." Walt responded. "Like . . . like. . . like my sister's room, that she painted pink and orange because she wanted it to be unique, even though my dad thought it was hideous. Like . . ." Walt searched for other, more meaningful examples, but none were coming. "Like Friday night pancakes."

"Friday night pancakes?"

"When my mom disappeared," Walt explained, "the only thing my dad could cook was pancakes, and so we'd have them three or four nights a week until grandma came to live with us. But we loved pancake dinners so much that we were always bugging him for it. So, finally, he declared every Friday night 'pancake night' and so that is what we do—have pancakes every Friday night for dinner."

Walt smiled at the recollection and he saw Ling smiling, too. "That sounds like a good memory," Ling said.

"It is," Walt assured him. "And there are a thousand and one little things just like it that make me feel . . ." Walt searched for the word. "Make me feel . . . connected, I guess."

"Tell me some others," Ling prompted. He was still smiling and seemed to be taking pleasure from Walt's recollection of his life's details.

Walt thought hard. Even if this wasn't helping Ling's recall, at least it was amusing him. "Oh," he continued. "There are a million things. My dad, for example, has had the same winter coat since I can remember, and it smells like his office and . . . like him, and when I was little he and I used to play hide and seek and I'd hide in the hall closet, wrapped in his coat. I love to remember that smell."

"Another good memory," Ling commented, wistfully, as if wishing for pleasant memories of his own.

"And my mom," Walt went on, getting caught up in his own recollections, "I always think of the birthmark on her neck. When I was sick as a little kid and she would hold me, I would look up at the birthmark. She thought it was big and ugly, but my dad would tell her it was the most beautiful thing about her. Once, she said she was going to have it removed by a doctor somehow and I cried because I couldn't imagine my mom without her birthmark. So I cried until she promised she would not have it removed. My sister, Acey, has a mark, too—not really a birthmark. It kind of looks like a vaccination mark. It's on her leg and..."

Walt stopped. Ling's face had suddenly gone blank. His skin was ashen and a quiver of fear rode up Walt's spine for fear that Ling was going to be ill. "Are you okay?"

William, Celia and the Rememberer saw the change in Ling, too, and they hurried across the cavern floor.

"Ling!" William cried out.

"What happened?" Celia asked anxiously.

"I don't know!" Walt told her. "I don't know. I was telling him about my memories . . ."

"My aunt!" Ling called. "My aunt!"

"Your . . .?"

"My aunt, my Aunt Zi," Ling continued, staring straight ahead as if he were seeing his aunt's image before him. "She raised me after my mother died."

"He's remembering," William exclaimed.

"She . . . she had a birthmark." Ling put his right hand over his left forearm. "Right here. Right on her arm. She . . . she . . ." Ling spoke haltingly, the memories coming back slowly in bits and pieces. "She smelled of cinnamon. Her hands, they always smelled of cinnamon because she worked with the village baker in the afternoons."

"Yes!" William cried. "It's coming back!"

Ling sat up and looked at the four faces surrounding him. "I loved the smell of her hands and sometimes she would bring back a tiny crust of something with cinnamon for a treat."

"You did it!" Walt felt himself suddenly embraced by William in a squeeze so tight it took his breath away. "You did it, Walt!"

"I didn't . . ." Walt tried to speak but William only hugged him tighter and repeated "You did it! You did it!" He felt Celia's hand patting his back and saw Max Romannie smile knowingly.

"One precious memory," Romannie repeated the phrase he'd spoken earlier, "can bring back a thousand."

". . . my sister and I would fight over the piece of cinnamon bread and then my father would take it from us and split it into two even tinier halves and we'd each have just a taste, but it was so good." Ling laughed and rubbed his belly. "We fought over everything, my sister and I."

369

"It's coming back!" William repeated. "It's coming back."

"Easy now," Romannie interjected. "We don't want to get a headache. It is coming back. But we will need to work slowly now that Walt has started him on the way."

"I really didn't do anything," Walt told them.

"You're such a modest show-off, Walters," he heard Celia say.

"You have worked a miracle, Walt," the Rememberer assured him. "And I have a feeling you will work many more."

"I was just telling him . . ." Walt tried to explain.

But William was too anxious to keep Ling going. "What else do you remember?" he asked his old friend.

"My sister's name is Xiang . . ." Ling told him.

"That's one of your mnemonics," William interrupted. "A half hour ago you couldn't remember if you had a sister."

"She's two years younger than me," Ling reported.

"Ha-ha," William laughed.

Walt would have gladly listened for hours to Ling recall his past. A warm rush of feeling washed over him as he realized that, while he may not have done much, he seemed to have contributed—ever so slightly—to Ling's sudden return to recollection. He'd done something right and helped someone. It was a good feeling.

But before he could listen any further, he felt a tap on his shoulder and turned to see Romannie, backing away from Ling and William and signaling for Walt and Celia to follow. "We'll let them reminisce," Romannie said softly when they were several steps away. Ling was wholly absorbed in recounting his memory and William was totally wrapped up in listening. They did not notice the others backing away. William sat down on the stool next to his old friend and encouraged him. "We have a mother to rescue," Romannie reminded Walt and Celia.

Walt felt Celia squeeze his arm and whisper, "You did it!" and then turn her attention immediately to Romannie. This was the life of a hippo: taking only moments to enjoy each minor triumph before moving on to the next challenge. To defeat Sheron and NyXus, they would always be on the move.

"What's the plan?" Celia asked Romannie.

Max Romannie gestured for Walt and Celia to follow him as he walked toward the corridor leading to the front of the cave. Walt and Celia trailed him purposefully, but Walt could not help looking back at Ling and William before stepping into the darkness.

William was huddled close to his old friend, listening to Ling tell his history with great glee, as if he were recovering long-lost treasure. Walt turned to the darkness but then heard Ling call his name.

He turned back once more to look at the two faithful hippos. Ling was smiling at him, gratefully. "Walt," he said, grinning. "Remember . . . .. Zig zag."

THIRTY-TWO

Walt and Celia were startled when they reached the mouth of the cave. Six gnome probes hovered above the heads of two protectors, Achebe and Von.

"Look out . . . "Celia started to shout, but stopped herself when she saw that the gnomes were not preparing to slime the hippos. They were not doing anything, in fact, but floating benignly three feet above the protectors' heads. Straps dangled below the probes, tangled together, and Von and Achebe were attempting to straighten them out. Celia looked at the Rememberer who was smiling at her surprise. "How?"

Romannie laughed. "You remember Dr. Zabigni?"

"You restored him?"

"He is a hippo now." Max Romannie waved in the direction of the probes. "And doing many wonderful things for the resistance."

Celia marveled at the gnomes that had once been so menacing. Out of their attack posture, their buzzing motors reduced to a quiet hum, they seemed harmless enough, almost quaint. Romannie explained to Walt: "Dr. Zabigni is a mechanical genius from 19th century Italy. We finally managed to restore his hippocampus to a functioning capacity after a century of effort and he has been able to turn his mind and memory to our mechanical endeavors. The probes are his first successful project." Romannie looked at them proudly. "They will be enormously useful."

Achebe and Von had now managed to untangle the straps that cascaded from the gnomes and Walt could see that they were actually harnesses that hung between the probes. There were six gnomes and two of them were needed for each harness, which dangled between the pair.

Achebe grinned broadly as he stepped into the leg of one harness and secured safety straps across his waist and chest. "And," he added, "they're a lot of fun."

"We managed to capture a few probes along the way, and Dr. Zabigni has adapted them to our use," Max Romannie explained. "We will be able to travel vast sections of Paralleladise much more quickly, now. And they are quieter, so that we may travel less conspicuously."

Celia edged her way closer to the hovering probes, her eyes trained on them. She was fascinated but still did not wholly trust the once-dangerous weapons of Sheron. Romannie nodded to Walt, indicating that he should follow her.

"What do you . . .?" Celia started. "You fly them?"

Achebe laughed his deep, warm laugh. "That's the theory." He adjusted the straps one last time and then found the controls that hung from one of the harness straps right at his hand.

"Theory?"

Walt was seeing the gnome probes up close and in full light for the first time. They were very much like garden statues, with wide grins and pointed ceramic caps. From their backs, synthetic wings flapped at an incredible speed in a blur of movement. "How many times have you used them before?"

"For a rescue mission?" Achebe clarified. "Never."

Von held the harness from another pair of gnome probes open and indicated that Celia should step in. She moved forward like an apprehensive child approaching a scary carnival ride that might actually be fun. Von secured the straps around her.

"How many times have you used them for other kinds of missions?" Walt pressed, realizing that the last harness suspended between the two remaining hovering probes were for him.

Von turned to help Walt into the gnome probe apparatus. "Actually," Romannie explained, "this is the first time we've used them at all. But they're our best hope for freeing your mother. Sheron will not be expecting us for some time, but with the gnome machines we will be able to cover a lot of area in no time." Romannie smiled confidently. "And, of course, Sheron will never expect an air rescue."

Achebe interjected, "We will locate your mother and free her before Sheron is even aware we are on our way."

"Surprise, stealth, speed," Romannie summarized. "They are our best hopes for getting your mother back without being caught. We cannot afford to lose anyone of you." He looked from Achebe to Celia to Walt in order to emphasize the point. "So we must hurry." Now, Romannie turned deliberately to Achebe. "We'll rendezvous at the tower in two hours. In four hours we will move again. You know the sequence."

Achebe nodded like a soldier receiving orders and Romannie turned to Walt and Celia. "And you two, listen to Achebe, be alert and, above all, come back to us. If I am wrong—if your mother is not at your house, Walt, do not search elsewhere. Return to the rendezvous point and we will consider our options. Try to avoid letting Sheron know we have the gnome technology. If you can get in and get out without being detected, we'll retain the element of surprise for future missions."

"How will we fly Walt's mom out?" Celia asked. "There's no probe for her."

Achebe explained. "I should be able to take her with me. The probes will hold both of us." He smiled. "If I can hold on to her."

"But," Walt felt compelled to mention. "We don't even know how to fly these things." Von had finished securing Walt in the harness. He slapped the controls into Walt's palm and then grasped a silver handle that hung from the harness strap at Walt's shoulder. "This is how you get out," he said gruffly and, to demonstrate pretended to pull the silver handle.

"Achebe will give you the proper training to fly," Max Romannie assured them, pulling on the straps along Celia's back as if to test their reliability.

"We should go," Von said to Romannie. "You have stayed too long here."

"Quite right," Romannie agreed, but he was looking intently at Celia. "No heroics, my little girl," he told her. He turned to Walt, "And you either, young man. Remember, it is better that you return and we have a second chance to rescue your mother than that you do something foolish and get caught."

"I understand," Walt told him. He felt like a secret agent on a mission. A jitter of anticipation ran through his body. But Walt knew that, unlike a good secret agent, he would not follow the orders if he thought taking a risk would save his mom.

"We should go," Von repeated.

"Be very careful," Romannie cautioned once more. He touched Celia cheek with his cupped palm. "It's so good to have you back. I wouldn't want to lose you again."

"I'll be careful, Max," Celia assured him.

Romannie turned to Achebe. "Bring them back safely," he said.

Achebe nodded as Romannie turned determinedly with Von and walked into the darkness at the back of the cave. He did not look back and Walt understood that, as the Rememberer, he could not take time to fret. He must continue moving so he wouldn't be traced and he could not linger over things he could not control. Could Walt ever put aside his concerns for the ones he cared for to be a good Rememberer?

"Time for your training," Achebe said the moment Romannie and Von disappeared into the blackness of the cave. He turned and walked to the mouth of the cave. The hovering gnome probes turned with him, swinging on the harness tethers.

Walt and Celia exchanged an apprehensive glance. Then Celia shrugged, causing the gnome probes above her to bob and their wings to briefly grind against one another. She flinched an exaggerated "oops" and then followed Achebe.

"Try to keep your shoulders apart," Achebe called back.

When Walt turned, he saw that moving was not as easy as Achebe made it seem. He had to keep his body rigid to keep the gnomes from crashing together and the lift of the probes was greater than he'd imagined. Carefully, he pivoted and stepped between Achebe and Celia at the mouth of the cave, staying far enough away so that his gnomes would not collide with theirs.

"Lesson one…" Achebe announced. "And this is fun, so don't look so scared."

"I'm not scared," Celia replied, looking scared. Walt wondered if he appeared as worried as Celia.

"Lesson one," Achebe repeated, showing them the remote in his hand. "Up." He pressed a red button in the center of the remote once. His body immediately rose five feet into the air. The harness snapped into full tension creating a kind of seat for him as he dangled above Walt and Celia. "Up!" he repeated.

376

Walt and Celia looked at one another and then at their remotes. "Up?" Celia asked and then darted into the air as she pressed the red button on her remote. Suddenly she was hanging next to Achebe hovering above the ground. She looked down at Walt. "Your turn, Walters," she shouted, nervousness in her voice. "It's a . . . a hoot."

Cautiously, Walt pressed the red button on his remote. Instantly he shot up into the air and found himself alongside Celia and Achebe once more. After the initial jolt of ascension, he bobbed lightly in the air. It was like floating on a swimming pool raft.

"Woo hoo," Achebe said. "I told you it was fun."

Walt balanced himself into a sitting position. He dangled precariously five feet off the ground held only by straps and two flying gnomes, but as he settled into the harness strap seat he felt a little more secure. Surely, by the time Achebe finished training them, he would feel perfectly comfortably in this absurd flying contraption.

"Now, every time you need elevation," Achebe explained, "hit the red button and you'll ascend another five to ten feet."

Walt looked at the red button cautiously. It was definitely a button to mind carefully.

"Lesson two," Achebe went on without waiting for questions. "You see the arrow button at the top." Achebe covered the button on his remote with his thumb to show them.

Walt and Celia each placed a finger over the same button on their remote.

"Slowly depress the button," Achebe advised.

Simultaneously, Walt and Celia pressed the arrow button.

"Ahhh," Walt heard someone scream as he shot out of cave at tremendous speed. Then, he realized the scream was coming from him. "Ahhhhhh!"

Ten feet above the surface, Walt zoomed above the waters of the false sea outside the cave, flying very quickly, the wind blasting against his face. He thought he accidentally hit the wrong button on the remote or pressed it too hard, but then, from the corner of his eye, he saw Celia zipping along at the same speed ten yards away.

Celia's eyes were wide with alarm. Like Walt, she had not expected the sudden bolt from the cave. She'd released her remote and held on with white-knuckled determination to the harness straps.

"Up!" Walt heard Achebe call. "Up!"

Walt did not want to take his eyes off the landscape speeding by below, but slowly he looked up to see Achebe, cruising along above him and Celia.

"Up!" Achebe repeated. He was grinning broadly, taking delight in Walt's and Celia's surprise. "Get some elevation!" he cried. "Press the red button!"

The calm waters of the sea whirred beneath Walt's feet. There was nothing immediately ahead to run into and so, very slowly, he looked to the remote in his hand, found the red button and pressed it.

The first jolt of elevation took him up half the way to Achebe's altitude. A second press of the red button brought him to the same level.

"There you go!" Achebe called. The wind that roared by their ears as they zoomed along made it necessary to shout. "Now you've got the idea."

Celia suddenly popped up on the other side of Achebe. She had found her remote and, like Walt, pressed the red button for altitude.

"Didn't I tell you this was fun?" Achebe called to her. "Woo hoo!"

Celia's pale expression did not reflect "fun," but she grimaced a forced smile as she settled into her harness. "What about the training?" she shouted. "Romannie said there'd be training."

"That was it," Achebe responded. "You're trained." And then he pressed the arrow button of his remote once more to zoom out ahead of them, letting out a whoop of exhilaration at the power of speed and flight.

"That was the worst training I've ever had," Celia yelled after him, but then, in a competitive spirit she, too, pressed the arrow button to accelerate and keep up. Her gnome machine bolted ahead of Walt and, in a moment she was right behind Achebe.

"Ha-ha!" Achebe laughed, watching Celia catch up and seeing her determination. "Come on, Walt!" he called back.

This speed was way too dangerous, Walt thought to himself. His mom would never allow it if she could see him now. But he wasn't going to let Celia and Achebe leave him behind. He took a breath and pressed the arrow button three times in quick succession.

He felt as if he'd been shot out of a cannon as he blasted ahead, catching up instantly with Celia and Achebe.

"Woo hoo!" he heard Achebe call out as Walt approached. "Now, to turn, you pull down slowly on the strap on whichever side you want to go." Achebe shouted these instructions and pulled gently on one strap. The gnome probe on that side dipped slightly from the tug and Achebe glided in that direction. Then he released that strap and pulled on the other side, which brought him back to his original position. "Don't pull too hard. Gentle."

Walt and Celia both experimented, pulling cautiously on the straps that supported them and feeling themselves glide first in one direction and then in another. After only a few tries they had mastered slow turns though Walt was sure that the need for a sharp change of direction would send them into a tailspin.

Achebe watched them test their skills and nodded approval. Once he was certain they were in control of the steering, he shouted "Up!" once again and ascended another 20 yards. Walt and Celia followed, gaining confidence with each new maneuver.

Achebe pointed toward the horizon where the sea ended at what looked like a tiny fishing village. "That way," he shouted and the three of them changed course.

Walt looked down and watched as sea gave way to the fishing village and then open fields below. They were more than 100 feet in the air and from this vantage he could see across large expanses of Paralleladise. He realized how unlike the real world it was, for instead of the patchwork of fields and suburbs he might have seen from an airplane flying in the real world, Walt saw fragments, small mosaics of lifestyles beneath him. They flew over what appeared to be a French village and then, a moment later, they were passing above a snow-covered plain. Off in the distance he saw the Empire State Building towering up over a greatly abbreviated New York skyline.

With Achebe leading the way, they climbed another one hundred feet and from this height Walt could see in the distance the great Sphinx of Egypt with the peaks of a mountain range behind it. All of these places, he realized, had been created over millennia to replicate locations in the real world and deceive those who were kidnapped by Sheron until their memories were destroyed. The facades of buildings and houses only vaguely resembled their real world counterparts, but apparently it was enough to fool newcomers under the influence of lethemine.

Celia, too, Walt could see, was fascinated by this view of Paralleladise—its remarkable combination of ingenuity and falsity. The inadequacies of the replicas were obvious to the hippos, but the other victims of NyXus—some of whom Walt could see far below walking the streets and fields—were oblivious to the fakery.

They flew over mountains, plains, cities and suburbs in moments. Off to the left was a huge gorge surrounded by jungle. Could that be the cavern they had tried to cross when they were running from the banders? And the desolate field beyond that— was that Prairie Dog Flats where they escaped after the Assembly meeting? Walt saw how true Romannie's words had been: it would have taken days to walk through, around and over these different locales and terrain if they hadn't had the gnome flying machines.

He studied the horizon ahead searching for some place that resembled his hometown of Lexington. Soon, they might find his mother whom he hadn't seen in four years at the Paralleladise imitation of his home. What would she look like, Walt wondered? What would life in the hippo resistance be like with his mother at his side? Would the longing for family disappear even a little bit when they were together again? Or would they both continue to feel incomplete until they were joined together again with Zelda, Acey and Walt's father? It was all too unreal and unimaginable.

"There!" Walt heard Achebe shout. The big man was pointing off to the left where a clock tower arose out of a smattering of housetops and trees. It was a residential area and, as they drew closer, Walt recognized the tower as a replica of the Lexington courthouse on the square. He had only seen it from the ground and after nightfall on the evening of the Assembly meeting. He had not recognized then what a poor imitation it was, for the tower was only half of its true size and only the side facing the main street was complete. From the air, it was clear the other half was only scaffolding holding up the façade. Walt was fascinated by how easily he had been deceived under the influence of lethemine and, when they flew over Lexington Middle School a moment later, he marveled at how tiny the replica was. It could not have contained even half of the classrooms the real world original contained and yet, when he visited it in his lethemine haze, he had not even noticed its differences. "Descend," Achebe instructed, holding up the remote and showing them that, by pressing a black button at the back of the remote, he stopped moving forward and hovered, like a helicopter in slow descent.

"Walt!" Celia called out. She was smiling and pointing to the street just ahead. It was the replica of Walt's street and there was Walt's house, sitting quiet and abandoned in the empty neighborhood.

Walt pressed the black button on his remote and felt his forward momentum slow. Gradually, he began to sink over his neighborhood. From this height, it was still hard to tell where he might land.

"Circle," Achebe instructed, pulling on one harness strap so that his gnome machine made slow, wide circles as it descended.

Walt followed suit, trying to match Achebe's circling pattern with his own, and, just above him, he saw Celia moving into a similar descent. Within moments he recognized how expertly Achebe was guiding them, for on the ground, right in the middle of the circles they were making in the air was the roof of Walt's house.

Suddenly, Walt was very anxious to be inside like he was sometimes when the family returned from a trip and he longed to see that everything in the house was exactly as they had left it. Now, he knew that nothing in the house was likely to be a satisfying duplicate of the house he remembered, but the fact that his mother might be there created that same sense of urgency.

Achebe, Walt and Celia continued their cautious descent for several minutes until, finally, the roof of Walt's house was coming up fast.

"Red and black together, red and black together!" Achebe repeated.

It took Walt a moment to understand that Achebe was directing them to press the red and black buttons simultaneously and by the time he found and depressed them, his feet were practically on the roof. But when he did, the gnome machine stopped descending and hovered in place. Walt was only two feet above his roof.

Celia and Achebe hovered at the same height nearby and Achebe smiled as he pointed to the silver release clasp Von had showed them back at the cave. "Careful," he warned, pulling the clasp and dropping to the roof. His gnome machine remained in place, hovering within easy reach.

Walt and Celia imitated Achebe and dropped, less gracefully than the tall athletic man, onto the rooftop.

"Didn't I tell you it was fun?" Achebe asked, but before waiting for an answer he quickly turned his attention to the business at hand. "We've got to hurry now. I don't know if anyone saw us, but it's likely someone did and if they have any memory at all, they might retain the fact long enough to alert the patrols."

"Do you really think she's here?" Walt asked, peering over the roof, trying to determine the best way to get down. The street and entire neighborhood was quiet, abandoned, like it had been when Walt first awakened in Paralleladise, not realizing where he was. In his lethemine confusion, he hadn't found the desolation disconcerting, but now the emptiness was eerie, as if everyone in the neighborhood had disappeared at once.

"Only one way to find out," Achebe answered. "I think you'll be safe having a look. Sheron's too clumsy and over-confident to wait and lurk or leave a guard."

"Aren't you coming?" Celia asked.

Achebe shook his head and reached for his gnome probe. "I'll stand watch out here. That's where the threat is. If Sheron discovers you're here, he'll send the probes first. I'll alert you. If you hear me calling, come out quick."

"But what if they slime you?"

Achebe laughed. "I'm too fast for them. Now, don't worry about me. Just get in and get out. If your mom is in there you should know quickly. If you're not out in five, I'm coming in after you."

Celia nodded at Achebe's instructions.

"But how?" Walt asked. "If she's there, won't they have locked her in?"

"Probably," Achebe agreed. "But these phony houses—they make them fast and flimsy. It won't be too hard to get in." And then, without further word or warning, Achebe grabbed the straps of his hovering gnome machine and swung both of his legs into the air and then brought them crashing down on the rooftop in a powerful thrust. The roof beneath him gave way in a splintering crash as if it were a thin pane of glass. "See?" he said nonchalantly.

"Who needs a door when you have Achebe?" Celia said, smiling as she moved over the hole the big man had created.

"Now get in and get out," Achebe reminded them. "It'd be great if we could get her without anyone seeing us or the gnome machines."

"Right," Celia responded. She was standing at the edge of the hole in the roof and Walt watched as, without hesitation, she jumped through it and into the attic of the house.

Walt looked at Achebe amazed that adults were allowing him to do so many clearly dangerous things.

"In you go," Achebe told him. "Make it quick. I'll be here to help you get out."

Walt stepped over to the hole and looked in. Below, he saw Celia standing on the rafter beams of the attic looking up at him. "It's a snap," she called up. "Just remember to land on the beams so you don't fall through to the next floor." She smiled.

Walt looked at Achebe. It sounded much easier than it looked, but Achebe clearly wasn't concerned. He was studying the skies, searching for approaching gnome probes. "In and out. I'll be right here."

Walt looked into the hole once more, took a deep breath and jumped.

THIRTY-THREE

"Yaaah!" Walt let out an involuntary yelp as he plunged through the roof. He thudded into the attic insulation and fell forward. When he stood up a moment later he was surprised to find he had landed on one of the attic beams and then, falling forward, caught himself on another. Restoring Ling's memory, flying the gnome machine, leaping into attics--he was managing so many things he didn't know he was capable of.

"Smooth," Celia said of his scream.

"Five minutes!" Achebe shouted down. He'd climbed back in his harness and was hovering above the roof.

"Let's get moving," Celia said and together she and Walt turned to look for the exit. But, in turning, Walt's attention was caught by the glowing panel in the far corner of the attic. He pointed. "It's still there."

"Yes, it's your portal," Celia told him. "It will be here even after they tear this house down to build some other replica for a new arrival."

Though there was little time, Walt found himself moving toward the portal, fascinated. He remembered seeing it for the first time when his father set up a ladder to show him the attic. It had looked like a harmless plywood panel in the roof—a builder's patch over a construction error. And then, he saw it a second time—glowing bright with energy—when he found Acey standing before it, about to be dragged in. Now he approached it as if he were passing a car wreck—cautious, but unable to turn away.

Since being rescued by Ling and the other hippos at the Lexington Middle School, Walt had recovered most of the memories of his first days in Paralleladise under the influence of the lethemine. But he wasn't able to recall exactly how he had come through the portal or what had happened to him before he woke up in his bed in the replica of his Lexington home.

Above the glowing panel was the placard he'd finally remembered in the Weeper Village. The gilded symbols glistened as if calling to be deciphered. "That's the key," Walt said. "That's how you get back through."

Celia nodded but did not respond for a long moment. Finally, she said, "Walt, I'm sorry I got you into all this. I was so intent on bringing you, and your memory, to help the hippos."

"If you hadn't guided me here, Celia," Walt said when her voice trailed off, "I would never have known about my mom." He looked into her eyes. Her face was wrinkled in guilt and concern. "I would have never had this chance to save her."

She studied him another moment as if judging the sincerity of his forgiving tone. Finally, her expression lightened. "Guess we'd better find her then."

Walt smiled. "Come on."

They moved across the rafters of the attic. When they came to the access panel to the floors below, they paused. The panel was opened and pushed to the side. On the floor below, a chair had been positioned into Walt's closet. It brought back Walt's memories of the moments before he was dragged through the portal—the tremendous shaking of the house, scrambling into the attic and seeing Acey standing at the portal door.

"Someone's been trying to get up here," Celia said.

In a moment, they had both climbed through the attic opening and lowered themselves into Walt's bedroom.

"Mom?" Walt cried out.

"Mrs. Walters?"

There was no response and they hurried through Walt's room. Walt's eye briefly registered the many discrepancies between his room at home and this replica, differences he hadn't noticed under the influence of lethemine. He also noted the metal bars across the window, like those of an old western jailhouse. They had not been there before. They'd been put up recently to keep someone in, or out.

In the hallway, they found the doors to all the other rooms closed and since there was no window, the light was dim. They hesitated and Walt wondered whether Celia was remembering the dark hall in her own Mill Street home where the door to the attic was as she had described it in her diary.

But if the similarity was making her anxious, she didn't show it. She stepped with determination to the door to Walt's father's room across the hall, turned the handle and threw it opened.

"Mrs. Walters!" she cried out. The room was empty, without furniture or even a closet.

Adopting Celia's bravery, Walt walked to the next door and opened it with a solid push, letting it bang against the wall inside. There was a mattress and nightstand in the room, but otherwise it was as empty as the first.

"Mom!" Walt cried again. "Are you here?"

Silence greeted his call. Wordlessly, he and Celia approached the third door—the door to Acey's room—and Celia had just set her hand on the knob when they heard a sharp snap coming from below. They jumped, startled.

"Downstairs!" they shouted simultaneously and ran to the top of the stairs. There, they paused to listen for further noise.

"Could be someone who came in by mistake—couldn't remember if it was their own house or not," Celia cautioned. "Or maybe something just fell."

"Mom!" Walt called down the steps.

When no one replied, Walt and Celia bounded down the stairs. At the bottom, they rounded the banister, their eyes sweeping over the empty living room. Then they walked cautiously though the archway to the kitchen where the loud snap came from.

"Mrs. Walters?" Celia called, her voice full of trepidation.

The counter aisle that occupied the center of the kitchen, separating it from the dining area, still held the box of food Walt had been given by the grocer in the Paralleladise square on his first day of captivity. The bag of opened snack chips and the empty candy wrapper Walt left remained next to the box. Beside them, however, was a half-eaten apple, and Walt did not recall having left that there.

"Hello," he said loudly, but Celia put her hand on his arm. She brought an index finger to her pursed lips to pantomime a "Shhhh!"

Walt listened and heard distinctly what Celia was calling his attention to. It was the sound of someone breathing, slowly, hesitantly, as if trying to remain undiscovered. It was coming from the far side of the counter.

Celia pointed and, slowly, she and Walt began to walk around the counter.

"Hello," Celia said. "We hear you. We're not going to hurt you."

As they circled the counter, a figure leapt up in front of them, screaming.

"Stay back!"

It was a woman with long dark hair, wielding a broom above her head like a baseball bat. Her eyes were wild with determination, fear and fury. "Don't come near me!" she shouted, waving the broom menacingly. "Stay away!"

Walt recognized her immediately. She had not changed at all in four years, hadn't aged in Paralleladise. She was exactly as he remembered her.

"Mom," he said.

Mrs. Walters was taken to Paralleladise when Walt was eight years old. He had grown and changed a great deal since then and, at first, she did not recognize him. She opened her mouth as if to say she was not his mother, but slowly recognition dawned. She studied him curiously, the broom sinking from its threatening position above her head. Her understanding was evident in her changing expression.

Finally, she spoke, turning her head slightly to the side, as if disbelieving what she was about to say. "Walt?"

Walt was too stunned to move. He stared at the beautiful face of a mother he thought he'd never see again. He wanted to speak and run to her, to embrace her, but suddenly he could not move at all. He had come looking for her, hoping to find her, prepared to find her and yet he was thoroughly amazed that she was before him, alive and unchanged since the last time he had seen her when she sent him off to school four years earlier.

Walt's mother, too, seemed paralyzed by the surprise encounter. Perhaps she had been trying to get home to her family for so long that now, facing her son unexpectedly, she was frozen in amazement, having never truly known whether she would make it back. Her eyes were filled with wonder and then with tears as she understood that this was truly happening.

"Walt," she repeated. The broom dropped from her hands.

And suddenly, Walt was able to move once again for he found himself running across the kitchen floor and throwing himself into his mother's open arms, hugging her with all of his might.

"Walt, Walt," she said again and again holding him tightly as if she were trying to convince herself that he was real and he was there.

Walt tried to speak, but when he opened his mouth words would not come. Instead, he felt tears coat his cheek—his body releasing a cry of joy and relief at the reunion he had imagined so often but which was so much better in the reality.

"I can't believe it," Mrs. Walters was saying now and rocking him back and forth in her arms as if he were still a little boy. When she disappeared, he was still small enough to be wrapped into her body by an embrace, but now he was nearly as tall as she. "I didn't know if I would ever see you again."

"Mom," Walt finally managed to croak out, but found he had little more he wanted to say at this moment. Instead, he wished to stay in her embrace forever to make up for the years of lost hugs he had missed so much. Despite the passing of so much time, her hug was familiar—warm, comforting and loving—and Walt felt incredibly happy.

"Walt, Walt," his mother repeated, pressing his head against her shoulder, and Walt was content to be held and to hear her speak his name.

How long they stood in this embrace, Walt could not say, for everything else melted away—time, Paralleladise, the precariousness of their situation, the sadness and anxiety of the last four years. But finally, they were brought out of their reverie by the sound of Celia's voice.

It was the tentative voice of one who did not want to disturb them. "Walt? Mrs. Walters?"

Reluctantly, Walt's mother released her hold on her son as she brought herself back to the surroundings and the reality of the situation. She looked at Celia, puzzled, as if she thought that Celia, too, might also be one of her children, grown older and bigger since her disappearance. But she was calling her "Mrs. Walters," so it could not be Acey or Zelda. Still, Walt's mother's studied Celia trying to place where she knew her from.

"Mrs. Walters," Celia began again. Walt saw the trail of tears she shed watching Walt and his mother's reunion. "Mrs. Walters, you probably don't remember me . . ."

But a flash of recognition crossed Mrs. Walter's face. "Alice?" she asked.

Celia smiled more brightly than Walt had ever seen her smile. Her broad grin was accompanied by more tears of joy. "You're amazing," was the first thing Celia could say.

"You . . . how did you . . . you've grown," Mrs. Walters finally managed to say. Her mind was obviously still trying to unravel the mystery of the appearance of her son and this girl she had helped escape from Paralleladise, both several years older than when she had last seen them.

"I escaped," Celia said. "You got me out, remember? You pushed me through the portal into your own time."

"I . . . ." Mrs. Walters started still trying to reason it all out. "You went through my portal. I . . . ." The evidence of sudden recollection was obvious on Mrs. Walters' face. "You made it out?"

Keeping one arm around Walt, Mrs. Walters reached with the other pulling Celia to her and hugging them both one on each side. "I can't believe it," she whispered. "How . . .?"

"We can explain it all later, Mrs. Walters," Celia said, embracing Walt's mother tightly. "Right now, we've got to ..."

But before Celia could even finish her sentence, the house began to shake violently.

"What . . .?" Walt cried out.

"Oh no!" Celia called over the deafening rumble. "Sheron!"

At that same moment, the kitchen window came shattering in on them with a powerful crash and all three instinctively ducked to avoid the flying debris. Behind the crash was Achebe, slamming into the kitchen riding his gnome machine through the window and the hole in the wall created when he kicked it to batter his way inside.

"Get out!" he shouted before his feet even touched the ground. "Get out of here!"

Achebe's gnome machine, flying above his head, was unable to squeeze through the hole and clattered against the outside wall. Deftly, Achebe pulled the release on his harness to drop to the floor and swiftly crouched into a defensive position, spinning to face the gap he had just made. He looked to Celia. "Get them out of here. I'll try to hold Sheron off!"

But even as he spoke, the beam of light that was Sheron blasted through the opening like a giant searchlight and swept a path across the kitchen floor heading directly to where Achebe stood. The athletic man waited until it was almost upon him before he leapt to the side, rolling on his back and shoulders and then onto his feet a few yards away.

"Go!" Achebe shouted. "Go, go!"

393

Walt, his mother and Celia were momentarily stunned by the sudden events, but Celia quickly shook herself into action, grabbing Walt's arm.

"Come on!" she shouted and pulled his sleeve. It roused Walt and his mother and they followed in the direction she was pulling. "We've got to get out of here!"

Sheron's light adjusted instantly to Achebe's evasion and slithered across the floor after him. Again he waited until it was almost upon him before jumping up onto the kitchen counter staying just inches ahead of the tracking searchlight, ducking down to avoid the ceiling.

"Clear your mind!" Celia was shouting as Walt and his mother followed her out of the kitchen.

"But Achebe!" Walt yelled. Surely, they were not going to leave him behind.

"Just get out!" Achebe answered. "I'll be all right."

Yet, even as he spoke the words, Walt saw the beam of light arise from the floor. This time, however, it did something Walt had not seen it do before. It changed shape, transforming from a straight beam into a swirling cloud, like a smoke signal billowing into the air, touching the ceiling and spinning like a funnel cloud sending the box of food on the counter and every other loose object nearby flying across the room in a fury. Then, the light transformed again into a loose snaking pattern and Walt saw the end of the beam shift into the form of sharpened teeth. It looked like a serpent of light with the teeth of a shark. It paused briefly, the jaws swaying in the air at the ceiling, as if staring down at Achebe, its prey.

Achebe crouched below it on the counter, ready to pitch himself and roll away again as the light trailed him.

394

But, like a bolt of lightning, the bright beam shot down this time, catching Achebe in midair as he dove from the counter top, snatching the big man in its opaque jaws of light.

"Ahhhh!" Walt heard Achebe shout. It was a shout of dismay more than pain, filled with surprise and anger at having been caught.

The jaws of light clamped hard around Achebe who struggled against it. Like a giant snake with captured prey, the light beam swung Achebe around triumphantly in its jaws bringing him first up to the ceiling and then swiftly down to the floor again.

"Get out!" Achebe managed to shout again as he pounded his fist futilely against the jaws of light engulfing him.

And then, in a flash so quick that Walt's eyes could not even follow it, the serpent light with Achebe in its jaws disappeared through the open window.

THIRTY-FOUR

"Achebe!" Walt called out.

"We've got to get him back," Walt's mother cried running toward the window.

"No!" Celia shouted emphatically, stopping Mrs. Walters in her tracks. She and Walt looked at Celia who stared sadly at the opening through which Achebe had just disappeared. Tears welled in her eyes but determination sounded in her voice. She shook her head. "No!" she repeated. "We can't do anything for him." She looked at Walt's mother. "You know that," she added.

Mrs. Walters considered Celia's admonition for a long moment and then she lowered her eyes, "Yes."

"We have to get out of here," Celia told them. She drove the loss of a comrade from her mind, just as Walt had seen other hippos do. Like soldiers, they could not stop in the middle of a battle to mourn casualties. And right now, a hasty retreat had to be planned.

"He'll be back for us," Walt's mother agreed, referring to Sheron.

"We have maybe ten minutes before he returns," Celia explained. "We've got to get as far away from here as possible."

Walt shook from his mind the image of Achebe being dragged away. He had to concentrate on their precarious situation. "The gnome machines," he said.

"It's our best shot," Celia said, turning and dashing to the stairs in the living room. Walt followed at her heels.

"What are gnome machines?" Mrs Walters wondered, but she ran behind Walt and Celia up the steps.

Upstairs, they sprinted down the hallway into Walt's room. Celia quickly bounded on to the chair in Walt's closet and then turned toward the others. Lacing her fingers together, she crouched and held them as a stirrup before her waist.

"Come on," she directed. "Up!"

In other circumstances, Walt could imagine his mother taking issue with the safety of these acrobatics. But now he felt her hands on his waist lifting him as he pushed with one leg onto the chair and then put his other foot into Celia's cupped hands. With another thrust he was through the attic opening and turning to help Celia whom his mother had boosted to the access opening. Then, the two of them reached down to pull Mrs. Walters, who jumped from the chair and grasped the access panel frame to help hoist herself through with more athleticism than Walt remembered her having before she had spent four years trying to escape from Paralleladise.

Celia was up and making her away across the attic rafters before Mrs. Walters was on her feet. She hustled to the hole in the roof Achebe had made as an entry when they first arrived.

"Oh no!" she cursed, looking up through the opening.

Walt was at her side in a moment. He peered up through the hole and saw the reason for Celia's frustration. The gnome machines they had flown to get there were not hovering above the roof where they left them. Only the smiling, capped head of one of the gnomes was there, broken and lying on the roof shingles so that it peered down into the opening. The harness straps were tangled around what Walt could see of its torso, which was broken in half, its inner machinery smashed and scattered.

"Sheron must have destroyed them!" Celia surmised.

"We'll have to run for it."

"There's no time. We'll never make it."

"What else can we do?" Walt turned to face his mother only to realize she had not followed them to the hole in the roof, but was standing near the corner of the attic next to the glowing portal.

"Mom?"

Mrs. Walters did not respond. Her hands were on the symbolic forms of the placard that was adjacent to the portal. She was pressing them, one by one, and, as she did, they changed to other forms.

"Mrs. Walters?" Celia said.

Walt's mom did not take her eyes off the plaque, but called back to them. "The portal! We can escape through the portal."

Celia looked at Walt and they both hurried over. As they approached, Walt's mother explained, "I was up here last night. I almost had it. . . I'm sure of it." She continued to press the symbols as she spoke. The placard, Walt realized, was like a combination lock. Although the symbols appeared to be carved in solid wood, they changed when they were pressed. Then, they glowed for a moment and transformed into a different symbol. When they were aligned in the right combination, Walt guessed, the portal would open.

But Walt did not recognize any of the symbolic forms. They were of a different notation system, another alphabet, than any he knew. And his mother's changing of the forms appeared totally random.

"There's no time. Mrs. Walters," Celia was saying. "We've got to get out now or we'll be trapped when Sheron returns."

398

"Just one more . . ." Mrs. Walters continued pressing the symbols, disregarding the urgency. She pressed a final symbol several times until it changed to the one she wanted and then pulled her hands back from the placard expectantly.

The three stared at the portal in bated anticipation.

But nothing happened. The portal continued to glow in ebbing and brightening throbs of light. The placard's illumination faded into its gilded wood appearance, but the portal did not open.

"Ahh," Mrs. Walters let out a sigh of frustration. "I thought I had it." She began to press the symbolic forms again, not giving up.

"There's no time," Celia repeated. "I know of a place we can hide in catacombs about a mile from here."

"We'd never make it, Alice," Mrs. Walters told her. "There are patrols all over the streets. I've seen them from the windows. Sheron will be back before we could get to the catacombs. This is our only hope. She was depressing the placard symbols quickly now, trying random combinations in hopes of hitting on the right one. "I thought I had it. I thought I remembered."

"Mom." Walt put a hand on his mother's shoulder. "We can't go back."

His mother continued to change the symbols. "Yes. I almost had it ..."

"No, Mom," Walt interrupted. "You don't understand. We can't leave yet . . . even if you do figure out the key."

Walt's pronouncement stopped Mrs. Walters abruptly. She turned to him, her eyes filled with surprise. "Walt, what do you mean?"

Walt shook his head. "We've got to . . . I've got to stay."

"No, Walt." His mother wrapped his face between her hands. "Sheron will be back. We can't stay."

"You don't understand," Walt felt tears of frustration welling in his eyes. Only now, as he spoke the words did he realize his commitment to helping the other victims of Paralleladise. "I've talked to the Rememberer."

"You've met Romannie?"

"He wants us to . . ." Walt started. "He thinks we can . . . They think I can help them."

"Mrs. Walters," Celia interjected. "It's my fault. I brought Walt here."

"You brought him here? I don't understand. Why?"

"I'm sorry," Celia told her. "I know you were trying to protect me by sending me through the portal."

"The hippos, Achebe and others," Walt went on. "They've saved me more times than I can repay. I have to stay and help if I can."

"But Walt . . . Alice," Mrs. Walters said, deep compassion in her voice. "If we're caught, NyXus will surely destroy our minds. He knows I survived his memory-purge once. He'll have to destroy my memory altogether. And yours, too, just to be sure."

"Then we can't get caught," Walt told her.

Mrs. Walters stared intently into Walt's face. He could see by her changing expression the train of thought going through her mind: she wanted to protect Walt and Celia, to save them from a Paralleladise existence. But she saw, too, they were not the young children she had known. They were, perhaps, old enough to take the risk of staying to fight. And, yet, she could not let go of the desire to take them from harm's way and adult responsibility by escaping through the portal.

"It's not your key," Walt heard Celia blurt out in a surprised voice. He and his mother looked at her. Celia was pointing to the placard next to Mrs. Walters. "It's not your key," Celia repeated. Her eyes were lit up in discovery.

"What do you mean?" Mrs. Walters asked her.

"It's your portal," Celia elaborated, the full reasoning coming to her only as she explained it to Walt and his mother. "It's your portal, yes, the Lexington portal. It's your portal . . . and Walt's portal . . . and MY portal. But it's Walt key. The placard—it's Walt's key. Like yours, perhaps, but not. "

Mrs. Walters turned to look at the plaque once more. Understanding illuminated her features. "Of course," she said. "The same portal, but a different key." She turned to Walt. "A different combination. Your combination."

"When you sent me back through the portal using your key," Celia reasoned, "I went back to your time—not mine, even though this is my portal, too."

"And this key . . ." Mrs. Walters nodded at the placard.

"It would send you back to the moment Walt came through the portal."

"Four years after I came through."

"Yes! That's why your combination isn't working. It can't work on Walt's key."

"Of course!" Mrs. Walters exclaimed. She glanced at the placard and then at Walt. Her eyes were full of hope. "Walt, do you remember?"

Walt looked from his mother to Celia then at the placard. The symbols in gilded letters remained in the last combination Mrs. Walters had tried:

δεςειτσΥειλλθσιονσδεαραρισεσοφτ

Some of the forms looked vaguely familiar, but it did not make any sense to Walt and he had no idea if they were in the right order.

"Think, Walt," his mother said. "Concentrate. See if you can remember."

Walt shook his head. "I can't . . . "

"Try," his mother encouraged.

Walt closed his eyes. He tried to picture the placard as it had looked when he went to the attic and saw Acey being drawn into the portal. He cleared his mind as best he could to allow only the plaque to occupy his memory. But only a few odd shapes appeared in the gilded letters of his mind.

He opened his eyes and looked once again at the wooden symbols. "I . . ." he started and then he saw something. "It's . . . it's a word."

"What?" Celia asked him.

"It's a word," Walt repeated, pointing at the plaque. "Or several words maybe." For suddenly, Walt saw a pattern of repetition in the symbols that reminded him of the symbolic codes his father had shown him so many times. "It's a . . . message."

Mrs. Walters studied the plaque closely. She, too, saw the repetitions. "You're right!" she exclaimed, stepping up to touch the letter forms once more.

"There's no time," Celia reminded them. She turned to Walt and cupped his face between her hands, looking deep into his eyes. "There's no time to decipher it," she said, pleadingly. "Walt, you have to remember."

"I can't . . ."

"Please, try," Celia pleaded. "Please. Close your eyes."

Walt closed his eyes. Celia continued to cradle his face in her hands. "You're in the attic at home," she spoke in a low, soothing voice like a hypnotist. "Not this Paralleladise replica," she went on, "but the attic at home—with real dust and real cobwebs and mottled roof rafters where rain has come in."

The details were helping, Walt realized. Details had helped him to restore Ling's recollection and now Celia was using them to bring back the precise image in Walt's memory.

"It's dim and dusty," Celia went on, "except for the blinding light of the portal and the blazing letters on the plaque. You can see the dust particles dancing in the beam of light from the portal."

"Yes," Walt told her. He remembered the prevalent fog of dust lit by the intense glow from the portal.

"Acey is there," Celia continued in her steady voice. "And you can hear me behind you, but you don't know it's me. You're too busy pulling Acey away from the portal."

"Yes," Walt said again, the scene was coming back to him in its fullness and details. "It's cold," he explained, mentioning a detail Celia had left out. "It's a cold wind pulling us toward the portal."

"It's cold, yes," Celia echoes. "And Acey is staring at something next to the portal. You look, and you see it's the placard, and there are symbols on it."

Yes! Walt remembered holding Acey, trying to keep her from being dragged toward the menacing light. And, as he was pulling her from the powerful force, he saw she was staring at something—at the placard adjacent to the portal. Walt recalled knowing right away it had significance because of what he'd read in Alice Shaworth's diary—in Celia's diary.

"You tried to warn me!" he said to Celia, not opening his eyes, not wanting the recollection to slip away. "You were there! You told me to remember."

"Yes," Celia responded, excitement in her voice. "I told you to remember—so you would store the images in your mind, so that you could find your way out again."

"I remember you grabbed my hands."

"Do you remember the plaque, Walt?"

Walt thought hard. He struggled to block out all the images bombarding his mind and focus solely on the placard and the gilded symbols. The combination flashed before his eyes and he knew it was the right one. But then, just as quickly, it faded and Walt shook his head trying to bring it back.

"You can do it," he heard his mother say.

"Come on, Walt."

The dust and Acey's hair as he pulled at her waist trying to drag her to safety—he concentrated on these details and on the exact moment when he saw the plaque. It flashed again, this time more distinctly and it lingered in his mind's eye for several seconds.

"Do you remember?"

Walt did not answer but opened his eyes and stepped toward the plaque. His mother stepped to the side and Walt moved carefully, as if he were balancing something very fragile on his shoulders. He did not want to shake away the image returning to his memory.

He reached out to the first gilded symbol upon the plaque and pressed it firmly. It glowed warmly against his hand and then dissolved and reformed into a different character. This wasn't right, Walt could see, comparing it to the picture in his head. He

404

pressed again and then again and each time the form changed shape until, finally, it transformed into the symbol he recalled:

ο ε

"Is that it?" Celia asked. "Is that the first symbol?"

But Walt did not answer. He was afraid to speak, afraid to break his concentration. He moved on to the second symbol and pressed the gilded letter. It glowed and transformed and he pressed it repeatedly until it appeared as he recalled:

εσ

"I think you've got it," Walt heard his mother whisper. But Walt could not turn his attention away from the plaque. Any moment the image might slip from his hippocampus. If he could solve this puzzle of the placard, he might understand the secret to all the portal keys, he might know the trick to opening every hippo's portal. With Romannie's help and the knowledge of the keys, they might be able to free all the captives of Paralleladise.

One by one, Walt changed the symbols of the placard in front of him, pressing each letterform until it matched the image his brain had retained.

"Everything that has ever happened to us—from the moment of birth to the here and now—every face we've encountered, every word we've heard, every fact, every detail—we remember it all." Walt took comfort in recalling these words of Max Romannie echoing in the back of his mind. *It's all in there somewhere, ready to be brought back to life when we need it."*

Walt had managed, with Celia's help, to bring the placard forward out of his memory. Now, if only he could keep it there long enough to solve the combination.

εσαχέξςομσόκοάνχεοςξομσό

Only two more symbols to go, Walt realized, pressing the second-to-last form and believing for the first time that he might finish it.

Then, without warning, the attic began to shake with fury.

"Sheron! He's back!"

"Run!" Celia shouted over the deafening thunder that accompanied the quaking.

"I've almost got it," Walt tried to tell her and as he did, he turned the second-to-last letter form to the correct symbol:

$$\kappa$$

"Only one more," Walt cried out.

"Look out!" Walt heard his mother scream behind him and then felt her body smashing into him from the side, knocking him to the floor of the attic, into the insulation and on to the rafters.

Looking up, he saw a burst of brilliant light crashing into the spot before the placard where he had just been standing. It was Sheron's tracking beam and it had zeroed in on him. His mother had pushed him out of the way just in time. Now the light retracted, tracing its way along the floor attempting to locate his mnemonic signature again.

"Mom!" Walt said. His mother had landed to the side of Walt after pushing him to the floor.

"I'm all right!" Mrs. Walters responded, rolling and standing in one deft movement.

"This way," Celia called. She, too, had been knocked to her hands and knees and was scrambling across the rafters heading for the attic access.

"Celia!" Walt called to her. Sheron's beam had determined a course and was moving swiftly across the floor inches away from her. "Look out!"

Celia rolled to the side but, to Walt's surprise, the beam did not try to follow her. It passed only inches from her head and shoulders slowing down for only a moment before zooming for Walt and his mother.

"He's after you!" Celia shouted.

Walt was on his feet and moving away from the hostile beam of light in strides that carried him across several rafters at once. But he had not gone far when his mother caught him in her arms.

"Go back to the portal!" she shouted. "Open the portal!"

She pushed him firmly back in the direction he'd run from. Sheron's beam was bearing down but slowed, as if confused about which mnemonic signature to focus on.

"My oldest daughter is Zelda!" Mrs. Walters shouted in the direction of the beam. "Her birthday is June 29th. She was born at four-oh-seven on a Monday afternoon."

It took Walt only a split-second to realize what Mrs. Walters was doing. She was using her mnemonics to boost her signature signal, to attract Sheron to her and away from Walt.

"My youngest daughter is Acey! She is sweet and beautiful and born on April 23rd." His mother broke off the recitation to glance at Walt. "Go!" she shouted and then turned again to the beam. "Acey was born in the middle of the night."

Mrs. Walters' diversion worked. For a moment Sheron's beam of light hesitated as she and Walt went in opposite directions. But when she continued to call out her memories, she became too tempting of a target. The beam of light drew itself into the air, arching against the ceiling and transforming itself into a giant opened hand that then clenched into a fist and opened again before making a lightning-fast dash to grab Mrs. Walters.

She was prepared. Walt saw his mother take two steps and jump into the air, grasping onto one of the overhead rafters where Achebe had broken through the roof. She swung out of the way just as the hand would have caught her, eluding its grasp.

"Go, Walt, go!" she cried out, dangling from the ceiling.

Walt darted to the placard. Its forms had resolved themselves into the gilded wood letters once again, but remained in the order Walt had put them, except the last symbol which waited to be turned to unlock the portal.

Walt closed his eyes and saw the combination in his mind and placed his hand over the last symbol. It glowed underneath his touch and changed to another symbol—but not the right one.

"My only son is Walt," he heard his mother calling out in winded breath behind him as she tried to lure Sheron without being caught.

"Behind you!" he heard Celia cry as he pressed the symbol one last time.

And there it was—the final symbol of the combination:

$$\tau$$

What happened next transpired so quickly Walt could only watch. He had no time to react or fully absorb the entire chain of events.

He turned to help his mother, prepared to dash out of the way in case Sheron's beam were upon him. His peripheral vision registered Celia, running across the attic as if she intended to throw herself in front of Sheron's spotlight and block it from Walt and his mother.

But she was too late, for Mrs. Walters was ahead of Celia with Sheron's beam, still in the shape of an opened hand, surrounding her, ready to take her in its grasp.

Mrs. Walters was two yards from Walt and, as he turned to face her, she leapt into the air, diving in his direction, perhaps to knock him out of harm's way once again.

But, in turning, Walt had moved out of position and his mother sailed past him, her momentum carrying her directly toward the portal which, at that very moment, opened in a blinding gush of light and frigid wind which pulled her forward at an incredible speed.

"Walt!" he heard her cry as the draft from the portal seized her in mid-air and pulled her into the blaring light, briefly illuminating her body in a halo of brilliance before dragging her into the blinding intensity of the tunnel where she disappeared in an impenetrable glare.

"Mom!" Walt cried out, instinctively moving toward her, trying to save her, to pull her back, to keep from losing her. But in that split second Sheron's beam of light, clasped shut as if it were clutching Walt's mother, balling into a fist and colliding violently with the light blasting from the portal.

The collision created a lightning bolt so close and powerful that it sent Walt and Celia flying through the air and crashing against the angled roof of the attic.

Walt thudded against the roof beams and saw Celia fall to the floor before dropping into a layer of attic insulation.

"Uuhh!" He let out a groan at the bruising pain as he hit the floor. He expected at any moment for Sheron to turn toward him, and he knew he could not stand up quickly enough to turn away. He watched and waited to be captured.

And so, he was surprised to see Sheron's beam of light temporarily unmoving. Smoke steamed off the end of the beam that had been a fist but had now transformed again into a simple spotlight.

The spotlight remained motionless for a split moment and then, as furiously as it had entered, it retracted in the blink of an eye out the hole in the attic roof.

At once, the attic was quiet except for the whooshing high-pitched drone made by the open portal which continued to emit its brilliant ray.

Walt slowly pushed himself to a sitting position and saw Celia standing up, gingerly, on the other side of the attic. "What happened?" he asked.

The lightning explosion that tossed them both into the air had left Celia bruised, too. She limped toward him carefully, as if testing for sprains and fractures.

"Sheron's energy beam doesn't mix well with the energy from the portal," Celia explained. "He got too close and it caused a spark, like when two electric poles with the same charge get too close."

"That was quite a 'spark.'" Walt pointed out.

Celia was next to him now and reached down to help him up. Walt grasped her hand and was pulled to his feet. "I know," Celia smiled. "I think Sheron may have given himself a boo-boo."

Walt headed immediately over to the portal where his mother had been pulled in. He stopped as close as he could to the brilliant light without being drawn into the vacuum of the tunnel.

"He'll recover and be back," Celia went on. "Sooner than we expect."

Walt, squinting, peered into the brightness. "She's gone."

Celia nodded, watching Walt's face. "She'll emerge on the other side, in your attic, in Lexington. But it will be four years after she disappeared."

"She'll try to come back for us. She'll try to rescue us."

Celia shook her head. "I doubt NyXus will keep this portal active. First your mother came through, then you. . ."

"And you," Walt added, as Celia joined him next to the portal.

"It's too dangerous for him," Celia concluded. "He'll have to close it down."

Walt considered the implications. If NyXus did close the portal, Walt may never be able to return home. And yet, he knew he couldn't abandon all the victims of Paralleladise.

"That's why you should go now," Celia said softly, "before it closes."

Walt turned to her, shaking his head. "I can't. I have to stay and help." He pointed to the placard. "Now that we know the key is a code word, we might be able to help other hippos get back . . . if we can figure out what it says . . .what it means."

Celia smiled sadly. "You're a brave boy, Walt." She hesitated and drew a deep breath. "I can report back to the others. There are puzzle-solvers among the hippos. They will be able to decipher your key." She looked at the placard and put her index finger next to her forehead. She had memorized the symbols and sequence on the plaque. "It's all up here."

"No," Walt said. There was nothing he wanted more at that moment than to take Celia's hand and jump with her into the portal before it closed—to return to his home, to his family, to the life he was living only a short time ago, but which seemed ages in the past. There was nothing he wanted more than to wake up the next morning in his own bed, get dressed, go to school and lead the life of a thirteen-year-old boy. Every bone in his body longed to return home. But he knew he could not. "I have to stay," he told Celia. "I could never leave you here." He touched

411

her cheek. "Besides," he smiled, "who would become the next Rememberer?"

Celia studied him for a long moment. Then with a nod, she pursed her lips and leaned forward to kiss his cheek. "You're not the only one with a big hippocampus, Walters," she told him.

And only then did Walt realize what she was doing. Only then did he feel her hand pressed flat against his chest. Only then did he understand her plan, when it was too late to resist. For he felt the firm thrust of her palm, the powerful push that made him fall back into the brilliant pull of the portal.

The last image he had of Paralleladise was Celia Washroth watching in a sad goodbye as he was whisked away into the portal light.

Epilogue

Mr. Walters saw the light on in his son's room and walked down the hall to look in. Walt was sitting on his bed, reading from a book—an old, hardbound diary with a metal faceplate.

"Hey, Kiddo."

Walt looked up. "Hi, Dad."

"Getting late."

Walt nodded setting the diary to the side. "Guess I'm just not tired."

Mr. Walters crossed the room to sit on the bed next to his son.

"Thinking about Celia?"

"The more I read it," Walt touched the cover of the diary, "the more I realize all the stuff she put in there for me."

More than six months had passed since Walt returned through the portal, delivered back to his home at the exact instant he had left it. But things were still not quite right with him, Mr. Walters knew. He was still bothered at having left his best friend, Celia, behind, along with many of the new friends and others he felt bound and destined to help.

There was nothing Walt could do. Mr. Walters had heard the story several times from his son about how Celia had sealed his fate when she pushed him into the portal just before it closed, sending him home, saving him from years, decades or centuries of captivity in a world of emotionless forgetting.

Celia had predicted correctly the fate of the Lexington portal to Paralleladise. It was closed down permanently by the powers that ruled there, all traces of it—the portal and the placard—completely disappeared. There was no way to go back, no passage through which Walt could lead a rescue party. The feeling of helplessness gnawed at Walt's conscience. He was restless with the desire to do something, anything to help out, and yet he could think of nothing to do.

Mr. Walters picked up the diary. He'd read it more than once since learning from Walt of the fantastic adventure in Paralleladise. Walt told him of the role the diary played—how Celia had used it as a coded warning of what was to come. Mr. Walters had read over the diary in an effort to discover some way of helping Paralleladise prisoners, and as a way of better understanding the bizarre events his son and his wife had described, of making them more real.

"I've found a couple of things, too," Mr. Walters told his son, hoping to cheer him a little. "I think Celia threw them in just for you." He leafed through the entries of the journal until he found the page he was searching for. He held it open for Walt to see, resting a finger on the passage:

"Should I tell U.U. what a big crush I have on him?" Celia had written in an entry that was supposed to make the book seem like a real diary. Walt had probably read the passage a dozen times without considering its significance.

"A crush on U.U.," Mr. Walters read. "Two U's. Double U's." He paused and let it sink in and then added, "W."

Walt's eyes widened and he scooted to the end of the bed, next to his father, and took the diary from him, re-reading the passage. "I never noticed . . ."

"She's a clever girl."

Mr. Walters put his arm around Walt shoulders to offer encouragement. What a young man his son was growing into! And how fast! His experiences in Paralleladise had changed Walt in many ways. He had become more responsible, taking greater care in his school work, keeping his room tidier, and getting along remarkably well with Zelda, suppressing sibling antagonism even when she provoked him. The adventure seemed to have catapulted him overnight into young adulthood.

But with his growing maturity had come adult concerns, too, and Mr. Walters hated to see his son so burdened by the weight of leaving friends behind in Paralleladise, so consumed with guilt that he could not do more to help them.

"What are you two doing?"

Walt and his father looked to the door of Walt's room. It was Mrs. Walters, peeking in on her way to bed and finding father and son in conversation.

"Just reminiscing," Mr. Walters told her. Though months had passed since his wife had come through the portal, he had not yet fully gotten used to looking up and simply finding the love of his life before him, radiant and beautiful. Of course, she had come through the portal using Walt's key and so was transported back to the moment when Walt was abducted into Paralleladise —four years after she had disappeared. And she never seemed to tire of reminding her husband that, technically, she was now several years younger than he. That was okay, for having missed her so desperately for so long, Mr. Walters was happy to hear anything she might say.

"Looks serious," is what she had to say now. Mrs. Walters could see from their expressions that the topic of conversation between her husband and son was not a lighthearted one, and she recognized Walt's look of ambivalence. Because of their experiences in Paralleladise, she and Walt were very close and she could often tell when he was thinking about his captivity. Now, she knew, he was worried.

She felt the concern, too, of course. She and Walt were the only ones who truly understood the terrifying experience of being held by NyXus and Sheron and losing memories. She knew his feelings of futile helplessness because she felt them, too.

After she and Walt had come through the portal and were reunited with their family, Mrs. Walters called the police to alert them to the threat of NyXus. When an officer arrived, Mrs. Walters took him to the attic. But the portal was gone by then. Even the harmless wood panel that covered the roof where the portal had been disappeared and the police officer could only shake his head, bewildered at her story, and promise to write up a report.

For months, Mrs. Walters continued to press authorities to do something. She told local police, state prosecutors and federal agents her story, but always got the same reactions: curious stares, disbelief, and veiled suggestions that she might be imagining things. The more she told the story, the more unreal and fantastic it sounded, even to her. She could not blame the authorities for thinking it was preposterous.

Then, as police examined their records of Mrs. Walters' disappearance, four years earlier, they began to wonder if her incredible story of an abduction to an alternative universe where memories were annihilated was fabricated to cover-up some nefarious activity. Finally, she and her husband decided it was becoming dangerous to talk about the Paralleladise ordeal until they had better evidence of its truth.

So, Mrs. Walters knew the questions and feelings Walt was having—his ambivalence about being here, safe and sound, while scores of others suffered. She entered his room, now, and sat on the bed, sandwiching Walt between her and her husband. She rested a hand on his head and mussed his hair.

"You know," she offered, "what you discovered about the portal key—about it being a coded word or phrase…that may have been enough. The hippos may have already figured out how to use the information to get out."

Walt looked at her. She saw that he was trying to judge whether she believed this were truly possible or likely.

"Celia may already be home with her parents . . . in her own home, in her own time," she suggested, but could tell from Walt's sad eyes that the argument was not very persuasive.

Walt smiled, gallantly. "It's possible."

Mrs. Walters pulled her son to her in a hug. She so wanted to take away his sadness and guilt—to free him of the concerns that were robbing him of a happy youth. She wanted to take all feelings of responsibility off of his shoulders and on to hers. But if that wasn't possible, she thought, maybe she could help him by offering the consolations she had learned to take.

"When I was in Paralleladise," she told Walt, "I never gave up the fight to get back here. But there were many times when I didn't believe it would ever happen. I met so many who had lived lifetimes there and only kept up the struggle to escape because they knew of nothing else to do, even though they had long ago forgotten what they were hoping to escape to."

Walt was staring at the floor, but Mrs. Walters could see that he was listening.

"It's hard, I know" she continued, "to feel okay about being here, knowing so many others are still trapped. But I know, too, if I were to live now with my family—those I had most longed to escape for... if I were to live now in full possession of my memories and emotions... if I were to live here and dwell always on my captivity there, I would not have escaped at all, Walt. I would still, in many ways, be NyXus' victim." She paused, not sure if he understood. "And I think it would be a disservice to the memories of those we left behind, if I did not live and love this freedom of everyday life as fully as I could."

Walt did not look up and Mrs. Walters could tell that he was weighing her words, searching them for a way of understanding what he had experienced. She picked up the diary resting on the bed and ran her hand over the embossed letters "A.S" on its cover.

"Some things you lose and get back," Mrs. Walters said, pausing to gaze at her husband's face. She looked back at Walt. "Some things you lose and never see again. So the best thing is to love all things while you have them as much as you can."

After his parents had left his room and gone to bed, Walt got up and put the diary of Alice Shaworth back into the old portfolio it had first come to him in. As he lifted the flap to slide the diary in, he found the photo that he and Celia had come across the day they opened the portfolio. Looking closely, he realized it was a picture of Celia. He had not recognized her before, thinking he was looking at the image of someone who had lived long ago. Now he saw Celia's familiar features in the face of the girl in the picture—the wisdom of her eyes, the playful beginnings of a smart remark on her lips. She was holding a white terrier and Walt turned the photo over to read the description Celia had written there: "Me with dog."

Walt smiled and slid the photo in the portfolio with the diary. He opened his closet and put the old leather satchel on the shelf at the top of the closet.

He would take the diary out again someday, he thought, as he turned off the light and lay down in his bed—in a month or a year. But he would leave it there for a while, he decided, try not to think about it so often and concentrate on the things that were so important to him in his life now—his home, his family. And maybe, with time, he could grow used to the idea that he would never again see those he had met in Paralleladise or his friend, Celia Washroth. And maybe, with time, that would be okay.

But, Walt would see Celia again. And Achebe and other hippos. He would be drawn again into NyXus' empire and the struggle to liberate Paralleladise. He would, once more, battle with Sheron and fight to save his friends and family.

He did not know that then.

But, he knew that there were many people who had touched his life, who had come into it for years or moments and helped him, saved him, changed him, guided him, taught him what was true or important about himself and the world. And as he drifted off to sleep he felt grateful for all of them and promised himself, no matter what, that he would always, always remember.

Made in the USA
Monee, IL
03 July 2023

38464520R00246